PRAISE FOR T
Clarissa

Impossible Saints

"A rich debut. Grounded in a wealth of research into the suffrage movement, the book will please readers who enjoy detailed historical recreations. With insight and sensitivity, Harwood explores century-old social mores and challenges that still echo loudly today."

- Publishers Weekly

"This frustrating but tender romance, teetering between hope and despair, doubtless represents many relationships challenged by change. The story is best for readers interested in women's rights and the British suffrage movement."

- Historical Novels Review

"The perspective is refreshing in that the church is not the villain, nor are all the suffragettes cardboard cutouts. One interesting aspect is the novel's exploration of the contrast in ideologies between the more conservative, peaceful suffrage groups and the militant, property-destroying Women's Social and Political Union. This parallels the spectrum in today's protest-heavy atmosphere, lending the novel contemporary social relevance in addition to its romantic plotline."

- Booklist

"An engrossing historical romance. By 1928, all British women over 21 could vote; readers will root for Lilia and Paul's romance to have a similarly happy ending. For lovers of romantic historical fiction from the Brontës to Tracy Chevalier (*Girl with a Pearl Earring*)."

- Library Journal

"A simply riveting read from cover to cover, *Impossible Saints* is an original and consistently entertaining, narrative driven novel by a writer with a genuine flair for both originality and deftly crafted characters."

- Midwest Book Review

"Anyone pining for a passionate yet principled historical romance will fall hard for this impossibly readable story. It's the perfect thing for a long weekend. But months later, readers will still recall the harrowing descriptions of imprisoned, abused women. Lilia's pointed, challenging questions will linger even longer."

- British Heritage Travel

Bear No Malice

"A smart and highly civilized tale about love, temptation, and second chances."

- Kirkus Reviews

"Historical fiction fans with a penchant for complexity in their romances will appreciate this story of two ardent people overcoming the pasts they can no longer escape."

- Library Journal

"Harwood has taken the villain from her last novel and turned him into a sympathetic, if flawed, protagonist. Both historical-fiction and historical-romance fans will relish this novel, in which characterization is strong and realistically informed by backstories and in which two damaged people come to truly know themselves and find their missing pieces in each other."

- Booklist

"An impressively and deftly crafted novel that will engage the readers complete attention as the author presents more unanticipated plot line twists and turns than a Coney Island roller coaster."

- Midwest Book Reviews

"An intriguing study of a flawed man. All the characters in this novel, even the minor ones, are complex and surprising, and Harwood deftly blends social realism with fairytale lyricism in a way that is moving without being sentimental."

- Historical Novels Review (Editor's Choice)

"Readers who enjoy a tender love story will want to keep turning pages to learn these characters' secrets and find out whether and how they come together."

- HistoricalNovels.info

"From the Surrey countryside to the churches and drawing rooms of London, and on into England's illicit boxing dens and penitentiaries, Harwood pulls the reader into the Edwardian era as though she could actually transport us there to witness history with our own eyes. Harwood practices a delicate steadiness in drawing her characters and painting a time when supporting women's voices and protecting the vulnerable among us was beginning to transform institutions. Bear No Malice balances mystery and discovery from the first page to the last, making for a delightful reading experience. With expert pacing and intricately woven backstories, Harwood has crafted a rich story of heartbreak, redemption, grace, and love."

- InTheStacks

THE CURSE OF MORTON ABBEY

CLARISSA HARWOOD

Thornfield
Press

THE CURSE OF MORTON ABBEY

Thornfield Press

Copyright © 2021 by Clarissa Harwood

Cover design by Tim Barber of Dissect Designs
Interior design by Polgarus Studio

E-Book: 978-1-7777369-1-0
Paperback: 978-1-7777369-0-3

To Laura,

This book brought us together,
and you've been its best champion. Thank you!

Calm judgment and absence of partisanship are qualities which a solicitor ought to possess . . . and those are qualities which are not commonly found in a woman.

- Lord Halsbury, House of Lords debate, 1917

1

⚜

LONDON: FEBRUARY 1897

I stacked the three piles of paper side by side on the desk, their edges as straight as if I had lined them up with a ruler. Taking a new page and dipping my pen in the inkwell, I started a third copy of the contract. Father always said a solicitor must keep three copies of everything. He used to praise my neat, regular handwriting, saying it was as uniform as typewriting.

If only he were still in the study with me, muttering over an endless deposition or shifting in his chair when his bad knee troubled him.

But everything had changed. Even the room didn't smell the way it ought to. Instead of a combination of old leather and the camphor-based liniment Father would apply to his knee every morning, the room, ready for the new tenants, smelled of lye soap. And I knew if I looked up at the walls, they would be empty of books and bookshelves. The corner where the massive leather armchair used to be was bare. The painting that used to hang above the desk, of a meadow dotted with wildflowers, was gone too. I knew every brush-stroke of that painting, and for good reason: I had spent most of my life in this room. I used to look at the painting to rest my eyes from the copy work I had begun at the age of six.

No matter. I didn't look up. If I kept my eyes on the desk and the papers in front of me, I could pretend for a few more minutes that nothing had changed.

A knock at the door startled me. Bloody hell. When Father was alive, nobody interrupted his work. Why must I be interrupted? Perhaps if I ignored it . . .

But the knocking continued, accompanied by Mother's voice, sharp with impatience: "Vaughan, what are you doing in there? Open the door."

I sighed and set the pen in its stand, then rose and limped to the door, my left foot dragging a little under my skirt. The special, heavy shoe made my limp less noticeable, but it was difficult to manoeuvre when I was tired, as I was now.

Mother stood there. She ought to have been a queen, with her tall, majestic figure and beautiful face. Even at two-and-sixty, she was lovely. I inherited nothing from her except stubbornness.

"What are you doing?" she repeated, her brow furrowed.

"I'm copying Father's last contract."

"You've already done that."

"No, the one I copied yesterday was for the Highsmith case," I said. "This one is the Gittings contract."

"There's no need to do any of this," she said. "Your father's colleagues will finish anything he left undone." Was she looking at me with pity? Father would never have done that.

"This is my work, and I need to finish it," I replied. I returned to Father's desk and pulled out the large drawer, where I had filed the work he left unfinished when he died three months earlier. I was pleased by the look of the neatly-organized folders.

Father used to call me his reference book, for I could recite many of the statutes relating to contract law without having to refer to the texts. I had only to read a page once with concentrated focus, and I would remember every word.

"It's not your work any longer." Mother came into the room and laid a hand lightly on my shoulder, making me flinch. "Come to the drawing room. We must talk."

I had no desire to do as she asked, but the truth was that there would be nothing more for me to do after I'd finished the Gittings contract. I could have completed it days ago, but it was my last link to what I knew I could do perfectly. And my last link to Father.

I reached into my skirt pocket to reassure myself the letter was still there. It was. At least I hadn't imagined this miraculous offer of employment.

Mother led the way out of the study and into the drawing room. As a child I had loathed this room, and even as an adult I spent as little time in it as possible. It was a site of unfathomable social rituals and women in ridiculous hats staring at me as if I were a living curiosity. A museum exhibit like Leonine the Lion-Faced Lady.

The drawing room was Mother's domain. It used to be filled with delicate ornamental tables and her spun-glass hummingbird collection. But now most of the furniture and ornaments were gone, already packed up and sent on to my sister Elizabeth's house in Bayswater. On the one hand, I was glad there was less likelihood of tripping over something. On the other, the relative emptiness of the room only magnified the effect of the green and white wallpaper, which looked like hundreds of squinting, critical eyes.

I wedged myself into one of the two delicate, spindly-legged chairs left in the room. The letter crackled in my pocket, and I reached down to smooth it.

"Have you packed your things?" Mother asked, settling herself in the chair across from me. "Elizabeth is expecting us tomorrow morning."

"I'm not going."

"What are you going to do, then? Sit in the study until the new residents throw you out?" She set her lips in a hard line. "You know perfectly well they are moving in within the week."

"I've accepted Sir Peter Spencer's offer, Mother. You know that. I'm going to Bradford tomorrow."

"You're being ridiculous. Even if you manage to take the correct train, you have no idea how to conduct yourself in the world, and you are not a solicitor. I cannot imagine what possessed the man to hire you."

"It's Yorkshire, not Siberia," I countered. "And I'm a solicitor in everything but name. Father trained me—"

She waved her hand dismissively. "He trained you to copy documents. That's all. Besides, you must be able to see how suspicious the position is. Why would this Sir Peter offer such a large salary for fairly simple work? And why does he require your presence for three months? Preparing the papers for the sale of an estate is surely a matter of a few days, not a few months."

The chair's armrest was digging into my side, and I shifted uncomfortably. "Sir Peter wrote that the legal documents must be organised before the estate can be put up for sale. That's why the process will take longer than usual."

"How do you know this man is who he says he is?"

"I'll find out, won't I?" I hadn't met Sir Peter, as Mother well knew. "He won't be at Morton Abbey when I'm there, anyway, at least not for the first couple of months. I may not even meet him until the spring."

"That's even worse. Why would he offer the position to

someone he's never met? He might be a murderer, for all you know. What has gotten into you, Vaughan? You've led a sheltered life, but you are eight-and-twenty. You ought to have more sense."

I wouldn't admit that I shared her suspicions. "Sir Peter is in Italy and can't meet me right now. Father's colleagues gave me a good character, so I imagine Sir Peter considered that adequate, along with my own description of my abilities."

Mother frowned. "Didn't the advertisement also specify that some physical strength would be needed? Aside from the question of why physical strength would be needed for legal work—"

"No doubt it's merely a matter of lifting boxes and stacks of papers."

"You cannot even do that. You obviously did not inform him of your affliction."

Sir Peter was unaware not only of my bad leg but also of my sex. It was the first time I'd used my ambiguous name to deceive someone. Father's colleagues had kindly agreed not to reveal I was a woman in the letters they had written on my behalf. The very fact that I *had* an employer after months of fruitless searching was proof of the success of this strategy.

"I know I can do the work," I said with more confidence than I felt.

Mother softened her expression through a Herculean act of will. I could tell it wasn't easy because each feature seemed to move, one by one, into an artificially relaxed position.

In a quiet but strained tone she said, "My dear, I'm just trying to protect you. You can't possibly do the work, and even if you can manage some of it, you won't be able to work fast enough to please your employer. Nobody will be as patient with you as your father was. Come with me instead. Elizabeth has plenty of room, and you can help with the children."

I couldn't imagine anything worse than living with my sister Elizabeth and her four brats. Beautiful, elegant Elizabeth, a copy of Mother.

"No," I said, my teeth clenched to stop the words I really wanted to say. Living with Elizabeth and Mother in the same house would kill me.

She stared at me. "What is the matter with you? Have you given no thought to what your father would have wanted? I know what I want doesn't matter to you, but I thought you would care about his wishes. Though perhaps you have no feelings at all. When I think of your reaction to his death, compared to your sisters, it makes me shudder. You were his favourite, but you didn't shed a tear. Not one tear."

She'd voiced this criticism before, and I had to bite back a sharp retort every time. Showing emotion was frowned upon in my family, so I found it hypocritical of her to expect it as proof of love. I had indeed shed tears in the privacy of my bedroom, where she couldn't judge their quality or quantity.

"I think he would want me to work," I said slowly. "He always said I could do anything I put my mind to."

"Oh, my dear girl," Mother said with merciless softness. "Don't you understand? He said that merely out of pity. He knew you could never hope for what other women have, so he said what he thought would make you happy. Come with me, Vaughan, and try to be content with your lot."

It wasn't the first time Mother had said this, either. I didn't know if it was true or not, but it could no longer hurt me. My heart was a stone that was unmoved by the pelting rain of her pity.

I looked at Mother. The prison she wanted me to choose was tiny and crowded, with no room to breathe. If I went there, I would never escape.

I reached into my pocket again. The letter was still there. I didn't ask for freedom, just for a more spacious prison. What had I to lose?

2

WEST YORKSHIRE

My journey was long and arduous, but contrary to Mother's expectations, I did take the correct train to Bradford. Once I disembarked at the station, I expected the hired carriage sent from Morton Abbey to be waiting for me, but this was not the case. I stood with my luggage outside the station's front entrance, shivering with cold and watching other passengers scramble into the few waiting carriages and leave. It was early evening, and the winter darkness had already settled in. The gas lamps at the station were all that seemed to stand between me and an unknown wasteland.

I approached the nearest porter, who stared openly at my feet as I limped towards him.

"Is there more than one entrance where the hired carriages wait for passengers?" I asked.

"No. Where are you trying to get to, Miss?" he asked.

"Morton Abbey," I said.

He looked aghast. "Why'd you want to go there? You must be mistaken."

I thought him incredibly rude. Surely he wouldn't have questioned a man in such a way.

I drew myself up to my full height, which was regrettably

not much above five feet, and said coldly, "I am not mistaken. Is there a fly I can hire if the carriage I'm expecting doesn't arrive?"

"Nobody I ken will take you to Morton, Miss. Happen to Netherton—that's the nearest village to Morton—but it's too late in the day for that now. You can take a fly to the Bradford Inn tonight and go on to Netherton tomorrow."

"That won't do."

As we were speaking, a shabby carriage was pulling up to the station, and the driver called out, "Mr. Springthorpe!"

"That's my carriage," I said hurriedly. "Please bring my luggage."

The porter looked from me to the carriage and back again with amazement, but fortunately he obeyed me without further protest.

The driver didn't look at me as I approached, merely throwing open the door. Once my luggage was loaded, I looked to the porter for assistance to climb into the carriage, but he just stood before me looking mournful with his arms at his sides.

Thinking he must be waiting for a tip, I reached into my reticule, but he leaned forward and said in a hoarse whisper, "I'd sooner accept a coin to send an innocent soul to hell. Don't go to Morton Abbey, Miss."

"Are you coming or not?" the driver demanded. I wondered if everyone who served customers in the area was as rude as the people I'd met so far and if anyone ever gave them tips.

"I am," I said, "but I'll be damned if I have to climb into the carriage without help."

The porter offered me his arm at last, and as I climbed up he added, "You will be, either way, Miss."

I was too shocked to reply, and I had no sooner sat down

than the driver slammed the door and the carriage jolted into motion. The carriage was uncomfortable and draughty, and while I knew that Sir Peter probably wouldn't send a private carriage for a mere legal assistant, it didn't bode well that such a decrepit vehicle was considered suitable for me. There was a threadbare rug with which I tried to cover my legs, but it did little to keep me warm.

It seemed to take forever to reach Morton Abbey, and I was exhausted and numb with cold, which made it seem all the longer. I couldn't stop thinking about what the porter had said, and even though I hadn't yet reached my destination, I felt as if I'd made an irrevocable decision. What had I gotten myself into?

Finally, the carriage stopped with a jolt and the driver opened the door. I forced my frozen limbs to move, stumbling as my feet touched the ground. He didn't trouble himself to help.

After depositing my trunk on the ground beside me, the driver jumped back onto his seat and drove away as fast as if a pack of wild dogs were in pursuit, making a tremendous clatter.

I stood shivering before an imposing stone edifice. The entrance was a gaping archway that looked like a monstrous mouth. Nobody seemed to have tried to beautify the building in any way. A huge grey block with smaller blocks attached on each side, it looked as though it had been a weary builder's last task before he died, and he had merely shoved the walls in place and washed his hands of it.

The surrounding landscape was no better. In the moonlight I could see a few scraggly trees along one side of the building, and nothing else but a vast grey emptiness. Surely there must be other buildings close by. Perhaps the estate would look better in daylight.

I left my trunk and walked through the archway, which led to a massive oak door. As I made my way towards it I was swallowed up in near-darkness. I wasn't a timid woman, but I didn't like the atmosphere of this place. I hoped the inside would look more welcoming.

It took me a while to find the bell-pull by the door because of the dim light. I had to feel for it, my fingernails scraping against cold stone; then, when I found it, I had to exert all my strength to budge it. I wondered when it had last been used.

As I waited, I mentally rehearsed what I would say. Everything depended on my ability to convince my employer's people I was capable of doing the work required of me, despite my sex. I had never been very good at persuasion.

After several minutes the door opened slowly, creaking all the way, to reveal a tall, stoop-shouldered old man in a black frock coat and, oddly, a resplendent green cravat. He stared down at me in silence.

I bore his scrutiny as long as I could, then said, "I'm Miss Vaughan Springthorpe. Sir Peter Spencer is expecting me."

He frowned, then took a monocle from his front coat pocket, raised it to his eye, and examined me again.

"Sir Peter has hired me as his legal assistant to prepare the papers for the sale of the estate," I said.

"Sir Peter is expecting *Mr.* Springthorpe," he said in a piercing, reedy voice.

"Yes, I understand." I took the letter from my reticule and held it out, though I had no intention of relinquishing my hold on it. "This letter confirms I'm the person Sir Peter has hired."

He didn't look at the letter, and his frown deepened. "You may come in, but you'll have to wait while I speak with Mr. Spencer."

"Speak with him?" I exclaimed. "I thought he was in Italy." I had hoped to impress Sir Peter with tangible proof of my competence before meeting him.

"Sir Peter is not here, but his brother Nicholas is. Come this way." He reached out to take my carpetbag.

"That won't be necessary," I said quickly, tightening my grip on the bag. "It's not heavy. But you might have a servant bring in my trunk."

He made no reply but, still frowning, pointed to a wooden chair in the small antechamber just inside the entrance. "Wait here," he said.

While he was gone, I wondered whether the presence of my employer's brother would work for or against me. Sir Peter's letter had led me to believe the estate was uninhabited except for a few servants. But perhaps Nicholas Spencer would prove an ally, or at least give me a chance to convince him of my competence.

The antechamber was chilly and musty-smelling, and I drew my cloak more closely about me, glad that the butler, if that's what he was, hadn't offered to take it.

The old man didn't return for a long time, and when he did, my limbs were aching from the cold and from the hard wooden chair.

"I'm sorry, miss. You can't stay here."

I rose to my feet as quickly as I was able. "This is ridiculous. I have proof that Sir Peter has hired me. I've come all the way from London and I'm not going back now."

"We were expecting a man. We haven't got a room suitable for a woman."

"What does that matter?" I struggled to keep my temper. It wouldn't do to fly into a rage. "You must have a room ready for the man you were expecting. I don't require anything more. You may consider me a man for all the difference it will make."

He looked at me blankly.

"I insist that you take me to see Mr. Spencer. I want to speak to him directly."

"Certainly not. Mr. Spencer is very ill. He sees no one."

I eyed him warily. Would he try to remove me bodily from the house? Despite his height, he was frail-looking. I was willing to put up a fight, but I didn't want to injure an old man. At the same time, he might be stronger than he looked.

One of Mother's favourite phrases popped into my head: "You'll catch more flies with honey than with vinegar." Putting on a sweet, coaxing manner was as alien to my nature as intellectual debate to a dormouse, but I was desperate enough to give it a go.

Forcing my lips into a smile, I said, "What is your name?"

"Bedford."

I taxed my brain trying to think of what Mother or my sisters might say in such a predicament. "Mr. Bedford, I've come a very long way. I don't mean to cause any trouble. All I want is to do the work Sir Peter has hired me to do, and I'll work so quickly and quietly that you won't even know I'm here."

Another blank stare. He didn't have the benign, watery eyes of an old man. His were hard and dark. Malevolent.

I heard quick footsteps approaching, and a rotund, motherly-looking woman appeared at the entrance to the antechamber. Looking at her grey hair and her deeply-lined face, I judged her to be old, perhaps as old as Bedford, but she moved with the quickness and vigour of a much younger woman. She wore an apron over a plain black woollen dress.

"What's takin' thee sae lang, Bedford? Where's the young

man?" the woman asked in a broad Yorkshire accent. When she saw me her eyes widened. "Who's this?"

"This is *Mr.* Springthorpe," Bedford said grimly.

"I'm Miss Springthorpe," I said unnecessarily, about to launch into the same explanation of my presence that I'd given Bedford.

Before I could do so, the woman gave me a quick, comprehensive look and said, "Tha's Sir Peter's new assistant?"

"Yes."

"I'm Mrs. Wilson. Tha' look chilled right through, tha' does. Tha' mun be hungry too. Come to the kitchen and have summat to eat."

With that, the brisk little woman turned and led me through a great hall, heels clicking at a smart pace. Relieved that someone in the house was willing to accept me, I followed, wishing my heavy shoe wouldn't make such a loud scraping noise on the floor. The great hall was more impressive than the exterior of the house had led me to expect, with tapestries richly-embroidered in jewel tones and a massive central staircase.

Mrs. Wilson ushered me down a short flight of stairs at the back of the great hall that led to the kitchen, then disappeared into what must be the larder. I went to the cavernous hearth and put out my hands to the disappointingly weak fire, then looked about me. The kitchen seemed medieval in its size: the few furnishings, from the fireplace to the worn wooden table, were so large that I felt like a dwarf in a fairy tale about to be gobbled up by a giant. I had the strange feeling that I was the only person aside from Mrs. Wilson to enter the kitchen in years.

Mrs. Wilson returned with a small iron pot, which she set over the fire, and a roll, which she placed before me.

I thanked her, sat down and began to eat, too ravenous to care that she was staring at me curiously. It wasn't clear whether the look was caused by the speed at which I was eating or simply by the fact that Sir Peter's new legal assistant was a woman.

"Will Sir Peter be coming home soon?" I asked when I'd finished the roll.

Mrs. Wilson went to the fire and stirred the pot. "We don't expect him. He lives in Italy during the winter, and even in the summer he's rarely here." She poured the contents of the pot into an earthenware bowl and set it on the table. "Does he know tha's a woman?"

I paused to think about how honest I wanted to be and to take a mouthful of soup, which turned out to be delicious and creamy, with chunks of potato and a hint of thyme. "No, not exactly."

Mrs. Wilson paused also, head to one side, considering. "He might not let thee stay. All the same, if tha' can do the work . . . he's a generous man."

"Is he?" Based on the salary he'd offered me, I already suspected this, but I hoped to learn more about him.

Fortunately, Mrs. Wilson seemed pleased to have someone new to talk to, and she didn't disappoint me. "Generous to a fault, I always say. I've known him since he was a lad. No man is kinder or more generous than Sir Peter. And handsome too. It's a pity he never married—a great favourite with the lasses, he always were."

"Is his brother like him?"

The housekeeper's expression darkened. "Not at all. The younger brother's temper is as sour as his brother's is sweet. Just between us, tha' understand. Not that I don't pity Mr. Spencer."

"Why do you pity him? Because of his illness?"

"Illness, my eye!" Mrs. Wilson exclaimed, then added more quietly, "I haven't seen him lately, mind. He hasn't left his room for months and sees nobbut Bedford. I make his meals, and Bedford takes them up to him. But I hear things. The man's not ill but barmy."

This didn't bode well for my plans. If what Mrs. Wilson said was true, there was no point trying to win over Nicholas Spencer.

"Sir Peter could send his brother to an asylum," she continued, "but he's a right generous man, he is, letting Mr. Spencer live here and have owt he wants. Not that he asks for much, but I worry about Bedford. He's too old to care for a sick man—sick in the head, mind."

"Is Mr. Spencer violent?" I asked.

"Don't know, miss. At least he stays in bed most of the time—so Bedford says—but happen he's dangerous. Be sure to lock thy door at night."

I was sceptical. Mrs. Wilson seemed inclined to be overly dramatic, though it wouldn't hurt to err on the side of caution and listen to her warning. Was the handsome salary I'd been promised meant to compensate me for having to share the house with a madman?

"Did many other people apply for this position?" I asked.

A guarded look came into the housekeeper's eyes. "No. The situation of Morton Abbey is too lonely for most folks."

"Even considering the generous salary?"

"Aye." Mrs. Wilson paused, pursed her lips, and added, "I'll be frank with thee, miss. Tha' seems like a plain-spoken, honest woman and I hope tha'll stay. Tha'll be company for me in these dreary winter months. Before tha' came, Sir Peter hired three young men, one after the other, for this position. None lasted more than a week."

"Why?"

"'Tis hard work. Tha'll see tomorrow. Tha' won't be moving papers around a desk for a few hours, then at thy leisure. There's much that needs putting to rights before tha'll get to the papers, and even then it won't be easy." After a pause, she added, "And strangers don't like this house. To my mind, folks let their fancy run away with them, but some say they see and hear strange things, mostly at night."

"Ghosts?" I smiled.

Mrs. Wilson cleared away my empty bowl and went back to the fireplace. With her back turned, she answered, "Nowt so interesting as that. Happen all they heard was the creaks and groans of the house. They weren't used to such an old, lonely place."

"I'm not afraid of hard work. I've worked all my life for my father, and he was a hard taskmaster. And I'm not afraid of ghosts . . . or madmen."

Mrs. Wilson returned to the table and nodded. "I believe thee. Tha's had to bear some hard things already, doin' a man's work, and with thy bad leg. What made thee lame?"

Surprised by her boldness, I stiffened. "I was born this way. Mrs. Wilson, I'm very tired. Would you show me to my room, please?"

"Aye. I've blethered on long enough. Come along—there are many stairs. I hope they won't be too difficult for thee."

"I'll manage."

Mrs. Wilson continued to talk all the way to my room, which seemed to take forever to reach. I was so exhausted I couldn't focus on what she was saying—it was something about the

Spencer ancestors—and could only stumble after her down several corridors and up two flights of stairs. Along the way Mrs. Wilson had to unlock doors between passageways, which she locked again once we had passed through. I couldn't understand why this was necessary, since she would only have to unlock them again when she returned to the main part of the house. Was Nicholas Spencer more dangerous than she had let on?

Finally, I was alone in my room. It was nearly as bare and inhospitable as the antechamber into which Bedford had first shown me. A washstand, a plain but serviceable wardrobe, a cold, ash-filled grate, and a small bed were the main furnishings. At least someone had brought up my trunk, and at the far end of the room there was a window large enough to offer a promising view. The view would have to wait until morning, though, and I didn't bother to undress or even remove my cloak in the icy room. I removed my shoes and lay down on the bed, the springs creaking loudly in protest. I no sooner pulled the bedclothes over myself than I fell asleep.

A loud noise, similar to the report of a gun, awoke me in the early morning, just as dawn was breaking. I struggled to sit up, my head feeling leaden and achy, and my limbs stiff. I'd been dreaming that I was riding a horse through cold, dark water. The water was high, up to the horse's neck, and rising rapidly. I was terrified I would drown, but instead the water lowered and we reached a bank where there was a large, flat rock and a single willow tree. Just as the horse scrambled onto the bank, a shot rang out and I felt the impact of the bullet slamming into my chest.

I rarely dreamed, and even when I did, my dreams were

never so vivid or violent. As a child I'd had recurring dreams of drowning, but it had been more than twenty years since I'd experienced such nightmares. The ominous atmosphere of the house, as well as Mrs. Wilson's story about the mad Nicholas Spencer, must be the cause.

I shook my head. This was ridiculous. I wouldn't allow myself to be caught up in fanciful stories or wild imaginings of danger, even in my dreams. I was not a fanciful woman. Everything I had accomplished in my life so far had been due to my clear head and pragmatism.

Throwing back the bedclothes, I rose and limped to the washstand across the room. I lifted the pitcher and tipped it into the bowl, but no water came out. Peering into the pitcher, I realized there was a crust of ice on top of the water. I reached in and tried to break the ice with my hand. It didn't budge.

"Hellfire and damnation!" I burst out. The difficulties of carrying out my morning ablutions aside, it felt good to be alone and use language nobody would chastise me for. "You speak like a navvy," Mother said once. "Where in the world do you hear such language?" Father had never cursed in front of Mother or my sisters, but he did in my presence. I'd picked up the habit from him.

There must be a maidservant in the house who would bring me hot water for washing and start a fire in the grate. I was merely awake too early. No matter—I would wash later when the other inhabitants of the house had risen. In the corner of the room was a tall, narrow shaving stand with an adjustable glass attached to the top. They had put me in a man's room, after all. I went to the stand and saw that the glass was, as I expected, tilted upward to accommodate a person much taller than myself. I made no attempt to adjust it. There was something freeing about not having to worry about my appearance. Even though I could tell my hair had loosened from its plait and become frizzed from sleep, I turned away from the glass.

It took a few minutes to put on my shoes—my fingers were too stiff with cold, and the heavy shoe on my left foot required extra lacing—but at last I was ready to explore my new surroundings. I left my room and moved carefully across the darkened landing to find the staircase I knew was nearby. When I found it, I clung to the balustrade, descending slowly, worried my skirt or my own feet would trip me. A tiny window set into the wall on the way down the stairs allowed a modicum of light, but I wished I had lit a candle.

Just as it had the night before, the house smelled damp and mouldy, like ancient ruins. It seemed inconceivable that anyone would wish to live there. When I reached the landing of the ground floor, there was a door on my right and another on my left. I tried the right-hand door. It was locked. So was the door on the left. I knocked loudly on both doors but was met with silence. Standing on the narrow landing, with no way to move but to return up the stairs the way I had come, I was overcome with frustration. Was I a prisoner in this house?

I returned to the second floor. There were two other doors across the landing from my bedroom, but they were both locked. There was also a dark alcove tucked away behind my room that I hadn't noticed before. As I went to look at it, I realized that it housed another set of descending stairs, this time a wrought-iron spiral staircase. Although my leg was already aching, I didn't want to stay in my room until Mrs. Wilson came to find me, whenever that would be, and the stairs were the only other option. I felt dizzy as I followed them—they seemed to go on and on endlessly. Finally, I reached another door at the bottom of the staircase. Holding my breath, I tried the door handle, and a moment later a gust of cold air hit me. I was outdoors, squinting into a grey fog that was beginning to lift, showing glimpses of the expanse of moor surrounding me.

Despite the cold mist, I was grateful for the open spaces and the increasing light. I walked fifty paces or so, then turned around to look at the house, trying to get my bearings. My room was in the east wing, and the door from which I had emerged was at the back of that wing. From the back, the house looked even larger and gloomier than it had the evening before.

There was a path leading around the back of the house and through a maze of hedges, in the middle of which was a decrepit stone structure with a headless statue. I made my way towards the structure, which I realized as I drew nearer was an old fountain. The statue appeared to depict a Greek or Roman goddess, and the jagged line of the neck suggested that it used to possess a head. It was a pathetic sight: a frozen, disused fountain presided over by a headless goddess. How my sister Letitia would love this place, I thought—she was forever reading Ann Radcliffe novels and imagining sinister monks and fainting ladies. But the sensational possibilities of the atmosphere were hardly to my taste. I would have preferred a hearty breakfast in front of a blazing fire. But I was curious about the inhabitants of this place. Were there no servants besides Bedford and Mrs. Wilson? And was Nicholas Spencer the only other person who lived here?

I followed the path to the back of the west wing, and a movement at one of the first-floor windows caught my eye. I was too far away to be certain, and the fog didn't help, but it looked like a face—a gaunt, white face. A second later it disappeared. It couldn't have been ruddy, round-faced Mrs.

Wilson or the ancient bushy-browed butler. Was it Nicholas Spencer?

I approached the nearest door, intending to find out for myself who it was, but I was thwarted once again. All the doors at the ground floor were locked, not only in the west wing but also at the centre of the house. Having walked too far already with an empty stomach, and with my lame leg aching intolerably, I gave up my explorations for the moment and went to the main entrance at the front of the house.

It was the first time I'd seen the front of the house in daylight, and I noticed a Latin inscription carved into the archway above the entrance: *aut Caesar aut nihil.* Caesar or nothing. If this was the family motto, I was in for a difficult time indeed.

I yanked on the bell-pull with all my might and waited for a full five minutes before Bedford appeared.

"Oh, it's you, miss," he said with a baleful stare. He didn't seem inclined to let me in.

"I'll come in and have my breakfast now," I said in the most imperious tone I could muster.

As he moved aside to let me pass, I added, "I insist on knowing why the devil . . . er, that is, why is it that every door in this house is locked?"

If my language surprised him, he didn't let on. "Where in the house are you trying to get to, miss?"

I glared up at him. "Anywhere besides my room, really. I assume there's a library or study where I'll be working. I can't even get to the kitchen from my room. I can only go outside."

With the slow emphasis of an oracle, he said, "Away goes the devil if he finds the door shut against him."

3

I'm sorry about the locked doors, miss," said Mrs. Wilson as she bustled around the huge kitchen. "It was my mistake. I should've left them open for thee to get to the middle of the house."

I was focused on my bowl of porridge and merely nodded. It was a great relief to be near the fire, which made the whole room seem more cheerful, and to have my insides warmed by hot food. It was also a relief to escape the malevolent presence of Bedford. Mrs. Wilson, on the other hand, seemed like a relatively normal person.

"I'll be going to the village in an hour if tha' has any letters to post," she said.

"No, I have nothing yet. I'll be writing to Sir Peter later today, but that letter can be posted tomorrow."

"Tha'll be writing to thy family too, I expect. They'll miss thee, bein' so far away."

I didn't reply. I was quite certain none of my family members aside from Letitia would miss me.

"Does tha' have brothers and sisters?"

"I'm the youngest of five sisters."

"Is that so? No brothers?"

I shook my head.

"Are thy sisters married?"

"Yes. Well, almost. My fourth sister, Letitia, will be married this summer."

"Ah, so tha's the only one left to be a comfort to thy mother and father."

"My father died three months ago. My mother is living with my eldest sister and her family." I was beginning to think I'd prefer the company of the taciturn Bedford after all.

"Mrs. Wilson, will you show me the library?" I asked. "I'd like to get to work as soon as possible."

"Certainly, miss."

As I followed the housekeeper out of the kitchen, I remembered the ice in my pitcher that morning and asked, "Is there a housemaid who can bring up some hot water for me to wash with in the mornings?"

"No, nobbut me and Bedford indoors. There's a gardener who helps us with the heavy lifting, but he stays outside. I'll bring hot water up for thee. This morning tha' was already up and out of the room when I came. Tha's an early riser."

"Not usually. This morning I awakened early because I heard something." I couldn't see Mrs. Wilson's face, but I was alert to any hesitation or change in her pace or bearing. There was none, but neither did she appear to be curious about what I had heard.

"Does Bedford go out shooting in the mornings?" I asked.

She turned and stared at me. "Shooting, miss? Birds and such like?"

"Yes."

"My word, no. He's too old for that."

"Does Mr. Spencer shoot?"

Mrs. Wilson laughed. "My word, miss, that's all we need— a barmy man with a gun! No, even when he was wick, Mr.

Spencer was no sportsman. He never joined the hunting parties his father and Sir Peter would have. Squeamish at the sight of blood, Mr. Spencer always was, no matter if it was his own or an animal's. Too nesh for a man, to my mind. His brother, though—"

"I'm certain I heard the report of some sort of gun this morning," I persisted.

Mrs. Wilson shook her head. "Tha' must've dreamed it, miss. Come, the library's just off the great hall."

I wasn't convinced by her explanation, but all thoughts of guns and madmen fled my mind a few moments later when Mrs. Wilson opened a set of massive doors to reveal a room in the worst disarray I had ever seen.

What must have been a beautiful library many years, perhaps decades, earlier was in shambles. Black oak bookshelves lined the walls from floor to ceiling, but only the top two shelves were neatly arranged, filled with books of similar size and colour. The books that presumably belonged on the other shelves were helter-skelter, some precariously perched on the edge of the shelves, some on the floor. Only small patches of the crimson Turkey carpet were visible. Piles of books were stacked against the long windows at the far end of the room, obscuring what little natural light there was. It looked as though the books had been used as weapons in a battle, and the victor had forgotten them in his haste to celebrate.

The state of the library was an assault on my love of books as well as my love of order. I bent down to look at what appeared to be a bloodstain on the pages of a book by my feet, but it was only a trick of the light.

"I told thee the work wouldn't be easy," said Mrs. Wilson gloomily.

"The room must be straightened before I can hope to find

the documents," I said, half to myself, "much less sort them."

"Aye."

I took a deep breath. "I'd better start at once."

"I'll call you for lunch, miss."

"Could you bring my meal here instead? I haven't got any time to lose."

"Aye. Good luck to thee." Mrs. Wilson scurried away so quickly she must have been worried I'd try to enlist her help.

All morning I laboured, moving stacks of books and papers, coughing and sneezing as I disturbed layers of dust. It was just as well I hadn't had the opportunity to wash that morning. When Mrs. Wilson brought in my lunch, I asked for a dusting cloth, having realized that by moving the books, I was only moving the sediment from one place to another.

By mid-afternoon I was exhausted. I wasn't used to physical labour, and I felt as grimy as a charwoman. In his last letter, Sir Peter had written, *I ought to warn you the estate account-books and legal documents are not in order. Before examining them you will have to organize them.* At the time I couldn't have known how optimistic his words had been. Organize them, indeed! I'd have to *find* them first. Was this the reason physical strength was a requirement of the position? Shoving a stack of books aside, I collapsed on what appeared to be the only chair in the room—there might be others that needed to be unearthed, but I had no energy for further excavations—and surveyed the library.

There was no material difference in the appearance of the room compared to when I'd first entered it. Sir Peter might as well have asked me to spin straw into gold. No wonder the other assistants he had hired left after a week, and no wonder he hadn't asked many questions about me. Anyone who could survive this work was welcome to the handsome salary, and it was clear I'd be using all my strength to earn every penny.

I was no fool. I hadn't expected the work to be easy, and tasks that would cow a weaker woman—or man—wouldn't deter me. At Father's request, I'd once translated all five parts of *Consolatio Philosophiae* into English over a period of four days. I hadn't slept much during that time, but I'd completed the task. Father had laughed delightedly when he saw the huge pile of pages. "You're like an intelligent ox, my dear," he said. "You put your neck to the yoke, and no matter how heavy the load, you push it with all your might until it budges. What can't you accomplish through sheer willpower?"

It was the highest compliment he had ever paid me. At the time I said merely, "Everything I can do is because of your training."

Now I would put my neck to the yoke again, and this time I'd have monetary compensation for it. Taking a deep breath, I rose to my feet, determined to work for another hour or two. As I did so, I heard voices in the corridor. Moving as quietly as my heavy shoe would allow, I crept closer to the half-open door and listened.

"This isn't what he asked for." It was Bedford, speaking in a thin monotone.

"He asked for a potato and a chop," replied a harassed-sounding Mrs. Wilson. "That's what's on the plate."

"He requested gravy with it."

"There's no gravy at the moment, and I haven't the time to make it."

"He's having a bad day. Surely you could—"

"I'm in no mood to cater to His Nibs' whims today. I'm already run off my feet having to go up and down the stairs in the east wing." In a lower voice, she added, "It would've been so much easier to put Miss Springthorpe in the west wing."

"You know we couldn't do that."

"Not before we met her, no. But with that lame leg, she can't make much trouble." Her voice was light, almost joyful, with relief.

Their conversation continued for a minute longer, but it was too muffled to make out their words. Then I heard Mrs. Wilson's brisk footsteps heading down the corridor towards the kitchen. A moment later, Bedford's slower, shuffling walk indicated he was moving in the opposite direction. I opened the door a little wider and peered round it. Bedford was carrying a tray towards the door leading to the west wing. At the door, he set down the tray on a small table, then pulled a ring of keys from his pocket. He unlocked the door, opened it, and reached for the tray again.

I waited to see if he would lock the door behind him again, but he didn't. My first impulse was to follow him, but then I decided to wait and see how long he was gone. I was curious about the west wing, but not keen on the idea of being locked into it should Bedford's visit be a short one. The library clock had struck three while I was eavesdropping on the conversation between Mrs. Wilson and Bedford. I returned to my work but stayed close to the door so I'd hear him return. When I heard footsteps in the corridor and peered out to see Bedford locking the door to the west wing, I checked the time again. It was half-past three.

There must be a pattern in Bedford's visits to Nicholas Spencer. Once I determined what it was, I'd explore the west wing for myself. I wondered what sort of trouble Mrs. Wilson and Bedford thought I might make that caused them to put me in the east wing instead of the west. The way Mrs. Wilson had spoken of my leg chilled me. Why was it so important to keep me out of the west wing? Although I would have much preferred to focus on my work, I wanted to gather as much information as I could about Morton Abbey to minimize interruptions and unpleasant surprises.

That night was a particularly cold one, with the wind howling and beating against the house. Even though the windowpane in my room rattled in protest against the wind, I fell into a dreamless sleep the moment I lay down, exhausted by the day's labour. But just like the night before, I awoke suddenly because of a noise. This time it happened in the middle of the night, not early morning, and it wasn't a gunshot. It was the sound of footsteps in the corridor outside my room. I stared into the darkness, trying to distinguish the sounds of my surroundings from the loud thudding of my heart.

The footsteps were slow and shuffling, but not heavy, as if the person outside my room were on tip-toe. As the person reached my door, there was a silence, then what might have been a sigh or a quiet exclamation, and the creak of the door handle being turned.

"Who's there?" I called, sitting up. I was fairly certain I'd remembered to lock the door when I went to bed, but the possibility that I'd forgotten suddenly seemed very real. And very frightening.

There was no answer to my question, but I must have locked the door, for the creaking sound stopped, followed by the footsteps fading away into silence.

Anger replaced my fear. I pushed back the covers and got out of bed, lighting a candle as quickly as I could. Not caring that I was in my stocking feet and nightdress, I limped across the cold floor, unlocked the door, and swung it open.

I was too late. Holding my candle aloft and peering across the landing, I saw nothing. The door to the spiral staircase was closed, but I didn't think the person would have gone that way: I would have heard him or her descending. The footsteps seemed to have come from the main staircase. I started towards it but hesitated at the top. Without the shoe that balanced my lame leg, it would be dangerous to navigate the stairs.

In frustration, I shouted down the stairs, "You'll be sorry if you do that again!"

I was almost disappointed when there was no response. Stumbling back into my bedroom, I shut the door with as much force as I could, locked it, and dove back under the bedclothes, shivering.

Damn him. I thought it unlikely that Mrs. Wilson was behind this attempt to frighten me, nor did I believe in ghosts, so it must be either Bedford or Nicholas Spencer. It was becoming abundantly clear that I needed to see Mr. Spencer for myself to assess how dangerous he was.

The next day was without incident. When I met Bedford on my way to the library after breakfast, I asked him if he had spent a quiet night and met his gaze with what I hoped was a piercing look. He replied mildly that he had. I didn't believe him.

I worked all day cleaning the library, this time taking only a few minutes' break for lunch and dinner. Mrs. Wilson brought both meals to me and admonished me not to overtire myself. I paid no attention. I wasn't an ox, as Father had said. I was a machine. A determined, efficient machine that wouldn't stop until its task was completed.

I was rewarded for my efforts late that evening when I finally allowed myself to sit down and survey my progress. Unlike the day before, there was a definite change in the room. There were still disorderly piles of books and papers around the perimeter, but the middle was now clear, revealing the rich crimson expanse of the carpet and the polished beauty of the black oak desk in the centre of the room.

I hadn't forgotten about the west wing. Bedford had made two trips to the invalid while I was in the library, once at eleven o'clock for only a few minutes, and again at three o'clock for half an hour. It seemed the afternoon visit had the most potential for my explorations, so I decided to attempt the west wing the next day.

That night there were no gunshots or footsteps, or perhaps I was so exhausted that I didn't hear them.

On my third day at Morton Abbey, I took two breaks from my work. The first was to write a letter to Sir Peter. I took care to infuse my words with competence and optimism, assuring him that even though the library was in a disorganized state, I would soon put it to rights and ensure that the documents were in order. I didn't mention the fact that someone clearly didn't want me there. Instead, I apologized for not telling him sooner I was a woman, but as I had all the necessary qualifications, I didn't think it would make a difference.

I spent my second break in the west wing, looking for Mr. Spencer. As soon as the door to the west wing closed behind Bedford that afternoon, I crept out of the library. I was carrying my shoes—it was impossible to move quietly about the house while wearing them—and I limped as quickly as I could down the corridor, opened the west wing door, and slipped inside.

Thankfully, the west wing corridor was dimly lit, and I stayed close to the door until my eyes adjusted. Bedford's footsteps echoed along the far end of the passage, then stopped.

I heard what might have been a door opening, then nothing.

There were three doors on each side of the corridor and another at the far end. The first door on the left was locked, but the second wasn't. I went in.

It was a feminine room, with pink and white wallpaper and a lace-trimmed coverlet on the bed. The coverlet was thrown back to reveal pink satin sheets. An embroidery hoop lay on the bed with a half-finished cross-stitch pattern of a spaniel: it wasn't very well rendered, and I thought the person responsible for it wise to turn her attention to a different task.

The room was completely different from the others I had seen so far in this house: it seemed vibrant, pulsing with life, and I glanced behind me, worried that its occupant was present and resentful of my intrusion. But I was alone in the room, and I gazed at the open jewellery box on the toilet table overflowing with pendants and pearls, the gilt-edged hairbrush, and the open wardrobe door where velvet cloaks and silk dresses in bright colours hung. There was a faint scent of rosewater in the air. It was as if she—whoever she was—had been there only a moment ago.

I backed out of the room and closed the door quietly. As curious as I was about the woman who inhabited this room, I didn't want to invade her privacy.

There was a newspaper lying on the floor near the third door on the left, and I heard the murmur of men's voices. I went to the door opposite to it on the right side of the corridor and tried the handle, thinking it might be useful if I needed a quick place to hide.

The door was unlocked, but when I went inside, the room was not what I expected. There was an empty table in the middle of the room, and cabinets were set against the walls.

Drawing closer, I saw rocks inside them. They were all fairly small, the largest no bigger than my fist, and they seemed to be just ordinary rocks in tones of brown or grey, the sort one might pick up from a field and then throw back. They weren't labelled, but they were placed in neat, orderly lines as if they had some special significance.

I left the room with more questions than answers about the inhabitants of the house. Although my hip was beginning to ache from limping around in my stocking feet, I approached the third door on the left again. I tried the handle, slowly and quietly, but the door was locked.

Hellfire and damnation! I hadn't heard Bedford lock this door behind him. The only way to get to Nicholas Spencer seemed to be either to convince Bedford to take me to him, which seemed unlikely, or to steal Bedford's keys, which was even less likely.

I pressed my ear against the door. One of the male voices was definitely Bedford's, but I couldn't tell what they were saying. As I considered what to do next, I heard footsteps approaching from within. I flattened myself against the wall— there was no time to do more—and hoped I wouldn't be seen in the dark corridor.

"Forgive me, sir," Bedford was saying as he unlocked the door and began to push it open. "I forgot about the newspaper. I will fetch it for you at once."

Hidden behind the open door, I watched as Bedford walked the few paces to the newspaper and bent to pick it up.

It was my only chance. Dropping my shoes, I flung myself through the open doorway, shut the door, and with shaking fingers, locked myself inside.

4

Miss Springthorpe! Open the door at once!" Bedford demanded.

I ignored him and took in my surroundings. The warmth was the first thing I noticed because every other part of the house, except the kitchen, was cold. There was a crackling fire on the hearth, and though it was daylight outside, the heavy floor-to-ceiling velvet curtains were firmly closed. A tray of untouched food was set on the night table by the bed. Sitting on the bed, propped up by pillows, was a man. Not much of him was visible. Despite the warm room, he was wearing a heavy dressing gown, a night-cap pulled low over his brow, and a thick muffler around his neck. Nevertheless, I believed his gaunt face was the same one I had seen looking out of the window the morning after I had arrived at Morton Abbey.

"Good God," he said. His voice was stronger than I would have expected from an invalid.

I took a step closer to the bed. My feet sank into a thick carpet, and the firelight played on the polished mahogany furnishings. Instead of the sickroom smells of medication and unpleasant body odours I'd expected, the room smelled faintly of sandalwood.

"I'm Miss Vaughan Springthorpe," I said.

"I'll be damned if you are. Come closer so I can see you."

I limped towards him, stopping a few feet from the bed. Whether he was mad or just ill, he didn't look strong enough to hurt me.

"What's the matter with your leg?" he demanded.

"Nothing that need concern you." To avoid his asking further unwelcome questions, I added quickly and unnecessarily, "I assume you're Mr. Spencer."

Now that I was closer to him, I noticed that his eyes were unusually light-coloured and fringed with thick black lashes. It was impossible to determine his age. From Mrs. Wilson's mention that she had known Nicholas and Peter Spencer when they were boys, I assumed they were both relatively young, but even in the dim light cast by the fire, I could see that this man's skin looked strangely like old parchment, and his beard was streaked with grey. Perhaps Mrs. Wilson had been only a girl when she first came to work for the Spencer family. If that were the case, the brothers could be in their late fifties or even early sixties.

"If you tell me your real name, I'll tell you mine." He looked towards the doorway, from whence the sounds of Bedford's protests still issued, and shouted, "For God's sake, Bedford, cease that racket! I'll take care of this."

Bedford complied.

"I told you my real name," I said.

"I've never heard anything so idiotic. Vaughan is a surname. Have you no Christian name?"

"I don't know why you should care one way or the other." I did indeed have a Christian name, but nobody ever called me by it, and I wasn't about to tell him what it was.

"I *don't* care. Perhaps you could suggest an appropriate subject for conversation between a sick man who is trying to get some rest and an intruder who has locked his trusted servant out of his room." He coughed, then pointed to the glass of water on his bedside table. "Give me that."

Although I was irritated by his imperious manner, I handed him the glass, felt icy fingers brush mine, then stepped out of reach. I didn't want to be caught off guard in case he lunged at me. "What's your illness?" I asked.

"It is none of your business. What are you doing here?"

"By 'here' do you mean in this room or at Morton Abbey?"

"In this room, of course. What sort of fool do you take me for? I know you are at Morton for my brother's money. That's why all the so-called solicitors come here. You'll last no longer than the others. A few more days at most."

"You're wrong," I said firmly. "I'll stay until I've completed the work, no matter what you or anyone else in this house does to try to frighten me away."

"You're wasting your time. Has it not occurred to you that the salary my brother has offered is too good to be true? It is another of his many false promises. You won't see that money."

This was the first thing anyone at Morton had said that really did frighten me, but I tried not to show it. "You're lying. Sir Peter has already paid me a handsome advance."

"Has he? Well, that's the only money you'll get from him. Unless, of course, he's made a fortune at the gaming tables."

His sardonic tone made it clear there was no love lost between him and his brother. I had suspected as much from what Mrs. Wilson had said.

"I don't believe you."

"Look around the estate, woman! The buildings are crumbling, including this house. Everything is in disrepair. Do you see any evidence that its owner has money?" He lay back against the pillows. "Get out of my room. I want to sleep."

I would have been only too happy to obey him, but I had no intention of leaving without trying to obtain answers to my questions, especially after expending so much effort to get to Mr. Spencer. Concentrating on maintaining a civil tone, I said, "I'd be obliged if you could tell me what your objection is to my working here. Perhaps we could come to some compromise whereby I don't interfere with your life and you don't interfere with my work."

"Get out," was the response.

"Mr. Spencer—"

"Get out," he repeated. "I have neither the time nor the energy for an ugly, crippled, money-hungry spinster who pokes her nose into other people's business—and breaks into their bedrooms."

The enormity and childishness of the insult took my breath away. With as much dignity as I could muster, I turned and made my way back to the door, more aware than ever of my ungainly walk and wishing I had worn my shoes.

I unlocked the door, opened it, and handed the key to a bewildered-looking Bedford, who was still waiting outside.

"I apologize for locking you out," I said. "It won't happen again."

He stared at me, not blankly as he usually did, but with astonishment.

Gathering up my shoes, I left the west wing. Although my hip was aching, I didn't put my shoes on until I was safely back in the library.

I sat down at the large desk, most of which was still cluttered with papers and books, and dropped my head in my hands. I was too shaken by the encounter with Nicholas Spencer to resume my work immediately. Despite what Mrs. Wilson had told me, I saw no evidence that he was mad, though I'd heard madmen could pretend to be sane for short periods of time. He did seem to be ill, or at least very weak. Why hadn't he been afraid I would hurt him, locked in that room alone together? Perhaps he was stronger than he looked and merely exaggerated his illness as an excuse for his bad behaviour. Never had I met a more disagreeable, churlish, horrible old man, and I was glad he had shut himself up in the west wing where I wouldn't have to see him.

But two worries nagged at me. First, by making an enemy of Nicholas Spencer, I may have hurt my chances of keeping my position. Although Sir Peter and his brother might have their differences, they were family, after all, and he might not take kindly to an employee who forced her way into his brother's room. I had no other job prospects and nowhere else to go. Even if I could stomach the idea of living with my mother and Elizabeth, I'd rather die than give them the satisfaction of seeing me fail. I hoped Sir Peter would reply quickly to my last letter. I didn't know how fast the post moved in this isolated part of Yorkshire, but it couldn't move fast enough for me.

The second worry had to do with what Nicholas Spencer had said about Sir Peter's not paying the salary he had promised me. Could there be any truth in it? It was clear enough from the neglected state of the house and the dearth of servants that Sir Peter wasn't putting money into the estate. But that didn't necessarily mean he had none. He may be spending it on other things. Hopefully not on gambling.

I shuddered. I knew there were titled families with entailed estates and no money. Although Morton Abbey wasn't entailed—indeed, it couldn't be, if Sir Peter was selling it—were the Spencers in a similar position? If Sir Peter was as charming as Mrs. Wilson claimed, why hadn't he married an American heiress? Isn't that what the impoverished landed gentry did?

I finally shoved my worries to the back of my mind and returned to work. Finding the account books and legal documents would answer some of my questions, but there was still much clearing and organizing to be done. The only account books I'd found so far were so outdated they were useless.

Instead of eating alone in the library at dinnertime, which was becoming my habit, I decided to join Mrs. Wilson in the kitchen in hopes of learning more about the family.

"I met Mr. Spencer this afternoon," I said as I sat down at the table.

"Aye. I heard." Mrs. Wilson set a steaming bowl of stew in front of me. The housekeeper didn't seem as garrulous as usual, and I was worried my only apparent ally in the house had already turned against me.

I took a moment to consider what to say next. "I wanted to meet him, but I'm afraid I didn't go about it in the right way. I shouldn't have locked Bedford out of the room."

Mrs. Wilson settled herself at the table across from me with a bowl of lentils and started to pick through them. "I wish I'd seen Bedford's face when tha' locked him out," she said with a flicker of amusement. "That's nivver happened to him before."

"Is he angry?"

"No, just surprised. He said tha' likely got an earful from Mr. Spencer and won't want to see him again."

"That's certainly true."

"What does tha' think of Mr. Spencer?"

"He's as bad tempered as you said. I was shocked by his rudeness. I pity Bedford—it must be difficult to take orders from that man."

"Aye. Thank the good Lord I have little to do with him mysen. But he treats Bedford better than other folks. Mr. Spencer is a clever man when he's not in one of his fits, clever enough to be mannerly when he wants summat." She threw a handful of bad lentils into an empty bowl.

"Has he always lived here?"

"No. After he finished his studies at the university, he lived in London for some years. That's where he met his wife."

"He has a wife?" I thought of the pink-and-white room in the west wing. "Where is she?"

"Don't know, miss. Nobbut Mr. Spencer knows."

I suppressed the urge to laugh. Surely any wife of Nicholas Spencer would be stashed away behind one of the many locked doors in this house. Dead, of course. Bluebeard was alive, if not particularly well, and living at Morton Abbey. But it was no laughing matter, really. Perhaps there was something truly sinister in the west wing that I'd be sorry to discover.

"He was different as a young man," Mrs. Wilson continued. "Never as charming as his brother, but nice looking and pleasant enough. Mind, he was prone to melancholy and not one for talkin'. Always had his nose in a book. A few years after he married, he brought his family back here. The bailiff at Morton had just died, and Sir Peter was looking for a new one. Mr. Spencer was tired of London and took over the work. He's been here ever since."

"What was his wife like?" I asked.

"A bonny lass. Hair as black as a raven's wing. Mr. Spencer went daft with love for her. The way he acted, she might've been an angel straight from heaven, but she'd been spoiled by her rich family, and she made the servants step lively around here. We had more servants at Morton in those days, but even so we were kept busy fetchin' and carryin' for her at all hours."

"There's a woman's room in the west wing," I interposed, my curiosity outweighing my reluctance to admit I'd been snooping. "The one with pink and white wallpaper. Was it her room?"

Mrs. Wilson paused, looking startled. "Aye. I go in to do some dusting from time to time, but I try not to move owt. You'd best not go in again. It's not been used since the day she left. Mr. Spencer's orders."

"How long ago did she leave?"

"Heavens, mun be ten years. Maybe more. I don't remember. Some folks saw her in the village getting into a carriage with a strange man. There was plenty of talk about who he might be, but nobody knew for certain. Mr. Spencer didn't say a word to anyone, just shut himself up in his room. He used to come out in the daytime and read in the library or walk about the grounds, but that happened less and less. Now he nivver comes out."

I pondered this.

Mrs. Wilson pushed the bowl of lentils aside and looked at me wearily. "The saddest thing was seeing the bairn who was left behind. I suppose it wouldn't have been good for the child if Mrs. Spencer took her, but it was no better to leave her here. The poor little mite had to fend for herself. Mr. Spencer ignored her."

"That's terrible."

"Little Frances had a nanny, of course, but she was a very active and curious child, and she was left alone too much. I tried to convince Mr. Spencer to let her play with the village children, but he wouldn't. The lass ran wild, stuck in the house as she was and with no other children to play with. She tried to get her father's attention, as children will—runnin' up and down the corridor outside Mr. Spencer's room and that sort of thing. Once she broke a lamp and her father came out and shouted at her. I heard the din and went to see what was the matter, but when I got to the corridor, Mr. Spencer was in his room again with the door locked, and the poor little lass was on the floor, all crumpled up and bawlin' with her face against the door. Oh, it was a sad sight, miss."

"Where is Frances now?" I asked.

Mrs. Wilson paused to dab at her eyes with her handkerchief. "In heaven. Drowned in the pond. Nobbut Mr. Spencer knows what happened that day. He found her. Poor little lass was only eight years old."

I was too horrified to reply at once. I wished we were not in the kitchen, which always made me feel small. Out of the corner of my eye, I saw an insect fly into the weak fire on the hearth, sizzling briefly as it died.

"How did Mr. Spencer react to his daughter's death?" I asked.

"I saw no change. He stayed in his room as he always did. Even Bedford said there was no change in him. About a week after Frances died, Bedford was poorly and I took Mr. Spencer's dinner up to him. I told him I was sorry he lost his daughter, and does tha' know what he said?"

I shook my head.

"He said, 'It's better this way.' I didn't know what he meant, but I was afeared by his look. His eyes were hard and ugly, like a murderer's, like he didn't have the feelings of regular folks. I'll tell thee the truth, miss—I hated him then."

"I can understand that."

"I know tha's curious, miss," she said, leaning forward and

looking at me with more gravity than she'd shown thus far, "but tha'll be safer askin' me questions than pokin' about in the west wing. Mr. Spencer's stronger than he looks, and he's not above attacking folks when he's in one of his fits."

What I'd seen in my brief meeting with Nicholas Spencer was consistent with the picture Mrs. Wilson had painted of a harsh, miserable man. Certainly he had experienced tragic events in his life, but I knew of others who had endured worse losses and had become more compassionate because of them.

That night I had the same dream as I had the first night I arrived at Morton. Once again I was riding a horse through dark water, and once again the water rose so high I was afraid I would drown. Once again there was a large, flat rock and a willow tree on the bank. But this time, instead of the water lowering and the horse reaching the bank, the horse disappeared and I began to sink. Strangely, I could breathe normally in the water as if it were air, and I could see another person under the water about ten feet away. It seemed to be a child, wrapped up in a cloak or blanket from which she was struggling to free herself.

She sank lower, and I swam over to her—I could swim in the dream even though I couldn't in reality—and tried to unwrap the cloak to free her. But when the child's face was revealed, it wasn't a child at all: it was Nicholas Spencer, with his strange pale eyes and parchment skin. I tried to escape, but the water slowed my movements and he caught me painfully by my lame foot. He dragged me down, deep into the water until I was overcome by a choking darkness.

I awoke and sat bolt upright, gasping for breath. I felt cold and wet, and at first I thought I really had been drowning. But then I realized I was perspiring and must have pushed off the bedclothes while I slept. The cold air on my damp skin must have awakened me. Getting out of bed, I changed into a fresh nightdress.

As I was about to return to bed, I heard a distant high-pitched wailing, as if a child were crying somewhere in the house.

"I must be dreaming still," I said aloud. It was too cold to stand in the middle of the room in my nightgown, so I got back into bed and huddled under the covers, shivering. The wailing seemed to grow even louder, and I pulled the pillow over my head to try to drown it out.

"It must be the wind," I said, my voice muffled by the pillow. I didn't believe in ghosts. Obviously the tragic story Mrs. Wilson had told me had been in my mind when I fell asleep, which led to my dream, and my dream had influenced the way I heard ordinary sounds.

But no amount of reasoning or burrowing under the bedclothes helped. Even though the sound was barely audible and far from my room, it was all the more unsettling for that.

"Bloody hell." I pushed aside the blankets and got out of bed for the second time. Lighting a candle, I put on my shoes and my woollen wrapper and left the room to investigate.

I made my way slowly down the stairs to the ground floor. Mrs. Wilson had been true to her word: after the first night she had ensured that the doors at the bottom of the staircase leading to the centre of the house were unlocked.

When I entered the great hall and passed the library in the direction of the west wing, the crying grew louder. I half-expected to see a sobbing child at the door to the west wing, but when I reached it, there was nothing there. Trying the door handle, I wasn't surprised to find it locked. I pressed my ear against the door. The sound was clearly audible. Could it be Nicholas Spencer? I didn't think so. A grown man wouldn't be capable of such a high-pitched, sustained keening.

As I straightened up and turned away from the door, I collided with a tall figure and felt a bony hand grip my arm.

I gasped and dropped my candle.

5

I watched Bedford stamp out the beginnings of a fire on the floor where my candle had fallen. Then he held up his own candle and peered at me, his bushy white eyebrows meeting above his long, thin nose.

"What are you doing wandering about in the middle of the night, Miss Springthorpe?" he said sternly. "You could have burned the house down."

"I wouldn't have dropped the candle if you hadn't startled me," I said. "I was trying to find out where the crying was coming from."

"What crying?"

I hesitated, but the house was silent. "I heard a sound, like a child's wailing. It awakened me. Didn't you hear it?"

"No. There is no child in this house. The wind is strong tonight."

Even though I had entertained the same thought, I said decidedly, "It wasn't the wind."

"Perhaps you were crying in your sleep and that is what awakened you."

"I don't cry. Besides, I continued to hear it after I awoke. I heard it all the way here."

"Do you hear it still?" He peered at me like a physician about to commit his patient to a lunatic asylum.

"No."

We stared at each other.

"Oh, what's the use?" I snapped. "I'm going back to bed."

"I'll escort you back to the east wing."

"No," I said again, sharply. The thought of walking through the house with the spectre of Bedford like some ancient vampire at my side was most unpleasant. And what was *he* doing wandering around the house in the middle of the night? But I didn't want to antagonize him, so I added in a more civil tone, "Don't trouble yourself. If you would merely light my candle for me, I'll find my own way back."

"Very well." He retrieved my candle and re-lit it, then handed it to me. "Be careful," he warned. "Some of the furnishings in this house are hundreds of years old and cannot be replaced."

"I understand," I said, trying to match his chilly tone.

"You had better not leave your room again at night, Miss Springthorpe. Even with a candle, you could easily miss your footing on the stairs and have an accident." His mouth stretched thinner into what might have passed for a smile.

I tried to suppress a shudder. Not trusting my voice to be steady enough for a response, I turned to leave.

As I walked away, he added in an undertone, "Be not curious in unnecessary matters." Another one of his proverbs.

As I made my way back to my room, I cursed Bedford, Nicholas Spencer, and Morton Abbey under my breath. How my sisters would laugh to think of me—the most prosaic, logical woman alive—in this bizarre situation. I was sorry I hadn't burned the house down.

I couldn't get back to sleep. It seemed like the longest night of my life as I lay in the darkness, listening to the wind, which didn't sound quite like the crying I'd heard earlier. The house creaked and groaned as if being tortured to reveal its secrets by the merciless battering of the gale.

I finally hauled myself out of bed at first light, exhausted and bleary-eyed. The view from my window was uninspiring—nothing but a vast, bleak greyness, a barren moor covered with a light, patchy blanket of snow.

The place was so isolated and oppressive—even aside from the strange sounds in the night—that any ordinary person wouldn't be able to bear it. And even though I was convinced I could bear more than an ordinary person, three months was definitely too long to remain in such a hateful place. I re-read Sir Peter's letter and noticed that he had offered the salary for the work he wanted done, not for a specific period of time. Three months was merely his estimate. I resolved then and there to work harder, through the nights if necessary, and finish the work within the month.

I put my resolve into action that day, and I spent the next few days closeted in the library, taking all my meals there and working late, sleeping only three or four hours each night. In my exhaustion I slept soundly, so if strange things happened while I slept, I was unaware of them.

By two o'clock in the morning on my seventh day at Morton Abbey, my head ached and my eyes stung, but I had finally organized the library and collected all the documents I needed to put the estate's accounts in order and prepare for the sale of the property. I left the documents in a few neat piles on the desk and went to bed.

When I awoke, I was surprised to find it was already ten o'clock. I ought to have expected my body to finally rebel against the schedule I'd set for myself. Mrs. Wilson had warned me more than once, "Tha'll make thysen ill, miss, workin' such long hours," but I'd paid no attention. At least I wasn't ill—I'd merely overslept. I could make up for the loss of time.

I hurried down to the kitchen to a cold breakfast of bread and cheese. Mrs. Wilson wasn't there, so I ate quickly, then made myself a pot of tea to take to the library.

When I opened the library doors, I couldn't believe what I saw. At first I thought I'd somehow entered the wrong room, that there was a second library in the house. But this room was horrifyingly familiar. It was the same room in exactly the same state of chaos I'd seen a week ago, my first morning at Morton.

Well, not exactly the same state. The dust had not reappeared, but once again, books were strewn everywhere, some lying open, face down on the floor, their pages crumpled. The same gaping holes in the bookcases leered at me. The same precarious piles of books were stacked against the long windows at the end of the room. Worst of all, the account books and legal documents I'd left in neat stacks on the desk were gone. Some papers were strewn about the room, but it was immediately clear there were fewer of them than there ought to be.

For the first time in my life, I felt my knees go weak. My vision narrowed to a single telescopic view of the far end of the library, and the tea things rattled on the tray. By some miracle, I managed to set down the tray without upsetting it. I sank to the floor on my knees, taking deep breaths. I had never fainted before and I wasn't about to do so now.

Slowly, my vision cleared. On my hands and knees, I crept to the nearest mess of papers. Picking them up leaf by leaf, I saw that they were blank. In an increasing frenzy, I moved to the next pile of papers, then the next. All the papers in the library were the same. I didn't dare look at any of the books for fear they too were filled with empty pages.

I no longer knew what was real and what was a trick of my imagination. Is this how it felt to be mad? Trembling violently, I rose to my feet and ran as fast as my lame leg would allow, out of the library, through the great hall, and out of the house.

I didn't stop running even when the blast of cold air hit me. I hadn't thought to put on my cloak, much less a hat and gloves, but I was in such a disordered state that I hardly felt the cold. All I could think was that I must escape.

I ran down the main carriage drive, then veered off across the snowy front lawn, narrowly missing a collision with the big chestnut tree, and onto the rougher ground of the moor. I ran for what seemed like miles. My body felt oddly suspended in time and space. By now, I thought, I must be out of sight of the house, and I allowed myself to look over my shoulder. But the house was still there, waiting like a demonic presence. I hadn't run far enough.

At that moment my foot struck something—a stone, perhaps—and I tripped and fell headlong. I didn't know how long I lay on the ground, but I slowly became aware of a sharp pain at my temple and of a chill seeping into my bones.

Then I heard heavy footsteps approaching. I tried to scream, but I could only emit a pathetic squeak. Now, I would be murdered on the spot.

Instead, I felt something warm—a cloak? a blanket?— enveloping me and strong masculine arms lifting me up and carrying me as if I weighed no more than a child.

I must have dozed or lost consciousness, for the next thing I knew, I was inside a warm room, being lowered gently onto some cushions.

"There, now," my rescuer said in a hearty baritone. "Are

you comfortable? You're chilled right through, so I thought I'd put you by the fire."

I looked up into the face of the most beautiful young man I'd ever seen. In truth, I hadn't seen many young men in my life—not so close, anyway—but this one was remarkable by any standards. His nondescript woollen coat and brown cloth cap worked to his advantage by setting off the bluest of blue eyes and unruly fair hair.

I put a hand to my head, which was throbbing.

"You've got a nasty gash. Will you let me put some balm on it?" There was an intriguing Yorkshire lilt in his voice, but his speech was that of an educated man, too cultured for the rural labourer he looked to be.

"Yes." My voice was hoarse, as if I hadn't used it in a long time. I supposed I hadn't.

He jumped up with an easy grace that belied his height and went to the other side of the room, then returned and knelt before me. With gentle fingers he smeared a cool ointment on my forehead, then tied a strip of cloth around my head as a bandage.

I looked around, for the second time that day not fully believing my surroundings were real. I was in a simple, one-room cottage that looked as comfortable and relaxed as my rescuer. It was a bachelor's dwelling, clean but untidy—clothing was thrown over a chair, and there were various tools I couldn't identify piled up close to the door. Beside the cheerful fire, not far from where I reclined, sat a large wiry-haired dog with hopeful brown eyes.

"Are you afraid of dogs?" the young man asked. "Welkin won't hurt you—he's friendly but he's a gentleman."

"No, I'm not afraid."

As if on cue, Welkin approached and lay down beside me. I reached out and he nuzzled my hand.

It all seemed so strange, like a dream. Or perhaps I was dead and this was heaven. The cottage and the dog were so very different from anything I'd seen at Morton so far that they seemed to belong to a different world. And this man who filled the room with his warm, open manner was everything an angel ought to be.

"Who are you?" I asked.

"I'm Joe Dixon, the gardener here."

"Here?" I was still disoriented enough to hope that "here" meant somewhere other than Morton Abbey.

"Yes, at Morton," he replied, dissolving my illusion.

"But it's winter. Surely there's nothing for you to do here now."

He grinned. "There are always things to do. I'll show you when you're feeling better. Are you staying at the house?"

I couldn't suppress a shudder. "Yes."

"What's your name?"

"Miss Vaughan Springthorpe."

He didn't blink an eye. "Pleasure to meet you, Vaughan." He ought to have called me "Miss Springthorpe." But far from offending me with his ready use of my familiar name, Joe Dixon melted my heart.

To my utter mortification, I felt tears welling up in my eyes. I couldn't remember a time when I'd allowed my emotions to get the better of me in front of another person. I covered my face with my hands, unable to prevent the tears from spilling over.

Joe waited silently beside me. Welkin stretched out at my other side and rested his head on my knee. When my weeping subsided, Joe gave me a handkerchief, which I took gratefully and mopped myself up as best I could.

"I'm sorry," I said shakily. "I never cry. I don't know what's the matter with me."

"You had a bad spill. From the way you were running from the house, I'd wager you had a shock of some kind too."

"You saw me?"

He nodded.

Floodgates of a different kind opened, and I told him what had happened since I arrived at Morton, surprising myself again. Talking at such length was no more natural to me than crying.

A shadow passed over Joe's sunny countenance as I told him about my encounter with Nicholas Spencer. When I reported that he'd called me an ugly, crippled, money-hungry spinster, the shadow turned into a quick flash of anger.

"That was cruel of him," Joe said. "Cruel and untrue." He didn't know me, of course, so he couldn't judge whether Mr. Spencer's words were true or not, but it was kind of him to say they weren't.

Welkin, whose head was still on my knee, looked from me to Joe and back again with sad eyes and a furrowed brow as if trying to mimic Joe's concern.

I told Joe the rest of the story, including what I had seen in the library that morning. When I was finished, I asked, "Do you think I could be imagining any of this? Is it possible I'm losing my mind?"

"No, I don't think so. I think someone—Mr. Spencer, most likely—wants you gone, that's all. Sir Peter ought to have warned you about him."

"I wish Sir Peter were here." It only just occurred to me that

Joe might know the Spencer family very well, despite his youth. "Have you met him?"

"Yes. He hired me last summer. He seems to be a good sort of man, but a restless one. He isn't really interested in the estate."

This was no more than I'd already surmised for myself.

"I've never met Nicholas Spencer," Joe added, "but from what you say, I'm glad of it. All the same, I can't help pitying him a little. He must have suffered a good deal."

"I have no sympathy for people who create their own suffering," I countered. "I wouldn't be surprised if he drove his wife and daughter away on purpose, or murdered them both."

"I hope not," he said. "What will you do now? Will you look for work elsewhere?"

"No. I told Mr. Spencer I'd complete the work no matter what he might do to frighten me away. And I will." I realized as I spoke that I had changed my mind since my flight from the house. My pride would not allow me to give up so easily.

"Are you certain? There must be similar work you could find that isn't as frustrating or difficult. Come to think of it, I can't imagine any work more frustrating than yours, considering the circumstances."

I raised my chin. "My father told me there was nothing I couldn't do if I put my mind to it. He trained me to be a purely rational person and gave me a man's education. My sheer pigheadedness—that's my mother's term—also helps."

"You're not like any woman I've met before. Nor any man, neither."

The admiration in Joe's eyes was gratifying, and I allowed myself to bask in the rare experience for a moment.

"I ought to go back," I said.

"Not yet, surely. You ought to rest a bit longer."

A sudden worry struck me that if I stayed even a minute longer I'd never want to leave. "No, I'm well enough to get back to work now. God knows I shouldn't waste another minute, considering the task ahead of me." Then, realizing my words might be taken the wrong way, I added, "Not that talking to you is a waste of time." I looked down at my feet, cursing my awkwardness and the heat that rose to my face.

"Will you let me come with you, at least part of the way?" he asked, not seeming to notice my confusion. "It's a long walk in the cold."

I nodded, still unable to look at him. "Thank you."

He helped me to my feet and reached for a green woollen blanket that was lying over a chair, then arranged it around my shoulders.

I was still shaky and my head throbbed, so it was a relief to lean on Joe's arm as we walked back towards the house. He was so tall that the top of my head barely reached his shoulder.

It took us only twenty minutes to reach the main carriage drive and gain sight of the house. In my panicked flight before I fell, I couldn't have gone far. How strange that my sense of time and space had been so confused.

"I can go on alone from here," I said. "Thank you for everything you've done. I don't know what would have happened if you hadn't found me."

"Any time you need me, I'll come," he replied, sounding so much like the perfect guardian angel that I would have smiled if he hadn't looked so solemn.

I began to remove his blanket, but he said, "No, keep it until we see each other again. I won't take it back unless I see you wearing a cloak next time—it's too cold to be without one."

In spite of my resolve to get back to the house and start organizing the library at once, I watched Joe turn and walk away. I pulled the blanket closer, hiding my nose in it. It smelled of wood smoke and pine needles, and I inhaled the scent deeply with an almost superstitious notion that it would give me courage for the task ahead of me.

Strangely, the main doors were unlocked and unmanned. Was there any other house with so many inside doors that were locked and outside ones that weren't?

I went inside, making my way through the great hall towards the library. On my way there, Mrs. Wilson popped her head out of one of the front rooms.

"Oh, it's tha', miss," she said, emerging from the room with a box of cleaning supplies. "I didn't hear thee come down for breakfast. My word, what's happened?"

I knew I must look a sight, enveloped in the green blanket, my hair awry, and wearing as a bizarre headdress the strip of cloth Joe had tied around my forehead.

"I went for a walk on the grounds and fell. It's nothing, really." I hesitated, then asked, "Mrs. Wilson, have you been in the library this morning?"

"Why, no, miss."

"Will you come with me to look at it, please?"

"Wouldn't tha' like to clean up a bit first?"

"I'll clean up after we go to the library."

"As you wish." She set down her box and followed me. If my odd appearance and admittedly unconvincing explanation of it troubled her, she hid it beneath her usual loquacity. "It's been a busy morning. Mr. Spencer had a bad night and Bedford's been tending to him, so I've been butler and housekeeper rolled into one. Bedford wouldn't like it that I've unlocked the front doors, but I can't be in two places at once."

Mr. Spencer had a bad night, did he? I had no doubt he was responsible for the state of the library and the loss of the documents, either by his own hand or by proxy. No doubt he was exhausted after spending the night destroying my week's worth of work. But it was best not to share my suspicions with Mrs. Wilson until I saw the library again and had a better sense of whether I could trust her or not.

When she opened the library door and stepped inside, she gasped. Even before I looked inside, that gasp ended the faint hope I was entertaining that the library would be in the state I had left it in the night before. It was as disordered and untidy—and the scattered papers as blank—as they had been earlier that morning.

"How did this happen?" cried Mrs. Wilson, staring at me.

"I wish I knew." I studied her face, looking for a sign that she knew more than she was letting on. If she did, she was a very good actress, for I saw nothing there but shock. I continued, "When I left the library last night, it was in perfect order. When I came in this morning, it was in disarray. It would have taken someone hours to create such a mess. Do you have any idea who could have done this?"

"No, miss."

"As far as I know, there are only three inhabitants of this house: you, Bedford, and Mr. Spencer. It seems to me neither Bedford nor Mr. Spencer is strong or healthy enough to throw these heavy books around the room." I didn't want to make an enemy of the housekeeper, but I couldn't trust anyone. "And I can't imagine why you would do such a thing."

"Me, miss?" Mrs. Wilson looked appalled. "I would nivver do such a thing. But there are four folks living here. Tha' didn't include thysen."

My eyebrows shot up. "Are you suggesting I did this?"

"No, not o' purpose, of course. But this house has a strange effect on folks, especially at night. Maybe in your sleep—"

"Whether awake or asleep, I didn't destroy this room. Why would I ruin my own work?"

Mrs. Wilson didn't reply, and we surveyed the room for a few minutes in silence.

"I'm going to my room to change," I said.

"Would you like me to order a fly from the village, miss?"

"What for?"

"I thought tha'd want to go home after everything that's happened. Nobody would blame thee."

"I'm not going anywhere. I'll be working in the library all day, as usual."

I went upstairs to wash my face and tidy my hair. The shaving mirror showed that I didn't look quite as bad as I felt, but I certainly didn't look good—tangled hair, hollow eyes beneath the ragged strip of cloth around my forehead, a scratch on my left cheek.

I removed the makeshift bandage. The gash on my forehead had stopped bleeding but looked ugly and swollen. Going to the washstand, I washed my face gingerly, then brushed my hair and pinned it into a knot at the nape of my neck. My ablutions made me feel a little better. I sat down at the small desk near the bed, took paper and pen, and wrote a brief letter.

Dear Mr. Spencer,

I am writing to request the return of the documents that were taken from the library. I don't know who took them, but I believe you do, and you know as well as I do that those documents are necessary for my work. If you don't return them

within twenty-four hours, I will be forced to resort
to measures you won't like in order to locate them.
I am a patient and persistent woman, and I won't
give up until I find them. I assure you I will be
finished with my work and out of the house within
a month if you grant my request. If you do not, you
will find me very difficult to get rid of.

Sincerely,

Miss Vaughan Springthorpe

There. My threat was as politely worded as I could manage.
I knew I was taking a risk, especially since I still didn't know the
exact nature of the relationship between Nicholas Spencer and
his brother, but it seemed reasonable to think Sir Peter wouldn't
want the work he hired me for disrupted or made more difficult
than it needed to be.

I gave the note to Bedford to deliver to Mr. Spencer, then
went to the library and began the weary work of returning the
books to their proper places and searching for any legal papers
my enemy might have missed in his rampage. I was determined
that nobody would drive me away from Morton Abbey. It
wasn't even about the money. I was going to do the work I was
hired for if it killed me, just to prove I could.

6

The next few days brought no reply from Nicholas Spencer to my note. I had questioned Bedford about the library, but as I expected, he denied playing any part in the destruction. Only one event occurred to break up the tedium of my work: a letter came from Italy. Finally, Sir Peter had written.

Dear Miss Springthorpe,

I apologize for my delay in replying to your letter. I've been travelling on the Continent and couldn't write until now. You may be at ease on the subject of your sex. All that matters to me is that you can do the work, and you came so highly recommended by Mr. Jameson and Mr. Kent that I have no worries on that score. I am impressed with your initiative and hard work so far. (Mrs. Wilson has written to me also and says you are so dedicated that you do not even stop to eat most days. Please do take meals and rest breaks as often as you can— it is not easy work, and I would not wish to starve, however indirectly, any of my employees!)

Allow me to apologize also for not telling you when I hired you that my brother lives at Morton. Because he has been ill and keeps to his room, I didn't see the *necessity of it, but I ought to have informed you. He will not be any help to you since he is opposed to my selling the estate, which you probably already know. Please pay no attention to any attempts on his part to convince you that he has possession of legal documents proving the estate is his, not mine. This is part of his madness. You will see from my father's will that the estate is fully and legally mine. I haven't had the heart to send my brother away, but if he causes any trouble for you, I can have him removed.*

    Do let me know if you have any further questions or concerns, and believe me when I say how pleased I am to find a dedicated legal assistant at last.

    With warmest regards,

    Sir Peter Spencer

I considered this letter not only a welcome relief from my worries but also a valuable weapon in my arsenal. Sir Peter seemed the kindest and most reasonable of men. What other man would allow his insane brother to live rent-free in his house, especially a brother who was actively opposing his decision to sell his own property? With Sir Peter on my side, Nicholas Spencer could do his pathetic worst. He might delay me, but he couldn't stop me.

I was also glad that my sex made no difference to Sir Peter. In the three months of searching for employment after Father's death, I had heard everything from "you'll take work away from the male clerks" to "go home and keep to your needlework." My qualifications and offers to work without pay for a time to prove my competence had been brushed aside. Sir Peter's decision to hire me might have had more to do with the fact that the other legal assistants had been frightened away than with his belief that a woman could do legal work, but it didn't matter. I felt truly secure in my post for the first time, as frustrating as the situation and the work itself was.

The third morning after the library had been ransacked, Bedford appeared at the library door to inform me that Mr. Spencer wanted to see me.

"He wants to see me?" I felt a mixture of alarm and relief. "Now?"

"Yes."

I was running out of things to do in the library without access to the legal documents. But I also sensed that Mr. Spencer wouldn't give them up without a fight, and I wasn't interested in arguing with a madman. Even if he wasn't mad, he'd been so horrid to me the last time we met that I could hardly stomach the prospect of seeing him again.

Bedford led the way to the west wing, unlocking the two doors that separated Nicholas Spencer's room from the centre of the house. I was glad I didn't have to creep about or try to outwit Bedford this time. I was especially glad I didn't have to remove my shoes. Having to reveal my deformed foot to the merciless eyes of Mr. Spencer had been one of the worst things about my first encounter with him. This time I wouldn't be vulnerable in any way.

Bedford ushered me into the inner sanctum and left immediately, closing the door behind him. The room looked exactly the same as before and was just as dimly lit. Despite the slivers of sunlight at the edges of the heavy curtains, they were firmly closed. Once again there was a blazing fire in the grate, and the room smelled faintly of sandalwood.

Mr. Spencer wasn't dressed as warmly as the last time. He wore nothing on his head, and I was surprised to see that his hair was dark, with only a few streaks of grey, unlike his beard. When I came in he was sitting propped up against pillows, with his head back and eyes closed. He didn't change his position even when I approached the bed. Was he asleep, or only pretending?

"Mr. Spencer," I said.

His eyes flew open. "You needn't shout. I'm not deaf."

"I see you intend to be as civil to me as the last time we met," I said briskly. "Why don't you simply tell me where the documents are so I can remove myself before we repeat that unpleasant conversation? Or I could go at once and you could send me the information in a letter instead." I turned back towards the door.

"No, that won't do. Come here. Sit down." After a few seconds' pause, during which I didn't move, he added, "Please."

It was the first polite word I'd heard from him. I took the chair he indicated, which was close enough to the bed that I could see his ghastly parchment-like skin. Something was the matter with him, certainly, but I was still unsure whether it was physical or mental. Perhaps both.

He was looking at my forehead. The gash on it had begun to heal but was still unsightly. "What happened to you?" he asked.

"I fell. It's nothing."

"Oh. I wish to apologize for my conduct the other day. I was in a great deal of pain, and it led me to speak in a discourteous fashion."

"Discourteous" is not the word I would have used. "Nasty" or "cruel" would be nearer the mark. While I found it interesting that such a disagreeable man would venture to apologize to me, it was even more interesting that the apology was delivered in the same imperious tone he used when he ordered me to sit down. It was clear enough he didn't mean a word of it, but why had he bothered to even attempt an apology?

"Well?" he prompted, still in the same tone. "Have you nothing to say?"

"Nothing, sir," I replied dryly.

"It is customary for both persons to apologize when they have insulted each other."

"I apologize only when I'm actually sorry, or when I'm convinced the other person is. Neither is true in this case."

He glared at me.

"Mr. Spencer, do you intend to return the documents or not? I have work to do and haven't got time to waste on useless conversation."

"You may have the documents," he said slowly, "but they are incomplete."

"What do you mean?"

"Haven't you read them?"

Now it was my turn to glare at him. "How could I, when I'd only just found them before you took them and laid waste to the library?"

If I'd been hoping he would admit his part in the devastation or that his face would give him away, I was disappointed.

"The account books and legal papers relating to the property that were in the library are old documents from when my father was alive," he said. "He changed his will several times, but due to the incompetence of our previous family lawyer, most of those amendments have been lost. I have the most recent papers that you'll need."

"Very well. I'll take those too. Where are they?"

"Slowly, Miss Springthorpe. I have a proposition for you,

but I must explain something first. You probably think I dislike you, but my dislike is not personal—I don't even know you."

"You may be surprised to learn that I don't care whether you dislike me or not."

He cursed under his breath. "Are you capable of listening to what I have to say? It will be exhausting trying to explain my proposition if I'm interrupted every few seconds. You must remember I'm not well."

"I'll do my best," I replied. Nicholas Spencer was just the sort of invalid I found most trying—imperious and self-pitying by turns. Why did he think anyone would wish to obey his commands or feel any sympathy for him?

"The reason for my objection to you ought to be obvious," he went on. "Your business is to turn me out of my own home. Naturally, I don't want the estate sold while I'm still living. I have given up trying to control what happens to it after I die. I know you think the estate belongs to my brother, but if you knew how he has plundered it to finance his mindless amusements—"

He began to cough, and I automatically reached for the glass of water on his bedside table. When I handed it to him, my fingers brushed his. Just like the first time, his skin felt as cold as ice. As cold as death.

He leaned forward and took a sip. "Thank you. I won't bore you with the details of my brother's extravagant way of life. Suffice it to say he has never cared about the estate as I do. He has contributed nothing to it, whereas I poured everything I had into it—my energy, my time, my money—before I became ill. This house is only a shadow of its former self, but if you had seen it then, you would have thought it a fine place. Everyone thought so."

I shifted impatiently. When would he get to the point?

"This estate is mine. There's no need to frown in such a disagreeable way, Miss Springthorpe. I do not suffer from delusions, despite what some people say. In his last recorded will, my father left the estate to my brother. But he made another will shortly before he died, leaving the estate to me."

I couldn't suppress an unladylike snort. If I had a penny for every client who made that claim to Father, I'd be rich. "Where is this will?" I asked, trying to keep a straight face.

"I don't know. It's somewhere in the house, but I haven't been able to find it. And you needn't smirk about that, either. I am neither well enough nor stupid enough to try to dispute the matter in court. I have one request of you, and if you'll agree to it, you may have all the documents and I won't get in the way of your work."

"What is it?"

"I will die soon." He looked across the room at the heavily-curtained windows. "There are things I want done with my possessions in this house before that happens. I am asking you to help me with those tasks and to delay the sale of the estate until after my death. I will pay you for the work, of course." He leaned back against the pillows as if he'd offered a thorough and reasonable explanation of what he wanted me to do.

My eyebrows shot up. "You'll forgive me if I have a few questions about your proposition, Mr. Spencer. First, when exactly do you expect to die?"

"Good God, you're direct. Not to mention heartless."

"I don't know what sort of lawyer you think I am, but I won't act against Sir Peter's wishes. He wants the estate sold as soon as possible, certainly within three months."

"I am not asking for much longer than that. I would be surprised if I live another six months."

I frowned. "Did a doctor tell you that?"

"I don't need a doctor to tell me."

"What is your illness?"

"I'm suffering from mortification."

In a flash of anger, I shot back, "Don't play games with me, Mr. Spencer. I'll never make an agreement with you that depends on waiting until you die, and I can't work for you when I'm already working for your brother. He is my client."

"I am not asking you to do legal work for me, so there is no conflict in that regard."

"What are you asking me to do, then?"

"I have a collection of minerals that must be categorized and labelled."

"Are those the rocks in the room down the corridor?" I asked, remembering too late that I'd gone into the rooms in the west wing illicitly.

He looked at me with narrowed eyes. "You haven't leave to go in there. If you've put anything out of order—"

I couldn't resist. "That's *your* specialty, isn't it? You create chaos out of order. I do the opposite."

He acted as if he hadn't heard me. "Those minerals are valuable and I'll know if even one of them is missing."

"I'm not a thief." I stood up stiffly. "You ought to hire someone else who understands you and who has the time to carry out your orders. I already have an employer and enough work to keep me occupied for a long time."

I was nearly at the door when he spoke again.

"There is no one else I can ask." His voice had lost its overbearing tone, taking on a note of desperation.

I turned around.

"I am sure you know that my brother hired others before

you. Whether they were discouraged by the amount of work involved or by the strange goings-on in this house, they left within a week. You're different. No obstacle appears to discourage you. I didn't have to worry about the estate's being sold until you came." He ran a hand through his hair, then continued, "The truth is that I need help. I cannot catalogue the minerals on my own. My vision is not what it used to be and it takes very little to strain my eyes. Will you please consider taking on this work? There is a cheque for one hundred pounds in the top drawer of the desk by the window. Every month I'll pay you the same amount. It's a very good salary for what will amount to only a couple of hours of work every day."

I glanced at the desk but made no move towards it. He already thought me money-hungry, so what did it matter if I accepted it? But my hesitation wasn't because of the money. I didn't want to displease Sir Peter, and I didn't want to work with Nicholas Spencer. He would be very trying to my nerves. On the other hand, the money would be useful, especially if there was any truth in what he'd said about Sir Peter's inability to pay the rest of my salary.

"Will you put this offer in writing?" I asked.

"I haven't got the strength to write, but you can write it down yourself. I'll sign it, as long as the terms are agreeable to me."

"I'll need a day to think about it. I'll take the documents on my way out, if you please."

"You may take the papers that were in the library. They are in the top of that chest of drawers." He watched me retrieve the papers, then sighed and closed his eyes. "I'm tired. You can go now. Come back at precisely three o'clock tomorrow afternoon."

I chafed at the return of his imperious tone. I had no

intention of being treated like a servant or of following his orders to the letter. I wasn't ready to leave yet, either. "Does anyone else live in this house besides you, Bedford, and Mrs. Wilson?"

"No."

"But you mentioned the strange goings-on in the house. I assumed that you, or perhaps both you and Bedford were responsible for trying to scare me away—the chaos in the library, the footsteps outside my bedroom door, the gunshots in the middle of the night . . ." I paused, hoping he'd give himself away, but he didn't react. ". . . but I don't understand how you or any other adult could have made a sound like a child crying."

He sat bolt upright. "You've heard it too?" His voice was filled with a sudden frenzied energy. "Bedford and Mrs. Wilson don't hear it. At least they say they don't."

A cold chill snaked up my spine. I said flatly, "I don't believe in ghosts. If there is a child locked up somewhere in this house, you ought to own up to it."

But he was staring straight ahead as if in a trance, not listening. After a long, suspended moment, he slumped back against the pillows.

"Why are you still here?" he snapped. "I told you to leave."

I left.

7

At two o'clock the next afternoon I looked up from the desk in the library, bleary-eyed from reading the mountain of legal papers in front of me. So far, what Mr. Spencer had told me about them was correct. They all dated from well before the death of his father, Sir Peter Spencer the elder, and there was nothing in them to cause concern about legal irregularities. The estate was not entailed, but old Sir Peter had followed tradition by leaving it to his elder son. Strangely, he had left his younger son very little, just an annual sum of five hundred pounds, which to me was a great deal of money but was meagre in light of the old man's assets. Even if there was no truth in Mr. Spencer's claim that his father had changed his will on his deathbed to leave his whole estate to his younger son, the old man must have known he was setting his sons against each other. On the other hand, I had seen many wills in the course of my work with Father, and I was often amazed by the testator's blindness to the divisive effects of his will. The Spencers' case was clearly an extreme one, but I supposed that where there was more property, there was more greed.

I wondered if Nicholas Spencer had kept some of the papers with the intention of feeding them to me one at a time, like treats for a dog, in order to keep me under his control. I wouldn't stand for it. I hadn't decided yet whether to accept his offer of employment, and I would see him when I was good and ready.

Through the long windows at the far end of the library, a movement caught my eye, and I went to investigate. The ubiquitous grey mist enveloped the house, but through it I could make out a human shape, followed by a smaller four-legged shape, moving around the low shrubbery. More by instinct than by sight, I knew it must be Joe and Welkin.

I hurried back to the desk and scooped up the papers—I knew better now than to leave them unattended in the library. I made my way to my room as quickly as I could, left the papers on my bed, and left, locking the door behind me.

I was worried I'd taken too long getting outside, but when I went to the spot where I'd seen the moving figures, they were still there, about twenty yards from the house.

"Joe?" I called, feeling awkward. What if I were mistaken? Or what if he had done his duty by coming to my rescue the other day and didn't particularly want to see me again?

"Vaughan? What a pleasure to see you!" He banished my doubts at once with his hearty greeting as he appeared out of the mist. From behind him, Welkin uttered a short bark and came bounding to meet me.

Since my first meeting with Joe, I'd begun to doubt whether he was as wonderful as I remembered; perhaps I had exaggerated his positive qualities because of my desperate state that day. Now I knew I hadn't. It wasn't just his good looks. The energy and warmth radiating from him was irresistible, and I was happy merely to be in his presence.

"I'm glad to see you're wearing warm clothing today," he said. "Do you feel better?"

"Yes, much better, thanks to you." I couldn't think of anything else to say and was annoyed with myself for feeling so tongue-tied and shy. After all, he was only the gardener, and his manner was so frank and open that I must be the only person on earth who could feel ill at ease around him.

"I was just on my way to check some of the plants," he said. "My garden almanac says there'll be another cold spell before spring, and I wanted to make sure they're safe. Would you like to come with me?"

"Yes," I said almost before he'd finished asking the question. I would have agreed to nearly any offer from him, especially after spending so much time in the darkness that was Morton.

Joe led the way to a part of the estate I hadn't explored yet, near the west wing of the house. On the ground there were several rows of burlap-shrouded, snow-covered lumps. Nearby was a stone wall about six feet high.

Some of the coverings had come loose from the plants, and Joe bent down to rearrange the little shrouds. One covering had come loose altogether, exposing a shrivelled stick.

"That one's dead, isn't it?" I said.

"Maybe. Maybe not." He crouched down and examined it, then replaced the covering as gently as if the plant were a baby. "We'll have to wait and see."

I gazed out over the landscape. Most of the mist had dissipated, but I still couldn't tell where the garden ended and the barren moor began. It all looked dead and ugly to me. "I don't know anything about plants or gardens."

"Don't you?" Joe looked up at me. His eyes were very blue under the brim of his cloth cap. "Doesn't your family have a garden?"

"No. We always lived in London, and we had only a bit of

grass and a shrub in front of our house."

"A shrub?" He laughed. "Just one?"

"Yes. A very ugly one."

"I'll teach you about gardening, if you like. There's nothing more satisfying than a garden you've tended with your own hands."

"If you say so." I wasn't convinced, but I was willing to listen.

"Come, I'll show you the rose garden. That's the best part."

I followed him to the stone wall. There was a wrought-iron gate set in the middle of it, and as he opened it, the rusty hinges squealed.

I passed through and found myself inside a small walled garden, no more than twenty feet square. It smelled like dead leaves and other rotting vegetable matter. Except for a bench at the far end, there was nothing to see. Nothing remarkable, anyway. There were more burlap-covered lumps on the ground. Vines hung along the wall, sodden and drooping from the snow and rain.

"I suppose it must be pretty in the summer," I said hesitantly.

"Pretty! You'll never see anything more beautiful, I promise. June and July are the best months for the roses. Then you'll see climbers on the walls and blooms on the bushes too—pink, yellow, red, white." Joe's voice was filled with excitement as he beamed at the garden, then at me, as if willing me to see what he saw.

June and July. By then I'd be long gone, or such was my original plan. But if I accepted Nicholas Spencer's offer, I might still be there. Although I'd never cared much for flowers or gardens, suddenly it seemed crucially important that I see the roses in full bloom.

"If the estate sells before summer, I won't see the roses," I said slowly. "You won't either, will you?"

A shadow crossed his face. "Oh. I suppose not."

"Where will you go when the estate is sold?"

He shrugged. "I'll find work somewhere. It won't be difficult. Sir Peter will recommend me."

As he examined the plants, I wandered over to the bench. It matched the wrought-iron of the gate but was more intricate in its detail, with insets of woven vines and leaves. At the centre of the backrest was a heart-shaped medallion with two initials. The initials were so ornately detailed that it was difficult to make out what they were, but I eventually deciphered them: N & A. Was the "N" for Nicholas? Mrs. Wilson hadn't told me what Mr. Spencer's wife's Christian name was, but I'd wager it began with an "A."

I sat on the bench. "Mr. Spencer wants me to do some work for him."

Joe looked up, giving me his full attention. "Does he, now? What sort of work?"

"Labelling rocks. But I think that's just a delaying tactic. He doesn't want the estate sold until he dies."

Joe frowned. "Is he dying?"

"He seems to think so." I chose not to report Mr. Spencer's claim that he was dying of mortification. If it had been an attempt at black humour, I didn't find it amusing.

Joe came to sit beside me on the bench, resting his arm along the back of it. I was distracted by the thought that if he were to move his arm slightly forward, it would be around my shoulders.

"Are you going to accept his offer?" Joe asked.

"I don't know. I certainly won't delay the sale of the estate on his behalf, since that would be acting against Sir Peter's wishes. And I find Mr. Spencer so difficult, no compensation would make his offer worthwhile." I wanted to tell Joe about the crying sound, which was more disturbing to me than anything Mr. Spencer had said or done, but I was afraid he'd think I was mad.

"It sounds as though you've made your decision, then."

I hesitated. It seemed ridiculous, given all the troubles I'd encountered in the short time I'd been at Morton Abbey, but now that I was outside in the fresh, bracing air with Joe, I wanted to prolong my stay. Not because Nicholas Spencer wanted me to, but because Joe's enthusiasm for the garden was contagious. Or perhaps because my interest in Joe was keener than it ought to be, and I wanted more time with him. It was silly. We'd only just met, and for all I knew, I wouldn't see him again except perhaps from a distance.

"I suppose it would be acceptable if I didn't have to work too closely with Mr. Spencer," I said. "If he gives me instructions and then I can work alone, I could bear it." I added, more to myself than Joe, "And with the salary he's offered me in addition to my regular salary from Sir Peter, I could rent a flat in London and start my own legal practice."

"Is that what you want?" he asked.

I flushed and looked down at the ground as if I'd revealed my most intimate secret. In a way, I had. It had always seemed such a far-fetched aspiration that I hadn't fully admitted, even to myself, how much I wanted it. "Yes. I've heard of a woman solicitor in London who's done it, so it's not impossible. Her name is Eliza Orme and she apparently has enough conveyancing work to support herself."

He nodded thoughtfully.

"I want to be independent," I went on. "I don't want to live with my mother and sister, but they think my plans are selfish, as well as just plain odd."

He was silent.

"Do you think I'm being selfish? Or odd?" I surprised myself by asking the question, but now that it was out, I watched his face anxiously as if his opinion would be the final pronouncement on my character.

"No," he said, "but then I live by myself, if Welkin doesn't count, so maybe I'm selfish and odd too." His smile returned as he met my gaze.

"It's different for men. Nobody thinks it odd for a man to live alone."

"I suppose not. But I'm six-and-twenty, and my mam thinks I ought to be married with a family of my own by now. She wants grandchildren."

I did wonder why he wasn't married, since he could have no shortage of female admirers, but I certainly wasn't going to ask. Instead, I said, "Does your family live nearby?"

"Yes, in Netherton, the nearest village in the valley. I visit them once a week, and a rowdier group you won't find anywhere. I have three young brothers, and they don't know the meaning of "quiet." I love them, but I also love my peaceful little cottage."

I smiled back at him. "Then you do understand. I have four older sisters, and they all like to talk at the same time."

"I hope you'll get what you want, Vaughan."

He was looking at me so warmly that I felt shy again. "I ought to go back to the house," I said.

"I'll walk with you."

We walked for a while in a companionable silence, Welkin trotting at Joe's side. As we left the gardens and turned towards the house, I noticed something dazzlingly white on the muddy bank that sloped down to the main carriage drive.

I pointed. "What's that?"

"Let's find out."

As we drew nearer, Joe let out a whistle. "Would you look at that? I didn't know there were snowdrops here. I've never seen them before in this area."

"How lovely." I stared down at the small patch of bell-shaped white flowers, the inner petals marked with green at the tips. In contrast to the mud and dead grass that surrounded them, their purity and brightness seemed miraculous.

"Have you ever seen a whole field of them?" Joe asked.

I shook my head, almost afraid to look away from the snowdrops in case they disappeared.

"There's one a few miles from Morton. In a fortnight or so they'll be blooming. When you have a day off I could take you to see them."

He was only being polite, of course. Why would he wish to spend a day with me? But I replied, "I'd like that," just in case he really meant it.

I lingered over the flowers for a few minutes more, then turned back to the house. Welkin, who had kept a respectful distance from the snowdrops, pushed his nose into my hand, and I patted his head.

"There's a saying in my family," Joe said, "about the fate of the person who sees the first snowdrops of the year."

"What's that?" I put no stock in superstition, but I was inclined to be indulgent with Joe.

"Good fortune will come to that person within the year."

"Good fortune?" I smiled up at him. "That's not very specific. What sort of good fortune?"

"It depends on what the person needs most. To judge from generations of my family, it's usually money or love."

"Oh." I hesitated, nonplussed by his earnest look. Did he really believe in such fanciful notions? "I hope it will be money, then. It's ever so much more substantial and reliable than love, isn't it?"

He didn't reply. With a smile and a wave, he walked away, Welkin trotting after him.

I regretted my words. I knew nothing of love except by watching my sisters. When the men they made sheep's eyes at didn't respond the way they hoped, they were in torments. Torments that were exceeded only by worse suffering if said men *did* respond the way they hoped. As a child, I had thought such goings on very stupid, and time hadn't changed my opinion. I had been raised not to desire or expect love or marriage, but money I could work for, and I did believe in its substance and security. But I wished I hadn't said so, not to Joe. It made me sound cold. Mercenary. Even money-hungry.

Reminded of Mr. Spencer's insult, I frowned and turned towards the main doors of the house. Bedford was there, his baleful stare more intense than usual. Today he was wearing a bright red satin cravat.

"Where have you been, Miss Springthorpe? Mr. Spencer has been waiting for you for over an hour."

I raised my chin. "I've been looking at the gardens with Joe Dixon. Not that I need explain my whereabouts to you or to Mr. Spencer."

His bushy eyebrows met in the middle, and he let out a harrumph.

"You may tell Mr. Spencer I'm not ready to see him today," I added crisply. "I haven't made a decision regarding his offer and will need another day to think about it. I'll see him tomorrow at three o'clock."

"He won't want to wait."

"He must. I have nothing to say to him today."

I swept past Bedford and went to my room.

The oppressiveness of the house weighed on me more than usual that evening. It was such a contrast to the open air—even the grey winter sky was more welcoming—and the congenial company I'd enjoyed that afternoon. The house was like a giant parasite trying to drain me of all energy and hope.

All the same, a crystal-clear image of the snowdrops stayed in my mind. There was something about them I couldn't put into words, something powerful that the stifling atmosphere of the house couldn't touch. It was the snowdrops more than anything else that helped me make up my mind about Nicholas Spencer's offer. Before I went to bed that night, I wrote out a two-page contract and laid it on my bedside table, ready for his signature.

"You've made it appear that the only work you're to do is cataloguing and labelling the minerals."

Nicholas Spencer was holding a candle in one hand and the contract I'd written in the other. He was hunched over, holding them both so close to his face that I expected the papers, and possibly his eyebrows as well, to burst into flame at any moment.

"You haven't told me what other work I'll be doing," I said, "so I couldn't put it in the contract. It's a beautiful day—I'll open the curtains so you have more light to read by." I rose from the chair by his bed and approached the windows. It was the first day of full sunshine I'd seen since I'd been at Morton Abbey, and it was painful to see the curtains in Mr. Spencer's room as firmly closed as ever.

"No," he said sharply. "The light hurts my eyes. This candle is enough."

With a sigh I returned to the chair, already regretting my decision to accept his offer. To be fair, he hadn't put up as much resistance to my terms as I'd expected. What surprised me the most was that he hadn't argued with the clause that required him to turn over to me all the documents in his possession relating to the estate.

"There are a variety of tasks I wish you to do," he said. "It would take too much time to list them all."

I found this explanation unconvincing, but I said nothing.

"Something more must be added," he said. "Perhaps, 'The work will include, but not be limited to, cataloguing and labelling the minerals.'"

"I'll add that only if 'subject to the employee's agreement' follows it."

"Very well." He returned his attention to the contract. After a moment he read aloud, "'The employee reserves the right to terminate this agreement without notice and without having to supply a reason.' You drive a hard bargain, Miss Springthorpe. You also have a way with legal language, which I suppose shouldn't surprise me."

"My father was a solicitor."

"Ah, he's the one who taught you about the law. I wondered how you learned it. It is unusual for a woman to know these things."

I noted that he couldn't bring himself to call me a lady. It would have been a polite fiction if he had, but his words made my hackles rise anyway. "My education was unusual," I said, unable to prevent a note of defensiveness from creeping into my voice. "My father wished me to learn the law, history, science, and some of the classics. I haven't been taught the useless accomplishments of a lady." I emphasized the last word to show him I was aware he hadn't used it for me.

He looked at me curiously. "So you received a gentleman's education."

"You might say that. But my education was more practical than that of most gentlemen. Less emphasis on the classics and languages. More emphasis on bookkeeping and the sorts of things that are useful in the business world."

"But he must have known how difficult it would be for a woman to find employment with such an education. You are not exactly . . . appropriate for typewriting positions, and most other positions in business are held by men."

I was only too aware of this. "I don't think my father expected me to have to seek employment. He trained me to help him with his work. It saved him the expense of hiring an assistant."

"Why do you not still work for him?"

"He died four months ago."

"Oh." After a moment's hesitation, he added, "Had he not thought of what would happen to you after he died?"

Although I was pleasantly surprised that Nicholas Spencer was capable of conversing like a normal human being, I didn't like the personal turn the conversation was taking. "As I said, he didn't expect me to be thrown upon my own resources. He probably thought I'd live with one of my sisters after he died."

"But you don't wish to do so?"

"I don't. If you're finished reading the contract, I can make the necessary amendments and we can both sign it."

He handed me the contract and put the candle on his bedside table. I felt his scrutiny as I made the changes. The advantage of the dim light was that he couldn't read my eyes or my expression easily, but I was impatient with his insistence on near-darkness. If I had to read or write in such conditions on a regular basis, I would ruin my eyesight in a matter of weeks. It was no wonder his vision wasn't, in his words, "what it used to be."

The contract was signed with no further quibbles. I rose and said, "I'll take the documents now, if you please."

"They are in the top drawer of the desk by the window, along with your first month's pay."

I went to the desk and opened the drawer. The cheque for one hundred pounds lay on top of a pile of papers, but there weren't as many papers as I'd expected. I picked them up and returned to his bedside but didn't sit down.

"Are these all the documents?" I asked. "Including the most recent ones?"

"Yes, of course," he said, reverting to his usual sardonic tone. "Do you think I would renege on the terms of our agreement before the ink is dry?"

Without replying, I made my way to the door. Just before I opened it, he said, "I have some preparations to make, so we can't begin today. Meet me in the room down the corridor with the minerals at seven o'clock Sunday evening, and we can start. I presume you know the room I mean, since you have already taken the liberty of going into it."

Dismayed, I said, "But I thought . . ."

"What is it? Is that your day off?"

"No. I don't take days off. I thought you'd give me instructions and I'd be working alone in that room."

"If you thought I would leave you alone with valuable minerals and gemstones, you thought wrongly."

I slapped the pile of papers down on the nearest surface, picked up the cheque and advanced towards the bed. I held up the cheque before his eyes, poised to rip it in half. "If you think I will bear your insults merely because you are paying me, *you* think wrongly. I've agreed to work for you, but I haven't agreed to be abused or treated like a criminal."

I began to tear the cheque, but he caught my wrists in a painfully hard grip. For an invalid, he was surprisingly strong.

"Don't be stupid," he said. "Keep the money and I'll try to keep a civil tongue in my head."

"Is that an apology?"

"Obviously."

"Then it's the worst one I've ever heard."

"You must make allowances for my illness."

I wrenched my hands out of his grasp. "You and your illness may go to the devil! If indeed you are ill."

We glared at each other. We were at an impasse and we both knew it. He needed my help and I needed his. I could walk out of the room and behave as if he didn't exist, preparing for the sale of the estate with the documents I had, but my better judgment told me if I could get him to trust me, or at least give me all the documents he had, my job would be easier. And the money wouldn't hurt, either.

But would working with him be worth the constant friction? Could I keep my temper in his presence for an hour or more? I doubted it. At the same time, there would be little to lose by trying.

"I haven't got the strength for this," he said at last, averting his face. "You may take or leave my offer."

I said coolly, "I'll see you Sunday evening."

8

I spent most of the next day in the library burying myself in legal documents. By midafternoon I could no longer pretend to be focused on my work, for I was spending more time gazing out the library windows than at the papers in front of me. I decided to go for a walk.

It was a cold day, but in my warmest cloak, hat, and gloves, I was tolerably comfortable. I didn't try to convince myself I had no destination in mind. I followed the path Joe and I had taken the last time I saw him, towards the west wing and the rose garden. When I opened the gate and went in, I couldn't help but feel disappointed. Joe wasn't there, and the garden seemed even more desolate than usual, frozen and abandoned.

I left the garden and began to retrace my steps, but I hadn't gone more than a few feet from the garden gate when I saw Joe striding across the snow-covered lawn towards me. My disappointment turned to delight, but I tried not to show it.

When we were close enough to speak, we exchanged greetings, then he asked, "What are you doing out on such a cold day?"

"Just walking. I needed to get away from my work for a bit. Are you going to the rose garden today?"

"It's too cold to do much, but I like to check on it every day. Will you join me?"

I nodded and followed him.

He gave the garden one sweeping, comprehensive look, poked at a couple of plant covers, then turned to me. "Everything's fine. There isn't anything more to do at present."

I was half-hoping he'd offer to show me the field of snowdrops he mentioned the last time we saw each other. I didn't have the courage to suggest it myself, and he didn't seem to want to stay in the garden, so I resigned myself to what would inevitably be a short conversation and a quick return to the house.

But as we turned back to the gate, I realized that with his knowledge of the grounds, Joe could satisfy my curiosity about some aspects of the story Mrs. Wilson had told me.

"Joe, where is the pond?"

He frowned. "What pond?"

"The one where Mr. Spencer's daughter drowned."

"Ah. It's beyond that grove of trees." He pointed vaguely westward, but there were several groves of trees and it wasn't clear which one he meant. "It's a longish walk from here, farther than it looks."

"I'd like to see it."

He looked startled. "Why?"

I realized he must be thinking I was one of those people who revelled in tragedy and loved to hear all the gruesome details, and I hastened to say, "Not from idle curiosity, I assure you. I think it's best to find out everything I can about the family and this place. Whoever's been trying to frighten me seems intent on keeping me in the dark."

He gave me an admiring look that warmed me down to my toes. "You're a brave woman."

He didn't know about my nightmares or my fear of water, so I silently agreed that I was brave, indeed. But I believed what I'd said: if I confronted the people and places that frightened me, just as I had done with Mr. Spencer and the west wing, no doubt my fears would dissipate and I would be more comfortable at Morton.

He offered to take me to the pond, and I readily agreed. It would be easier to be brave with a companion like Joe.

We left the garden gate and walked further away from the house towards the grove of trees. I was surprised it was so easy to keep up with Joe until I realized he had slowed his pace to match mine.

I began to regret my decision well before we gained sight of the pond. The grove of trees looked somehow familiar, even though I'd never been to this part of the estate before. But surely any grove of trees, especially in winter without their leaves, would look very like another, so I tried to dismiss the idea and the uneasy flutter in the pit of my stomach.

The water wasn't visible until we reached the trees, and even then, wisps of mist hung in the air, partly obscuring the view. Joe offered me his hand to help me step over some loose stones, and I took it gratefully. Watching the ground to avoid losing my footing, I didn't look up until I was only a few feet from the water's edge, and what I saw then astounded me so much that I dropped Joe's hand and stared.

I knew this place. Impossible, yet true. I didn't want to believe it, and at first I focused on the details that were different: the leafless trees with their stark black branches against a grey sky, the mist, the snowy patches on the ground. But it was increasingly difficult to ignore what I *had* seen before: the odd, horseshoe shape of the pond, the flat rock near where we stood that was large enough for two people to sit on, and even the willow tree close to the water's edge.

I was trembling from head to foot. This was the pond where I drowned in the nightmares I'd been having since my first night at Morton. What my rational mind told me was impossible was an indisputable fact. In my dreams it was summer, not winter, and Joe wasn't there, but the place was the same.

I took a few steps back, jarring my heel painfully against a stone, but I righted myself without falling. Something else was different from my nightmares: there were footprints in the snow, near the willow tree. Small footprints, the sort that might be made by a child's boots.

My heart was thudding erratically and I couldn't catch my breath. I turned my back on the pond and the eerie footprints and hurried away as fast as I dared, scattering loose stones in my wake.

In my haste I was deaf to movements behind me, so when I felt restraining hands on my shoulders, I cried out in shock and lurched away.

It was only Joe, trying to get my attention. "What's the matter?" he asked.

I couldn't reply. The edges of my vision darkened and I thought I might faint, as I had nearly done when I saw the library in disarray.

"Come," he said, leading me to the nearest tree and sitting down with me at the base of it. He slipped his arm around my shoulders, and I leaned into him as I tried to breathe again, grateful for his support.

When I was able to speak, I said, "I drowned in that pond."

Understandably, he stared at me as if I'd lost my senses. "What do you mean?"

"Since I came to Morton I've been having nightmares about drowning in a body of water. This is the same pond as the one in my dream."

"You've been to the pond before," he said slowly, still looking puzzled.

"Only in my nightmares."

I forced myself to look at the pond now that I was a safer distance away. It didn't look particularly ominous, just cold and still. The trees were too close to it, though. I imagined a little girl running through the trees, dense with summer foliage, and coming upon the pond too late to stop. Or perhaps she wandered through the trees and saw the water in time, but perhaps she saw a butterfly alight on a stone or twig near the water's edge, and with a typical child's curiosity, she moved closer, lost her balance, and fell in. I shuddered.

Joe was studying my face. "Perhaps there was a photograph or painting of the pond somewhere in the house," he said, "and you forgot you'd seen it."

"No."

"Perhaps the housekeeper described the pond to you—"

"No, she didn't." I spoke more sharply than I intended.

"I'm sorry," Joe said. "I shouldn't have brought you here."

"You've done nothing wrong," I said in a softer tone. "It was my idea."

"Shall we return to the house? You needn't go near the water again."

"Let's wait a little." Now that the initial shock had passed, I thought it best to stay for a bit longer. There was nothing sinister about the place besides what my mind had invested it with. And perhaps Joe was right, that I'd seen a painting of the pond without really noticing it and it had lodged itself in my mind, then entered my nightmares. If not, there must be some other rational explanation.

"I need to look at the pond again," I said.

He gave me a doubtful look. "Are you sure?"

"Yes. I'm not afraid anymore." This wasn't exactly true, but I was determined to master the lingering anxiety I still felt. "And I thought I saw footprints. I want to be certain."

"Footprints? That's odd. I didn't notice that."

We returned to the pond, Joe a few steps behind me. I stayed well away from the water, intent on finding the footprints. It wasn't difficult to see the small boot-prints circling from the willow tree to the water's edge, then back again. They disappeared where the snow had begun to melt, but under the willow tree they were well-defined.

"Do you see that?" I said to Joe in a hushed voice. "And look, there's another set of footprints beside the smaller ones." The larger set of footprints were harder to see and didn't join the smaller ones in the circling pattern, but their outlines were clear near the tree and beyond it, as if an adult had called the child away from the water's edge and walked with her from the tree, back in the direction of the house.

Joe was silent, and I looked over my shoulder at him. He looked troubled, and his gaze flickered away from mine.

"Do you see them?" I said again.

"I see the small ones," he said slowly.

"Look over here," I said, pointing to the larger footprints.

He humored me by looking, but I could tell he didn't see them. In truth, they were melting into the ground even as I pointed, and I couldn't be certain even then of what I had seen.

"Vaughan—" he began.

"It doesn't matter," I interrupted, wanting to prevent any opportunity for a discussion, however well-meaning, of my mental state. "You see the small ones. They look fairly fresh, don't they? Do you think they were made today?"

"They must have been. It snowed early this morning, so any prints made yesterday would have been covered. Let's go, Vaughan. You look cold."

I took the arm he offered me and we went past the trees, back towards the rose garden and the house.

"Do you know of anyone besides you who might have reason to walk on the property?" I asked, careful not to specify whether such a person might be an adult or a child.

"No. I suppose it could be anyone, even a vagrant or poacher."

I doubted this. Nor could I picture Bedford wandering around the pond in the cold, which left Nicholas Spencer, but again, he couldn't be as ill as he claimed to be if he could walk all the way to the pond. And even if the larger footprints were made by one of them, it still didn't explain the smaller footprints.

When we reached the rose garden gate, Joe stopped and took my gloved hand, turning to face me. "You'll forgive me for taking you to the pond, won't you?" he asked.

"There's nothing to forgive." I couldn't fathom why he seemed so troubled. The strange experience had been mine alone, and I would have expected him to be worried for my sanity, if he was worried at all. "You've done nothing wrong," I added.

"I'm glad you're not upset," he said. "I don't want anything to frighten you away from Morton."

I frowned. "Why? I don't understand."

He squeezed my hand and smiled. "Can't you guess?"

I didn't dare to guess. I bade him farewell, then slowly made my way back to the house. I didn't know what to think about anything—my strange experience at the pond, the child's footprints, the adult's footprints that Joe couldn't see, Joe's unaccountable interest in me. I remained in an unsettled state for the rest of the day.

❧

To my relief, working with Mr. Spencer didn't turn out to be as difficult as I expected. Every evening at precisely seven o'clock, Bedford conveyed Mr. Spencer to the mineral room in a wheel-chair. Then Bedford would open the glass cases that housed the specimens, cast a suspicious eye on me, and leave. Mr. Spencer would examine each mineral—always by candlelight, which I thought was ridiculous—and tell me its scientific name, along with the place where it was found and the date. Some minerals were from dealers, in which case I would write the name of the dealer on the card as well. Then I'd take the specimen, wrap it in special paper provided for the purpose, add the card, and pack it away in a box.

Mr. Spencer preserved a businesslike tone during these proceedings, and neither of us spoke more than necessary. He offered no additional information about the minerals, and I didn't ask. I considered it my good fortune that he chose not to be disagreeable, and it was safer not to converse. Sometimes he would examine a specimen in silence for a long time, but even this I considered a blessing—I could close my eyes and rest or just let my mind drift.

The minerals looked like so many dark blobs to me, except for the crystals, which reflected what little light the candle provided. I didn't understand how Mr. Spencer could tell the difference between them in such dim light.

One evening a few days after I started working with him, I noticed a small box at the back of one of the glass cases and pulled it out. There were several small stones in the box, and one larger one, but they all seemed to be the same type. I picked up the larger one. It felt smooth and warm in my hand.

"Why is this stone warm?" I asked.

Mr. Spencer had been examining another stone, which he set down in order to take the one I was holding out. "That's amber. It's not a mineral—"

"I know," I interrupted, pleased that I wasn't entirely ignorant. "It's hardened tree sap, isn't it? But I don't understand why it's warm."

"It's resin, not the same as sap. And it isn't really warm on its own, but it has a low heat capacity, so it takes on the temperature of its surroundings. Your hand is warm, so the amber takes on your body heat."

He gave it back to me. It felt even warmer now. I liked the way it felt in my hand. It seemed alive and comforting somehow, not like the other stones.

"You may keep it if you wish," he said. "The amber isn't part of my collection. It belonged to an acquaintance of mine who didn't want it when he found out it wasn't valuable. The best amber is transparent, but these specimens are the more common cloudy sort."

This information made me like the stone even more. I held it up to the candle to examine it more closely. "It doesn't have any insects trapped in it, does it?" I asked. "I wouldn't like that." I had seen an amber pendant in a shop once with a large ant inside it.

"No, I don't think so. Are you afraid of insects?"

"Not at all. I feel sorry for them. It's terrifying to think of being covered in a liquid that paralyses one as it solidifies. It's even worse than drowning in the pond."

I realized immediately what I'd said, and my heart made a

strange little jump as if it were skidding to a halt.

His reaction was immediate as well. He looked at me sharply and demanded, "What pond?"

"I didn't mean . . . that is, I was . . . speaking generally."

"No, you weren't. You didn't say 'a pond.' You said 'the pond.' Are you referring to the pond here at Morton?"

I hadn't been thinking of his daughter's death, only of my nightmares and my eerie experience at the pond with Joe. My first feeling was guilt that I'd inadvertently reminded him of his daughter's death. My second was fear. If he'd had something to do with her death, I could be in danger now, alone with him in the dark room.

He held the candle up to my face, so close I could feel its heat, while his face receded into the shadows. I forced myself not to shrink away even though I felt like a patient about to be operated on by an angry surgeon.

"Have you seen our pond, Miss Springthorpe?" he asked, his tone still sharp.

If he had been annoyed by my going into the mineral room without leave, he would doubtless be enraged by my going to the pond. Nevertheless, I replied in the affirmative and steeled myself for the consequences.

"How did you know where it was? Did that meddlesome housekeeper tell you?"

"No. Joe, the gardener, was showing me around the place and we were near the pond, so he took me there."

Before he could subject me to a second barrage of questions, I said, "If you intend to set me on fire, will you be quick about it? I can't carry on a conversation with a flame two inches from my nose." Part of me believed that he would indeed have no scruples about setting me on fire.

He set down the candle on the table between us. His hand was shaking.

We were both silent for a moment. Then he asked, "What did it look like?"

"What?"

"The pond. I haven't seen it in years."

I needed only to recall my recurring nightmare to describe the place in detail, but I had no desire to do so. "I don't know. Cold. Wet."

"The pond has nothing to do with your work, Miss Springthorpe." The low, measured tone of his voice made him sound far more sinister than when he was openly angry. "You'll be very sorry if you poke your nose into matters you know nothing about."

"I wasn't aware Morton's grounds were forbidden to me," I replied. "Surely I may go for a walk if I wish."

"What sort of fool do you take me for?" he snapped. "You've been listening to Mrs. Wilson's tales and no doubt enjoying the sensational possibilities. Morton Abbey is not part of a ghost story to titillate listeners on a rainy night. This is my home. My family has owned this place for hundreds of years, and I am not going to stand by while ignorant onlookers mine it for sport."

"I have no interest in the kind of sport you speak of," I said. "I don't like mysteries or ghost stories, and I positively hate Morton Abbey. I'll be only too happy to turn my back on it forever once my work here is done."

He lowered his head, his beard sinking into his chest as if he were deflating. "I'm too tired to continue with the minerals this evening. I want to go back to my room."

Relieved to escape the uncomfortable conversation, I rose to summon Bedford, and when he came to collect Mr. Spencer, I went to my own room for the remainder of the evening.

9

A fortnight passed without any unusual occurrences. I continued to work in the library during the day and in the mineral room with Mr. Spencer in the evenings. Neither of us mentioned the pond or any other disquieting topic again, and I was troubled neither by strange noises nor nightmares, though I did notice that Bedford was always in the west wing when I was there, watching my comings and goings with the attentiveness of a bird of prey. With his eyes always on me, it was impossible to explore further.

Although March had arrived, there were few signs of spring in the air. The atmosphere both inside and outside the house was as dark, cold, and gloomy as usual. Worst of all, I didn't see Joe, despite the fact that I went to the rose garden every afternoon. I wondered whether I had frightened him away with my strange behaviour at the pond. Even if I had, surely now that the weather was getting warmer, he would need to work longer hours in the garden. I tried going out at different times— one day at one o'clock, the next at two, the next at three. But my hope would turn to disappointment when I found the rose garden as empty as ever.

One morning after breakfast I went to the library as usual but was lured outside by the sunshine and the sight of yellow crocuses in full bloom on the lawn outside the long windows. It was the first time I'd gone out in the morning, and I didn't intend to spend more than a few minutes away from my work. But as soon as I left the house, the heady light scent of spring in the air made me linger. I wandered across the lawn, thrilled by the sight of the leaf buds sprouting on the chestnut tree and a robin tugging determinedly at a worm.

I was near the west wing, about thirty feet from the rose garden, when I heard the garden gate creak and saw Joe emerge. It instantly flashed through my mind that he may not want to see me—after all, he wouldn't expect to see me outdoors in the morning. Perhaps he had purposely changed his schedule to avoid me. I moved to hide myself behind the nearest tree, but as I did so, he turned in my direction and our eyes met.

I froze with my hand on the tree trunk. What if he thought I was following him?

Joe approached me at once. "Vaughan, you're out early today! How are you?" His greeting was as hearty as usual.

"I'm fine," I said, not quite meeting his eyes. "I ought to be working, but it's such a beautiful day, I had to come outside." Why couldn't I speak in a normal tone instead of this strange, defensive one? Forcing myself to sound casual, I asked, "Are you working in the gardens today?"

"No. I can't spare more than a few minutes for Morton today because I promised my family I'd visit them."

"Oh."

"Will you come with me?" he asked.

I blinked up at him. "Come with you? To visit your family?"

"Yes. Why not? I've already told them about you, and they'd love to meet you."

He'd told his family about me? "But my work . . . I haven't done any work yet today."

"Can't you take the day off?"

His words were blasphemy against my Gospel of Work. I never took a whole day off. But somehow, coming from Joe, the suggestion seemed eminently reasonable.

I hesitated. "I'll need to tell Mrs. Wilson or Bedford where I'm going so they don't think I've just disappeared."

"Go ahead, then. But don't be long. And don't even think about making any changes to your appearance. You're perfect just as you are."

I was indeed thinking about making myself look more presentable. But I didn't know what more I could do with my usual uniform of long black skirt, white blouse, and my hair in a knot at the nape of my neck. Dazzled by Joe's smile, I went back into the house and told Bedford I was going to Netherton for the day, assuring him I'd be back in time to work with Mr. Spencer that evening.

When I returned to Joe, we walked to the end of the carriage drive, where a gig and placid-looking grey mare were waiting. Joe helped me into the light carriage, swung himself up beside me, and we set off at a pace that belied the horse's calm appearance. For a moment I allowed myself to imagine I was leaving Morton Abbey behind forever, and I nearly urged Joe to drive faster in the rush of exhilaration the fancy produced. But after a while I was content merely to observe my surroundings.

The moor still looked largely dead, with brown gorse everywhere, but here and there patches of green marked the approach of spring. I had always expected the moors to be flat, but there was considerable variation in the landscape—little hills and valleys, rocky plateaus, even groves of trees. I sniffed the air as eagerly as a rabbit, closing my eyes. I opened them again when I heard Joe laugh.

"You look as though you're drinking the air," he said.

"I am. Oh, look! The sun's coming out from behind that cloud." I pointed to the eastern sky. "I'm desperate for light. If I were a plant I'd be dead after all the dark hours spent in the house. Did I tell you Mr. Spencer refuses to have the curtains opened in his room?"

"Yes, you did."

"And he does everything by candlelight—even working with the minerals. I don't know how he can distinguish between them. It's horrible."

"Is he any kinder to you now?"

"I wouldn't say 'kinder,' but he's not as disagreeable as he was. I think it's only because we don't really talk to each other. It's very dull working with him, but I bear it the best I can."

"Are there still odd things happening in the house? Any rooms in disarray or strange sounds?"

"No. Bedford is as taciturn as ever, but nothing really strange has happened lately. I consider it proof that Mr. Spencer was the instigator of all of it. Now that I'm useful to him he doesn't want to scare me away."

Joe looked at me with a thoughtful expression. "What do you think about asking Mr. Spencer to come to the rose garden with us some afternoon? The fresh air might do him good."

Startled, I said, "He never goes out."

"You said he has a wheel-chair. I could push it into the garden for him."

"I doubt he'd come."

"You're probably right. It was just an idea." The horse had slackened its pace, and with a flick of the reins, Joe urged it on.

I disliked Joe's suggestion very much. Although he and I hadn't spent much time in the garden together, I'd already come to think of it as ours, and I didn't want anyone else to intrude. Especially not Nicholas Spencer. In the unlikely event that he was willing to go outdoors, he would inevitably bring the bleak oppressiveness of the house with him, and I couldn't bear that.

Netherton was closer to Morton Abbey than I expected. We hadn't been on the road for more than three-quarters of an hour before we approached the little village nestled in a valley. The brown cottages with their slate roofs seemed dwarfed by the overpowering moorland, but once Joe stopped the gig and we began walking down the high street, I felt as if I'd entered a bustling medieval town from a folk tale. Ruddy-faced women gabbled happily in clusters in front of shop windows; portly men called out friendly greetings as they passed one another on the street; an adorable little boy was standing on a street corner with his arm slung around the neck of a big fluffy dog. The street sounds in London were harsh, the smells noxious, the poverty of the street people heartrending, but here, in this magical village, everyone seemed happy and well-fed. A group of little boys ran past Joe and me, playing a game of bandy with someone's hat. Joe took my arm to guide me out of the way, calling a good-natured warning after them.

We stopped in the village square so Joe could make some purchases for his family—a bag of candied ginger for his brothers, flowerpots and cooking utensils for his mother. The shopkeepers greeted Joe like a long-lost son, and he returned the greetings in kind. Nobody shot me uncomfortable stares, not even seeming to notice my leg as I would have expected people in a small village to do: they seemed to simply accept me as Joe's companion. It was all I could do not to stand in the middle of the street and gape at everything.

"Everything is so . . . clean," I said inanely to Joe at one point. He smiled. "You like Netherton, do you?"

"I do." But even as I said the words, I realized they weren't quite true. Netherton was too perfect, somehow. It didn't seem real, and I kept waiting for something ugly or wrong to cross my path to remind me that this was real life. I would have felt better if there were just one person who seemed cross or upset.

"We've won the 'Prettiest Village in Yorkshire' title every year since I was a lad," Joe said. "It's a point of pride with everyone now to keep everything looking tidy."

I realized that the strangeness must be more in me than in the place. After spending so much time in the gloomy atmosphere of Morton, no doubt any ordinary village would seem unusually happy and bright.

I began to feel anxious as we finished our business in the square and returned to the gig. I never enjoyed meeting new people, and if Joe's family members were all at home and as noisy as he claimed, it would be overwhelming. Adding to my nerves was my desire to make a good impression.

There was little time for my anxiety to grow, for we arrived at Joe's family's cottage in minutes. All the cottages in the area were made of a coarse sandstone—gritstone, Joe called it—but this one was remarkable for the row of windows spanning the length of the top floor.

Joe saw me gazing up at the windows and said, "Those are weaver's windows. Netherton is a mill town, and some of the cottages were built with those windows to allow more light to weave by. It's my mam's glass house now: she calls it her conservatory. She loves those windows because she can grow more varieties of flowers up there, especially her prize orchids."

I was surprised that Joe's mother was involved in what I

thought of as a hobby only for the wealthy, but perhaps I had confused orchid collectors with orchid growers. I knew very little about the subject.

As soon as we went inside, we were enveloped by warmth and light and happy exclamations. It was as if his family hadn't seen Joe for months, even though I knew he visited them at least once a week. Three boys hurled themselves at Joe, nearly knocking him over, and they all began to talk at once.

"Joe, where've you been?"

"We've been waiting for the *longest* time!"

"What's in the bag?" This was from the youngest boy, who looked about ten. "Is it a present for me?" He made a grab for it, but Joe held it above his head.

"Must I bring you a present every time I see you, Billy?" he demanded in mock frustration.

"Aye. You always do."

Joe lifted Billy off his feet and turned him upside down, holding him by the ankles, which seemed terrifying to me but made the boy giggle happily. When Joe set his brother upright again, he said, "Try to behave yourselves, now. You don't want my friend to think you're savages, do you?" Turning to me, he introduced his brothers to me and gave Billy the bag of candy. Billy and David, the middle boy, greeted me pleasantly enough but were far more interested in the candy. Johnny, a gangly adolescent of about fifteen, merely gave me a sidelong glance and nodded. I was absurdly pleased that they seemed like ordinary boys instead of picture-perfect ones that the village had led me to expect. There were dirty smudges on Billy's face, and the two older boys had unruly dark hair that looked as though it hadn't been combed in a while.

The three boys looked nothing like their elder brother, but

when Mrs Dixon entered the room, there was no question which parent he must resemble. She looked to be in her mid-forties, younger than I expected, and she was lovely, with pale golden hair and the same stunningly blue eyes as Joe's.

"How do you do, Miss Springthorpe?" she said with a smile. "Come into the kitchen away from the mayhem and have some tea." She spoke in a quaint, old-fashioned way, with only a hint of Yorkshire in her voice, as if she'd been raised in a London schoolroom in her parents' generation instead of her own.

On the way to the kitchen I noticed a cabinet crammed with family photographs. There were several photographs of what I took to be aunts, uncles, and cousins, and even more of the three younger Dixon boys. I saw no photographs of the whole family or of Joe's father, but the one that charmed me most was at the front, of an impossibly young and beautiful Mrs. Dixon with a cherubic, tow-headed little boy on her lap.

"Yes, that's Joe," Mrs. Dixon said, seeing the direction of my gaze. "Wasn't he the sweetest-looking child?"

"Yes, he was," I agreed.

"You'd never know what a holy terror he was from looking at that innocent face," she said, laughing.

"Mam!" Joe exclaimed in mock protest. "You're already ruining the impression I wish to make on Miss Springthorpe."

I was used to hearing Joe call me by my familiar name, and the formality of "Miss Springthorpe" seemed paradoxically intimate. I liked it very much. Probably too much.

The kitchen, like Mrs. Dixon herself, was warm and inviting. The blazing fire with a rocking chair placed before it, the pots and pans teetering precariously on the shelves, dishes and cups scattered helter-skelter on the counter—all created an atmosphere of cheerful clutter. Something was bubbling in a pot on the stove that smelled of cinnamon and cloves.

Joe and I sat at the kitchen table as his mother moved with the grace of a dancer around the room, preparing the tea.

I felt at ease at once. It helped that Mrs. Dixon had a quiet manner, and I was glad she wasn't the sort of woman to overpower a guest with questions or mindless chatter. It also helped when she said, "It's about time Joe brought you for a visit. He's always talking about you."

I didn't dare look at Joe. I couldn't imagine what he had said about me. He knew so little, really.

When she sat down at the table with us, she asked me about myself, seeming especially interested in how I'd learned so much about the law. After I'd told her about my background, she said, "I never thought I'd see the day when a woman could work as a lawyer."

At first I couldn't tell whether she approved of the idea, but then she added, "You ought to be proud of what you've accomplished. And you'll give other women hope. Perhaps someday there will be no distinction between men's and women's work."

"Thank you," I said. "The next step, of course, is for women to be allowed to qualify as solicitors. At present we can work only in an unofficial capacity." I couldn't help but compare Mrs. Dixon to my own mother, who believed a woman's worth could be measured by the number of expensive gowns and important acquaintances she had.

"How are you managing at Morton?" she asked. "That place is not for the faint of heart."

"Oh, have you been there?"

"I was a maidservant there when I was young."

I was surprised. Joe hadn't mentioned this.

"You were there only a couple of years, weren't you, mam?" Joe put in.

"Yes." She gazed out past my shoulder towards the window with a dreamy, faraway look that made her look like a lost princess in a fairy tale. "It was a grand place then, the grandest in Yorkshire. The dinner parties they'd have. And the dancing. I'd sneak a peek into the great hall to watch the dancers: the dresses the ladies wore made them look like angels, I thought." She laughed and returned her gaze to us. "Not like angels in the Bible—more like fallen ones."

"My mother ought to have been the gardener at Morton, not an indoor servant," Joe said to me. "She taught me everything I know about plants."

"Yes. I love plants, especially flowers, but midwifery was my true calling," she corrected him. Turning to me, she said, "I brought most of the babies in this village into the world. That's far more important than growing plants."

She went on to tell me about her work as a midwife, which she was clearly proud of, as well as her gardening, but I couldn't help but notice that neither brought the sparkle into her eyes that was there when she spoke of Morton in its heyday.

"I've nattered on long enough about myself," she said at last. "You didn't say what you think of Morton."

"It's dark and gloomy, but I can imagine it brighter and happier in former days," I replied. "So much of the atmosphere depends on the inhabitants, and Mr. Spencer is quite dark and gloomy himself. Did you know him when you worked at Morton?"

"Yes. Not well, of course, but he did seem strange. I'd be cleaning a room thinking I was alone, and then I'd notice him in a corner peering at me over the top of a book. He was as still as a watchful cat, which I thought odd for a lad. His brother and father were different. Bright, vigorous men who were always moving."

It startled me that Mrs. Dixon had called Mr. Spencer a "lad." She must have been very young herself when she worked at Morton. Was he younger than he looked?

Before I could ask more questions, Joe's three brothers burst into the kitchen demanding their tea, and the room was filled with several conversations at once. I was relieved that nobody singled me out. They included me in their conversation, but they also allowed me to sit back and watch them. It was almost like watching a play. Every member of the family had a role. Billy and David were the funny ones, telling jokes and laughing at each other. Johnny was the peacemaker. Mrs. Dixon was the doting mother. And Joe was the framework around which this family was built. That was clearer than anything else. I couldn't imagine the family when Joe's father was alive, for it seemed complete now.

After our tea was finished, all the boys helped with the washing-up, which impressed me. Their methods were unusual, though: David would wash an item, then toss it over Billy's head to Johnny, who would catch it in his dish-towel and dry it. Then he'd give it to Billy to put away. Joe laughed at my expression as I watched this dangerous process.

Beside me, Mrs. Dixon said in an undertone, "That game of piggy-in-the-middle is the only way to get the boys to help in the kitchen."

"It's brilliant," I said, "but don't you lose a great deal of crockery?"

"Johnny's always the catcher, and he doesn't miss many." But as David held up a freshly-washed cup to throw to Johnny, Mrs. Dixon sprang forward to take it from him, exclaiming, "No, Davy! That's Dora's cup."

I would never have noticed anything odd about her innocuous-sounding words, aside from idly wondering who Dora might be, had the atmosphere in the room not suddenly and dramatically changed. Everyone's behaviour remained the same: Johnny handed the cup in question to his mother, and the boys went on washing up. Joe continued to watch the process with an impassive expression. But the light-hearted mood was gone, and Mrs. Dixon cradled the cup in her hands, gently dabbing at the wet spots with her apron. It was an ordinary earthenware cup with a floral design: not a very good design, either, because I couldn't tell which flower it was meant to be. Something round and pink, perhaps a rose, but the petals weren't detailed enough to be certain.

I gave Joe a quizzical look, but he avoided my eyes.

"Who used this cup?" Mrs. Dixon asked. Her tone was not demanding—indeed, I couldn't imagine her using such a tone—but rather a plaintive one, the hurt showing plainly on her face.

Nobody answered her, but I thought I detected a guilty look on the two youngest boys' faces.

Mrs. Dixon looked disappointed, but not surprised, by the silence. "Well, I suppose there's no harm done. Dora won't need it until she comes home."

Joe went to his mother and slipped an arm around her shoulders. "Why don't you put the cup in the china cabinet, mam? That way nobody will use it by mistake."

"Now, Joe, that makes no sense," she said. "How can Dora use it if I do that?" Her gaze met mine, and she smiled. "My daughter has been away at school, but she'll be coming home soon. She's my only girl, and I miss her dreadfully."

"How old is she?" I asked. Why hadn't Joe told me he had a

sister? He'd mentioned only his brothers, and he'd been so open about everything else, this seemed like a shocking omission.

"She's six."

"Oh." I was surprised that such a young child would be at a boarding school when her brothers were not. It was clear to me that something was amiss.

The tension in the room hadn't dissipated: in fact, it seemed to thicken. The boys finished washing up and slunk out of the kitchen, single-file and with downcast eyes, as if they were on a chain gang.

Joe turned to his mother with an artificial edge to his usual brightness. "May I show Vaughan your orchids? You needn't join us if you have things to do here."

"Of course," she replied. "And I do want to join you."

She led the way up a narrow staircase that opened out into the window-lined room. A ledge along the windows was filled with flowering plants in various stages of growth. On the floor were taller plants, and there was a long table at the far end of the room filled with empty pots and gardening tools.

Mrs. Dixon proudly showed me her plants. Some were medicinal herbs she'd used in her work as a midwife, but I could tell the orchids were her favourite: she waxed eloquent about the different varieties and how to care for them. If I'd first met her when she was with her orchids, I would have mistaken her for a garrulous woman.

"This one is just starting to bloom," she said, pointing to a resplendent purple flower.

"It's beautiful," I said.

"My mam has won awards for her orchids," Joe said proudly. "One was even named after her: phalaenopsis dixonii."

"I grew it without a stove house, right here on this window

ledge," she said, adding, "Joe, will you fetch the certificate they gave me? It's downstairs in the front parlour."

He assented and went downstairs. As soon as he was out of earshot, she said furtively, "May I show you a photograph of my daughter? Joe doesn't like me to show it."

"Of course," I said, mystified all over again.

She reached behind a stack of flowerpots and pulled out an ornate picture frame, then handed it to me.

"Isn't she beautiful?" she said proudly.

I couldn't reply at once because I was too shocked. The little girl depicted was beautiful indeed, but she couldn't have been Mrs. Dixon's daughter. It had been taken from a magazine advertisement: the child was the well-known face of Pears soap.

Mrs. Dixon was looking at me expectantly, so I choked out, "Yes, very beautiful."

She took the picture from me and looked at it for a long moment, then turned to me and said, "I know it's not Dora, not exactly her, but she looks very like this girl. And I can't find any photographs of Dora, even though I know we have some. Joe says we never did have any, but I know he's wrong about that. When she comes home, I'll be sure to have new photographs taken."

We heard Joe's footsteps on the stairs, and Mrs. Dixon hurriedly put the picture back in its hiding place. Joe showed me the certificate and spoke of his mother's flower-growing accomplishments with pride and his usual warmth.

I spent the rest of my time at the Dixons' house in a dazed state, struggling to follow the conversations. Mrs. Dixon was perfectly bright and natural when we returned downstairs, and when it was time to leave, she expressed delight at having met me, urging me to visit her whenever I liked.

I had much to think about on the ride back to Morton with Joe. He seemed preoccupied too, and I didn't interrupt his reverie until we had left Netherton and were on a quiet country road listening to the steady clop-clop of the horse's hooves.

"Are you all right?" I asked.

Looking directly at me for the first time since we left his family's house, he said, "Yes, of course."

"Why didn't you tell me you have a sister?"

After a short silence, he said, "She died about a year ago."

"Oh. I'm sorry." Given the odd scene in the kitchen, I wasn't entirely surprised, but Mrs. Dixon's behaviour still puzzled me. "Then why does your mother . . ."

"She's never accepted Dora's death. At first my brothers and I tried to convince her of the truth, but she'd become so upset that her nerves wouldn't recover for days. After a while we decided it was better to let her believe Dora was alive and just away at school."

"She showed me a picture," I said, feeling oddly disloyal to Mrs. Dixon. "She said it was a photograph of Dora, but it was an advertisement from a magazine."

He sighed. "She still has that?"

"She said she used to have photographs of Dora but she can't find them. Is that true?"

Shrugging, he replied, "I don't know."

It seemed odd to me that there wouldn't be photographs of Dora when there were so many photographs of other family members in the house, but I didn't want to bombard Joe with questions. I knew well enough how much I hated it when outsiders spoke of my father and intruded on my private grief. But there was one more question I had to ask.

"How did Dora die, if you don't mind telling me?"

At first I thought he wouldn't reply. He seemed far away again, staring straight ahead at the road. We had reached Morton's gates, but instead of passing through to the house, Joe reined in the horse and the carriage stopped.

"She was playing in a field by some train tracks," he said, looking down at the reins in his hand. "It appears she went onto the tracks and didn't hear the train coming."

The thought of a child dying in such a horrible way chilled my blood. "I'm so sorry, Joe."

"Someone had to identify her body," he went on. "I didn't want my mother to see it. You can't imagine—" He broke off and took a deep breath. "Last year my mother was ill, and I sent her to Switzerland for treatment. She loved it there, and she improved greatly both in body and mind after three months."

"She was there for three months?" I was amazed that he could afford this on a gardener's salary.

"Yes." He must have heard the astonishment in my tone, for he added, "I'm fortunate that Sir Peter pays me so well."

As his words sank in, I felt relief mingling with my concern for him and his mother. What Nicholas Spencer had said about Sir Peter's lack of money must not be true. I could expect to be paid the rest of the money he'd promised me if he was so generous to Joe.

Then I chastised myself for thinking of money at a time like this. I was truly sorry for Joe, and I leaned over and put my hand on his arm. "Your mother is fortunate to have a son like you," I said. "She nearly burst with pride every time she looked at you."

"Thank you, Vaughan."

Then he did a very strange thing. He turned and kissed me on the mouth. It was a very light, brief kiss, but I was so shocked that I froze. There was no time to think what to do. Should I kiss him back? Slap him? Exclaim in haughty outrage that he was taking advantage of me? What would my sisters do? I had no idea, really. Their stories of encounters with men didn't involve unexpected kisses from anyone they weren't engaged to.

I certainly didn't want to slap Joe or even exclaim in haughty outrage, but I didn't know if I ought to kiss him back, either. I merely sat back in stunned silence.

"I hope I haven't offended you," he said. "I've wanted to kiss you since the day we met." He couldn't be serious. The day we met I was a mess of scrapes and bruises in addition to being in a mad frenzy to escape from Morton. I was hardly at my best. And I was willing to bet money on the fact that no man even half as handsome as Joe would want to kiss me upon our first meeting, no matter how propitious.

"Why?" I asked. It was the only thing I could think of to say.

He laughed. "I don't think I can answer that question right now, not until I know whether you're offended or not."

"I'm not offended," I said. "It's only . . ." Only what? I didn't know.

"It was just a kiss," he said. "But if you didn't like it, I won't do it again."

He was teasing me. Playing with me. Enjoying my confusion. And I *was* confused, that was certain. It might be just a kiss to him—no doubt he had kissed many women—but it was the first time a man had kissed me, and it mattered. At least I had the wits about me to realize it mattered more to me than it likely did to him, and I decided to treat the incident casually, as he was doing. I wasn't quite brave enough to invite him to kiss me again, which seemed to be what he was hinting at, but

I contented myself with saying, "I didn't say I didn't like it."

All I could think about as Joe urged the horse forward and drove to the house was that I was in over my head.

10

That night I was awakened by two sounds, though in my half-conscious state they melded into one. The first was a loud knocking at my bedroom door. The second was fainter but distinct enough—the same sound that had awakened me once before. The sound of a child crying.

I sat up in bed and pushed my hair out of my eyes, then rose to slip on my wrapper and go to the door. "Who's there?" I called.

Although I half-expected to receive no answer, Mrs. Wilson's voice came through clearly from the other side. "It's me, miss."

I unlocked the door and swung it open.

Mrs. Wilson was wearing a thick woollen wrapper and nightcap, holding a candle and looking agitated. "Miss Springthorpe, I need thy help. Mr. Spencer is having some sort of fit and fell out of bed. Bedford is poorly and can't help him, but he won't let me in his room. Will tha' come?"

"Yes, of course." I didn't expect to be any more welcome than Mrs. Wilson, but I would at least try to do what I could. I went back into my room to put on my shoes, then followed the housekeeper.

On the landing the crying sound was louder. I stopped and shuddered. It wasn't the sound a child made when it was hungry or tired or just being disagreeable. It sounded like the intense anguish of loneliness.

"What is it, miss?" Mrs. Wilson had begun to descend the stairs but turned back to look at me.

"Surely you can hear that sound," I said.

"What sound?"

"The crying."

If Mrs. Wilson thought I had lost my mind, she didn't let on. "I hear nowt but our own voices and footsteps."

How was it possible she couldn't hear the crying? It permeated the house and became louder as we made our way towards the west wing. At first I thought the sound was coming from Mr. Spencer's room, but as we approached his door, it seemed that the sound was issuing from another room at the far end of the corridor.

"What's in that room?" I asked, pointing at the door.

"It's just a staircase leading up to the second floor, where the day and night nurseries and servants' rooms used to be. There's nowt up there now baht old furniture and things that belonged to old Sir Peter and Lady Spencer. Come, miss—we mustn't lose more time."

I was certain that Mrs. Wilson was hiding something, but I set my suspicions aside for the present and turned back to Mr. Spencer's door, which was ajar. I knocked, then pushed the door wider, not knowing whether I felt more trepidation about what lay behind this door or the one that led to the second floor.

The bedclothes were in disarray, and Mr. Spencer was lying on his left side on the floor beside the bed. One of the bed sheets was wound around his legs, presumably the cause of his fall. But why couldn't he get up on his own?

I approached him cautiously, as if he were a wild animal.

When I was at his side, I spoke his name.

He shied away and uttered a string of curses that would have quailed a more timid woman.

I merely waited until he was silent, then said, "Let us help you back into bed."

He raised his head to look at me. "Oh, it's you," he said, almost civil again.

I decided to consider this an acceptance of my suggestion, and I beckoned to Mrs. Wilson, then bent down to untangle the sheet from his legs.

But as Mrs. Wilson approached, Mr. Spencer cried out, "Not her! That woman is trying to poison me, and I'll be damned if I let her near me." He seemed to be struggling to get up, but something was wrong with him, for he couldn't seem to move his left leg even though the sheet no longer impeded it.

"Calm down," I said loudly and firmly. "I can't help you if you're going to behave like a lunatic. And I need Mrs. Wilson's help to lift you. Nobody is going to poison you."

Miraculously, my words seemed to have their intended effect. At any rate, he stopped struggling and allowed me and Mrs. Wilson to manoeuvre him up and onto the bed. He was thin and frail, but it still took all my strength, and probably the housekeeper's too, to complete the task.

I pulled the bedclothes over him and sat down heavily in the chair beside the bed. "Send for a doctor," I said to Mrs. Wilson.

"No doctor," Nicholas Spencer growled from the bed.

"You're not in a position to argue," I snapped. To Mrs. Wilson I said, "How far is the nearest doctor?"

"There's one in Netherton, miss. T'will take more than an hour for him to get here at this time of night."

"Fine. Send for him, then, if you please. You can go now.

I'll let you know if I need anything."

The housekeeper didn't have to be told twice. She was gone the second I finished speaking.

In the commotion of trying to get Mr. Spencer back into bed, I'd forgotten about the eerie crying. It was still audible, though fainter than it had been when I was in the corridor.

Mr. Spencer was breathing raggedly and shaking, and there was a sheen of perspiration on his face.

"Are you in pain?" I asked. "Is there any medicine I could give you while we wait?"

"No. I'm so bloody cold."

There was a folded blanket on a nearby chair, and I retrieved it and put it over him. He shifted awkwardly, raising his right arm over his head, and I realized he was trying to cover his ears with the pillow.

"Do you hear that crying?" I asked. What did it matter if he thought me insane for asking?

"Of course. It's driving me mad." He groaned, then went still. "Wait. You can hear it?"

"Yes."

He said nothing more, but his breathing became more regular and he released his stranglehold on the pillow, closing his eyes.

I pitied him, even though part of me would sooner put him out of his misery than try to prolong his life. Had it been like this in Father's room as he was dying? I didn't know, for Mother hadn't allowed me to see him once he took to his bed. He had died of a cancer that acted quickly—mercifully for him—but it seemed to me that he was perfectly fine one day and dead the next.

I reached out to take Mr. Spencer's right hand, holding it

between both of mine. At first I noticed only that his skin was cold, but then I realized it wasn't wrinkled or gnarled, not the hand of an old man. It was a smooth-skinned, elegant hand, with long, tapered fingers. I thought of what Mrs. Dixon had said about him being "odd for a lad" when she worked at Morton.

I tried to study his face, but with only one candle and no fire there was even less light than usual. His nightcap and beard covered so much of his face there wasn't much to be seen anyway.

"What's the matter with your left leg?" I asked.

"It isn't just my leg. It's my whole left side. I can't feel it, much less move it."

"You can't feel it at all?"

"No."

Alarmed, I asked, "Has this happened before?"

"Yes, but it happens more often now and lasts longer." His hand gripped mine and he gasped in pain.

"What is it?" I asked.

"My head."

"What can I do?"

"Distract me. Talk."

I stared at him in dismay. Making conversation was hardly my forte. "What shall I talk about?"

"Good God, woman, this isn't a dinner party. Just talk. Quietly, if you please."

I hesitated, then began to tell him about Joe and the garden. I thought it best not to mention my trip to visit Joe's family, but I thought it might be comforting for Mr. Spencer to hear how much Joe loved the gardens at Morton.

I talked about the plans Joe had for the gardens, warming to my subject as I saw everything he'd described in my mind's eye. "As soon as the weather is warm enough, Joe is going to fix the trellis in the rose garden. We've already seen tiny green shoots in the ground. Joe says he loves to see new plants growing in places he didn't expect, especially wildflowers."

I realized belatedly that I probably shouldn't have mentioned the rose garden. If it had belonged to Mr. Spencer's wife, he might object to my poking about in it. But he neither moved nor spoke, leaving his hand in mine, so I continued.

"Even though it's still cold outside, in the sunshine I can smell the earth. It's a rich, moist, green smell, if that makes sense."

"I remember," Mr. Spencer said.

"Perhaps on a day when you're feeling better, you could come out to the garden with us," I said, surprising myself with the invitation. "Joe is strong—he could push you in your wheelchair."

"I'm not an invalid," he said. "I can walk. Usually."

This was news to me. If he could walk, why did he have Bedford push him less than twenty feet from his bedroom to the mineral room in his wheel-chair every evening?

"Listen," he said. "The crying has stopped. Hasn't it?"

I listened. The house was silent. "Yes, it has. Do you feel any better?"

"A little. But it still feels as though a knife is wedged in my temple. At least it's staying there and not stabbing me repeatedly." He shifted a little and I loosened my hold on his hand in case he wanted to withdraw it. Instead, his fingers tightened around mine. "I don't like gardens. There is too much death in them."

I frowned. "I don't see how you can say that. They die in the winter, I suppose, but some only seem to die. Joe says even the most dead-looking plants are really alive inside, just waiting for spring."

"I'd better meet this paragon of gardening wisdom."

"You needn't be sarcastic."

"I'm not. I'm merely accepting your invitation."

Nicholas Spencer was full of surprises. One minute he could be the most disagreeable man on earth and the next he was civil, almost friendly. His contradictory nature couldn't be fully accounted for by his illness, either.

"How old are you?" I asked.

"I'm ancient."

"How ancient?"

"Why do you want to know?"

"Mere curiosity."

"I'll tell you if you tell me your age," he said, "though I'm well aware that no woman over five-and-twenty is likely to tell the truth."

"I'm eight-and-twenty, and I don't care who knows it."

"Well, that's an honest answer. I'll reciprocate—I'm forty."

"I don't believe you. When did you turn forty?" Aside from his hand, everything about him—the way he looked, the way he moved, the way he spoke—suggested he was much older.

"Today, as a matter of fact. Will you not offer your best wishes on this auspicious occasion? It's a good round number. You must be honoured that I am sharing my final birthday with you."

"What a horrid thing to jest about."

"It's no jest."

"Whatever your age really is, you'll hasten your death by thinking that way."

I was spared what would undoubtedly be his sharp retort by

the arrival of the doctor, who was shown into the room by Mrs. Wilson.

I withdrew my hand from Mr. Spencer's and stood up.

"I'm Dr. Foster," said the white-haired little man, holding up a candle and eyeing me as if I were his patient.

A burst of manic laughter erupted from the actual patient, startling everyone. "Ha! The irony is surely obvious."

I ignored this outburst and said to the doctor, "Mr. Spencer has a pain in his head and he's also lost the feeling in his left side. He fell out of bed."

"And you are . . . ?" the doctor prompted.

"Miss Springthorpe. I'm Sir Peter Spencer's legal assistant."

"Doesn't anyone in this house have a sense of humour?" Mr. Spencer interposed. "Or are you all illiterate?"

What was the matter with him now? If he wasn't mad, he was certainly creating a believable impression of madness.

The doctor asked me and Mrs. Wilson to leave the room while he examined the patient. On my way out, I heard Mr. Spencer say with another laugh, "Oh, Foster, is that your name? I thought it was Faustus."

Joining Mrs. Wilson in the corridor, I shivered and pulled the collar of my wrapper closer around my neck.

"I shouldn't have left thee alone with him, miss," Mrs. Wilson said. "He's a madman, and no mistake. Thank the good Lord tha's unharmed."

I wasn't convinced about Mr. Spencer's madness, which he seemed to turn on and off at will. I hoped he'd have the sense to explain his symptoms clearly to the doctor, at least.

"How is Bedford?" I asked. "He isn't very ill, I hope."

"I don't think so, just an attack of rheumatism. Happen old age catchin' up with him. Since the doctor's here, though, we could ask him to see Bedford when he's done with Mr. Spencer."

"Yes, let's do that." The housekeeper's mention of old age reminded me of what Nicholas Spencer had said about his own age. "Do you know how old Mr. Spencer is? He told me he's only forty, which I find difficult to believe."

Mrs. Wilson hesitated, staring at the ceiling as if numbers were written there. "Aye, that's about right. Sir Peter was fifteen when I came to work for the family, and Mr. Spencer about ten. I've been at Morton thirty years."

Despite this corroboration of Mr. Spencer's claim, I couldn't help feeling sceptical.

"He does seem older," she continued, "but bein' barmy and bad-tempered will do that to a body. Did tha' hear him say I'm trying to poison him?"

I nodded.

"I don't mind telling thee, miss, if I knew a way of poisoning the man without getting caught, I would've done it a long time ago."

"I can't say I would have blamed you." But even as I said the words, I felt strangely disloyal, though why I would feel the need to be loyal to Mr. Spencer I had no idea. Perhaps it was because I had heard the fear in his voice and believed he really was suffering.

"Tha' can go back to bed, miss. I'll talk to the doctor when he's finished."

"No, I'll stay. I'm wide awake now, anyway."

I didn't entirely trust Mrs. Wilson to give me an accurate report of the doctor's words. I was also curious to know what his diagnosis would be.

When Dr. Foster emerged from Mr. Spencer's room, he told us, "I don't know what the cause of his head pain is. It could be a cancer. It could be just migraine. I told him he ought to see Dr. Stanhope, an oculist in London, but he says he's seen a specialist already. In Mr. Spencer's words, the specialist was 'as useless as the rest of you.'"

"Damn his stubbornness," I said, earning a disapproving look from the doctor. "What about the paralysis?"

"What paralysis?"

"I told you, he's lost the feeling in his left side."

"That's not what he said to me. He said he had a bit of numbness, but that's all."

I couldn't believe it. What sort of game was Nicholas Spencer playing?

"Mr. Spencer is a strange man," Dr. Foster resumed. "I wouldn't be surprised if he's invented his illness, even the head pain."

"No, that can't be right," I said, ignoring a second affronted look. "I think he really is in pain. There's no reason why he should invent—"

"Miss Springthorpe," Dr. Foster interrupted, looking as though he'd just eaten something rotten, "I know more about medical conditions than you do. I've also seen my share of perfectly healthy people who fancy themselves ill for a myriad of reasons, though such patients are usually female. It is my professional opinion that whatever is the matter with Mr. Spencer is mainly in his head."

Mrs. Wilson interposed then to ask the doctor if he would see Bedford.

I didn't think twice. I returned to Nicholas Spencer's room, not bothering to knock first, and went to stand by the bed, on the left side this time.

He was lying on his back with his eyes closed, but he opened them as I approached. "What is it?" he asked.

"Lift your left arm," I said.

"What?"

"You heard me."

"Leave me alone, Miss Springthorpe," he said wearily, closing his eyes again.

"If you don't do as I say, I'll push you out of bed and you'll be in exactly the same predicament as before."

He stared at me. "Have you lost your mind? You're madder than I am."

"Don't think I won't do it." I made a sudden movement towards him, my hands outstretched.

He reached across his body with his right arm, holding it up against my perceived attack. His left arm didn't move.

It was enough to confirm my suspicions, and I let my hands fall to my sides. "Why did you lie to the doctor about the paralysis?"

"Oh, for God's sake. I'm dying. What does it matter what I say to that old fool of a doctor?"

"Damn you!" I cried, so angry I was shaking. "How can you be such a coward? You're just giving up and turning your face to the wall instead of trying to find a cure or even just enjoying the time you have left. It isn't fair! Other people who want to live die too soon, and cowards like you who want to die just keep living."

I'd said far more than I intended to, and I felt confused and disoriented and breathless. I expected a blast of anger from him, but he was silent.

After a moment, he said quietly, "There's no need to cry."

"I'm not crying." But there was a tightness in my throat and possibly some moisture in my eyes. I swallowed hard. It would be humiliating to cry in front of him.

"You don't know my history," he said. "I've seen many doctors over the years and none of them knew what is the matter with me. I've been diagnosed with all manner of strange ailments and treated with various potions, none of which did any good. These attacks are becoming more frequent, and I have indeed given up on finding a cure. I suppose I am a coward, but despite what you believe, I don't want to die."

My nerves were strained to the breaking point. I couldn't bear further talk of death or illness or anything else with Nicholas Spencer, despite his calmer tone. I couldn't even speak.

"Go to bed, Miss Springthorpe," he said. "We've both had enough excitement for one night, and you look as exhausted as I feel."

I stumbled out of the room. It seemed like a very long way to the east wing, and when I reached my bedroom I barely had the strength to lock my door and remove my shoes before collapsing into bed.

Despite my exhaustion, I couldn't sleep for a long time. I kept thinking about the crying sound. Why were Mr. Spencer and I the only people who could hear it? Whatever relief I might feel to know the sound wasn't only in my head was mitigated by the fact that I shared this experience with a possible madman. On the other hand, perhaps Bedford and Mrs. Wilson did hear it and were lying. They had no reason to tell me the truth, but why would Bedford lie to Mr. Spencer, to whom he was obviously loyal? Nevertheless, I couldn't ignore the possibility that there was a real child in the house, and such a possibility required further explorations.

11

I've changed my mind," I said grumpily as Joe and I made our way up the carriage drive to the front entrance of the house. "I don't want him to come with us."

I knew I sounded like a sulky child, but I couldn't help it. It was a glorious afternoon, the first truly warm spring day, with a brilliant blue sky and the gentlest of breezes that diffused the scent of hyacinth, lilac, and warm, moist earth. I'd been with Joe in the gardens for an hour, watching him work and helping him with simple tasks such as clearing away dead leaves, and I didn't want to stop, especially not to see Nicholas Spencer.

I hadn't seen Mr. Spencer since the harrowing night a week earlier when he'd fallen out of bed. He'd sent me a note to tell me he needed to suspend our work in the mineral room until he felt well enough to resume it, and I didn't hear from him again until he sent another note a few days later stating that he was well enough to come out to see the gardens with me and Joe. This afternoon at three o'clock was the time fixed for our outing.

"It won't be as bad as you think," Joe said. "How could it be, on a day like this?"

"The only way it will be better than I think is if he changes his mind and doesn't come." I took one last, longing look at the sky, as if the arrival of Nicholas Spencer would instantly obscure it with dark clouds.

Bedford and Mr. Spencer were waiting just outside the front door.

Mr. Spencer snapped, "Where have you been? I've been waiting twenty minutes, at least." He was in his wheel-chair, wearing a large black hat, a green cardboard shade over his eyes, and a heavy blanket over his legs.

"We came as soon as we could," I retorted. "There is much to do in the gardens and we don't always notice time passing." I added, "This is Joe Dixon."

Neither Mr. Spencer nor Bedford acted as if they heard me, and neither of them looked at Joe.

With his bushy eyebrows drawn together, Bedford said, "I trust you will ensure that Mr. Spencer doesn't catch cold. You must also keep the wheel-chair on the gravel path and away from the mud. It isn't easy to dislodge if it becomes stuck."

It was all I could do not to express my desire to push the wheel-chair directly into a patch of mud and leave it there. Not to mention the likelihood that Mr. Spencer would suffer heatstroke rather than a cold, considering the way he was dressed. But I remained silent—showing admirable restraint, I thought—and merely nodded, my jaw clenched.

"You may go, Bedford. Thank you for all you've done," Mr. Spencer said in a tone so civil and gentlemanly that I could hardly believe it.

"May I push your chair, Mr. Spencer?" asked Joe, coming forward. "I'll be careful."

"Yes, yes." He reverted to his usual irritable tone. "We'd better be on our way or it will be nightfall by the time we reach the gardens."

I felt angry on Joe's behalf. First Bedford had ignored him completely, and now Mr. Spencer was treating him like a slave.

Joe manoeuvred the wheel-chair down the front steps and down the gravel path as carefully as if he were pushing a baby carriage. He remained just as patient—a stunning feat, in my opinion—during the barrage of pointed questions Mr. Spencer asked him about his origins and education.

"If you're a Yorkshire man, why don't you speak like one?"

"I was fortunate to have a bachelor uncle in London who wished to educate me like a gentleman. He arranged for me to go to Harrow."

"That's a very good education for a gardener."

"My uncle didn't want me to be a gardener. He had higher aspirations for me."

"What did you do after Harrow? Did you return to Yorkshire?"

"No, sir. I went to university. Oxford."

I hadn't known this. As much as I disliked Nicholas Spencer's method of questioning—more of an inquisition, really—I was learning more about Joe in a few minutes than I had in all the hours we'd spent together on our trip to Netherton and in the gardens at Morton.

"Now that's odd," Mr. Spencer said. "An Oxford-educated gardener."

"I didn't do well at university," Joe said. "My heart wasn't in it, but I wanted to please my uncle. I was sent down after a year and returned home. Eventually my uncle understood I wouldn't be happy unless I was gardening."

"When did you start working at Morton Abbey?"

I shot Mr. Spencer a suspicious look. I'd told him this information already. Was he trying to catch Joe in a lie?

"Sir Peter hired me last summer. It was fairly late in the

season, so I couldn't do much. I'd be happy to show you what I've done so far this spring. Vaughan has been a great help."

"Vaughan?" Mr. Spencer glanced from me to Joe. "Do you mean Miss Springthorpe?"

"Yes, sir." Joe looked embarrassed, and my desire to push the wheel-chair into a patch of mud revived.

"All my friends call me Vaughan," I said. Not that I had many friends.

Of course, "friend" wasn't quite the right word for Joe, but it would have to do. I'd been with him a few times in the gardens since our trip to Netherton, but neither of us had mentioned the kiss again, and we both seemed content pretending it hadn't happened. If it meant anything to Joe, he didn't say so to me, and it wasn't for lack of opportunity.

We reached the path that led to the rose garden.

"Where would you like to go, Mr. Spencer?" asked Joe. "We've been working in the rose garden lately if you'd like to see it. There isn't anything blooming there yet, of course, but you'd be sheltered from the wind."

"Very well."

Welkin came bounding to meet us a few minutes later, his paws covered in mud.

"Welkin, where've you been?" demanded Joe. "Chasing rabbits into the woods again, I'll wager. Do you mind if my dog comes with us, Mr. Spencer?"

"No. I like dogs."

At the rose garden, I held open the creaky gate as Joe pushed the wheel-chair through, followed by Welkin. I went inside and sat on the bench, calling Welkin to my side. My leg was aching and I felt unaccountably chilled, so I was glad to sit in the sun. Looking at the intertwined initials on the bench, I wondered what Mr. Spencer's reaction to the garden would be, but he merely listened as Joe wheeled him around the perimeter of the garden, explaining the work he'd done so far.

There were burrs in Welkin's fur on his side and haunches. "Look at you, silly dog," I said. "Hold still." I bent over him and began to pull out the burrs.

It wasn't long before Joe joined me, bringing the wheel-chair to a halt at a right angle to the bench and sitting on the ground on the other side of Welkin to help remove the burrs.

I glanced at Nicholas Spencer. He had pushed the blanket off his knees and removed his hat but was still wearing the heavy coat. Surprisingly, he had also removed the green sunshade. He returned my gaze, and I saw that his eyes were a very light grey, the irises ringed with black. The beauty of his eyes, framed by thick black lashes, was startling in contrast to the sickly pallor of his skin, which still looked oddly like parchment.

But his unusual appearance didn't make as much of an impact on me as the fact that he wasn't even squinting, despite the bright sunlight. How could he complain of pain from the smallest sliver of light from the curtains in his bedroom when full sunlight didn't hurt his eyes? Had he been lying? If so, to what purpose?

"I had forgotten what it's like here in the spring," he said slowly. "The smells. The colours. The greening of the trees and shrubs."

"Yes," said Joe, who had given up on Welkin's burrs and was leaning back against the bench, hands behind his head. "And it'll be even more beautiful when the roses are in bloom."

"I prefer the buds," Mr. Spencer said. "The blooms die too quickly. The buds hold the promise of beauty, which is better than the full flower. I like the potential, the possibilities. The mystery of not knowing what colour the flower will be. When a rose blooms it's already well on it's way to dying."

Dear God, I thought. Was I going to have to listen to another of his paeans to death?

Fortunately, we were all distracted by a blackbird's song, clear and flute-like, high above our heads.

"Where is it?" I whispered.

Joe pointed. "There, in the oak tree." The bird was so high that it wasn't clearly visible, but it continued to fill the air with trills and chirps as if performing for us.

I closed my eyes in order to listen better. It was a moment of utter perfection, and I wanted to draw it out as long as I could.

Welkin broke the spell by stirring under my hand, which had been resting on his back, and walking away.

I slowly opened my eyes. Joe was still looking up at the sky. Surprisingly, Welkin was leaning against Mr. Spencer's legs with his head on the man's knee.

Even more surprising was the fact that Nicholas Spencer was crying. He made no sound, but tears were running down his face and into his beard.

I didn't know where to look. Nobody in my family ever cried in front of anyone else. Even when my sisters and I were children, we understood that we must leave the room if there was any possibility we could lose control of our emotions. And I had never seen a man cry.

Increasingly uncomfortable, I looked at Joe for some sign to guide my actions. He had known what to do during my own embarrassing outburst when we first met.

Joe did nothing except glance at Mr. Spencer, then down at the grass, which he began to smooth meditatively.

I sat, tense and silent.

After what seemed like forever, Mr. Spencer fumbled in his coat pocket, retrieved a handkerchief, and blew his nose. "Forgive me," he said. "I haven't been outside the house in more than five years. It's overwhelming."

"It would be," said Joe, still supremely calm.

"You said you tried to please your uncle by going to Oxford," Mr. Spencer said. "I did the same thing, in a way. I went into politics to please my father. The younger son must have a profession, you know. He thought it was the highest work a man could do, and at first I agreed with him. As a young man I thought I could change the world to fit my ideals, and political life seemed the best way to do it. When I stood for a Liberal seat in Westborough, nobody was more surprised by my success than I. But it didn't take long to become disillusioned. Doubtless the same thing would have happened no matter which party I had joined. I went to my father, intending to tell him the truth—that I had been mistaken in thinking political life was right for me.

"Before I could say anything, he told me how proud he was. He had never taken much notice of me before. My brother had always been his favourite. But now he was telling me of the hopes he had for my political career. I think he expected me to become Prime Minister. Thus, I tried to make a go of it." He sighed. "My God! How I hated the deceit, the manipulation, the artificiality of it all. It was also far too public a role for me. Too many people around me all the time. I was constantly anxious, constantly performing for somebody. I could never be myself.

"I achieved some modest success. People voted for me, and I became a Liberal MP. You needn't look so surprised, Miss

Springthorpe. I was better at making speeches and ingratiating myself with people back then, as much as I hated all of it. By that time I was married, and my wife wanted me to have a brilliant political career even more than my father did, so I felt utterly trapped."

He reached down to scratch Welkin's ears.

"Then it all fell apart," he continued. "One of my political rivals accused me of accepting a bribe. I hadn't done it, but it didn't matter. My enemies managed to blacken my name, and my career was over very quickly. I do not mean to suggest I was morally above reproach. I made mistakes—many of them— just not the one I was accused of making.

"I couldn't hide the fact that I was relieved to be free of politics. My father and my wife were horrified by my failure and even more by my relief in response to it. They saw me as lazy, unambitious, hopeless. Needless to say, my marriage was never the same after that. But I am presenting an inaccurate picture. My wife never loved me, so whether I was a success or failure in my career wouldn't have changed that."

I looked at the intertwined initials on the back of the bench. "What was your wife's Christian name?" I asked.

"Alicia. Yes, those are our initials. But why do you say 'was'? It is still her name."

"I assumed she was dead."

A shadow passed across his face. "She is very much alive," he said flatly.

I wasn't certain I believed him. I tried to picture Alicia Spencer. Was she beautiful and elegant, a woman with sparkling wit who couldn't bear her husband's gloomy, dark moods? Was she an ordinary woman with extraordinary ambition who would have sought a political career herself had she been a man and who was trying to live out her ambition through her husband? Had she really left him for another man? Was she still with that man? Or had Mr. Spencer murdered her? I still considered this a logical possibility. If he hadn't murdered her, why hadn't he divorced her? Divorce was neither expensive nor difficult for a man of his class, especially if his wife had committed adultery. He must still be in love with her. But of course I couldn't ask about anything so private. It was already surprising that he had disclosed as much as he had about his personal life.

"What would you have done if you hadn't become a politician?" Joe asked Mr. Spencer. "Did you have other dreams?"

"I had many dreams. Before political life took all my time and energy, I thought about becoming a musician, a poet, a writer—all of which would have sent my father to an early grave had I been serious about them. I also thought about taking my interest in minerals further, perhaps becoming a professor of geology and mineralogy. But I was a dilettante in all of those areas. I was happy when I first moved back to Morton after my failed political career. Although working as my brother's bailiff was frustrating at times, I loved the estate and was glad to be back, taking care of it. My wife was unhappy, though, and things went wrong very quickly."

He turned to me and asked, "What of your dreams, Miss Springthorpe? Is there something you've always wanted to do with your life?"

"I've always wanted to be a solicitor," I replied. "Not my father's assistant, though that was fine for a while. To have my own legal practice and support myself. To be independent of my family."

"Is that all?" he replied, looking disappointed.

"It's a great deal to me," I shot back, affronted. "Do you know many women lawyers?"

"No. I didn't mean it isn't a worthy goal." Mr. Spencer paused, as if he was struggling to find the right words. "But it is a goal, an ambition, not a dream. You must have dreams that are not so . . . prosaic."

"I'm a prosaic woman."

He gave me an appraising look. "Perhaps you don't know yourself as well as you think you do."

I didn't like his superior tone. He didn't know me and was hardly in a position to judge how well I knew myself. But before I could express the sharp retort on the tip of my tongue, Joe intervened.

"Your father was fortunate to have you as his legal assistant for so many years," he said to me with a smile. "How did he manage to chase away your suitors to ensure that you wouldn't marry while he was alive?"

I forgot my annoyance with Nicholas Spencer in my attempt to comprehend what Joe had said. The very thought of Father having to beat back hordes of men who wanted to marry me was ludicrous.

"There was no need," I said finally. "My father knew I wouldn't marry. My whole family did."

"How could they possibly know such a thing?" Joe looked puzzled.

Did I really have to spell out the reality of the matter? I couldn't bring myself to point out my deficiencies to Joe, but I had to say something.

"I'm neither wealthy nor beautiful," I said, "and a woman needs at least one of those assets to attract suitors. My father used to jest about the way the beauty in our family wasn't evenly distributed. My eldest sister received the largest share of it, and each sister after that received a gradually diminished share until there wasn't any left for me."

"Your father said this?" Mr. Spencer interjected, looking shocked.

"It's a favourite family story. Everyone likes to tell it, especially Elizabeth, my eldest sister." I glanced at Joe, who also looked shocked. I had expected my listeners to laugh at the jest as my family always did.

After a minute of silence, Joe said quietly, "I have no doubt there's more than enough beauty in your family to go around, Vaughan."

He had spoken so gravely, so different from his usual light-hearted tone, that it took me a few seconds to realize he was complimenting me. To mask my confusion, I said quickly, "Beauty isn't important to me. For my dream—or my goal, as Mr. Spencer calls it—a quick mind and ability to work hard is far more important."

Nicholas Spencer was looking from me to Joe carefully, speculatively. He said to Joe, "I suppose you'll be glad to be finished your work at Morton as soon as possible so you can move on to a permanent position."

"No, sir," Joe said. "I'll be sorry to leave Morton."

"Why is that?"

"There's so much I'd like to do with it—make a herbaceous border along the carriage drive, clean up the shrubbery along the front of the house, enlarge the old kitchen garden—" He stopped abruptly, then continued in a more restrained tone, "I worry that the estate will be sold to someone who doesn't care about the gardens."

"I see," Mr. Spencer said.

Joe glanced at me, then said to Mr. Spencer, "I hope the estate won't be sold until the end of the summer. That would give me time to get the rose garden looking as it ought."

"I'm glad you feel that way."

"Are you tired, Mr. Spencer?" I asked. "Do you want to go back to the house?" I confess I wasn't concerned about him so much as hoping to spend more time alone with Joe.

"No. It does me good to be here. In fact, I'd like to come out regularly in the afternoons when the weather is fine." He looked at Joe. "I won't interfere with your work. I could even help with some of the gardening—the lighter work—if you don't mind."

He wasn't speaking to me, but I minded very much. Although I no longer considered Mr. Spencer an enemy, I still didn't trust him and didn't want him to intrude on my precious hours alone with Joe.

"Of course I don't mind," said Joe enthusiastically. "We need all the help we can get, as long as you don't overtire yourself."

"Thank you. I'll welcome the chance to be in a place where my speech and movements won't be so closely watched." After a pause, he added, "Will you both call me Nick? Nobody has called me by my Christian name in years." He turned to me. "And may I call you Vaughan?"

"I suppose so," I said. It was a strange request from someone I hardly knew, but given the class differences among us, it was far stranger for him to want Joe and me to call him by his Christian name. Nobody could stop him from calling us anything he wished.

We spent another surprisingly companionable hour in the garden, and when Mr. Spencer was safely back in his wheelchair, we set out for the house. After bidding farewell to Joe, Mr. Spencer said to me, "We'll have to postpone our work in the mineral room tonight. I'm too tired to do anything more today."

"Certainly." It was rare to have a free evening, and I intended to enjoy it by finding a book to read in the library.

I found a life of Jeremy Bentham that ought to have kept me engrossed, but I kept thinking I ought to have tried to stop Mr. Spencer from over-exerting himself. I hoped he would experience no ill effects from the excursion. Then I wondered why I cared.

12

I don't think Joe Dixon is who he says he is," Mr. Spencer proclaimed one evening a few days later. He and I were working in the mineral room. Despite the evidence from our day in the garden that he could survive and even enjoy bright sunlight, the room was lit, as usual, by only one candle.

"What do you mean?" I asked.

"It's just a feeling. Don't you ever have intuitions about people?"

"No," I replied tartly. "I believe most people at least try to be honest with others, present company excepted."

"Ah, how you drive the dagger home! Are you quite well, Miss Springthorpe?" It seemed just as difficult for him to call me Vaughan as it was for me to call him Nick, notwithstanding our agreement the day he came to the garden.

Ignoring his question, I said, "Why were you so interested in spending time with us in the gardens if you find Joe so suspicious?" Truth be told, I wasn't feeling entirely well. My leg and hip were aching from too much walking and working in the gardens, and I felt generally fatigued. The letter I'd received that morning from Mother hadn't helped, either. She'd included a long list of tasks waiting for me to do for my sister's wedding that I doubted my sister herself wanted done.

"I didn't say I dislike him," Mr. Spencer replied. "He's pleasant company, but I cannot help wondering why such a young man would want to work here. He has all the advantages of education, intelligence, and good looks. No such person is going to want to work at Morton for the pittance my brother is likely paying him. Why work at a place with no future when he could be the head gardener at some well-run, prosperous estate? He must be hiding something."

While there was some logic in what he said, I thought it was unfair to be so suspicious of Joe when he had been nothing but kind and patient with Mr. Spencer. "I think it's perfectly plausible he's doing exactly what he wants to do," I replied. "He lives so simply that he doesn't require a large salary, and perhaps he'd rather work alone than supervise under-gardeners. Perhaps he also likes the challenge of working at Morton." I knew Joe was sometimes frustrated by the enormity of his work, but most of the time he seemed happy.

"Perhaps." But Mr. Spencer didn't sound convinced.

"I have to go to London in June," I said abruptly.

"Why?"

"To attend my sister Letitia's wedding."

"Oh. I suppose it will be good for you to see your family." He pointed to a large mineral in the open case beside us. "Hand me that, would you?"

I did so, but my silence must have communicated more than I thought, for he asked, "Don't you wish to go?"

"Not really. I don't want to upset Letitia—she's my favourite sister—but I'd just as soon stay away from my mother. She was opposed to my coming here, and I'll be subjected to endless lectures about what a horrible daughter I am."

"What exactly did she object to about your coming here?"

"She didn't think I could survive on my own." Seeing his surprised look, I added, "She has a dim view of my ability to take care of myself. And she thought the work itself was suspicious."

"Regarding her first concern, she must not know you. I cannot imagine a woman who could take care of herself better than you can."

"Thank you." A compliment from Nicholas Spencer was a rare thing. "What of her second objection?"

"I'll admit there is reason to be suspicious. Has my brother paid you for this month's work?"

"No. Not yet." In fact, Sir Peter hadn't paid me anything since the first advance. He had written to apologize for the delay, promising to pay what he owed me as soon as he arrived at Morton. The only trouble was that he was still unsure when he would arrive. I was worried, but I didn't want to give Mr. Spencer an opportunity to say, "I told you so."

Fortunately, he didn't press me. He set down the larger mineral and handed me a small stone the size of a robin's egg with one jagged edge. "That is corundum. It is a particularly good one from Burma."

"What makes it a good one?"

"Its hue, mainly. That rich red colour is called 'pigeon's blood.' It would make a brilliant ruby if it were cut and polished."

I held it up to the candle and squinted at it. "I can't see the colour properly in this light."

"You may light the lamp, then."

I was surprised he would allow more light into the room without an argument, and I lit the gas lamp quickly before he could change his mind. With the additional light, I could see that the stone was red, but it wasn't as deep a red as I expected.

"Is it polishing that makes it brilliant?" I asked.

"That, and the cut. The cut is even more important because of the way light reflects off the facets."

"Don't you want to have it cut and polished?"

"No. I prefer it in its natural state. It interests me far more like this than cut into an artificial shape just to hang about some worthless woman's neck."

I wondered if he was thinking of a particular woman's neck, or if all women who wore gems were by definition worthless. I thought of the pendants and other jewellery I'd caught a glimpse of in the pink-and-white room in the west wing. Where was Alicia Spencer now?

We continued with our work, which I began to enjoy now that I could see the minerals better and that Mr. Spencer was telling me more about them. But after twenty minutes or so, he asked me to extinguish the lamp.

"Why?" I asked, dismayed.

"It hurts my eyes."

"I don't believe you."

He set down the stone he was holding and sighed. "Miss Springthorpe, I'm not in the mood to argue with you. We are finished for the day."

But I couldn't resist asking the question that had been lingering in my mind ever since the day he came to the garden. "I want to know why light hurts your eyes when you're in the house but bright sunlight doesn't. You took off your eye shades when we were in the garden the other day and the light couldn't have been brighter."

"You wouldn't understand."

"Give me a chance."

After a pause, he said, "When I have one of my headaches,

all light hurts my eyes. Candlelight is all I can bear."

"But you haven't got a headache now, do you?"

"You don't give up, do you? You're like a rat terrier." He rose from the wheel-chair and put out the lamp himself, then sat down again.

"I'm just trying to understand."

"I don't understand it myself, so you will not. I seem to be losing my eyesight. Sometimes I can see well enough, but other times . . . there is an obstruction at the centre of my vision. You don't know how distressing such an experience can be. It happens without warning. Most days I prefer not to know whether the obstruction is there or not. That is why I keep the lights low."

The meaning of his words slowly penetrated my mind, and I felt a confusing mixture of frustration and sympathy. "But Nick, don't you want to take advantage of the times you can see? Don't you want to just look and look at everything and try to burn it all into your memory before it's too late?"

"I haven't wanted to in the past," he said slowly, "but I did feel that way in the other day in the garden."

There was a long silence, during which I realized I had called him by his Christian name. It had just slipped out. I wondered if he'd noticed.

"Why don't you see the specialist in London that Dr. Foster told you about?" I suggested.

"I don't want to. I've seen specialists before and they merely wasted my time."

"You're the most stubborn man I've ever met."

"I prefer to think of myself as firm of purpose."

"Of course you do."

"Will you go to the library with me?" he asked.

"What? Now?"

"Yes. Have you any objection?"

"No, I suppose not. Shall I call Bedford to push your chair?"

"There's no need. Mrs. Wilson isn't usually about at this time of day, though perhaps you will allow me to lean on you if she happens to walk by."

"Very well." I didn't think his attempts to deceive Mrs. Wilson about the state of his health were necessary, but there was no point arguing when he knew Mrs. Wilson and his brother better than I did.

As we left the mineral room and headed down the corridor towards the centre of the house, he rested his hand lightly on my shoulder. It surprised me, but perhaps he was uncertain of his footing in the dim light—once again, all we had was a candle—and he wanted to be near me in case Mrs. Wilson came by.

I smiled to myself to think of the strange appearance we must make. The lame leading the blind. I didn't dare say it, though.

When we reached the library, Nicholas Spencer sank down into one of the leather armchairs by the fireplace, breathing unevenly.

"Are you unwell?" I asked.

"No. Just give me a moment."

I sat in the armchair next to his and waited.

He looked around the room. "You've done wonders with the library. Everything is in perfect order."

"Thank you." I considered reminding him I had had to put the room in order twice, but that would have been harsh, even for me.

"Do you see that shelf on the other side of the room with the red leather-bound books?" he asked. "It's just above your eye level, I think."

"Yes."

"Go over there, please, and take out the volume of Wordsworth's poetry."

I did as he bid me, but when I returned with the book and held it out to him, he waved it away.

"I'd like you to read to me," he said.

I hadn't expected this. "I . . . I can't."

"What do you mean? I know you can read."

"I haven't got a good voice for reading aloud, and I don't know anything about poetry. I wouldn't read it properly."

"Let me be the judge of that. Give it a go."

I set my teeth. "Is this part of my employment?"

"Mercenary little wretch. Yes, if that's the only way to convince you to do it."

I sat down again and opened the book. "Where shall I start?"

"Wherever you like."

I turned the pages, frowning as I skimmed a few lines here and there. The poems were filled with long, tedious descriptions of nature and rural people.

"Do you actually like this rot?" I couldn't help saying.

"I don't think that line is in any of the poems. I didn't ask for your commentary. I asked you to read something to me, and you won't understand any of it if you read so quickly. It's meant to be read slowly. Savoured."

I gave him a sceptical look.

"Give it to me." He held out his hand, and I relinquished the book. After a moment of searching, he passed it back to me. "Here's one you might like."

"'The child is father of the man,'" I read. "Now that's ridiculous."

"What did I say about commentary?"

Doggedly I began to read. It was both tedious and depressing, not only descriptions of nature but also mournful laments about losing one's appreciation for nature. I had heard of Wordsworth before, of course, and I knew he was once England's poet laureate. But that was many years ago. Surely his poems were out of fashion now, even among people who liked poetry.

I read as fast as I dared, expecting Nick to interrupt me at any moment with criticisms of my voice or reading style. I had never liked my voice—it was flat and a bit nasal. But he was sitting with his head back and eyes closed, enduring my poor performance with good grace.

It was a long poem with all the sentimental excesses I expected—rainbows, roses, laughing shepherd boys—but it also seemed to contain some Platonic philosophy. I knew nothing about poetry, but I had studied the ancient philosophers. While I didn't like the idea of decorating philosophical theories with poetic flourishes, my interest was sparked.

Something changed when I read the seventh stanza. I couldn't have defined what it was exactly that captured my attention, but there was something about a child who was stunted somehow, who learned to conform to the demands of the world and who lost . . . what? I wasn't sure. When I read the last lines of the stanza, "As if his whole vocation / Were endless imitation," I realized my pace had slowed and there was an odd feeling in my throat.

Nick didn't move or open his eyes.

I kept reading slowly, feeling as if I were under a spell. I still didn't like the poem—I was quite sure I didn't like poetry at all—but I pressed on, my mind and body feeling strangely suspended:

> *What though the radiance which was once so bright,*
> *Be now forever taken from my sight.*
> *Though nothing can bring back the hour*
> *Of splendour in the grass, of glory in the flower;*
> *We will grieve not, rather find*
> *Strength in what remains behind;*

My voice forsook me, and for a horrible moment I thought I might cry. I couldn't think of anything worse than crying in front of Nick.

After a few seconds of silence, without opening his eyes, Nick continued,

> *In the primal sympathy*
> *Which having been must ever be;*
> *In the soothing thoughts that spring*
> *Out of human suffering;*
> *In the faith that looks through death,*
> *In years that bring the philosophic mind.*

He opened his eyes and looked at me intently. "It's beautiful, don't you agree?"

I nodded, not trusting myself to speak. I couldn't believe I was becoming emotional about poetry.

He leaned forward, staring into the cold, empty fireplace. "I've always loved that poem, and over the years it's become even more meaningful to me. Especially the lines about the radiance being 'taken from my sight.'"

"Doesn't it depress you?" I managed.

"No. I find it comforting."

"I don't understand what he means by 'the philosophic mind.'"

"I think it's a mind at peace, a mind that can contemplate the universe with equanimity. Something I've never been very good at. I like to think there's still hope for me, though."

"I don't see how it's possible to have a peaceful mind if one allows oneself to feel too much, or even think too much. That's the trouble with poetry."

"Is it?" He sat back and smiled like an indulgent parent with an ignorant child.

"Poetry encourages morbid introspection. It isn't healthy."

"You sound like Plato wanting to ban poets from the Republic. Is there no place for feelings in your life?"

"Not very much. They ought to be subject to logic and reason."

"And do you consider yourself a logical person?" he asked.

"Yes."

"Do you always act rationally?"

"Don't be absurd," I said. "Nobody acts rationally all the time."

"You concede that people are irrational some of the time."

"Of course. But if a person is taught to act rationally and to subject his passions to his reason, he will do very well in life. You can't argue with that."

"I can and I will." He leaned forward again, but now he was looking at me, his grey eyes intense. "Our passions can tell us a great deal about ourselves. Our most irrational moments will reveal the truth in a way that no amount of reasoning ever could."

"I don't know about that. In any case, why is it necessary to know so much about oneself? I know enough to live a satisfactory life."

"Is that all you want? A satisfactory life?"

"Of course. Why should I want anything more?"

"I see we've come once again to the subject of dreams. Do you really mean to tell me you've never had wild, impossible dreams, even as a child? Haven't you ever wanted what was out of your reach?"

I looked away. "I didn't grow up with the privileges you did. Although my family wasn't poor, my sisters and I were taught to be content with little. Being the youngest of five girls as well as having . . . physical limitations made it clear to me there was no point having impossible dreams."

"I see. So you never allowed yourself to wish for more. Very sensible."

I turned narrowed eyes on him. "Are you mocking me?"

"No, Vaughan," he said quietly. "I just wonder if you have limited yourself too much, if there is some part of you that longs to be free but doesn't even know it's imprisoned. Rather like that strand of hair starting to come loose at the nape of your neck."

I reached both hands to the back of my neck and pulled my hair flat, feeling for a pin to stab it with.

"Must you treat your poor hair with such violence?"

"I don't see why it should matter to you what I do with my hair." My voice came out colder than I intended.

He shrugged. "It doesn't. Will you read a little more? You haven't finished the poem."

"I don't want to read more of that one. I'll find another." I sat down and began to read like an automaton, careful not to think about the meaning of the words. Instead, I thought how absurd it was that he should think me imprisoned. He was so clearly the prisoner, with his locked doors and dark rooms and secrets.

13

O ver the next few weeks, I finished most of the legal
work and put the documents in order, and Nick and
I finished cataloguing and packing away his
minerals. But there was much to do outdoors. It was an
uncommonly warm spring, and Joe was busy in the gardens
every day. I spent every afternoon with him, and Nick came too
on his good days, which became more frequent. I spent the
evenings reading with Nick in the library. I usually read to him,
but if his eyesight permitted, we read separate books in silence.
Other times we talked. Once we were finished with the
minerals, I refused to accept a salary from him. After all, it was
hardly work to read or talk to him, and while I wouldn't have
called him a friend, exactly, I didn't mind his company.

One day, Nick had ordered Bedford to unlock the door to
the second floor in the west wing and invited me to see for
myself that no real child was there. But when I looked up at the
impossibly narrow, steep staircase and uneven steps, I knew I
couldn't manage them on my own. Not with my lame leg. And
I couldn't in good conscience suggest that Nick try to ascend
the stairs when he was still using his wheel-chair, despite the
ambiguity surrounding whether or not he really needed it.

"Surely this isn't the only staircase leading to the second
floor," I said.

"The grand staircase used to lead there too," Nick replied, "but it needed repairs that were never done. Because it wasn't safe, the part of it between the first and second floors was sealed off. That was probably twenty years ago."

That night I was awakened by the sound of childish laughter instead of crying. I sat up in bed and pinched my arm hard enough to bring tears to my eyes, to be certain I wasn't dreaming. But I definitely heard a giggle, much nearer than the crying had ever been. It sounded as though it was just outside my room. I got out of bed as quietly as I could, lit a candle, and put on my wrapper. Another laugh, a clattering sound, and then light footsteps, as if a child were running back and forth on the landing.

I drew back the bolt and flung the door open, my heart quaking.

There was nobody on the landing, but I thought I heard a movement on the staircase. I took a step towards it, but my unshod foot stepped on a small, sharp object, and I cried out in pain.

I bent down to examine what I'd stepped on. It was a jack from a children's game: the pointed metal objects were scattered about the landing, and the ball was there, too. I gathered up the nearest ones and limped back to my room, fastening the door securely. I had stepped on the jack with my good foot, so I was doubly lame now, but the pain would likely fade by morning, unlike my worries. Either there was a real child playing jacks in the middle of the night, which seemed highly unlikely, or one of the inhabitants of the house had placed the jacks there. If the latter, it was an unmistakable warning. I was lucky I hadn't been closer to the staircase when I stepped on the jack: it would almost certainly have thrown off my balance and pitched me down the stairs.

The next afternoon I was in the garden with Nick and Joe, trying to decide whether to mention the child's laughter and the jacks. It was a perfect late-spring day that made it hard to believe that anything strange or mysterious was happening in the house.

"I think the pink roses will bloom soon," Nick said.

Joe and I looked at the bush Nick was pointing at. The fat buds indeed looked as though they were about to burst from their green containers.

"You're right," Joe said. "And the others won't be far behind."

Joe and I had been clearing away some weeds and dead leaves. Ready for a short rest, I rose to sit beside Nick on the bench, moving slowly because of the lingering soreness in my foot.

Nick glanced from my face to my feet, then back again.

Before he could ask the question I could see forming in his eyes, I said quickly, "I don't want the roses to bloom. Not now."

"Why not?" asked Joe. He stretched out on the ground nearby, resting back on his elbows and raising his face to the sun.

"I'll miss it. I'm leaving for my sister's wedding in London next week."

"So soon?" The disappointment in Joe's voice was gratifying. "I thought that visit was a long way off."

"So did I." Seeing that Joe's eyes were closed, I allowed my gaze to linger on his sun-browned face.

"I'm going to London next week as well," Nick said. "Perhaps we could travel together."

"You are?" I couldn't imagine Nick leaving Morton for any reason. "Why?"

"I decided to see the specialist that you and that old fool Foster are always going on about."

"Oh." I was too stunned to point out that I had mentioned the specialist to Nick only once, as had Dr. Foster, as far as I knew.

"I'm taking the nine o'clock train from Bradford on the fourth," Nick said. "Would it suit you to travel that day?"

"Yes, I suppose so."

"Has my brother mentioned to either of you when he intends to return to Morton?" Nick asked.

Joe shook his head.

I said, "I wrote to Sir Peter last week to tell him I've found an irregularity that must be investigated before we can move forward with the sale of the estate."

"What sort of irregularity?" Nick asked.

"A claim against the property." At his look of surprise, I hastened to add, "It's probably a mistake. Erroneous liens are filed all the time, and it ought to be fairly easy to clear up. It will delay the sale of the estate a bit longer, though, so your wish is coming true in spite of all my efforts."

I was smiling, but Nick didn't look as pleased as I expected.

"Sir Peter is still in Italy, anyway," I said. "In the last letter I received from him, he said he'd be going to France on his way back to England and would likely stay there at least another month."

Again, I expected Nick to express satisfaction with this information, but he was silent.

"I'd better get back to work," Joe said, jumping up. "Those trellises won't mend themselves."

"I'm going back to the house," Nick said. Then, as Joe moved to retrieve the wheel-chair, which stood near the gate,

Nick added, "There's no need for that. I'm feeling better, and I've deceived people long enough. I'll walk back."

After he left, Joe and I exchanged surprised looks. Nick had been so careful to feign illness and weakness whenever Mrs. Wilson might see him, and we understood why he felt it was necessary. What had changed now, that he was willing to let her see him walking without assistance?

"You'd think he'd be worried about Mrs. Wilson telling Sir Peter he can walk," I said.

"Perhaps it doesn't matter anymore," Joe said. "He may have come to some agreement with Mrs. Wilson or even with Sir Peter that we don't know about."

"What do you mean? An agreement to delay the sale of the estate?"

"No, I doubt that. But now that summer is nearly here and you've told us Sir Peter's plans, it might not make much difference if he finds out now or later that his brother is in better health than he thought."

I frowned. "Do you think Nick is in better health than he was?" I no longer believed that Nick was hiding anything about his health from me and Joe, but I couldn't tell if the apparent improvement was real or merely a result of Nick's new honesty.

"Of course. Can't you tell? He has colour in his face now, and he has far more energy than he did. Just the other day he planted those funkias by the south wall. He could never have done that a month ago."

"That's true."

"Will you come with me so we can keep talking while I work?"

I followed him to the west wall where the broken trellis was, and I watched as he unwrapped a coil of wire. The events of the night before still loomed large in my mind, and it occurred to me that Joe was the only person at Morton young and able-bodied enough to make a thorough search of the house.

"Joe," I ventured, "Something odd happened last night."

"Oh? What was it?" He glanced at me, pausing to stretch out the wire, one end towards me. "Could you hold this end for me?"

I took the wire, deciding that sharing the story with Joe was worth the risk of his thinking me mad. He was so calm and steady, more trustworthy in my eyes than anyone else at Morton. It was also easier to tell him about the child's laughter and the jacks while he was working on the trellis than if he'd been idle and looking me in the face.

When I'd finished my story, he frowned and said, "That sounds frightening, Vaughan. Is your foot all right?"

"Yes, just a bit sore. I was wondering . . . would you be willing to go into the house and look for the child?"

"Do you really think there's a child in the house?" He sounded surprised, but he didn't pause in his work, wrapping his section of wire around the broken trellis.

"I don't know. I can't imagine why everyone would lie to me about it, if that's the case. If Mrs. Wilson or Bedford, or even Nick, has kidnapped a child, the crime must be reported."

"Of course." He took my section of wire and secured it, then looked up at me from where he knelt on the ground. "I think what you've experienced is reason enough to search the house, but I'll need to think of a plausible excuse for doing it. I don't want to sneak around or jeopardize my position here if I can help it."

"I understand." Nervously I added, "I would never ask you to do such a thing if I didn't feel it was necessary."

"I know. It was courageous of you to ask." He looked at me gravely. "There's something I'd like to ask you, too, but it's very personal, and I haven't had the courage. Not yet."

I was struck dumb as my mind began to spin. He was too serious to be flirting with me, but we didn't know each other very well. If he intended to propose marriage, surely he would express his feelings for me or ask what mine were for him before taking such a momentous step. And despite his optimistic, relaxed attitude, Joe wouldn't propose marriage to anyone without ensuring that he had some sort of gainful employment after Morton was sold.

I must have looked as panicky as I felt, for he said, "Forgive me. I didn't mean to worry you. Shall I ask the question and get it over with?"

I nodded, though I had no idea how I would answer him if the question was what I . . . feared? Hoped for? I realized I was unacquainted with my own feelings on the matter.

My panic only increased as Joe, remaining in the kneeling position he was in from working on the trellis, turned to me and held out his hand.

"Vaughan, will you . . . lend me your shoe?"

"My shoe?" I repeated.

"Yes, your special shoe. I'd like to borrow it, just for twenty minutes or so."

It was a strange request, but I trusted him enough to believe he wouldn't make it without good reason. "Very well," I said. I bent down and removed the shoe, hiding my deformed foot under my skirt. When I handed the shoe to Joe, I was embarrassed by how large and ugly it looked in the sunlit garden, with its steel reinforcements and heavy leather straps, like a monstrous, wingless, artificial bat.

"Thank you. I'll be back shortly." Joe left the garden with the shoe.

I sank onto the bench and gave myself a stern talking-to for imagining even for a moment that Joe was going to ask a different question. But I was glad for the opportunity to think about the nature of my feelings for him. I enjoyed Joe's company. I admired his enthusiasm and even temper and good looks. He was kind and hard-working. There was nothing whatsoever the matter with him. I didn't think I had romantic feelings for him, but I wasn't a romantic person, so perhaps I wouldn't feel those for anyone.

Joe returned a quarter of an hour later with my shoe, promising I'd find out in a few days what he needed it for and that he'd search the house as soon as a good opportunity presented itself. Then he was gone.

I returned to the house in a state of confusion. What I needed, I realized, was a good, strong cup of tea. I was glad to see Mrs. Wilson carrying a tea tray to the kitchen table.

"Is that a fresh pot?" I asked. "I'd love a cup, if you don't mind."

"I don't mind." She looked at me with raised eyebrows. "Where's tha' been, miss?"

I put my hand up to my dishevelled hair and blushed as if I'd been caught in an illicit act. "In the rose garden." I sat down at the kitchen table.

Mrs. Wilson set down the tea tray, poured a cup of tea, and handed it to me. Then she poured one for herself, but instead of sitting at the kitchen table with me, she stood looking at me with a strange expression, a mixture of wariness, curiosity, and judgment.

"Please sit down," I said, "unless you're too busy."

She sat. "I've hardly seen thee this last month."

"I've been spending the afternoons outdoors now that the warmer weather has come."

"Aye. And in the evenings tha' reads in the library with Mr. Spencer."

"Not every evening," I said quickly, then was annoyed with myself for sounding so defensive. I was on edge, not knowing if she had seen Nick walk back to the house that afternoon. "Sometimes he likes to read in the library while I work."

"That doesn't trouble thee?" She peered at me over the edge of her teacup.

"No. Why should it?"

"Most folks wouldn't feel safe alone with a madman." Her tone was mild, but her manner was guarded, quite different from what it used to be.

I said carefully, "I don't think he's well enough to hurt me, and even if he is, I can defend myself. I couldn't keep him out of the library if he wishes to be there, anyway. It's his house."

Her response was quick and sharp. "It's Sir Peter's house."

"Yes, of course," I said. "I only meant Mr. Spencer lives here and I'm merely an employee."

But it was too late to amend my words. Mrs. Wilson's countenance plainly showed that I had switched sides in a war and now was allied with her enemy. It was ridiculous. I hadn't even met Sir Peter and didn't think I'd taken a side at all, if a side must be taken.

"I'm quite looking forward to meeting Sir Peter," I said, hating the false brightness of my tone, but anxious to try one more time to convince Mrs. Wilson that I wasn't the traitor she thought me. "He seems very kind and understanding in his letters. Is he the same in person?"

She settled back in her chair, her shoulders relaxing. "Aye. He's good at making folks feel comfortable, too. When he talks to thee, tha'll feel like the most important person in the world. The house always comes alive when he's here. He often brings guests with him, and we'll have extra servants here too. Tha' won't recognize the place, so full of noise and merry-making."

This didn't sound particularly appealing to me, but I wasn't about to object now that Mrs. Wilson was talking to me in a friendlier manner. "Will he bring guests this time, though?" I asked. "Surely he won't bring people here when the estate is to be sold so soon."

"Happen not. We'll have to wait and see. No doubt there will be a gathering of some sort, knowing Sir Peter."

I hesitated, not wanting to put Mrs. Wilson on her guard just when she was starting to warm to me again, but I felt she was the only person in the house I could ask about the jacks, since Bedford never answered any of my questions, and I didn't want to upset Nick. And the physical objects were tangible, at least, unlike the crying or the laughter. I drew the jacks out of my skirt pocket and placed them on the table between us.

"Do you recognize these?" I asked her.

Her face closed, but she nodded briefly. "Aye. They belonged to Mr. Spencer's daughter, Frances."

"Do you know where I found them?"

"In the nursery, I presume."

"I can't use the stairs to the nursery," I said, only just stopping short of adding *as you very well know*. "I found them on the landing outside my room. Can you explain how they got there?"

"No, miss. How could I explain it?" The guarded look was back in her eyes, and she began to gather up the tea things.

"Mrs. Wilson, wait. Please." I didn't know if it was the desperation in my voice or just that she wasn't fast enough to walk away, but she paused, her expression still closed.

"It appears that someone is trying to frighten me. If you know who this person is, I want them to know that I can't leave until the sale of the house is completed, but I promise I'll do so immediately afterwards. I am doing what Sir Peter hired me to do, and I can't complete that work if I'm injured by tripping over children's toys that inexplicably appear outside my room."

She rose from the table with the tea tray and turned away without a word. I sighed in frustration and put the jacks back in my pocket. Why had I thought she would answer me? She was no more forthcoming than Bedford.

But she set down the tea tray near the kitchen sink, then returned to the table and sat down again. With a look of resignation, she pressed her lips together.

"I didn't want to say anything, Miss Springthorpe, but you ought to know the truth."

With dawning hopefulness, I waited.

"You've noticed that Mr. Spencer is more wick now," she began.

I nodded.

"When he feels better in his body, he feels worse in his mind."

This was not consistent with what I had noticed. Nick seemed healthier in both body and mind. But I said nothing.

"I see from thy face tha' doesna believe me," she went on, "but the same thing happens every time he's troubled in his mind: his wee daughter's toys and games appear all over the house. He goes to the nursery and brings them downstairs, scattering them about so that it seems she's alive."

"He knows she died."

"He knows it as a fact, aye, but underneath, he can't accept it. He never could. I told you how cold he was when the lass died. He didn't cry. Any love he felt for that child was buried. Happen it's his guilt coming out in his actions."

"I don't see toys scattered everywhere. The jacks were placed outside my room. Deliberately. As if to frighten me."

"That may be. As tha' ken, he doesn't want the house sold, so happen he is trying to scare thee. But there's no ghost here, and nobbut him has a reason to do it. Make of it what you will."

When she left the kitchen, I remained at the table, toying with the jacks in my pocket and wondering if there could be any truth in what she'd said. Grief did make people behave strangely: I had only to think of poor Mrs. Dixon and her Pears soap girl. It was possible that Nick was moving Frances's toys around the house, but I no longer believed he was trying to frighten me away. And there was still no explanation for the sounds in the night, which I believed were connected to the toys. I resolved to find a rational explanation for both, hopefully with Joe's help.

14

The day before my trip to London, Joe asked if I'd like to accompany him to Netherton for another visit to his family, and I agreed enthusiastically. I was looking forward to seeing his mother: even knowing of her troubles, I found her a warm, comfortable person, the perfect antidote to the coldness of Morton. If anything, I felt more sympathy for her because of her loss. Her refusal to accept her daughter's death was a more extreme version of my own difficulty acknowledging that my father was gone forever. Even now, I found it hard to accept that he wasn't in London with the rest of my family, waiting for me to return.

It was a warm, sunny day, with the curves of billowy white clouds in sharp relief against the blue sky, no breeze, and the leaf buds on the trees bursting into an early green bloom. I was glad to leave Morton and its mysteries behind as we bounced along in Joe's gig. I determined to let myself fully enjoy the weather and the company.

I marvelled at the change in myself that had coincided with the change in season: I talked easily with Joe and wasn't anxious or self-conscious as I usually was with people, especially people I wished to impress. My spirits were lighter, which I attributed to Joe's friendship. A few days earlier, Joe had cleverly invented a problem with the rain gutters that required him to not only climb up onto the roof but also check the rooms on the second floor of both the east and west wings. None of the inhabitants of the house had protested, not even Nick, despite his suspicious nature and obsession with privacy. Perhaps he had come to trust Joe as much as I did. But Joe found no child in his explorations, nor did he have an explanation for what I'd heard. I was disappointed, but at least the fruitless search didn't seem to affect his opinion of my sanity.

When we reached Netherton, I noticed again that it seemed too perfect and too clean. There were more people outdoors this time because of the warm weather, and they too seemed unusually happy. Once again, I marvelled at the hearty greetings men offered to anyone who passed them in the street, the smiles on women's faces as they gathered near shop windows to exchange the latest news, the boys running about.

There was definitely something strange about this place. It was clearer to me this time because of my happier state of mind. The last time I'd been here, I couldn't distinguish between the strangeness in myself and the strangeness in the place, but this time the village seemed very odd indeed. I decided to look for people who didn't seem happy or buildings that didn't look clean, but in vain.

We drove past a park where some sort of children's festival or game was going on. Several groups of boys were playing games and running about. This too struck me as odd.

As we stopped in the village square, Joe gave me a quizzical look. "Are you all right, Vaughan? You look troubled."

"Oh, it's nothing, really."

He leaped lightly down from the gig and came to my side to help me down. Distracted by his hand gripping mine and his other hand lightly on my waist, I said no more, but he was still looking at me with a question in his eyes.

"You'll think I'm silly," I said finally, "but I'd feel better if I saw one person who didn't look happy. Or something that's not perfectly clean." I wanted to say that Netherton seemed eerie, but compared to Morton, there was nothing eerie about it, and Joe would certainly have thought me peculiar had I said it.

"That's easy," he said. "You'll find both in that little boy over there." He pointed to a small boy who was approaching a sweet shop window. "Do you see his shoes?"

His shoes were indeed dirty, as if he'd been walking through mud, and his face was blank rather than happy. But I still felt unsettled.

I thought of the boys playing in the park and asked, "Is there some sort of boys' club event or festival going on today?"

He shrugged. "I don't think so. Why do you ask?"

"The boys playing games. We drove past them. There were only boys there." I looked around us, and with a dawning realization, added, "and even here in the square there are only boys. Where are the girls?"

He laughed. "Vaughan, you're seeing what you wish to see. Don't you see the girl over there, pushing that pram? And the one in her brother's arms across the street?"

He was right, but the first girl was an adolescent, nearly an adult, and the second was very young, no more than two years old. There were no girls in sight between the ages of two and fifteen.

I mentioned this to him, and he shrugged. "At this exact moment, I suppose that's true, but it doesn't mean there aren't any. Besides, girls don't roughhouse and play outdoor games as much as boys do."

I gave him a suspicious look.

"You're from London, Miss Solicitor," he said teasingly. "In rural Yorkshire, girls and boys are treated differently."

"Do you think that's as it should be?"

"Aha, now you sound like my mam. What I think isn't important. This village holds old-fashioned views, and trying to change them would be pointless."

I frowned.

"I think it's splendid that you're a lawyer," he added warmly, "and I think girls ought to be allowed to play outdoor games if they wish to. Is that enough?"

I nodded, but I paid very close attention to the relative numbers of boys and girls as we went into a couple of shops to buy food for his family and made our way to the Dixon house. My observations about the lack of school-age girls continued to be correct.

At the house, Mrs. Dixon welcomed me like a long-lost relative, taking my arm and drawing me into the kitchen for tea and a chat while Joe went about the house making minor repairs to the furniture and windows, as well as carrying potting soil upstairs to his mother's conservatory. I tried not to let him distract me from my conversation with Mrs. Dixon, but he was working in his shirtsleeves and looked more attractive than usual.

At one point, Mrs. Dixon caught my sidelong glance at Joe as he left the room with hammer and nails. She smiled as if she knew exactly what I was thinking.

When he was out of earshot, she said proudly, "My Joe is worth ten of the best men in London. Nobody pays me any mind when I say that because I'm his mam, but still."

"I agree with you," I blurted out. As I felt heat suffuse my face, I stammered, "not that I've met many men in London, but he is so very . . . kind. And helpful."

"You can imagine how many village girls have set their caps at him," she said. "But I've never needed to worry. He's flirted with them, of course—what man won't flirt with a pretty girl? —but he's never been serious. Until now."

It was on the tip of my tongue to ask which girl he was serious about when I realized what she meant from the knowing way she was looking at me. I didn't think my blush could intensify, but it did.

She patted my arm reassuringly. "I know he's said nothing to you yet, and perhaps it's too soon for him to know his own feelings—men are so slow that way—but he's never brought a girl home to meet me before."

"We're just friends," I choked out. "He felt sorry for my difficulties at Morton and wanted to lift my spirits, that's all."

"Perhaps, but I know my son, and I've never seen him look at a girl the way he looks at you. And I don't mind telling you that you're exactly the sort I'd choose for him. A sensible, intelligent woman with a good head on her shoulders. That's what he needs."

I was in an agony of embarrassment. While it was wonderful to have his mother's approval, that would mean nothing if Joe himself didn't feel the same way, and I had no proof that he did. My own feelings were as confused as ever.

The hammering sounds from the parlour were interspersed with muffled thumps and an occasional curse.

"Do you like living here in Netherton?" I asked her, desperate to change the subject.

She gave a shrug so much like Joe's that I couldn't help smiling, and said, "No, not really, but it's home. Would you like another cup of tea?"

"Yes, please."

She poured me a cup and then another for herself. "I thank the good Lord every day that Joe isn't like his father," she said.

Joe had told me nothing about his father, aside from the fact that he was much older than his mother and had died several years earlier of apoplexy, or perhaps a heart attack: I couldn't remember which.

"Was Mr. Dixon a . . . cruel man?" I asked tentatively, reluctant to pry into family secrets.

She blinked and gave me a surprised look, as if she'd forgotten I was there, but then recovered her equanimity. "I won't lie to you, Miss Springthorpe. On the surface he acted the part of a good husband and father, but when he drank . . . yes, he was cruel."

"I'm sorry," I said.

"No need to be. Our lives have been much better since he died, and that was years ago, mercifully." She sighed. "Netherton has no scarcity of men like him, though, so perhaps it's right to be sorry."

This surprised me. "The village looks so perfect. Everyone seems happy."

"It's easy to scrub the surface clean; harder to erase the ugliness underneath."

"And there are so few girls. Little girls, I mean. Do you know why?"

"It's the curse," she said with another sigh, as if that explained everything.

"What curse?"

"Everything all right in here?" Joe asked, poking his head into the kitchen.

His mother and I both jumped like startled horses. She was quicker to recover. "We're fine, Joe dear," she said.

"I'm nearly finished, but I wanted to check a window in the conservatory before we leave." He looked at me. "Can you wait a bit longer?"

"Yes, of course," I said. "Take your time."

When he had gone upstairs, Mrs. Dixon drained her tea cup daintily and set it down, then leaned closer to me. "Joe doesn't like me to talk about the curse—he calls it an old wives' tale—but I know every family in this village. A midwife knows people's secrets. Many men here beat their wives and daughters, and their sons grow up to be just like them. It would serve them right if Netherton becomes a village of only men. Then it will die. It all started with that poor little drowned Spencer girl."

"Frances?" I exclaimed. "Her death was an accident."

"Not everyone believes that."

"I don't believe her father would have hurt her—" Although I didn't speak as strongly as I felt, I wondered at my instinctive desire to defend Nick. What had happened to my vaunted reasoning abilities? I had no evidence one way or the other.

"I know very little about him," she said, "and I don't accuse him of anything, but after his daughter died, hardly any girl babies were born in Netherton. Only boys."

Joe walked into the room. "Mam, you promised you would keep those silly stories to yourself," he said. It wasn't clear how much he had heard, but he looked exasperated. "Our village has more boys than girls, aye, but there's no need to keep the ghoulish superstitions about it alive. Vaughan hears enough nonsense at Morton and doesn't need more of it from you, too."

She looked affronted. "You don't know this village as well as I do, Joe."

"True, but that doesn't change what I said. Anyway, it's time for us to leave."

"What about the surprise for Vaughan?" asked Mrs. Dixon.
I didn't like the sound of this. In my experience, surprises
were usually unpleasant.

"It's ready," he said, "but I thought I'd give it to her later."

"Please give it to her now. I want to know if she likes it. I'll
make myself scarce upstairs, and you can call me down when
you're ready."

Joe agreed. I would have been worried if Mrs. Dixon hadn't
smiled beatifically at me on her way out of the kitchen.

"Stay where you are," Joe said as I started to rise to my feet.
"I'll bring it in."

He left the room and returned a few seconds later with a
large box, which he laid on my lap. I almost laughed aloud
when I saw it, for I didn't realize until that moment that my
conversation with his mother had led me to expect a much
smaller box.

"Open it, please," Joe said, his expression hopeful and even
a bit anxious.

I did so. The box was lined with crumpled newspaper,
which I had to move aside to reveal a pair of shoes.

One was an ordinary ladies' black dress shoe, but the other
was uniquely designed to fit my misshapen foot. It had been cut,
shaped, and reinforced in a way that would fit me.

"You made this?" I lifted my eyes to his, amazed.

"Aye. I had an idea for a shoe that would be lighter than the
one you usually wear, and I practiced with my mam's shoes. I
owe her three pairs of shoes now, but I'm pleased with the
result. Will you try it on?"

I bent down to remove my heavy shoe as Joe politely averted
his eyes. Then I slipped on the new shoe. It was a little loose at
the heel, but otherwise it was a perfect fit.

I rose and walked slowly back and forth across the room a few times.

"Does it feel comfortable?"

"Yes. It's wonderful. I've never had a shoe like this."

"I thought I ought to give it to you before you go to London so you could have a proper cobbler adjust it there."

"Thank you." I sat down again, too shy to look at him. He knew the contours of my deformed foot in intimate detail, yet it must not have disgusted him because it hadn't changed his behaviour towards me.

"May I call my mam back in? She'll want to see the shoe on you, if you don't mind."

"Of course."

Mrs. Dixon returned, and I obliged her by walking back and forth through the room again. I'd never had so much non-medical attention given to my feet before and wouldn't have believed myself comfortable with it, but comfortable I was with Joe and his mother in the short time I'd known them. Truth be told, I was more at ease with them than I was with my own family.

I thanked Mrs. Dixon for sacrificing her shoes on my behalf, and she surprised me by embracing me warmly. I was as little used to maternal affection as I was to people watching me walk, and at first I endured the embrace rather stiffly, but then I softened and returned the hug.

On our way back to Morton, I thanked Joe again for the special shoe, still feeling a little shy with him because I felt I'd revealed too much, not just physically with my foot but also emotionally. My defences were low, and I didn't trust myself.

"There's no need to keep thanking me," he said. In a more serious tone, he added, "Please don't pay attention to my mother's stories. She likes to speak of ghosts and curses, but its all nonsense."

"Is it?" I surprised myself by saying. "I noticed you admitted to her that there are more boys than girls in the village, but you didn't say that when I asked about it."

"True. I get tired of the subject, to be honest, and there's a perfectly reasonable explanation."

I raised my eyebrows. "What's that? Something in the water?"

He laughed. "No, though perhaps that's how it started. Think about it, Vaughan. That story about the curse has been circulating since Frances Spencer's death, and it spooked people. Especially people with little girls. Even if they put no stock in superstition, it would make any little girls' parents uneasy to live among people who believe and tell such stories. They must have moved away. Parents of boys felt no need to leave."

"Of course." I couldn't believe I hadn't thought of this explanation myself.

"That's why I hate it when my mam tells that story. If you tell a lie—and that's what I think of that story—often enough, it sounds more and more true. And I don't want more people to move away from Netherton."

"Perhaps you can find a family of daughters whose parents don't believe in old wives' tales and convince them to move here."

"That's a good idea." He smiled, then added, "I've been thinking, why don't we—you, me, and Nick—plan a celebration when you return from London? We could have a picnic in the rose garden. No doubt Nick will appreciate something to look forward to as well, no matter what diagnosis he receives from the specialist.

And the roses will be in full bloom then."

I agreed enthusiastically to this suggestion, and we spent the rest of the ride back to Morton planning the picnic. I was in such a good mood when I went to bed that I slept long and soundly. When I awoke, I decided that Joe's explorations in the house, or perhaps simply the influence of his warm reasonableness, had banished the ghostly night child forever.

15

In spite of the bustle and hurry of last-minute preparations for the journey to London—ensuring I'd packed everything I'd need, waiting for Nick to organize his own belongings and give final instructions to Bedford, waiting for the fly he'd hired to take us to the train station—I couldn't stop thinking about my conversation with Mrs. Dixon. I didn't believe for a second in any curse, but I was more curious than ever about the manner of Frances Spencer's death. I still didn't believe Nick could have hurt his own daughter, but perhaps someone else had. As a result of my ruminations, I was only half-aware of Nick's presence on the short trip to the train station in Bradford.

It was only when we reached the train station and Nick and I were standing with our luggage on the platform that I noticed how quiet he was. He hadn't said a word from the moment we left Morton.

Before I could ask if he was unwell, a porter approached us and asked if we wanted him to take our bags.

"Yes," I said at exactly the same moment as Nick said "No."

I stared at him. "But—"

"We don't need your assistance," Nick said to the porter, waving him away.

"I hope you don't expect me to carry our luggage," I said. I had two small bags, and Nick had only one, but I still didn't want to play the role of porter.

"Of course not." He looked past me at the people boarding the train. "I'm not going."

"What do you mean? Are you ill?"

He did look paler than usual, but he shook his head. "No. I've merely changed my mind."

"I don't understand," I protested, trying to mask my disappointment. I'd hoped the appointment with the oculist would be a turning point for him. "You've made all the arrangements—"

"They can be unmade. You'd better go. I don't want you to miss the train. Have a good trip." He didn't meet my eyes during this extraordinary speech, instead looking off into the distance, away from the crowd and back in the direction we had come.

I stood in silent thought for a moment, gazing at him, then at the train and passengers. It was like any other railway station. People were pushing past one another to be first in the queue, others were saying loud farewells to their friends, porters were rushing by with clattering carts. It was jarring even for me after three months of relative silence and seclusion at Morton Abbey.

I took a step closer to Nick and touched his arm to get his attention. "What's the matter?"

He met my eyes but said nothing. His mouth was drawn into a tight line.

"Is it the people? The noise?"

"Yes," he admitted.

"I have an idea," I said. "There's still time before the train leaves. Will you wait here for a few minutes?"

"Vaughan—"

"Will you try to trust me, just a little?" I spoke as gently as I could.

He hesitated. "Very well."

We already had two first-class tickets that Nick had paid for. I took them and went to find the guard, who watched me approach him with the glance at my leg that strangers always gave me. At Morton, I was an anomaly among other anomalies. I felt accepted there in a way I wasn't anywhere else. Now I was reminded I did not fit in with normal people or regular society, but I realized I could make use of that position, uncomfortable as it was.

"Excuse me," I said to the guard, holding out the tickets. "I'm travelling with my . . ." I looked back towards where Nick was standing some fifty feet away. I wasn't sure what to call him. My friend? My employer?

The guard followed my gaze. "Your father?"

Gratefully I seized on the suggestion. "Yes. But he's not well and can't bear noise of any kind. Could you arrange for us to have a compartment to ourselves?"

He looked at the tickets. "I can't promise you'll be alone in a compartment all the way to London."

"We'd be most grateful for anything you can do," I said, handing him half a crown. I was loath to part with the money, but if it would achieve the result I wanted, it was worth the loss.

When I returned to Nick's side with a porter following at a respectful distance, I said, "Everything is arranged. We have a compartment to ourselves, and we needn't board the train until the other passengers are on it."

Bemused, he said, "How did you manage that?"

"Persuasion," I replied. He didn't need to know that a large part of the persuasion was of the monetary sort. "Now will you come with me?"

He looked at the train and took a deep breath, then nodded.

Once we were comfortably settled in our compartment, I began to relax. I had never travelled first class before, and the royal blue velvet seats seemed sinfully large and luxurious, with matching draperies over the windows. And to have a whole compartment for just the two of us seemed just as indulgent. It was an old-fashioned compartment with no corridor and six seats. Nick and I sat facing each other by the window.

The guard put his head in just before the train set off. "Do you have everything you need, sir?" he asked Nick.

"Yes, thank you."

Touching the brim of his hat and nodding to me, the guard said, "I hope you and your father have a pleasant trip."

The second the guard left, Nick repeated, "Your *father?*"

"Yes." I couldn't help smiling at his offended tone.

"Did you tell him I was your father?"

"I allowed him to think so."

"How ridiculous. He must be blind."

I didn't reply.

"Why are you smiling like that?" he demanded. "Do you think I look old enough to be your father?"

I couldn't help enjoying Nick's displeasure. It was good for him to be distracted from his anxiety. "Well, your beard is very grey. It makes you look older."

"Does it?" He reached up to touch the offending facial hair.

"And perhaps it was meant as a compliment to me. Perhaps I look younger than I am."

"I think you do," he said, looking at me meditatively.

The train pulled out of the station, lurching a little before picking up speed. I pulled the curtain aside to look out the window, then glanced across at Nick.

"Would you prefer the curtains closed?" I asked. Even

though he'd been allowing more light into rooms lately, I'd become accustomed to his preference for dim light.

"No. You wish to look out, don't you?"

"Yes. I haven't been on many trains in my life. It's exciting to watch the landscape go by so quickly." I gazed at him appraisingly. "Are you all right now? No signs of a headache or any other pain?"

"Yes, I'm fine." He removed his hat and held it in his lap, smoothing the brim. "I apologise for my behaviour earlier. You must have thought me ridiculous. I thought I'd be able to manage, but when I saw all the people and . . . the noise and rushing about . . ."

"Not at all. I expected you to be anxious. It's been a long time since you've been away from Morton, hasn't it?"

"Yes. Five years, as a matter of fact. The last time I left Morton was a disaster."

"What happened?"

"Alicia was in London and sent a letter asking me to meet her at a hotel. After Frances's death she moved to the Continent, and her visits to England were rare. Stupidly, I thought she might have seen the error of her ways and wanted a reconciliation." He sighed. "Now you'll know what a fool I am. Despite all the evidence that she never loved me, despite knowing about her infidelity, I thought perhaps she had learned to appreciate me—if not love me—after all."

I was surprised on two counts. First, I'd been assuming his wife was dead, even that he might have murdered her, but I realized now that my imagination had run away with me. Second, he had never been so frank with me about his wife or his feelings for her, and I had never heard him say his daughter's name.

"Why did she want to see you?" I asked.

"She wanted a divorce." He stared out the window with unfocussed eyes.

"And you refused?"

"I did. It wasn't the first time she asked."

Uncertain whether to probe further when he was already telling me so much, I said mildly, "If she admitted to . . . taking lovers, or if you have proof that she did so, you could obtain a divorce quite easily and be free of her. Legally speaking."

"I can never be free of her," he said flatly. "In any case, I don't want a divorce. The very thought of the scandal—my family's name dragged through the mud, every detail of the case in the newspapers—sickens me. It is bad enough that Mrs. Wilson is so free with her stories. Wretched woman." He looked at me, adding, "You can know nothing of such sordid dealings. I shouldn't have told you."

"You forget I'm a solicitor." I sat up very straight, as if my posture proved I was a professional. "In the course of my work with my father, I heard about marital problems all the time. But surely no real scandal would touch you for long. Your name and reputation would be unsullied. Only your wife's reputation would suffer, but isn't that as it ought to be, given that she was the unfaithful one?"

"It's not just the scandal. There are other reasons why I cannot divorce her."

I waited for him to elaborate, but he was staring out the window again. It was incomprehensible to me that a man would wish to remain married to a woman who had cuckolded him, especially if she had no intention of returning to him. He must still be in love with her.

We were both silent for a time. I looked out at the landscape:

the moors were gradually giving way to gentle rolling hills and hedgerows. The rhythmic chugging of the train began to lull me into a drowsy state, which Nick interrupted with a question.

"Did you ask Joe to search the house the other day?"

I blinked, unsure how much to tell him. I thought he'd been convinced by the broken gutter excuse.

"I didn't believe he was in the house because of the gutters," he added. "Was he looking for the source of the sounds we've been hearing?"

"Yes," I admitted. "I didn't think you'd approve of him poking around on the second floor."

"On the contrary, I was relieved. It's about time a sane person who doesn't live at Morton went up there to investigate. I assume he found nothing."

"You're right. I had hoped he would, especially when he checked the rooms in the east wing, because of the new sounds I heard outside my bedroom." Joe had told me that he'd convinced Bedford to unlock the two rooms across the landing from mine, but they turned out to be just empty servants' rooms with iron bedsteads and little else.

"What new sounds?" Nick asked, instantly alert.

"Laughter." I pasted an expression on my face that I hoped passed for calm reason, or at least blankness rather than insanity.

Frowning, he said, "Maniacal laughter?"

"No. Happy laughter. The sound a child makes when she's playing or . . . I don't know. Just happy."

He looked confused. "When was the last time you heard it?"

"I heard it only once, about a week ago. And it was accompanied by other sounds, like jumping and running."

He appeared to be deep in thought.

"When was the last time you heard the crying?" I asked.

"About three weeks ago."

I looked down at my lap. "I know it sounds silly, but I'm hoping that Joe's presence on the second floor banished whatever it was. Not that I believe in a supernatural explanation."

The idea of Nick's daughter's ghost hovered in the air, but there was no way in hell I'd be the first to mention it.

"There's another explanation we haven't considered," he said.

My head snapped up. "What's that?"

"A psychological one." Ignoring my sceptical look, he went on, "Neither of us had happy childhoods. We were both kept indoors and in seclusion to some degree: you because of your leg and I because of my illnesses. Can it be a coincidence that I've heard a weeping child whose loneliness was palpable, and you've heard a happy child leaping and running about in a way you never could?"

I didn't like this explanation one bit. "That doesn't make sense. If I heard the child I wanted to be instead of the child I was, why wasn't it the same for you?"

"I'm not saying this possibility works perfectly for everything we've heard. But you have already heard the crying, and I may yet hear the laughter. There is some logic to it. Don't you think so?"

Logic was not a word I would apply to any part of this conversation, but I was silent.

"I know you don't like the idea," he went on. "But there are many respected physicians and scientists who believe that the mind and body are far more connected than previously thought. Henry Maudsley, for example. You needn't give me that look, Vaughan. You know I'd be the last person to say anyone's illness is all in their head. But this is not an illness. It's a . . . manifestation of a deep truth. An emotional truth."

This possibility was more outlandish to me than any other. I'd sooner believe in ghosts. Taking refuge in the more tangible aspects of the mystery, I asked, "Have you seen any toys in odd places about the house?"

He raised his eyebrows. "Odd places? No. Frances's toys are kept in the nursery, and I've seen no others."

I told him about the jacks and the ball I'd found outside my room, ending with, "Even if there's some merit in your psychological explanation, I don't believe our minds would pick up toys and place them in different rooms."

I watched him carefully as I spoke. If he knew anything about the toys, much less moved them himself, he gave no sign of it.

"I don't like the sound of that," he said, leaning forward with a look of concern. "And it's quite different from the sounds we've been hearing. The only explanation is that someone— not a ghost, and not our own minds—has been trying to frighten you. Or even hurt you."

"Why would anyone, aside from you, be trying to frighten me? You're the only person who wanted me to leave Morton. The only person who tried to prevent the sale of the estate."

"The only *obvious* person. There may be reasons others don't want you there." I must have looked sceptical again, for he added, "Yes, I'm the most obvious person, but I gave up trying to make you leave a long time ago. Now . . . I can't imagine Morton without you."

The sudden warmth in his tone and his eyes surprised me. He seemed unaware of it, for he continued, "and Mrs. Wilson is so loyal to Peter that she'd never interfere with anyone he hired."

"Bedford is very loyal to you." I pointed out. "Perhaps he

did it."

"I doubt that." But he hesitated, then added, "I'll talk to him when I return from London."

"Thank you."

"Are you in love with Joe?" he asked.

The question was so unexpected and so direct that I was surprised into telling the truth, vague as it was. "I . . . I don't know," I stammered. I looked out the window again to avoid his eyes.

"I don't mean to pry," he said, sitting back and looking out the opposite window. "You needn't tell me."

"It's not that. I really don't know. I've never been in love, so I don't know how to recognize the signs."

"Do you feel as though a vulture is eating your liver?" he asked.

I stared at him. "What?"

He met my eyes and smiled wryly. "Perhaps that's too Promethean. The way I felt with Alicia was more as if a wild animal had torn out my heart and was gnawing on it. I was still alive even though my heart was out of my body, and I fancied I felt every tooth mark as my heart was slowly being shredded into mincemeat."

"That's the most repulsive thing I've ever heard."

"Yes. Well." He raised his hand to his mouth, and I had the distinct impression that he was trying to hide a smile.

"I don't feel that way about Joe," I said with a shrug. "I just enjoy his company, and when I'm with him I feel . . . I don't know . . . like a cat basking in the sun."

"Perhaps that's what being in love feels like for you. It's different for everyone. Do you know what Joe's feelings are for you?"

"No."

"He flirts with you outrageously. Until he speaks seriously to you, you ought to guard your heart. I shouldn't like to see you hurt."

I was both touched that Nick cared enough to give me this advice and offended by his assumption that I was the one who would be hurt. Why wasn't he concerned that I might hurt Joe? Was it so obvious that Joe's attractions far outweighed mine?

In as neutral a tone as I could manage, I said, "I think I'll read my book now."

He made no objection, and we both settled down to read. Nick was reading a book of poetry—not Wordsworth for a change, but a poet I'd never heard of—and I was reading a guide to the finer points of English inheritance law. Although I'd finished the bulk of the legal work relating to the sale of Morton, I wanted to ensure I hadn't made any mistakes.

After a while the words began to swim and blur before my eyes, and I laid the book in my lap and leaned my head back, closing my eyes. I meant to rest for only a few minutes, but a longer time must have elapsed because when I opened them again, I had the fuzzy-headed feeling of awakening out of a deep sleep. We were pulling into a station that I assumed must be Leicester, but a sign for King's Cross Station assured me we were already in London and only minutes from our destination.

Nick had put aside his book and was watching me. In fact, he was watching me so intently and with such a strange expression on his face that I felt uncomfortable. It was an inscrutable expression, neither critical nor admiring. Rather as if he were trying to figure me out.

"Why are you staring at me?" I asked him.

His eyes flickered away, then back again. "I'm merely taking your advice."

"I don't know what you mean."

"Do you remember when we were talking about my eyesight and why I used to prefer dimly-lighted rooms? You said, 'don't you want to just look at everything and try to burn it all into your memory before it's too late?' I'm trying to burn you into my memory."

"Oh." I looked wildly about for something to do. My book was still on my lap, so I took my time packing it carefully into my reticule. "Perhaps you won't lose your eyesight. It hasn't become worse in the last few months, has it? The oculist may give you good news."

"I prefer to prepare for the worst."

"I know you do."

The shrill sound of the train whistle cut into our conversation, and as the train slowed, I wondered if Nick would be able to bear the noise and bustle of London. The noise at the Bradford station had been difficult enough.

"Is anyone meeting you here?" I asked.

"No. I'm going to take a cab to my hotel. Is anyone meeting you?"

"Yes. My sister Elizabeth."

The train stopped, and Nick put his book in his bag and started to rise, but I reached out and laid my hand on his arm. He sat down again and looked at me questioningly.

"Would you like me to come with you?" I asked.

"Come with me?" he repeated. "Where?"

"Anywhere. I mean . . ." I stopped in confusion. He had taken my hand and was looking at me with more than usual intensity. "I mean, to the specialist's office," I continued. "If you'd prefer not to go alone."

"Oh." He released my hand and said with sudden formality, "You needn't worry about me. I am neither infirm nor elderly and can take care of myself."

I thought his words and tone needlessly cold, since he must know I had been thinking only of his comfort. I turned to collect my bag. This time I was the one who half-rose and he was the one to stop me.

"Vaughan, wait." He didn't touch me, but his tone had returned to normal. "Forgive me. I know you wish only to be helpful."

I nodded, feeling too unsettled to reply, and we collected our things and disembarked.

Somehow, in the rush and hurry of the crowd on the platform, Nick and I became separated. I wanted to wish him luck with the specialist and say a proper farewell, but when I finally caught sight of him again he was walking away, and the next moment I was surrounded by Elizabeth and her children clamouring for my attention.

16

Family business delayed me in London for a fortnight. The first week was such a flurry of activity I had little time to think: as the only unmarried sister and maid of honour, I was expected to be available to everyone at all hours of the day and night. Whenever there was a problem, I was the one asked to fix it, whether it was the wrong item on the menu for the wedding breakfast, an oversight at the dressmaker's, a housekeeping problem, or merely the expectation that I would listen patiently to my family members' troubles. Nobody asked me about my time in Yorkshire except Letitia. Mother merely expressed surprise that I was managing to do the work expected of me at Morton Abbey.

Letitia ought to have been too preoccupied with her wedding to bother with me, but she took me aside for a sisterly chat one evening. I told her about the mysterious aspects of Morton Abbey that I knew she'd enjoy, omitting the night child's behaviour, which I thought would disturb her too much. She was especially interested in Joe, exclaiming delightedly, "I'm so glad you're meeting interesting people and not working all the time." I enjoyed her wedding more than I thought I would: it was an uneasy compromise between the simple ceremony Letitia wanted and the ostentatious pageantry my mother had tried to impose, but it was a love match, and seeing the way she and her new husband looked at each other made me think romantic love might not be so ridiculous, after all.

My second week in London was easier physically but more difficult mentally. Mother professed herself ill after the wedding and took to her bed, requiring me to carry out her orders. She wouldn't hear of my returning to Morton until she felt better, and I couldn't in good conscience leave her as she was, especially since my sister Elizabeth had gone to Bath for the week. In reality, there was little for me to do aside from writing a few letters for Mother and waiting for her next summons. My mind was allowed to drift, and it always drifted to Morton. I wondered if the roses were in bloom. I wondered if Joe missed me. I wondered how Nick's visit to the oculist had gone.

London no longer seemed like my real life. My life was at Morton, and as frustrating as I found the house and its mysteries, it felt oddly distressing to be separated from it. Despite the difficulties I'd experienced there, I was longing to return. It wasn't just the bonds I'd formed with Joe and even with Nick: the place itself had cast a spell on me. I hoped my unreasonable feelings would resolve themselves once my work there was done.

Finally, I was free to return to Morton. In the fly from Bradford, I was as excited as a child on her first trip to the seaside when I caught sight of the house and grounds. The trees were in full leaf and the birds were twittering merrily. The sunlit lawn was perfectly trimmed, begging for a game of tennis or bowls, and two people, one tall and one short, were standing together in the shade of the chestnut tree. As the carriage drew closer, I saw that they were Joe and Mrs. Wilson.

I called to the driver to let me out and asked him to continue to the house with my bags. Though I was tired and rumpled from travelling, I was so happy to see Joe that I didn't care. He and Mrs. Wilson were conversing so intently and seriously that they didn't seem to notice my approach.

Mrs. Wilson saw me first, and I pointed at Joe and shook my head to indicate that I wanted to surprise him. But she ignored me and said, "Here's Miss Springthorpe back from London," just as Joe was saying firmly, "It needs to stop."

"What needs to stop?" I asked from behind him.

He turned around, and for a fraction of a second, there was an expression on his face I'd never seen before. Displeasure? Anger? I knew it wasn't meant for me, but it was still surprising in someone with such a sunny disposition.

The dark look gave way to delight when he saw me. "Welcome back!" he exclaimed, lifting me off my feet in an enthusiastic embrace.

"Put the lawyer down, there's a good lad," Mrs. Wilson said.

As he released me, he said ruefully, "I've dirtied your cloak."

"It doesn't matter," I said. He could have covered me head to toe with dirt and it wouldn't have dampened my spirits.

I greeted Mrs. Wilson, who looked less pleased to see me, or perhaps she only disapproved of Joe's manner of greeting me. It was odd to see her out of doors.

"Tha'll be sure to deliver those vegetables to the kitchen, then?" she said to Joe as if I hadn't interrupted their conversation.

He nodded.

"I'll be getting back to the house with Miss Springthorpe," she said, looking at me expectantly. "No doubt you'll want your tea."

It was too early for tea, and I had the distinct feeling she didn't approve of me talking alone with Joe, but I wouldn't pass up the opportunity to do so, especially after being away from him for a whole fortnight. "No, thank you. I had a late lunch, so I won't need tea today."

She nodded curtly and turned back to the house.

As Joe and I walked to the rose garden, I asked in what I hoped was a casual tone, "What were you and Mrs. Wilson talking about when I arrived? Is anything wrong?"

He shrugged. "Not really. She's been suspicious of me ever since I went in the house on the pretext of checking and fixing the broken gutters. It turns out it wasn't as convincing an excuse as I'd hoped."

For the first time since I'd known Joe, I didn't believe him. He had sounded upset, or at least displeased, with Mrs. Wilson, not she with him. But I didn't want to pry, and I doubted there was anything seriously wrong: it was just something he didn't want to talk to me about.

The rose garden was in full bloom, filled with brilliant reds and yellows and pinks. I breathed in the heady scents, overwhelmed by the garden's lush beauty. It was even more wonderful than I'd imagined, a paradise I never wanted to leave.

The only truly dark cloud on the horizon was Sir Peter's imminent arrival. Joe told me Sir Peter had informed the household he would be arriving at Morton the following week, and he'd already sent some of his own servants ahead of him to help with the preparations. As curious as I was about Sir Peter, his presence made losing Morton too real, though it was ridiculous of me to think of losing Morton when I'd never possessed it in the first place. And Sir Peter's presence would do nothing for Nick's mood.

"Have you seen much of Nick since he returned from London?" I asked.

Joe shook his head. "We had one brief conversation, but he seems preoccupied with his brother's visit and hasn't been out much."

"I'd better go inside," I said, though I was loath to leave the garden.

"What do you think about having our picnic here tomorrow?" Joe said. "I need to go to Netherton in the morning, and my mother has offered to send me back with a basket of food."

"That would be wonderful," I said. "I'll mention it to Nick." I was glad Joe hadn't forgotten his idea about the picnic.

After going to my room and tidying my hair, I went in search of Nick, who was surprisingly difficult to find. Bedford, who looked as unhappy as ever to see me, informed me that Mr. Spencer had gone for a walk.

I went to the library and sat in my usual chair with a book, but I couldn't concentrate. Just when I decided to go outside once more before dinner, Nick came in.

It was difficult not to stare at him. His beard was gone, and he looked so different clean-shaven that it was difficult to believe he was the same person. He looked his age now, instead of ten or even twenty years older. His dark hair was greying only at the temples, and although nobody would call him handsome, he was certainly striking. His angular, almost sharp features were softened by full, well-shaped lips.

He approached me, then stopped about ten feet away and said quietly, "You've come back."

"Yes." I was so startled by his appearance I could think of nothing more to say.

"Do I look very different?"

"Yes, very."

A tiny smile appeared at the corner of his mouth. "Better or worse?"

"Better." I silently berated myself for being so tongue-tied.

He came to sit in the chair beside mine and asked about my visit with my family. It helped loosen my tongue, and I told him more than he needed to know about the wedding and Mother's illness: my awkwardness was making me alternate between the extremes of silence and loquacity. As I talked, he took out his pipe and filled it, then lit it. The familiar nutty scent of his pipe tobacco filled the room.

I managed to interrupt my own flow of words by asking what I most wished to know. "What did the oculist say?"

"As I expected, he gave me no definitive diagnosis. He did say the problem would be easier to diagnose if it could be isolated from the headaches. If what I'm having are severe migraines, which seems likely, the visual disturbance they cause could be masking another eye disorder. He had no explanation for the paralysis."

"Did he suggest anything that might help?"

"Just ergot, a common treatment for migraine. And of course he said to avoid distressing or difficult situations, which is laughable, considering I'm about to lose my home."

"Will you try the ergot?"

"If I need to. I've been feeling so much better lately that it may not be necessary."

"I'm glad," I said.

He took a slow, deep puff from his pipe. "I don't expect my good health to last, of course."

"Of course you don't."

Perhaps I had spoken too quickly or complacently, for he darted a suspicious look at me. "You're mocking me," he said.

"Never." But I couldn't help smiling.

"Your trip to London has made you mischievous."

He was wrong: it was the return to Morton that made me so.

"Yours hasn't changed you a bit," I said.

"Touché. Yet you seemed to think me quite changed when I first came in."

"Only in appearance. Otherwise you're as determined to be gloomy as ever."

"I have good cause. My brother will be here in a week."

"I know. Joe told me." Seeing Nick's expression darken, I said, "Let's not think about it until we're forced to. Joe suggested a picnic in the rose garden tomorrow. Will you come?"

"Are you sure you want me there?" He looked genuinely uncertain.

"Of course."

I didn't understand why he was hesitating. "Don't you think it would be good to set aside your worries for a day?" I persisted.

"I suppose so."

Later that evening when I was preparing for bed and thinking about the events of that day, I realized it really was the return to Morton that made me not just mischievous, as Nick had said, but happy. And though I'd chaffed Nick about his melancholy attitude, I knew I too would be sorry to see the estate sold, especially because it meant that Joe, Nick, and I would go our separate ways.

That night I dreamed that I was in the rose garden. A picnic blanket laden with mouth-watering delicacies had been spread on the lawn, and I was sitting on the wrought-iron bench, wearing Letitia's wedding gown and veil, waiting for someone to join me. I heard a male voice just outside the garden gate, a voice that made my heart lift with joy, but a sudden clap of thunder frightened me, and the next instant the sky went dark with rain. I stood up, intending to run for shelter, but my veil wrapped itself around my legs, and I fell headlong. The rain poured down, flooding the garden and sweeping me up in a torrent of water and broken flowers.

17

When I awoke the next morning, I was dismayed to hear a steady rain pelting the roof. It was nothing like the downpour in my dream, but when I went to the window, the sight of a soggy, drenched lawn confirmed my fears. There would be no picnic that day.

I went down to breakfast in a mood that rivalled any of Nick's blackest ones. It was all I could do to be civil to Mrs. Wilson. Then I closeted myself in the library with the legal documents. The lien filed against the property had indeed been an error, as I'd suspected. It was meant for a neighbouring estate, and now that I had cleared up the mistake, there was no legal reason to delay the sale of Morton any longer.

I checked and double-checked my legal reference books against Morton's documents to ensure I hadn't made any mistakes. Then I tried to read a novel, but I couldn't concentrate. I wandered aimlessly around the library for a while, then returned to the desk.

I must have fallen into a reverie, for the next thing I was aware of was a light touch on my shoulder and Nick's voice saying my name. His voice sounded so much like the male voice in my dream the night before that I sprang to my feet like a startled cat, nearly upsetting my chair.

"It's you!" I exclaimed. "What are you doing here?"

"I live here." He looked surprisingly bright and cheerful. "Not in the library, of course. I just wanted to remind you about our picnic. I'm sorry I startled you."

"But it's raining. Isn't it?" I squinted at the grey mist visible through the long windows.

"I've talked to Joe and Mrs. Wilson, and we're going to have the picnic in the drawing room," he said. "It isn't the rose garden, but we can make it pleasant. I'll even open my grandfather's ancient bottle of claret for the occasion. Will you meet us in the drawing room at seven this evening?"

"Yes." I turned to leave the room.

"Wait," he said. When I turned back to him, he handed me a little white box. "I have something for you."

"What is it?" I asked.

"Just a small gift, to thank you for putting up with me all these months."

Speechless, I looked down at the box in my hand.

"Open it," he urged.

I raised the lid. At first all I saw was a fine gold chain, but as I lifted it out, I realized an amber pendant hung from it. The amber was transparent and set in an intricate gold filigree leaf pattern. I had never owned anything so lovely.

I looked at Nick, whose expression was inscrutable, and thought of what he'd said long ago about adornments around the neck of a worthless woman. What did he mean by such a gift?

"It's nothing, really," he said. "Amber isn't valuable."

"You needn't remind me of that," I said, feeling somehow as if he were commenting on my worth as well as that of the stone.

"I didn't mean it that way," he said. "I know you like amber, and your eyes—" He broke off, then added, "I thought it would suit you. That's all."

The stiff formality of his manner confused me, especially in light of the obvious care he had taken to choose such a gift.

In my hand the gold filigree was cool, but the amber was warm.

"It's beautiful," I said quietly. "Thank you."

"You're welcome. I'll see you this evening."

I watched him leave the library, wondering why my interactions with Nick were still so volatile after all this time.

By early evening I had talked myself into a calmer, more hopeful state. The rain hadn't let up, but I refused to let it depress me. Putting my confusion and my worries about the future aside, I resolved to enjoy the evening.

Because the picnic would be indoors, it was easier to justify wearing the dress I'd worn at Letitia's wedding. It was a cream watered silk gown with a gold brocaded bodice. It suited my dark hair and eyes, if the compliments I'd received at the wedding were anything to go by. It was too formal for anything but a wedding or party, so I was well aware I'd brought it to Morton only out of vanity. Without my sister's maid to help me, it took longer than I'd expected to put on the dress. I struggled with my hair too, but eventually I managed to pin it up into a soft roll, managing to coax a few strands into curls that hung about my neck.

All I could see in the shaving mirror was my hair and face, which indeed looked well. My eyes seemed brighter, my lips fuller. I still wished the freckles across the bridge of my nose were not so prominent and that I were tall and graceful-looking instead of short and bosomy, but the dress, flattering as it was, couldn't perform magic.

The finishing touch was the amber pendant, which picked up the shimmering gold of the brocade. I wondered what Nick had meant to say about my eyes.

I went downstairs and entered the drawing room, delighted by the light, soft-soled shoe Joe had made, which allowed me to walk quietly and minimized my limp.

Nick and Joe were sitting in armchairs at right angles to each other at the far end of the room, engaged in a seemingly desultory conversation. At my approach, they broke off and stared at me.

All the pains I had taken with my appearance were amply rewarded by the look of admiration in Joe's eyes. Not general admiration, but the fascinated stare a man gives an attractive woman. I had seen men look at my prettiest sisters, Elizabeth and Anne, that way, but never in my life had I been the object of such a gaze. It felt wonderful, and a little frightening.

Joe rose and held out his hand to me. "You look beautiful, Vaughan. Doesn't she, Nick?"

I took Joe's hand and smiled up at him.

"She certainly looks nothing like the other lawyers I've known," Nick said dryly.

Joe led me to the sofa and sat beside me. "I'd get you a glass of claret if I could stop looking at you," he said with a grin. "Would you like one?"

"Yes, please."

"Since Joe has gone soft in the head, I'll see to the practicalities of our celebration," Nick said, going to the sideboard and pouring the claret. He brought me the glass and added, "This is my grandfather's much-prized claret, so I'd appreciate it if you could at least pretend to like it."

I nearly made a sharp retort, but he glanced at the amber pendant and smiled at me with a warmth that was at odds with his words.

I had been in the drawing room only once before, when Mrs. Wilson had given me a tour of the main rooms of the house. It had struck me then as empty and gloomy, with not enough furniture for its size and a huge portrait of a stern-looking old man dominating one wall. But it didn't seem empty now. A corner of the room had been whimsically set for our indoor picnic with a white cloth and place settings on the floor. Near where Joe and I sat on the sofa, by the large windows, stood a stately grand piano.

It wasn't the rose garden, but it had potential. And given my dream the night before, I was all the happier to stay indoors.

"Shall we eat?" said Nick. "Everything is ready. You'll spoil that fine dress if you sit on the floor, Vaughan, so you can stay where you are. Joe and I will bring you whatever you want."

"Yes, we'll be your servants for the evening," Joe added with a wink.

I rather liked the idea. Spreading out my skirt and settling back on the sofa, I began to feel like a queen. Joe brought me a plate of roast chicken, potatoes, and a delicious cucumber salad, and Nick ensured that my glass of claret never ran dry. I told Joe his mother was an angel to make all this food for us.

"Is that forbidding-looking man in the portrait your grandfather?" I asked Nick while we ate.

"Yes."

"He looks as though he could have used a regular glass of claret instead of hiding it away in the cellar all those years."

Nick laughed. "I believe he did have a glass every evening,

but it didn't do much for his disposition. I was terrified of him when I was a child. He had a deep, booming voice that seemed to reverberate throughout the house. The odd thing is that I was his favourite, though I didn't know it then. He wrote a letter to my mother near the end of his life—I was perhaps fourteen at the time—telling her I reminded him of himself and that I could do great things in the world if I could learn to take life and myself less seriously."

"Did you? Learn that lesson, I mean." I suspected he hadn't, and I was sorry for it. It was a pleasure to hear Nick laugh. I rarely saw him in a light-hearted mood.

He raised his eyebrows. "What do you think?"

"I can't say. You seem quite serious to me, but there's still time. I have hope for you."

"Do you? That's graciously spoken."

I found it easy to be gracious, given the circumstances.

The next few hours were unlike any I'd spent with Nick and Joe before. All three of us were in a sociable mood, and nobody mentioned potentially upsetting subjects such as Sir Peter's impending visit or whether the night child had caused any trouble while I was away. Joe was his usual agreeable self, but even Nick exerted himself by telling humorous stories of his years at Cambridge and his unfortunate foray into political life. I had never known Nick to be so witty. He was almost charming. Perhaps the free-flowing claret was the reason he felt comfortable showing this new side of himself. I was feeling rather charming myself, which was probably due to the same cause.

"The worst moment of my university years," Nick told us, "was when I decided I was destined to be a great poet, and I recited some of my verse to a roomful of fellow students."

Joe and I urged him to favour us with an example.

"Trust me, you don't want to hear it," Nick said.

"Yes, we do," I said. "Don't we, Joe?"

"Of course," said Joe. "Lay on—we promise not to laugh."

"I can't remember most of what I wrote back then," Nick demurred. "It was a long time ago."

"You can't escape so easily," I protested. "We insist upon hearing one poem."

"Very well. I'll recite the one I remember best: 'To a Fire-fly.'" He rose to his feet, took three paces and turned to face his audience. He cleared his throat and began:

Sometimes one must use excessive force.

No one wants to watch a creature in its death throes

Mutilated, suffering, dying.

Joe and I exchanged alarmed looks, and before Nick could continue, I interjected, "Don't you have a poem on a lighter subject? Something more suitable for the occasion?"

"Don't interrupt," Nick said briskly. "This one will do. Now, where was I?"

Neither I nor Joe offered to help him remember, but he didn't need our assistance. The poem was long but not as ominous as its beginning implied. The incident described in the poem was an accidental killing of a fire-fly. He didn't know what it was until its light flashed out when he killed it. This led to several lines of philosophical musings on the possibility of insects having souls. The poem ended with,

Guilty and ashamed, I slunk away.

Nobody need ever know, I thought.

But my crime changed me.

I see tiny brown things differently now.

And I have a new desire:

God grant that I may die this way

In a glorious burst of light.

In the silence that ensued, Nick returned to his seat and regarded us ruefully. "You may laugh," he said. "I never claimed to be a great poet. I just wanted to be one."

"I don't want to laugh," I said. "I like it. Especially the ending."

"I like it too," Joe added, "though I wish there weren't so much death in it. It reminds me of Wordsworth's 'Lucy Gray.'"

This naturally led to an animated conversation about Wordsworth's merits and demerits as a poet, to which I was surprised to find I could contribute intelligently. All those evenings reading poetry with Nick had paid off. And Nick, who had begun writing a life of Wordsworth during his university years, didn't dominate the conversation.

After we had exhausted the topic of poetry, we spoke of other things: gardening, art, music. During a pause in the conversation, Joe went to the piano and touched a key in the lower register, which resounded through the room with a rich tone.

"This is a fine piano," he said, glancing at Nick. "Do you play?"

"I used to. My mother was an accomplished pianist. She taught me to play, but I haven't touched it in years."

"Will you play something for us?" Joe asked.

"If you like."

As Nick went to the piano, Joe asked, "Do you play, Vaughan?"

"Badly." I shuddered at the memory of interminable piano lessons and even more interminable evenings playing at family social gatherings. "I'm no musician, but I was often pressed into service at the piano because my sisters love to dance."

Nick tried a chord, then another. A rippling arpeggio

followed, and Joe and I were instantly alert as the music filled the room. I recognized the music—it was a Chopin étude I had tried to learn for months, but my halting, slow rendition of it sounded nothing like this.

Nick's playing, on the other hand, couldn't have failed to please the composer. If it really had been years since he had touched the piano, his fingers had no trouble remembering the notes. He was hunched over the keys like a mad artist, swaying slightly on the piano bench.

The music cast a spell over me. Like the poetry Nick loved so much, his music made me feel things I couldn't name.

He played other pieces after the etude—a Beethoven sonata, a Schubert impromptu. Joe and I listened with rapt attention.

After an hour, Nick looked up from the piano and said, "I hope I haven't gone on too long. I had forgotten how much I love playing."

"It was beautiful," I said. "I'd be happy to hear more."

"So would I," Joe said, "but we've been sitting a long time. Do you know any dance music, Nick?"

"Yes. What do you want to hear?"

"A waltz. I'd like to dance with Vaughan."

No six words could have frightened me more, and my stomach gave a lurch. I stared at Joe, dumbfounded, as he jumped up from the sofa and extended his hand to me. "Will you?" he asked me.

Had he forgotten about my lame leg? "I—I can't," I said.

Joe took a step closer to me, still holding out his hand. "You needn't worry. That new shoe I made for you will help, and you can lean on me."

What I was feeling must have shown on my face, for Nick said, "Don't push her, Joe."

Joe kept his eyes on me. "I won't let you fall."

I don't know why I was willing to risk looking ridiculous. Perhaps it was Joe's confidence. Perhaps it was the prospect of being in his arms. Perhaps it was the claret. Whatever the reason, I put my hand in his and allowed him to help me up and lead me to the middle of the room.

Joe was true to his word. As Nick began to play a slow waltz, Joe slipped his arm around my waist—a heavenly feeling—and guided me around the room. I had never felt so light, so graceful. I hardly even noticed my missteps, for he caught me and held me closer whenever I started to stumble. I began to think stumbling was not such a bad thing.

We turned a little too quickly at the far end of the room, and I did stumble then.

"Forgive me," Joe said softly as he tightened his arm around my waist. "That was my fault."

We stopped dancing for a moment to right ourselves, and he looked down at me with an unusually serious expression. For one wild moment I thought he'd kiss me right there in the drawing room in front of Nick.

The music stopped abruptly, jolting me out of my trancelike state. Joe released me, and we looked across the room at Nick, who rose and stepped away from the piano.

"It's late," he announced. "I've played long enough."

"We've only just begun dancing," Joe protested. "Couldn't you play one more?"

"No. It's time I went to bed. Good night." Without waiting for a response, Nick strode past us out of the room.

Joe and I looked at each other.

"That was sudden," I said. "Perhaps I ought to go and see if he's all right."

"He's fine," Joe said, taking my hand as if he was worried I would run away. "Come and sit with me, Vaughan. There's something I want to ask you."

He led me back to the sofa and drew me down beside him, still looking very serious.

"What is it?" I asked.

"I need to leave Morton tomorrow," he said.

"You do? Where are you going?"

He took a deep breath. "I have some business in Manchester."

This seemed odd. "When will you return?"

"I don't know."

A dull ache settled in the pit of my stomach. It was true, then, that this evening was the beginning of the end of my time at Morton. Nothing would be the same without Joe. And as the day of Sir Peter's arrival approached, Nick would likely become more difficult, too.

"What did you want to ask me?" I said.

He hesitated. "If you should hear anything about me while I'm gone—anything that makes you doubt me—will you wait before judging me until I can explain my side of the story?"

I searched his face. "I don't understand."

"I know. But please believe I would never do anything to hurt you—or anyone else, if I could help it. I haven't told you everything about myself, and I've made some decisions I now regret, but I'm not a villain."

"Why can't you tell me your story now?"

"I'm bound by a promise I made to someone else, but eventually I'll be able to tell you. I know it sounds strange, but will you try to trust me?"

He looked so unhappy and worried, so unlike his usual self, that I said, "Yes, Joe. I'll give you the benefit of the doubt."

Relief flooded his face. "Thank you, Vaughan. You're an angel."

I made a move to rise, but he didn't release my hand.

"I have something else to ask you," he said, looking at me with those dazzlingly blue eyes. "Our friendship means a great deal to me, but I've realized lately that I want more than that. Will you consider becoming my wife?"

It was long past midnight, but I was still in the drawing room. After Joe had gone, I turned out the lamps and stood by the window overlooking the front lawn. The curtains were open, allowing the moonlight to stream into the room, giving it an otherworldly appearance. The remains of our picnic, with crumpled napkins and the white cloth on the floor, were proof that others had been there, eating and drinking and enjoying themselves. But the atmosphere belied that proof, making me feel as if I had only dreamed all of it—not only the eating and drinking but also the music and dancing and the feel of Joe's arms around me. I wouldn't have been surprised to awaken and find it had indeed been a dream.

I didn't know what to think about Joe's proposal. Even though I'd considered the possibility he might ask me to marry him, the reality of it took me by surprise. My immediate response to him had been an awkward stammering and a request for more time to think, which he took in stride. Of course I must think about it, he'd said. He wouldn't expect anything less. He took his leave, promising to return to Morton as soon as he could.

Staring out at the moonlit lawn, I slowly allowed myself to believe it was real. The kindest, handsomest man I'd ever met had asked me to marry him. I adored Joe, of course. I'd hardly be human if I didn't.

Despite the proposal, I wasn't certain what Joe's feelings were for me. He hadn't actually said he loved me, and even though he had kissed me before he left, it was the same as the first time, devoid of passion, as chaste as a child's kiss. Yet I knew he cared for me and enjoyed my company. Was that enough?

What I felt for Joe matched the warm regard he seemed to feel for me. It wasn't the sort of torture other people claimed to experience when they were in love. I thought of Nick's description of being in love and was glad I didn't feel as though a vulture were eating my liver. It was a relief, really. There was no danger of bursting into tears or throwing myself face-down on my bed in agony, as I had witnessed my sisters and the heroines in books doing.

I began to feel very sleepy, too sleepy to go up to my room and undress for bed. I lay down on the sofa with a cushion under my head, thinking I'd rest for a few minutes, then retire.

A scraping sound startled me awake. I lay motionless, disoriented, until I realized I was still in the drawing room, which was now bathed in a greyish early-morning light. I must have been asleep for hours.

A few quiet notes came from the piano, and I knew then that the scraping sound had been someone moving the piano stool. I sat up slowly and saw Nick at the piano. His hair was dishevelled and he was in his shirtsleeves.

When I met his eyes, he froze. "I didn't know you were still here," he said.

"I fell asleep." I put a hand to my hair, which was a tangled mess. My skirt was creased too. "I must look a fright."

"No." His eyes met mine for only a second, then flickered away. His face was pale and there were dark shadows under his eyes.

"What time is it?" I asked.

"Half five." He played a few more notes on the piano, then a slow progression of chords in a minor key.

I intended to go to my room and perform my morning ablutions. But I wasn't entirely awake yet, still feeling languid and dreamy from the events of the night before, and I leaned my head back against the sofa and closed my eyes, listening to the piano.

I would have liked to hear Nick play Beethoven or Mozart, which he'd played the night before, but he continued to play only fragments, a few notes here, a few chords there.

"Will you play something longer?" I suggested without opening my eyes.

"Very well." There was a brief silence. Then he began to play something heavy, slow, and sinister-sounding, still in a minor key.

"What is that?"

"Brahms. It's one of his *Balladen*."

I didn't like the piece in the least. It was far too gloomy and lugubrious for an early summer morning.

Perhaps Nick realized this as well, or perhaps he merely tired of it, for he stopped playing.

"Did you enjoy the evening?" he asked.

I raised my head to look at him. "Yes, very much. Did you?"

"Yes. For a while."

"Why only for a while?" I was sorry I asked the question before I'd finished asking it.

Staring down at the piano keys, he didn't reply at once.

Then he said slowly, "I don't like the way Joe treats you."

Now I was fully, painfully awake. I rose and went around the sofa to stand in the curve of the piano, facing him. Pushing my hair out of my eyes, I asked, "What do you mean?"

"He doesn't see you for who you are. It's as if you're . . . I don't know . . . a sort of pet." He was still looking at the keyboard.

A surge of anger rose in me. "So you object to his kindness? Or is it the fact that he treats me like a lady that offends you?"

"That's not what I mean. It's the shoe . . . and the dancing. His attitude is—" He broke off with a frustrated exclamation and stood up, facing me across the piano. "He's trying to change you, to turn you into an ordinary woman."

"You sound like my mother!" I exclaimed, my anger boiling over. "You can't bear it when someone treats me like a normal person and makes me forget about my foot. You want me to be content with my lot, to stay in the background and do what is expected of me—"

"Vaughan—"

"Damn you! Is it impossible to imagine that a man could find me attractive or want to dance with me? All I've ever wanted is to be an ordinary woman, and you'd take that away from me."

"You mistake me utterly!" he burst out. "You don't need to change, especially not to please anyone else. My God, how can you be so blind? You're an extraordinary woman, not an ordinary one."

I stared at him, shocked. He was visibly upset, breathing quickly, a tremor at the corner of his sensitive mouth.

My anger drained away.

"Forgive me," I said. "I misunderstood."

He swallowed hard, started to turn away, then turned back.

We looked at each other for a long moment. A very long moment. He was allowing me to read his eyes, to see the truth there. I had indeed been blind in thinking he was against me, or even indifferent to me. He was far from indifferent.

I was afraid. I said the only thing that could save me, the only thing that could save us all. "Joe asked me to marry him."

There was no change in Nick's expression, but there was a beat of silence before he replied. "Have you accepted him?" His voice was quiet, steady.

"Not yet. I've asked for time to think." My fear pushed me to say more. "But I don't need time to think. I intend to say yes."

This time he didn't hesitate. "No doubt you know what you're doing. If you'll excuse me, there are matters I must attend to."

He turned and left the room.

I sank into the nearest chair, feeling as if I had fought a physical battle but unsure whether I'd won or lost. So much had passed between me and Nick in that long, silent moment when our eyes met, an entirely different conversation from what we had expressed in words. Yet even now, when our exchange was fresh in my mind, it was easy to second-guess myself, to assume I'd been mistaken in what I thought I saw in his eyes.

My feelings were in such turmoil that I felt ill. The lack of sleep didn't help, either. It was all I could do to stumble back to my room, undress, and fall into bed, hoping the next time I opened my eyes, my head would be clear and my heart quiet.

18

I slept late that morning, and when I ventured downstairs, I took some bread and cheese from the larder and went back to my room, intent on avoiding Nick.

I needed to sort out at least some of what had happened the night before, though I refused to speculate about what I'd seen in Nick's eyes. Instead, I focused on Joe's strange request not to think worse of him if I should hear anything to make me doubt him. I wondered if his secret had anything to do with Sir Peter. Or perhaps it was related to the mysterious conversation I'd witnessed between Joe and Mrs. Wilson. To whom had he bound himself to keep his secret? I wondered, too, if Nick's suspicions about Joe had any basis in reality. I didn't agree that Joe treated me like a pet. Nick was a suspicious man, but it wasn't like him to make such outlandish judgments. Or was it possible I was so blinded by my feelings for Joe that I couldn't see him clearly? No doubt that's what Nick thought.

I stayed in my room for the rest of the day, avoiding mealtimes and hoping nobody would notice my absence. Mrs. Wilson and Bedford were working so hard to prepare for Sir Peter's arrival, along with the handful of servants he'd sent ahead of him, that they'd be glad I was out of the way. And no doubt Nick would be relieved as well.

By the time darkness fell, I was too restless to stay in my

room. I still wasn't ready to face Nick, so I went outside, behind the house where the headless statue presided over the broken fountain. It was dark enough that I would not be seen from the house, but even so, I was careful to stay close to the hedges that stood between the house and the fountain.

The cool night air calmed me a little. I breathed deeply and paced back and forth for a while behind the hedges, then sat on the bench with my back to the headless statue, looking at the house. It loomed large, dark, and silent in the moonlight. I had the strange feeling that I was completely alone at Morton, as if its inhabitants existed only in my dreams.

The strange feeling was exacerbated by the sound of a scream coming from the house. Although it was distinctly a human scream, I had become so used to strange sounds in the night at Morton that I didn't believe it was real at first. But then another scream brought me to my senses, and I rose and hurried to the house.

I was fairly certain that the scream had come from the east wing, so I went there. At the bottom of the staircase that led to my room, I saw a human form lying in a twisted position. It was too dark to make out who it was, and my heart thudded loudly in my ears as I approached. I hadn't brought a candle with me when I first came downstairs because of my desire to move about unseen, but now I regretted the absence of light.

A moan escaped from the crumpled figure. It was Mrs. Wilson. I rushed forward and knelt at her side.

"Can you speak?" I asked, touching her arm. "What happened?"

"Fell . . . down . . . stairs," she gasped. "My leg . . ."

Her leg was bent underneath her. She was clearly in pain and I wanted to do something to alleviate it, though I knew better than to try to move her.

"I'm going to send for Doctor Foster and get something you can rest your head on," I said, starting to rise.

She clutched at my arm. "Don't . . . go . . . upstairs."

"Why not?" I asked.

Before she could answer, the sound of hurrying footsteps announced the arrival of Nick, Bedford, and Betty, one of Sir Peter's servants. Thankfully, they were all carrying candles.

I rose to my feet and faced them.

Nick approached me with the wild look of a man awakened from a nightmare. "Are you hurt?" he asked, reaching out as if to put his hand on my shoulder, then withdrawing it abruptly.

"No, but Mrs. Wilson is." I stood aside so he could see Mrs. Wilson's prostrate form, and he knelt at her side just as I had done.

I felt a presence behind me and turned to see Bedford staring at me with a decidedly accusing look.

"Betty, send for the doctor," Nick said to the young servant. He gave her instructions and she hurried away.

Intending to get a pillow from my room to put under Mrs. Wilson's head, I began to ascend the stairs.

"No," Mrs. Wilson called weakly after me, and I paused.

"What is it?" Nick asked her.

"There's something up there," she said.

Nick and I exchanged puzzled looks. No doubt he was imagining all the frightening possibilities, as I was.

"I just want to find a pillow for her head," I said.

"I'll go," he said, rising to his feet.

Mrs. Wilson didn't object to his going, but I did. "Wait," I said to him, then turned back to her. "What's on the stairs, Mrs. Wilson?"

"Don't know," she said slowly. "I slipped on summat."

"I'll be careful," Nick said, and went up.

I knelt at Mrs. Wilson's side and took her hand, but I watched Nick until he disappeared and remained alert for any unusual sounds from above.

"This is your fault." Bedford's voice came from the shadows, making me start. I had forgotten he was there, and his tone was so unpleasant that I was afraid for my own safety.

"What do you mean?" I asked, trying to keep my voice steady and calm.

He didn't reply, and I was relieved when Nick reappeared a few minutes later, holding one of the pillows from my room. He helped me arrange the pillow under Mrs. Wilson's head, then sat on the floor beside her, opposite me, and said, "Bedford, there's nothing more you can do here. Why don't you go back to bed?"

"Very well, sir." The old man shuffled away, to my even greater relief.

"Are you more comfortable now?" Nick asked Mrs. Wilson.

"Aye." She closed her eyes. The candlelight made ghostly shadows on her face.

"Does anything hurt besides your leg?" I asked her.

"My back." Her eyes flew open and she said urgently, "Where's Joe? I mun talk to him."

Nick and I exchanged another puzzled look.

"Do you mean Joe Dixon?" I asked.

"Aye." She caught her breath as if stabbed by a sudden pain.

"He's in Manchester," I said. "What would you like to tell him? Perhaps we can send him a note, but I'll need to find out his exact address first."

"No!" she said, gasping. "I mun see Joe."

She seemed to be raving, but I promised to try to locate Joe the next day. I hoped the doctor would come soon. I felt useless,

THE CURSE OF MORTON ABBEY ～ 213

doing no more than holding her hand when she was in so much pain.

Nick said to Mrs. Wilson, "I was just thinking the other day of those ginger cakes you used to make for me and Peter when we were boys. Do you remember?"

"Aye."

"You wouldn't let Cook into the kitchen on those days because you didn't want anyone to interfere, and you were the only person who knew exactly how we liked them. You would make Peter's cakes in the shape of swords and mine in the shape of dogs—those were our obsessions at the time. We didn't fully appreciate your efforts then, typical self-centred lads as we were, but I think of those cakes fondly now."

I was touched by Nick's efforts to comfort Mrs. Wilson with these memories, especially considering the old animosity between them.

He went on to talk about other things from his shared past with the housekeeper: a kitchen maid who sneezed incessantly, a dinner party that was ruined by a drunken cousin who fell face-down into the syllabub, the day the Prince of Wales came to Morton to join Sir Peter's shooting party.

Mrs. Wilson seemed to be listening, but she also seemed to lapse in and out of consciousness, and I was glad when Dr. Foster came at last. He confirmed that her leg was broken, and after he set the fracture, Nick and I helped him move Mrs. Wilson to her own room at the back of the house near the kitchen. He cautioned us not to let her move again in case she had internal injuries.

The doctor gave Mrs. Wilson a sleeping draught, told us he'd check on her the next day, and left. Betty agreed to sleep in Mrs. Wilson's room in case she awoke and needed anything, so Nick and I left together.

It was past midnight. I turned towards the east wing and said, "I'll go up to bed, then. Good night."

"Wait," Nick said. "Have you forgotten about the stairs?"

In my weariness, I had indeed forgotten. "Was there anything there?"

"Yes." He put a few small, round objects in my hand.

I held them up to the candlelight. They were marbles, the kind a child might play with.

"These were on the stairs?" I said.

"Yes. I probably didn't find all of them, but I'll have another look in the morning. I don't want you to sleep in the east wing tonight."

"I don't mind. Now that I know what to look for, I'll be careful."

"It's not safe," he said. He took a step closer, holding the candle up. "Don't you understand? After what you told me about the jacks, and now this, I think someone in this house is trying to harm you. I'm not going to let that happen."

I was effectively silenced.

"Will you come with me?" he asked.

I nodded. He took my hand and led me to the west wing. For the first time since my early days at Morton, Nick locked the door that separated the west wing from the rest of the house, but this time I was locked in instead of out.

I thought of the pink-and-white room and shivered, visions of Bluebeard fluttering in my tired head. Would Nick lock me in his wife's room? I didn't want to sleep there.

But we went past the pink-and-white room and didn't stop until we reached the door of Nick's room.

"You can sleep here, just for tonight," he said.

I drew in my breath. "Here? In your room?"

He dropped my hand as if it had caught fire. "I'll sleep elsewhere tonight," he said stiffly.

"Oh." So many thoughts were whirling around in my head that I could say no more.

Nick opened the door for me, and I went inside. He remained at the threshold.

"Lock the door behind you," he said.

"I really don't think it will be neces—"

"Humour me, Vaughan," he said firmly. "When I leave, I want you to lock the door and draw the bolt. Don't open it to anyone until I return in the morning."

"Very well."

"Thank you. Is there anything you need in the house that can't wait until morning?"

I shook my head.

He bid me good night and left.

I followed his instructions and locked the door, a willing prisoner.

It was strange to be in Nick's room when he wasn't there. It was as dark and silent as a tomb. I felt my way to the windows, my fingers skimming along the smooth mahogany furnishings, and opened the curtains to allow the moonlight in. I would have liked to open a window as well, but Nick would no doubt object. A double-locked door was hardly effective against an intruder when there was a wide-open window in the room.

Was it possible Nick was right, that someone in the house was trying to hurt me? Bedford had never been warm towards me, but that was his way. Mrs. Wilson would hardly be the victim of her own plot. And Sir Peter, by way of his servants, wouldn't harm the person who was helping him sell his estate. Furthermore, what motive would anyone have? I could think of no logical explanation, and I refused to consider illogical ones. Perhaps someone else in my position would believe that the ghost of Nick's daughter had put the marbles on the stairs, but I never would unless I saw the ghost for myself. Perhaps not even then.

I removed the pins from my hair and undressed. Not having my nightdress with me, I left on my chemise and drawers, and the amber pendant, which I'd been wearing under my clothes, and climbed into bed. It was a huge bed, and the sheets were cool and slippery. I thrashed about like a fish, trying to get comfortable.

I hadn't been in bed more than five minutes when there was a quiet knock at the door.

"Who's there?" I called.

"It's Nick."

I shot out of bed and looked for something I could put on quickly over my underclothes. Nick's dressing gown was draped over a chair, so I slipped it on. It was much too big for me, trailing behind me like the train of a royal robe. I held the front of it closed at my breast, then went to the door.

When I opened the door, Nick looked past me instead of meeting my eyes. "I'm sorry to disturb you," he said in the same formal tone he'd used before. "May I come in? I forgot to collect some of my things."

"Of course." I stood back to let him pass, then watched him walk to his chest of drawers and retrieve some clothing.

"I thought perhaps you were testing me," I said.

"What do you mean?" he asked, still not looking at me.

"You said not to open the door to anyone until morning. Either I failed the test, or you didn't include yourself in the prohibition."

He turned to face me. "It wasn't a test. I only . . ." His voice trailed off, and even in the moonlight I could see that he was staring at my hair, which fell in loose waves over my shoulders, and the amber pendant that hung low on my neck, revealed by the gaping dressing gown.

We both froze.

Then he strode towards me. I raised my hands to ward him off, but I took a step towards him at the same time, and he pulled me into his arms and kissed me. The heat of his mouth on mine, one of his hands winding itself in my hair, the other at the small of my back, pressing me hard against him, sent thrilling sensations through my body. It did not occur to me to behave in a proper or even sane manner. Instead, I returned his kisses eagerly, hungry for more.

I was surprised by the strength of his arms around me, having thought of him for so long as frail and ill. There was no weakness in him now. I was the one who felt fragile, willing to yield to him completely.

It seemed scarcely a minute later when he ended the kiss, pulling away as abruptly as he had embraced me. I stared at him in confusion, dizzy and breathless. I knew at once that I could never subject this kiss to a cool, rational analysis as I had Joe's. Kissing Nick was like plunging into an open flame while hoping I wouldn't be burned.

"That was unforgivable," he said hoarsely. "I assure you it won't happen again."

But I wanted it to happen again. Immediately, in fact. I couldn't understand how he had managed to regain control of himself so quickly when I was sorely tempted to throw myself in his arms again and beg him to sleep with me. My fear of doing exactly that kept me silent and still as he returned to the bedroom door.

"Don't forget to lock the door behind me," he said. "And don't open it again, even for me." He left without another word.

If I hadn't been so stunned, I would have been amused by his parting injunction. Trembling all over, I locked the door, then stumbled to the bed and lay down, but I was still wearing Nick's dressing gown, and his scent of sandalwood soap and pipe tobacco seemed to mock me. I rose again and flung it off, then went back to bed, huddling under the bedclothes like a frightened child.

I slept fitfully, fragments of nightmares teasing me awake throughout the night. Some were similar to my old nightmares, sensations of falling into dark pools of water, struggling to breathe, feeling as though I must save not only myself but also someone else. But then the water disappeared and I was standing at the top of the stairs, not at Morton but at my family's old house, the one we lived in when Father was still alive. I felt myself slowly losing my balance and teetering on the edge of the top step, then falling. The fall was accompanied by a child's laughter and a great clattering sound, like hundreds of marbles poured down a flight of stairs.

The sounds in my dream jolted me awake, but as soon as I awoke fully, I heard not childish laughter, but instead, crying. It was the same sound I'd heard when I first came to Morton, only much louder and closer to my ears. The piercing cries were accompanied by a tapping or pounding, as if small fists or feet were hammering against the wall behind the bed.

I gasped and sat bolt upright, looking wildly around me.

The moonlight streaming into the room through the open curtains offered enough light to show that I was alone. I pressed my hands against the wall behind the headboard, calling out, "Who is it? Who's there?" There was no answer, but the sounds continued. I rose and walked around the room, looking under the desk, behind the curtains, and in the wardrobe to make absolutely sure there was nobody there. I checked the door and windows, which were still securely locked and fastened. Then I returned to the wall and waited for the sound to stop. Whether it was a real child or a ghost, surely it would tire of making these sounds.

I was right. The hammering stopped after a few minutes, and the sobbing subsided to a thin, piercing wail. I was shivering uncontrollably and wanted nothing more than to get back into bed and pretend nothing unusual had occurred, but instead I pressed close to the wall and said as loudly and clearly as I dared,

"I'll try to help you if you'll talk to me. Will you?"

The wailing stopped, but there was no other response.

"What do you want?" I persisted. "How can I help you?"

"I can't get out." It was a child's voice, muffled but clear enough.

I took a step back from the wall. I'd never been so frightened in my life. But it—she?—was talking to me for the first time, and I knew I may never get another chance.

Pressed against the wall again, I said, "Are you . . . in a room? Or a cupboard? Is there a door?"

"No."

"Do you remember how you got in there?"

She replied, but this time her voice was quieter and I couldn't make out the words.

"I can't hear you very well. Can you speak louder? Describe it to me, the . . . place you're in." *Please, God,* I prayed, *don't let the description sound like hell. Or heaven.*

"It's dark."

"Feel around with your fingers. Are there walls and a floor?"

"Yes. And . . ." some muffled words, followed by, ". . . a little bit taller than me."

"Very good," I said, feeling like a governess praising the child for doing her sums. "Do you feel any loose boards, or anything that seems like a lock or knob you could open?"

"No." The child began to whimper again.

"Try to stay calm," I said, as much as to myself as to the child. "I'll do my best to find you and let you out. I promise."

The child didn't reply, and I thought I'd lost her.

"Are you still there?" I called.

"Yes."

"What's your name?"

The muffled voice said something I couldn't quite understand.

"Ann? Did you say Ann?" I cried.

"Frances."

A cold chill froze my core, and I jumped away from the wall, my breath coming in gasps. The implications of that name were too overwhelming for me to comprehend. My mind simply couldn't accept it.

I forced myself to keep talking to her, but she didn't speak again or make any other sounds. I was afraid to go back to sleep, so I put on my clothes from the day before, pinned up my hair, and sat in the straight-backed chair at Nick's desk, waiting for dawn. As soon as the household was awake and there was enough light to search by, I intended to find the child—or her ghost—once and for all.

19

I must have slept again, for I awoke with my head resting on my arms at the desk and an aching back. The grandfather clock in the corridor was striking seven, so I tidied my hair and left the room. I didn't want to be alone with my thoughts or with Nick, and I was willing to risk being harmed by someone in the house rather than remain in his room. Before I left the west wing, I examined the wall and the floor in the corridor outside Nick's room, even lifting up the carpet to look for loose boards or cracks, but in vain. Then I went into Alicia Spencer's room, which was on the other side of the wall where I'd heard the child's voice.

It looked as it always did, the jewellery box overflowing with necklaces and pearls, the lacy coverlet thrown back as if its occupant had only just arisen from sleep, the scent of rosewater in the air. The poorly-rendered cross-stitch spaniel in the embroidery hoops was absent, but no doubt Mrs. Wilson had thought as little of it as I did and disposed of it.

This time I was so intent on finding the source of the night child's voice that I didn't worry about disturbing the privacy of Nick's absent wife as I had the first time. The wardrobe overflowing with rich fabrics was against the wall that was shared with Nick's room, and I tried to look behind it. The gap between the wardrobe and the wall was only a couple of inches,

222 ℝ CLARISSA HARWOOD

and I could see only dust and cobwebs: it hadn't been moved in years. I looked inside the wardrobe, pushing the clothing aside, thinking there might be a secret door or some other clue, but again I was disappointed.

With a sigh of exasperation, I pushed away from the wardrobe and stood up. As I did so, an untidy pile of clothing fell at my feet. I reached down to put it back, but then I realized the clothes didn't belong to an adult woman: they were the same rich fabrics as the woman's dresses in the wardrobe, but these were little girl's frocks, adorned with extra frills and with matching bonnets. The frock at the top of the pile caught my eye, and I picked it up: it was of pale blue silk with three tiers of lace ruffles and a matching pelisse, trimmed with dark blue piping. Even I, with my poor fashion sense, could see that the clothing, though finely-made, was at least ten years out of date.

Had Alicia Spencer brought Frances's clothes into her room after her daughter's death? I could imagine only too well a weeping, bereft mother clinging to her child's frocks, refusing to part with them. The room was infused with sadness, and even though I hadn't yet solved the mystery of the night child, I decided that if ever there was a case to be made for a ghost inhabiting a place, this was it.

Hastily, I put the clothing back in the wardrobe, hoping Nick wouldn't find me in this room or notice that it had been disturbed. I could no longer avoid thinking about what had happened between me and Nick the night before. The passionate embrace seemed unreal, as unreal as the conversation I'd had with the night child in his room. Now that I was thinking more clearly, I decided that the heightened emotional state we were both in after Mrs. Wilson's accident was the cause of our lapse in judgment. And perhaps that heightened emotional state had also led to my imagining the child speaking to me.

Trying to clear my head, I made my way to Mrs. Wilson's room. I was anxious to find out how she was faring, and when I entered, I was relieved to see that Betty was the only other person there.

"How is she?" I whispered.

"It's hard to say," Betty replied. "She was awake for part of the night, but she fell asleep two hours ago and hasn't stirred since." Betty was a little older and more self-assured than I'd thought her the night before, a plain, solid-looking girl of nineteen or twenty.

"I'm glad Dr. Foster will be checking on her later," I said.

"Mr. Spencer asked me to show you your new room in the west wing. He had your things moved into it early this morning. Would you like to see it now, miss?"

"Oh. Yes, please." I paused, then asked, "Where is he?"

"He left for Bradford about an hour ago. He said he had business matters to attend to there."

What business could he have in Bradford so early in the morning? All the same, I was relieved I wouldn't have to face him immediately.

Betty led me to the first room on the same side of the corridor as Nick's. It had always been locked, so I'd never been inside. Alicia Spencer's pink and white room was between my new room and Nick's.

The room was pleasant but smaller than the other rooms I'd seen in the west wing, containing only a bed, a dressing table, a small wardrobe, and an armchair by the window. The wallpaper was pale green with a darker green leaf pattern. It didn't look as though it had been used very often. The only item of interest in it was a vase of yellow roses on the dressing table.

Their rich, sweet fragrance filled the room.

"Did you put the flowers there?" I asked Betty. "Yellow roses are my favourite."

"No. Mr. Spencer did."

There was an odd little flutter in my stomach.

Betty was too well trained to allow her face to betray her thoughts, but I did see her give me one quick, assessing glance, lingering a fraction of a second too long at my feet.

"Betty, did Mrs. Wilson tell you why she went upstairs in the east wing last night? She doesn't usually go there in the evenings."

"She wanted to check on you because you'd been in your room all day."

I pondered this. "Did anyone else know she was going up to my room?"

"Not that I know of. I'd better get back to her now."

"Of course."

She went to the door but then paused and turned around. "Do you know who Joe Dixon is, miss?"

"Yes. He's the gardener here. Why?"

"Mrs. Wilson kept asking for him. She was agitated and wouldn't calm down until I promised to find him and bring him to her room."

"Did she say why she wanted to see him?"

"No, miss."

"I'll take care of it, Betty. Thank you. Oh, wait." I took the vase of yellow roses and handed them to her. "Please take these to Mrs. Wilson's room. She needs them more than I do."

"Yes, miss."

After Betty had left, I congratulated myself on my strength in giving the flowers away and determined to think rationally from now on.

As I made my ablutions, I decided I'd better make a trip to Netherton to ask if Mrs. Dixon knew how to reach Joe. If anyone would know, she would. But before I left, I had one more trip to make within the house, this time to the east wing to see the stairs leading to my old room.

Even in daylight, the staircase was dimly lit, since there was only the small window between the first and second floors. I moved slowly, staying close to the wall, looking for anything unusual on or around the stairs.

Reaching the second-floor landing, I sat down and felt along the top two stairs, including corners where marbles could be lodged. My hands touched nothing but cold stone and a little dirt.

I went to my old room, emptied of my things and looking less hospitable than ever. Sitting on the edge of the bed, I tried to work out the mystery of the marbles.

There must have been more marbles on the stairs when Mrs. Wilson fell. Nick could have removed the rest of them before he went out, but if he really believed foul play had occurred, why wouldn't he leave them until the police or a private detective came to investigate?

Was it possible I hadn't been in danger at all and the actual victim was the intended one? Nick had suggested no reason why I should be the target of anyone's hatred, and surely Mrs. Wilson was the more likely target. Joe had been upset, perhaps even angry, during the conversation I'd interrupted between them the day I returned to Morton. Was he angry with her, and was that anger connected to his secret and to her insistence upon seeing him now? Their faces and postures certainly had implied a more serious conversation than one about vegetables.

But I couldn't imagine Joe hurting anyone.

Could Nick be the culprit? The kindness he had shown Mrs. Wilson when speaking of the past as we waited for the doctor could have been meant to conceal his crime. After all, he hadn't been on good terms with her since he was a boy, and perhaps he was taking advantage of his improved health and desperate enough to keep Morton to hurt anyone who stood in his way. But he had seemed more at peace about losing Morton lately, not less so.

I hired a fly to take me to Netherton, and as the carriage rattled down the high street towards the Dixons' house, I thought how odd it was to be there without Joe. I also noticed that the villagers looked ordinary now, not as happy or perfect as they had before. It occurred to me that seeing Joe might have been what made them look unusually happy. His presence had that effect on me, so why shouldn't it be the same for others? Or again, perhaps the difference was in my perspective, and now that I was more used to the village, it didn't seem as odd as it did before. But I still saw no school-age girls: that, at least, was consistent.

When Mrs. Dixon opened her front door and saw me there, her momentary look of surprise changed to pleasure. She welcomed me with a warm embrace and led me into the kitchen before I could say a word.

"You look worn out, my dear," she said briskly, taking a pinch of different herbs from several containers and putting them in a glass. "Don't even try to speak until you drink this."

She added a greenish liquid to the glass and stirred it, then set it before me on the table.

"What is it?" I asked, giving it a dubious look.

"It's my cure for what ails you. I know it doesn't look

appetising, but trust me, you'll feel better once you try it." She smiled. "Joe says I ought to sell it instead of giving it away free to friends and neighbours. He thinks it would make our family wealthy, but he's hardly an objective judge."

I obliged her by taking a sip. It tasted better than it looked and made me think of the green smell of a summer meadow. There was mint in it, but I couldn't detect any other specific herb or flavour. Now that I was sitting down and in a warm, hospitable environment, I could feel my own exhaustion keenly. It wasn't just physical exhaustion from lack of sleep; it was mental fatigue, too, from my interactions with Nick and the night child and from trying to figure out the cause of Mrs. Wilson's accident.

"This is very good," I said, surprising myself by drinking the elixir down to the dregs.

"You needed it, poor dear," she said sympathetically, patting my arm.

I surprised myself again by starting to cry. I didn't know whether the tears were prompted by my fatigue, the sympathetic look on Mrs. Dixon's face, or just being away from the intense atmosphere of Morton—probably a combination of all three—but I didn't have the energy to control myself, so I simply covered my face with my hands until the tears had subsided. Mrs. Dixon placed a handkerchief discreetly on the table near me, then found something to do at the kitchen sink.

"I'm sorry," I said when I could speak again, mopping my face with the handkerchief. "I don't usually let my emotions get the better of me."

She sat down across from me again and said, "No need to apologise. Would you like to tell me what's the matter?"

"I'm looking for Joe," I said. "Do you know where he is?"

"He's in Manchester. He told me he'd be away for a week or so."

"Do you know where in Manchester he is, exactly? I need to get a message to him."

She hesitated, then said, "I do know, but he specifically told me not to tell you."

"What?" I exclaimed. "Why?"

"It's nothing bad. Just a surprise for you."

I'd had enough of surprises, both good and bad ones. "I don't want to cause trouble between you and Joe," I said, "and you don't need to tell me his address, but could you send him a message? It's urgent."

"Of course," she replied, looking alarmed. "What is it?"

"Mrs. Wilson wants to see him," I said. I explained what had happened to Mrs. Wilson and her refusal to tell anyone what she wanted to see Joe about.

When I'd finished, Mrs. Dixon said softly, "Ah, poor Jane." She seemed deep in thought, and after a pause, she went on, "Jane Wilson and I were good friends once. I was a frightened girl of fifteen when I went to work at Morton, and she was already the housekeeper there even though she was barely in her thirties. She took me under her wing and taught me everything she knew, enough to be the housekeeper myself if I'd stayed. But I was at Morton only a couple of years, and . . . Jane and I eventually lost touch."

"Do you have any idea why she needs to talk to Joe so badly?"

"That I don't, but of course I'll try to set her mind at ease. I'll send him a wire today."

"Thank you." I felt relieved already, and loath to leave Mrs. Dixon and her bright kitchen. The sun was streaming through the windows, illuminating the fact that there wasn't a speck of dirt to be seen anywhere, despite the surfaces cluttered with jars, bottles, and kitchen implements.

"Vaughan," she said, "would you like to lie down for a bit before you go back to Morton? You look as though you could use a rest."

The offer was tempting, but I hesitated.

"While you're resting, I can nip down to the post office and send Joe that wire. What do you think?"

My heavy eyelids made the decision for me, and I allowed her to lead me to a sofa in the parlour. I was dimly aware of her putting a blanket over me before I fell asleep.

20

I awoke in darkness and nearly fell off the sofa, thinking I was in my own bed at Morton. As soon as I remembered where I was, I got to my feet too quickly, before my head was ready. I sat down again, breathing deeply, and slowly realized that I felt completely refreshed, as if I'd made up for all the sleepless nights at Morton with one nap.

I found Mrs. Dixon in the kitchen, stirring a pot of delicious-smelling stew, and stammered my apologies for sleeping so late. She waved me off with a smile.

"What time is it?" I said. "I must be getting back to Morton."

"It's only six. You must be hungry. Have a bowl of stew before you leave."

My empty stomach made the decision for me. I returned to my seat across from her at the kitchen table and we began to eat together.

As we ate, she said, "I'd like to visit Jane when she's feeling better."

"Of course," I said. "In fact, I wish you could return to Morton with me now."

"Now?" Her eyes widened.

"Oh, I know you can't. I was just thinking aloud."

She hesitated, then said a little shyly, "I could, in fact. Johnny is old enough to take care of the younger boys, and I have no other duties here that can't be put off."

"I don't want to pressure you," I said, but I immediately felt better at the thought of Mrs. Dixon and her calming presence at Morton with me. Her warmth was second only to Joe's, and I felt instinctively that she could melt the chill of Morton and solve its mysteries.

"You're not pressuring me in the least. As long as Mr. Spencer wouldn't mind my presence there, I could even take over poor Jane's duties until she recovers. It's been a while, but I remember Morton Abbey well."

"That would be wonderful. I'm certain nobody would mind." Though I could never really be certain that Nick wouldn't object to a new face at Morton, I didn't care. We needed the help, and it would be far easier for someone who knew Morton to offer that help.

Mrs. Dixon made short work of arranging for Johnny to care for the younger boys, packing a small bag, and saying her farewells. We were on our way in a matter of minutes.

On the ride back to Morton, Mrs. Dixon said, "Joe told me he asked you to marry him."

I didn't know what to say.

"I oughtn't to have said anything," she went on, "but I want you to know how glad I am for both of you. I was hoping for this, but any mother knows not to push her children in the direction she wants them to go, or they'll just run the other way. Happily, I didn't need to say a word to encourage Joe. He sees your worth as clearly as I do."

"Thank you." I realized that she either didn't know or didn't care that I hadn't accepted Joe's proposal yet, but I was seriously considering it. After all, I felt calm and secure when I was with Joe and his mother, and I felt neither of those things with Nick or in the house at Morton. My behaviour with Nick the night before was an aberration. Even though he had instigated the kiss, I had behaved badly. Joe was the man I ought to have been kissing. Joe was unmarried and had no mysterious ties to other women or ghost children or crumbling mansions.

When we arrived at Morton, Bedford received Mrs. Dixon with his usual coolness. When she expressed her pleasure at seeing him again after nearly thirty years, he looked a little surprised, though whether he did so because he remembered her or not was unclear.

Nick hadn't returned from wherever he'd been all day, so I led Mrs. Dixon straight to Mrs. Wilson's room.

Betty was there at Mrs. Wilson's bedside, and the patient was asleep. Betty explained that Doctor Foster had been there a few hours earlier and had administered a powerful sleeping draught.

Mrs. Dixon sat in the chair Betty had vacated, gazing at Mrs. Wilson with tears in her eyes. "Poor Jane!" she said softly. "I've missed you, I have."

Betty relayed to us what Doctor Foster had said. Mrs. Wilson must stay in bed for at least another week. He hadn't liked the look of her: her skin was cold and clammy, and she seemed worse, not better. He was worried there were internal injuries, especially because her blood pressure was lower than it ought to be. He told Betty to watch the patient carefully and not to leave her alone, so Betty had had a long day of it.

"I'll stay with her," Mrs. Dixon said, dabbing at her eyes with her handkerchief. "Why don't you rest, Betty?"

Betty gratefully accepted the offer, promising to return in a couple of hours. Since I was at my leisure, I went to the library to escape the ever-increasing parade of Sir Peter's servants who were bustling about his suite of rooms, which were on the second floor of the centre part of the house. Instead of lighting a lamp, I found my way to my usual chair and looked out the long windows, watching the gathering darkness on the lawn. Despite the extra people in the house, it felt strangely uninhabited. I realized it would feel empty to me until Nick returned, for he and Morton couldn't be separated even in my mind. The house felt like a mere container, a shell that had lost its purpose.

I was still staring out the windows, lost in thought, when the library door opened and Nick came in. He went to the desk and lit the lamp, then turned to the nearest bookshelf and took out a book. He flipped the pages quickly—too quickly to read them—then tossed the book on the desk and turned back to the bookshelf. He took another book and did exactly the same thing with it.

He obviously didn't know I was there, and I ought to have stepped out from the shadows, but I was frozen in my chair, watching his mystifying behaviour. He repeated the process with several other books, letting them fall on the floor when he was done with them. It looked like the beginnings of the same mess that had greeted me twice in my first week at Morton, and I watched in speechless dismay. If he was losing his mind, I didn't want to witness it.

When all the books from one shelf lay in untidy piles on the desk and floor, Nick stopped, then placed his hands on either side of the shelf and leaned his forehead against it in a posture of despair.

I couldn't remain there any longer without his knowledge, so I rose and stepped into the light cast by the lamp.

He whirled around at the sound of my footsteps. "My God, Vaughan! You startled me. How long have you been here?"

"A while." I felt a little afraid of the wild look in his eyes. "I'm sorry. I ought to have said something as soon as you came in."

He looked down at the books strewn about, then at me. "I can imagine what you must be thinking."

"I'm thinking you've done this before," I said. "More than once."

"Yes. I am to blame for the state you found the library in during your early days at Morton."

"But you were so ill . . . how could you have done it?"

"Bedford and I did it together. It was exhausting, and I needed several days to recover."

"You love this room, and these books," I said, forgetting my fear in my desire to understand and taking a step closer to him. "Why would you do this?"

"My desire to find my father's will was greater—is greater— than my love for these books." At my look of confusion, he added, "My father's last will, the one he amended the day he died."

"So there really was another will."

"Yes. Let's sit down. I'll explain."

We went to our usual chairs by the fireplace, but before sitting down, he moved his chair several inches away from mine. I felt a stab of physical pain at this evidence of his detachment from me. Then I was angry with myself. Wasn't this what I wanted? The more rational and detached Nick was, the easier our interactions would be.

"My father was very ill, but still lucid, when he decided to change his will and leave Morton to me," Nick said. "You must understand that I took care of him during the last few years of his life. Peter didn't even trouble himself to visit. I spent many hours with my father, reading to him, listening to him, bringing him anything he wanted. It was the first time he seemed to notice my existence and to appreciate me. I'll admit I was glad Peter wasn't there."

He ran a hand through his hair and continued, "My father also noticed, apparently for the first time, how much I loved Morton. For years he'd been disappointed by Peter's lack of interest in the estate, but he still thought his elder son ought to inherit. Thus, I was surprised when he told me he wanted to change his will. No doubt most people would think I tried to influence him—even that I tried to convince him to leave Morton to me—but I didn't. Certainly I didn't hide my love for the place, but I never brought up the subject of inheritance or the will. In fact, I told him not to give me everything, that I could share the estate with Peter somehow. I don't expect anyone to believe that, either.

"The point is, he made a new will that day. It was properly signed and witnessed, but unfortunately he died before the will could be put into our lawyer's hands. I was emotional, obviously, and had little time to think about the will, but I was worried Alicia or even Mrs. Wilson would destroy it, so I asked Bedford to hide it inside a book here in the library."

I frowned. "Why didn't you just keep it with you until you could give it to the lawyer yourself?"

"I didn't want anyone to believe I had forged the will or my father's signature. It was so obviously in my favour that I was superstitious about touching it. It also seemed disloyal to my father even to think about the will that day."

"And Bedford did as you asked?"

"Yes. I have never had reason to suspect him of deceiving me. He has always been loyal to me, and he was devastated when he returned to the library and couldn't find the will. He thought he'd hidden the will inside a particular book of essays, but he'd hidden it hastily, and when he returned later that evening, he couldn't find it."

"I see," I said. Now the chaos in the library made sense.

Nick went on, "In the weeks following my father's death, Bedford and I searched every book in this room several times over. I kept telling him not to worry if we couldn't find the will, that he had better things to do, but he kept looking. We stopped looking for it when it appeared that Peter would allow me to live here undisturbed. But then you came, and you wouldn't leave despite the things I did to try to frighten you away. If you were staying, that meant Peter really could sell the place, so I started looking for the will again."

"The things you did to frighten me away," I repeated slowly. "Was everything in that first week your doing, then? Turning my door handle at night, the gunshots—"

"I paid a man to fire the gun outside your window. I'm sorry, Vaughan."

He looked genuinely contrite, and I knew his opinion of me had changed since those early days, but I still felt uneasy. He could have done other things that he hadn't admitted to. Had I trusted him too quickly?

"What about the child-related sounds?" I asked. "Did you have anything to do with the crying? Or the toys?"

"No. I still don't understand that. None of the sounds or odd things happening with Frances's toys make sense to me."

Now was the time to tell him what I'd experienced in his room the night before with the night child. But how could I tell this man that I'd spoken to his dead daughter? I still clung to the possibility that it had been an unusually vivid dream.

I ventured, "Have you heard any odd noises lately?"

He gave me a swift, sharp glance. "What sort of noises?"

"A child crying. Or speaking."

He paused, looking at me with an expression I couldn't interpret. "No," he said at last. "Why do you ask?"

"Just curiosity." To avoid dwelling on the unpleasant thought that I was now the only person who could hear the night child, I asked in my best lawyerly tone, "Who witnessed your father's amended will?"

"Bedford and a maidservant who left Morton shortly after my father's death."

"Have you ever tried to find her?"

"Yes. Her name was Susan Smith and all anyone knew was that she planned to find work in London. You can imagine the difficulties. I had no luck locating her."

"Did anyone else know about the amended will? Sir Peter, for instance?"

"I don't think so. He's never mentioned it, but of course it would be in his best interest to pretend it doesn't exist even if he does know."

I found myself looking at his lips and remembering how warm they'd felt against mine. Giving myself a mental shake, I asked, "Who else was in the house that day?"

"The servants. Alicia. Frances. She was about three years old at the time."

"Did your—did Alicia—know what was happening?"

"She knew my father was dying, of course, but she was feeling poorly that day and stayed in her room. I was relieved not to have to worry about her overhearing anything. My marriage wasn't a happy one, as you know, and by that time I'd stopped telling Alicia anything personal or important."

I wanted to ask him about his wife's room and whether he was still waiting for her, hoping she would return, but I couldn't bring myself to do so. Instead, I rose, went to the books he had dropped on the floor, and began to return them to the shelf.

Nick joined me, and for a few minutes we worked together without speaking or looking at each other. Even though we were side by side, I noticed he was careful to keep a proper distance from me, not even allowing his sleeve to brush against mine.

When all the books were back in their proper places, I turned to him and said, "I was surprised you were away from Morton all day today. Where were you?"

"I was in Bradford, asking questions."

"Asking questions of whom?"

"Most of Peter's servants who are here now are from Bradford, so I was talking to people who know them, who could give me an account of their characters."

"Why?"

"To find out if they are likely to be loyal to Peter to the point of harming anyone he wants harmed, of course. Have you forgotten about the stairs so soon?"

"I certainly haven't forgotten," I said, "but I thought perhaps you had. I went to look at them this morning and there was nothing unusual on them. No marbles."

"Yes, I know. Whoever put the marbles there in the first place must have been worried he or she would be caught and tried to get rid of the evidence." I must have given him a sceptical look, for he added, "Is it possible you don't believe me?"

"I don't know whom to believe."

"You still don't trust me," he said, sounding hurt. But then he uttered a bitter laugh. "Of course you don't. You have no reason to trust me after the way I behaved last night."

My face burned, and I stared at the bookcase in front of me. "Let's not discuss it."

"But I must tell you . . ." He hesitated, as if he were searching for the right words. "When I heard Mrs. Wilson scream, I thought it was you. It must have taken me only a few minutes to reach the east wing, but it felt like forever. When I realized you were unharmed, I lost my head and . . . behaved badly. You needn't fear anything from me of that kind again."

I didn't fear any such thing. Could he possibly be so obtuse as to think I did? Even now, standing so close to him, a wave of longing swept through me. He couldn't have failed to notice my response to his kisses, so he must now be playing the gentleman, pretending he was entirely to blame to save me from embarrassment.

"You do forgive me, don't you?" he asked.

I nodded, not trusting myself to speak.

"I went to see Mrs. Wilson this evening before I came to the library," he said. "Mrs. Dixon was there. She apologised for surprising me with her presence."

"Do you mind that she's here?"

"No. Why would I? We talked a little about what Morton was like in its heyday. I also offered her the use of one of the east wing rooms, but she said she'd prefer to be near Mrs. Wilson and that our former kitchen-maid's room—that tiny room adjoining Mrs. Wilson's—will do well enough. I thought that very kind of her."

I turned to look at him. "Do you remember her?"

"Yes. She wasn't here long, but I remember her following

Mrs. Wilson around and being very eager to learn." In a lower tone, he said, "I saw the roses in Mrs. Wilson's room. Why did you move them there? I meant them for you."

"You make it . . . impossible for me to tell you the truth," I said. It was perhaps the most honest thing I'd ever said to him.

"I know," he said earnestly, surprising me. "I am in a quandary, Vaughan, and you are suffering because of it. Perhaps we ought to be completely frank with each other—"

"I don't think that's a good idea," I interjected, coward that I was. Now that he had dropped the formal, detached tone, I was afraid to let him speak.

"You needn't worry," he said. "I have nothing to say that can hurt you. You're going to marry Joe and have a happy life with him, and I wish you both well—I really do. I ask nothing of you, and I can offer you nothing. Or rather, I can offer you nothing you would want. Surely there is no harm in telling the truth in such a situation."

"Yes, there is." I turned away from him, struggling to keep down the lump rising in my throat. "You can harm us both by . . . by saying too much."

He was silent for a moment. Then he sighed.

"You're right. Of course you're right. How could I forget what a sensible little thing you are? You don't want what you can't have. I will need you to help me be sensible too, especially when Peter is here."

I didn't know whether to laugh or cry. How could I help him be sensible, when it was all I could do not to make a fool of myself in front of him?

"When Peter comes," he said, "I think it would be best if you and I behave as though we are merely acquaintances."

I turned again to face him. "Why?"

He looked troubled. "If Peter suspects you and I are . . . friends, he will be as suspicious of you as he is of me. You don't want to make an enemy of him. For your own sake, he needs to believe you are loyal to him and his interests alone. I am already his enemy."

"Don't you think Mrs. Wilson or Bedford will tell him about the evenings we've spent together in the library?" My words sounded strange even to my ears, as if Nick and I had been engaged in illicit activities behind closed doors.

"They might, but I'll tell him you were merely answering my questions about the estate. It would be worse if he actually sees how much time we spend together."

"Very well." I spoke quietly to hide the tremor in my voice. "We'd better stop behaving like friends at once, then. Good night, Mr. Spencer."

I didn't wait for a response before leaving the library, unable to remain another minute with him without betraying evidence of my conflicting emotions. Did he really think I didn't want what I couldn't have? If he could have seen me rush to my room, lock the door, and burst into tears for the second time that day, for all the world like the silliest of my sisters, he wouldn't have thought so.

21

I spent the next few days holding my breath, or so it seemed. Everyone in the house was awaiting Sir Peter's arrival with varying degrees of anticipation and anxiety, and I felt the heightened tension keenly. Except for Betty, Sir Peter's servants seemed to consider me beneath their notice, but they were tolerant of, even obedient to, Mrs. Dixon. At Morton, she showed a different side of herself. She was still as kind and caring as ever with me and Mrs. Wilson, but she threw herself into the preparations for Sir Peter's arrival with a frenzied energy, concerned about the details of everything from preparing his rooms to planning the menus for each day of the week. I also marvelled at her incredible memory: she remembered where everything was, whether it be the good silver or the red damask tablecloth, without needing to be shown. When I remarked on this, she laughed and said that nothing had changed at Morton in thirty years, so it was easy to find everything she needed.

During the day I spent most of my time in Mrs. Wilson's room because Betty was now needed to prepare Sir Peter's rooms. Mrs. Dixon spent the evenings with Mrs. Wilson after her days' work was done, and I spent the evenings in my room, avoiding the library. If anyone at Morton meant to harm me, I gave him little opportunity to do it again. I saw Nick only in passing. He seemed as determined as I to pretend we were merely acquaintances.

The day before Sir Peter was due to arrive, I overheard an emotional conversation between Mrs. Wilson and Mrs. Dixon. Mrs. Wilson was not recovering as quickly as the doctor thought she should, and she slept most of the time, but occasionally she was lucid. I was just about to enter her room, but I hesitated at the door when I heard Mrs. Dixon weeping quietly and Mrs. Wilson saying, "I was wrong. I'm sorry, Rose."

I wasn't one to eavesdrop, but before I could decide whether to advance or retreat, Mrs. Dixon said through her tears, "Joe will fix everything. Don't worry."

I knocked then, lightly, and let myself in. Mrs. Wilson's face was an alarming shade of grey, and her eyes were closed. Mrs. Dixon was holding Mrs. Wilson's hand, but she released it to wipe her eyes when I came in.

"Forgive me for interrupting," I said. "Shall I come back later?"

"No, it's all right," Mrs. Dixon said. "We've been reminiscing, but Jane has exhausted herself by talking too much. She doesn't want us to call the doctor back again, but I think he ought to take another look at her."

"I agree. Would you like to send for the doctor or shall I?"

"I'll do it. Will you watch Jane?"

"Certainly. And don't forget to eat."

She smiled shakily at me on her way out, and I settled down to watch the patient, who was taking deep, labouring breaths.

"I know you and Mrs. Dixon are friends and have much to catch up on, but you ought not to talk," I said, touching her hand, which was cold and clammy. "You need to save your strength."

She opened her eyes wide at this. "Where is Rose?" she asked, looking distressed.

"She'll be back. She just went to get something to eat."

"Tell Joe . . ." she began. "No . . . Rose is here."

"I don't understand. Do you still wish to see Joe?"

"No. Tell Dora to find Joe." Her eyes were filled with confusion, and she was so agitated that she seemed to be trying to get out of bed, which alarmed me. I was worried that Dr. Foster had given her too much pain medication along with the sleeping draught and that she was hallucinating.

I managed to convince her to lie back in bed and go back to sleep. After a quarter of an hour, I noticed that she was very still. Too still.

Trying to keep my panic at bay, I reached for her pulse. I couldn't detect anything.

I rang for Mrs. Dixon, and as soon as she came into the room and saw Mrs. Wilson's face, she cried, "She's gone," and collapsed in her chair in a storm of weeping. I reached over to pat her shoulder awkwardly, but she was so distraught that she didn't seem to notice I was there.

I left the room and asked the nearest servant to find Nick and to send for the doctor. There was no time to consider what I was feeling, given Mrs. Dixon's distress. I had always been the person with the clear head when everyone else around me was upset.

Nick came in shortly afterwards. His eyes swept the room, taking in the prone figure of Mrs. Wilson, the hysterically sobbing Mrs. Dixon, and me standing silently beside her.

He came to me first and laid his hand briefly on my shoulder, looking into my eyes with such concern that my composure would have shattered had I not forced myself to focus on the crisis at hand.

"Mrs. Dixon needs help," I said abruptly, "and I think Mrs. Wilson has died." I ought to have mentioned Mrs. Wilson first, but Mrs. Dixon's state seemed more dire at that moment.

Nick asked me if the doctor had been sent for, and then he suggested that Mrs. Dixon go to her own room to lie down, but she refused to leave her old friend's side and promised to calm down.

"You don't need to be calm for us," he said to her gently, "only for your own sake." He gave her his handkerchief, which she took gratefully. I saw that there was a half-empty glass of green liquid on the table by the bed that looked much like the green drink she'd made for me at her house, and I rose to get it.

"Would you like some of this?" I asked her.

She shook her head. "Just a glass of water, please."

I went to get her a glass of water, and when I returned, Nick was standing by the side of Mrs. Wilson's bed, looking down at the housekeeper who had been no friend to him. I expected him to simply nod or glance at her as a form of respect, to acknowledge the place she'd held in the household, but he reached out to cover her hand with his, and I saw the glint of tears in his eyes. All my attempts to avoid him seemed ridiculous now. I wanted nothing more than to comfort him, and only the presence of Mrs. Dixon stopped me from doing something I'd undoubtedly regret later.

When Doctor Foster arrived, he confirmed Mrs. Wilson's death and questioned me and Mrs. Dixon closely, since we had spent more time with her than anyone else. I wondered guiltily if I hadn't watched her closely enough.

❧

The day after Mrs. Wilson's death was also the day of Sir Peter's arrival. I awoke feeling surprised to see sunshine outside. It didn't suit the gloom that had settled over the household. I was worried about Nick, given his reaction to Mrs. Wilson's death and the fact that he'd been dreading the sight of his brother for months, if not years. He didn't come down to breakfast or lunch, so I went in search of him. I didn't want another intense conversation with him, but how could it be otherwise, given the circumstances? I was anxious on my own account as well—after all, I would be meeting my employer that day face to face for the first time.

I found Nick in the library in his usual chair, contemplating his pipe. He didn't seem to hear me come in, and I approached him slowly, with the same caution I would use with an unfamiliar animal.

"May I ask you a question?" I began, stopping a few feet away.

He looked surprised to see me, but I couldn't tell if he was pleased or not. "Yes, of course," he said cordially enough. "Will you sit down?"

I stayed where I was. "I'll just be a minute. Mrs. Dixon told me earlier this morning that she needs to go back to Netherton just for the day because her youngest son was in a spot of trouble at school. She was upset that she won't be here to greet Sir Peter, but I assured her we can manage without her for the day. Is that acceptable to you?"

"Certainly. Peter's own servants are here and will see to anything he needs. Is she doing better today?"

"I think so. It's probably good for her to be away from Morton today." I hesitated. "I believe Mrs. Wilson had no family. Will you be making her funeral arrangements, or do you think Sir Peter will want to do it?"

"I'll discuss that with him when he arrives."

"Is there anything you'd like me to do to . . ." I hesitated. "To ensure that everything runs smoothly?"

"No. Thank you, Vaughan."

I started to turn away.

"Wait," he said. "Could you spare a few minutes? I have some legal questions for you about the estate."

"Very well." It was a little late for legal questions if he still meant to delay the sale of the estate, but I was relieved that he was calm enough to discuss them. I sat in the chair beside his.

"I know that my brother could legally turn me out of the house before the estate is sold, but my father's request that Peter accommodate my desire to live in the house is recorded in his will. Does that make a difference?"

"There is nothing binding in that request. If I'd been your father's lawyer I would have told him not to put something so vague in his will, something that depends on the cooperation of his heirs." I watched him take a pouch of tobacco from his pocket and fill his pipe. "Instead of delaying the sale of the estate, would you consider a compromise? Could you persuade Sir Peter to come to some agreement, perhaps to sell some of the land but allow you to keep the house? Or even sell the house to you?"

He lit the pipe and put it in his mouth. He wasn't one to try to talk around his pipe, so I had to wait until he took it out again. "He'll never sell me any part of the property," he said finally, "not unless I pay twice what it's worth, and I won't do that. And compromise, in case you haven't noticed, is a bad word in our family.'

"Yes." I thought of his family's motto: *aut Caesar aut nihil,* carved into the stone archway at the front of the house. "But when something you want so much is at stake, isn't it worth trying everything, even compromise, to get it?"

He looked at me with an inscrutable expression. "It probably is."

Then a thought struck me. "There is another possibility. You could find a buyer for the house yourself, someone who would be willing to sell it back to you."

"Ah. The only trouble is I don't know anyone who is likely to agree to such an arrangement."

"Then you could give the purchase money to someone you trust," I said, trying to keep the exasperation out of my voice, "have that person buy Morton, and after some time has passed, he could return the money to you and you could buy the property yourself."

"You're the only person I trust completely, but you're too involved in this business already."

I wondered if I'd heard him correctly. He had spoken casually, and he was sitting back in his chair, smoking his pipe and staring across the room. Did he really trust me so much?

I said, "I suppose Sir Peter wouldn't sell the house to someone you . . ." I paused, unable to find the right word. Trust? Care about? ". . . someone you know. If he wants to prevent your having any part of the estate, that is."

"Yes." He looked at me gravely. "It's likely too late, anyway. Regarding a different matter, didn't you say Mrs. Dixon sent Joe a wire last week? Have you heard from him?"

"I haven't, but she said he's on his way back from Manchester. Why do you ask?"

He hesitated. "I thought he might know something about the cause of Mrs. Wilson's fall."

"He left before her accident, so I doubt he'd know anything." I knew I sounded defensive, but I couldn't help it. "Besides, I thought you believed the marbles on the stairs were meant for me, not Mrs. Wilson. Joe wouldn't do anything to hurt me."

"I am trying to consider all the possibilities," he said, equally defensive, "but I shouldn't have expected you to do the same. One cannot be objective about the person one is in love with."

"I'm not—" I began, then stopped short, unsure what I'd meant to say. Not objective? Not in love?

I was saved from having to finish my sentence by a loud noise outside. It sounded like a strangled explosion, combined with a rhythmic mechanical chuffing sound.

Nick and I jumped up and went to the long windows, which offered a good view of the carriage drive.

"What in God's name is that?" Nick exclaimed.

"It's a motorcar." I had seen one once before, in London. It had been some distance away, and at first I'd assumed it was just an unusual-looking carriage, but then I'd noticed there was no horse and that a small crowd had gathered to look at it.

"I know what it is," he snapped. "What a ridiculous expense."

The vehicle came to a sputtering stop some ten yards from the main entrance. Two men were in it: the passenger was a slightly-built man in a tweed suit and cap, and the driver was a big man wearing a light, full-length coat, a leather cap, and goggles. He put me in mind of a creature from ancient myth. I watched, fascinated, as he extricated himself from the motorcar—no small feat because of his considerable height—and peeled off his cap and goggles, revealing hair that must have been bright gold in his youth, but now was mixed with white. All of Sir Peter's servants who had already been installed at Morton rushed outside and formed a queue to receive him, the one nearest him taking his motoring gear. He brushed himself off and strode towards the front door. The smaller man also alighted from the vehicle but remained where he was, looking at the tyres.

I didn't need to ask Nick which man was Sir Peter.

"Typical Peter," Nick said. "He always has to be the first one with a new toy. I hate to think what that contraption must have cost him."

"He's come early," I said. "Shall we go to the front hall to welcome him?"

"I suppose we must." But he didn't move.

"Nick, if you want Morton, you must try to be pleasant to him."

"Don't worry. I'll do my best to play the part of the admiring, dutiful younger brother."

"That's not what I said."

He gave me a rueful look. "Poor Vaughan. You're only trying to help, I know. I am not making it easy for you."

We arrived at the front hall just as Sir Peter was handing his coat to Bedford, who looked unhappier than usual, if that was possible, a deep frown furrowing his brow and his lips turned firmly downward.

Upon seeing Nick and me, Sir Peter strode towards us and shook his brother's hand vigorously, a look of amazement on his face.

"Why, Nick, old man, I hardly recognized you," he exclaimed. "You're looking well. Remarkably well."

"I am well," Nick replied guardedly.

I was struck by the contrast between the two brothers. The appearance and mannerisms of two family members could hardly be more different. Sir Peter's loud, hearty voice and florid complexion suited his careless, easy manner. Nick, on the other hand, was a spectral presence despite his improved health, with his thin frame, dark colouring, and quiet, controlled way of speaking.

Sir Peter turned to me and took my hand. "Miss Springthorpe, I presume."

"Yes."

"At last we meet, though I feel as though I know you already from your letters and the meticulous records of your work that you've sent me. The legal affairs of our family probably haven't been in such good order for centuries."

I was uncomfortable with such lavish praise, as well as by the way he was looking at me, with close, curious attention. It wouldn't have surprised me if he had looked at his motorcar in exactly this way before deciding to purchase it. He continued to hold my hand, as if he had forgotten it was in his possession, but he didn't release it even when I made a feeble attempt to withdraw it.

Nick came to my rescue, whether he meant to or not. "Have you had your tea already?" he asked his brother. "We usually don't have ours for another hour or so, but the servants could bring us an early tea in the dining room."

"No need," Sir Peter said, releasing my hand and waving his own in the air. "I've already arranged for our tea to be brought out on the lawn. It would be a shame to stay indoors when the weather is so fine. Besides, I've just been told of Mrs. Wilson's death and would prefer to stay outside for a while." A fleeting shadow passed over his face.

"Very well." Nick sounded as though he were speaking through clenched teeth.

"Come along, then. I'll show you my newest acquisition on

the way. You'll join us, of course, Miss Springthorpe." It was a statement, not a question.

It seemed to me as though the sheer force of Sir Peter's personality swept us outdoors along with him. I could imagine he wouldn't brook arguments when he was set on a course of action, and his tone, while cheerfully bombastic, also had an imperious note that I recognized. He and Nick were brothers, after all. But there was room for only one lord of the manor, and while it would have been kinder of Sir Peter to defer to Nick, at least for the first day or so, Nick must accept the fact that he wasn't Morton's owner.

I noticed Sir Peter glancing at my feet as I walked, and under his scrutiny I felt more self-conscious than usual about my limp. I wished I had worn the shoe Joe made for me instead of my heavy everyday shoe. Joe's shoe made my hip ache if I wore it for more than a couple of hours, but it was certainly more pleasing to the eye.

Once outside, Sir Peter introduced the small man hovering around the motorcar as Mr. Jones, his mechanic, then went on to say, "I brought this glorious machine from France, you know. It's a Peugeot. The Continent is far ahead of us in the design of automobiles, and this is one of their latest models, a Type fifteen."

"It looks like an ordinary carriage to me," Nick said.

I thought so, too. Aside from the steering column, a lamp on the driver's side, and the obvious absence of horses, it did look like a carriage.

"It's based on a phaeton, that's why." Sir Peter went on about flat-twos and transverse mountings, singing the praises of the vehicle in such technical detail that I quickly lost interest. However, I was struck by something familiar in the sweeping way

Sir Peter used his hands as he talked. I couldn't understand why it seemed familiar—Nick didn't have the same mannerism—but the feeling persisted that I had seen it before.

"Would you like to try it out?" Sir Peter looked first at Nick, then at me. "Jones and I could take you for a drive."

"No, thank you," Nick said coldly, looking as though he would rather be run over by the motorcar than get into it.

"Perhaps after tea," I said, to soften Nick's response.

"I see you still have no sense of adventure," Sir Peter said to Nick with the superior air of the elder brother.

Nick's face darkened, but thankfully a potential argument was averted by the arrival of two servants with trays.

We sat under the big chestnut tree on the lawn, Sir Peter gallantly offering me his arm and guiding me to the most comfortable spot where I could sit with my back against the tree trunk. Nick sat on my right, and although he was a few feet away, I could sense the tension in his body. On my left, Sir Peter stretched out on his side, looking the picture of comfort and ease.

"You said you brought the motorcar from France," Nick said. "I thought you were in Italy."

"I was. Most of the business I've been doing for the past year has been in Italy, but I've had to take shorter day trips. I was in France only for a week on the way back to England. I say, old man, what's brought on this splendid physical transformation? When I was here last—when was it? Two years ago?—you didn't leave your bed, much less set foot outside the house. Am I to attribute your improved health to Miss Springthorpe's presence? Are you a nurse as well as a solicitor, Miss Springthorpe?"

"No," I said quickly. "I hardly see Mr. Spencer." It was absurd, but I felt like Saint Peter after he had denied Christ, despite the fact that it had been Nick's idea to pretend he and I were merely acquaintances.

"Illness is a mysterious thing," Nick said. "I expected my condition to worsen, but my symptoms have been gradually improving instead. I'm well enough now to take on my old duties as bailiff."

I could tell that Nick was trying very hard to appear nonchalant, but I heard the note of hopefulness in his voice and silently willed Sir Peter to agree.

But Sir Peter laughed and said, "*Your* illnesses are always mysterious, that's certain. Nevertheless, as happy as I am to see you in better health, there won't be any need for you to do anything here. Not now." He popped a cucumber sandwich in his mouth and took a great gulp of tea. "Come, let's speak of more pleasant things. There will be time enough later to discuss money and property matters. Tell me, Miss Springthorpe, how have you managed to remain at Morton all these months without going mad? Don't you find it a gloomy old place?"

"I did at first," I said slowly, "but I became accustomed to it, and I've enjoyed spending time in the gardens whenever I wasn't working."

"And you didn't miss the company of others? No offence to my brother, but he isn't exactly the most sociable of men, eh, Nick?"

Nick stewed in silence, only lending credence to Sir Peter's words.

"Neither am I the most sociable of women," I said, mustering a smile, "So Mr. Spencer and I suit each other very well." I groaned inwardly, realizing my words hadn't come out the way I'd intended. I didn't mean to suggest that Nick and I were well matched in any way, only that we both liked solitude.

I added, "I don't feel much need for companionship."

"Is that so?" Sir Peter peered at me curiously. "I can't say I understand that. The more the merrier, as far as I'm concerned. I always found Morton unbearably dull unless there was a social event going on. The shooting parties were the best. Do you remember the parties Father used to have, Nick? He'd always invite at least twenty guests and they'd stay for weeks. Famous ones, too—Lord Carmichael and the Duke of Marlborough were regular guests. The Prince of Wales came once, too. It was jolly good fun. I suppose you wouldn't remember much, though, since you were always hiding in your room or the library with your books."

"I remember well enough," said Nick. "I couldn't wait until everyone had gone home."

Sir Peter shrugged. "I tried to follow Father's example after he died, but my parties were never as successful as his. Oh, they were all right, enjoyable enough. We did feast well"—he patted his belly in fond remembrance—"and the shooting was acceptable, but they weren't quite as exciting as in the old days. I suppose everything seems more vivid when one is a child."

Brushing the crumbs from his waistcoat, Sir Peter jumped to his feet more quickly and gracefully than I would have expected, given his large frame, and looked about him. "Morton's a pretty place in the summer, I'll say that for it." He looked down at me, extending his hand. "I think it's time to go over those legal papers, Miss Springthorpe. Will you excuse us, Nick?"

I allowed Sir Peter to help me up.

"What's the hurry?" Nick asked, shading his eyes with his hand as he looked up at his brother. "You said there would be time enough to discuss the property later."

"The truth is, old man, there isn't much time at all. But I need to discuss all of this alone with my solicitor first." He winked at me.

I couldn't help feeling pleased to be called a solicitor, despite my mistrust of Sir Peter. His charm was powerful enough to make me feel vaguely guilty for not trusting him instantly.

Nick sprang to his feet. "I have a right to know."

"All in good time, Nick," Sir Peter said smoothly. "All in good time. Shall we, Miss Springthorpe?" He offered me his arm.

I bit my lip. It was difficult to hide the fact that I would rather stay with Nick, even though he was no better company at the moment than an angry porcupine. I took Sir Peter's arm, but as we moved away I managed a look at Nick over my shoulder that I hoped was reassuring.

In the library, I went through the motions of showing Sir Peter the documents relating to the property and explaining how I had organized the family papers that had been in such disarray when I arrived. But I hardly listened to myself or to him. My mind was with Nick, wondering what he was doing. What he was feeling.

"Well, that's all we need to do, I think," Sir Peter said, bringing me back to the present. He leaned back in the chair at the desk with his hands behind his head. "I must say I'm very pleased with your work, Miss Springthorpe." He looked up at me—I was standing beside him, the better to show him the documents—as if he was trying to figure me out. "After seeing how, er . . . comfortable you seem at Morton, I was worried you might not want to leave any more than Nick does and that you might try to put obstacles in my path."

"I agreed to work for you, and I don't renege on agreements," I replied stiffly, "despite the fact that I haven't received a salary for the last three months."

"Forgive me. I've been remiss with your pay, but I can remedy that at once." He reached into his waistcoat pocket, pulled out an envelope bulging with bills, and handed it to me. I must have looked stunned, for he added, "No doubt my brother led you to believe I wouldn't pay you. Count it if you like. It's only half of what I owe you, but you'll get the rest soon enough, once your work here is finished."

He gestured to the chair beside him, and I sat. I couldn't bring myself to count the money in his presence, though my fingers itched to do so.

"Thank you," I said, "but I will trust your word as a gentleman."

"That's generously spoken. I'd be very surprised, though, if my brother hasn't tried to turn you against me. Hasn't he represented me as the monster who's turning him out of his home?"

I was silent. I felt unequal to my self-imposed task of persuading Sir Peter to compromise with Nick. It was obvious Sir Peter was too shrewd to be fooled by any of my attempts to embellish the truth.

"I'll be frank with you," I said finally. "Your brother hasn't hidden the fact that the two of you have a difficult relationship, though of course he hasn't told me details."

He raised one eyebrow. "Hasn't he?"

"No." This, at least, was the truth. "All I know is that you were your father's favourite, and he was jealous of that bond."

He shrugged. "Every parent has a favourite, whether they'll admit it or not. I was our father's favourite; Nick was our mother's. Those petty childhood jealousies are in the past. You're telling the truth, aren't you? You really do know nothing."

I nodded, and he looked meditatively at me as if wondering whether it would be worthwhile to tell me more. Although part of me wanted very much to know more, I preferred to hear about the Spencers' family history from Nick.

"I'm only the lawyer," I said. "There's no need for me to know personal details about your family."

"You're wrong on both counts," he replied. "I'm no fool, Miss Springthorpe. I can see you're far more than the lawyer, or at least you want to be. And in order to finish your work, it will be necessary for you to know some of our family secrets, sordid as they are."

I barely heard what he said after "at least you want to be." What did he mean? What did he see? My instinct told me I wouldn't like the answer if I asked. He was looking at me as if I were an adventuress. A woman who would take advantage of any opportunity to improve her position and financial status.

"Whatever bad blood there is between you and . . . Mr. Spencer," I said, remembering only at the last second not to use Nick's Christian name, "don't you think it would be better to try to put it behind you and start over? I know I'm ignorant of what happened in the past, but don't you think we ought to speak of the future? Your future. His future. The future of Morton."

"What are you suggesting?" He looked sceptical, but at least he was willing to listen.

"Mr. Spencer cares about Morton, and he's well enough to run it again."

"Well enough!" Sir Peter scoffed. "He's never been ill. He merely pretends to be when it suits him. That's how he's gained sympathy all his life."

I let that pass. "Nevertheless, surely you can't deny that he would take good care of the place, and instead of your having to pay him a salary if he became the bailiff again, you could sell Morton to him, perhaps not the whole estate but at least the house and some of the surrounding land."

He looked at me with narrowed eyes. "I could, indeed. But I won't."

"Why not?"

"I have no desire to do anything for Nick. He's held sway here long enough."

"But you could probably get more for the property from him than from anyone else." I was desperate now, grasping at straws. I wasn't good at this sort of negotiation.

"I'm not so sure about that."

Suddenly, he leaned towards me and plucked the envelope of bills out of my hand, holding it just above my head. I made a reflexive move to grab it, then realized how undignified I looked and quickly laid my hands in my lap.

He laughed unpleasantly, as if he'd discovered my ugliest secret. Placing the envelope on the desk in front of me, he leaned back in his chair again, never taking his eyes off me.

I felt humiliated. Small.

"Money is everything to a woman of your class, isn't it?" he observed. "That's why I can't for the life of me figure out what you stand to gain from trying to persuade me to sell the estate to my brother. And you don't seem like the sort of woman who would do anything without calculating the risks. Most of the work you've done for me will be useless if I sell to Nick. If I agree to do as you ask, will you return that money to me?"

"I've done the work you've asked me to do, regardless," I said, staring straight ahead and hoping he wouldn't notice the tremor in my voice. "I'm merely speaking on behalf of your family to try to make peace."

"What admirable unselfishness." After a pause, he added in a tone of mild surprise, "Why, you're rather pretty, aren't you? I didn't think so when I first saw you, but I suppose that unfortunate limp you have is the first thing people notice. I'd expected a woman lawyer would be a sour-looking mannish creature swathed in tweed, but you're not that at all."

I rose to my feet and took a step back from the table, ignoring the envelope that still lay there. As steadily as I could, I said, "I am still your employee and will complete the sale of the estate any legal way you wish me to. But I also think it's part of my work to urge you to . . . to consider the consequences of your decisions about the property and advise you based on what I think would be best for your family. If you truly don't wish to keep Morton Abbey in your family, you may sell it to anyone you like. I know neither you nor your brother has an heir who could inherit, but . . ." I paused to consider how to put the matter delicately, then went on, "that could change in time."

He laughed, this time as if I'd told him the best joke he'd ever heard. "You know nothing about us if you really believe that. I'm five-and-forty, with no intention of marrying a woman of childbearing age. And Alicia is forty. Considering her age, not to mention that she and Nick haven't shared a bed in years, I don't see any heirs coming from that union. Or were you thinking he might divorce her and marry again, a younger woman, perhaps?"

I stared at him. Was he taunting me? There was also something very strange in his tone when he spoke of Nick's wife. Why did he speak as if he knew about the most private matters between Nick and Alicia?

22

"I don't understand," I said.

But I was beginning to. Things I had considered strange were all coming together, forming a pattern. Nick's seemingly irrational hatred of his brother. The fact that Alicia Spencer lived in France. The fact that Sir Peter was away from England so often and had bought his motorcar in France.

"I see that Nick hasn't told you about me and Alicia," he said. "Sit down, Miss Springthorpe, and take your money. We're not finished."

I sat. I didn't touch the envelope, though, not willing to risk his whisking it away and taunting me again. His mercurial temperament kept me off balance, and I wondered if he had purposely cultivated it. One moment he was laughing like a man without a care in the world, and the next he spoke in a tone so commanding only the strongest soul would dare to defy him.

"I know what you're thinking," he said, "but I never intended to steal my brother's wife, and it was never a lark to me, or to her. It was love at first sight for both of us. If only I'd met her before Nick did, none of the misery we've lived with since then would have happened."

I wanted to tell him to stop. I didn't need or want to hear the details of this story. But my limbs felt frozen, as if I were under a spell—or curse—that wouldn't release me until the story was told.

"Don't worry," he said when he saw my expression. "I won't tell you more than is necessary. I tried to stay away from Alicia, but family events forced us to see each other regularly. She tried to be a good wife to Nick, but she was miserable. It was worse for her when they moved here from London: Morton was like a prison to her. It was worse for me too, since I had to see her more often when Nick began working as my bailiff. At last we reached our breaking point, and Alicia moved to France, where we could live together for at least part of the year."

"But . . ." I tried to remember what Mrs. Wilson had told me about Alicia's departure. "Wasn't Mrs. Spencer seen in the village with a strange man? If you were the man, people would have recognized you."

His eyes narrowed. "So you do know some of the story."

"Mrs. Wilson told me that. It's all I know."

"Obviously I couldn't allow myself to be seen alone with Alicia anywhere near Morton. I sent a trusted servant to meet her and bring her to me. That was one of the ways we tried to spare Nick's feelings. Alicia allowed him to think she had many lovers, and I did the same, so he wouldn't suspect us. But we've been together for nearly twenty years, and there's been nobody else for either of us."

I could imagine Sir Peter using his charm to win a woman's love. He must have been handsome in his youth, though he wasn't aging well, with extra weight around his middle and the complexion of a man who drank too much. But I couldn't imagine how any woman could leave Nick for Sir Peter. Despite his moods, Nick was a thoughtful, intelligent, good man. Sir Peter's charm was superficial and fleeting, his sense of humour childish, his morality questionable.

"Why are you telling me this?" I asked.

"Isn't it obvious?" he replied. "I'm trying to explain why I'll never sell Morton to my brother."

"Because you committed adultery with his wife?" Once the words were out, I regretted my sharp tone, but I couldn't take them back.

"No, Miss Springthorpe. Because he has wronged me far more than I've wronged him. Ever since he found out I was Alicia's lover, he's done everything in his power to revenge himself on us. Alicia and I have begged him to grant her a divorce more times than I can count, but he always refused. And his negligence caused the death of their child."

I couldn't imagine Sir Peter begging anyone for anything. "You think he refused the divorce just to spite you? But you couldn't legally marry your brother's wife anyway, so what would it matter if he and Mrs. Spencer were divorced?"

"It wouldn't matter if we'd stayed in England, but she and I could have married in France. If you ask Nick why he refused to give her a divorce, he'll give you a story about the sanctity of marriage and protecting the reputation of our family, but he's merely stubborn and vindictive."

I was silent. It was impossible to know how much of Sir Peter's story was true. As much as I didn't want to believe any of it, it did explain Nick's refusal to give his unfaithful wife a divorce and perhaps also his silence about Frances's death. Nick did have a vengeful streak, and finding out his wife and his brother were lovers could push any man to extreme measures. But I didn't believe he had caused his daughter's death, directly or indirectly. And it was astonishing that Sir Peter seemed to feel no remorse or responsibility whatsoever for his own part in the tragic events.

"We're quite the interesting little family, what?" Sir Peter quipped. Despite his light tone, his eyes were fixed on me with a calculating look. "But you needn't take my word for it. Ask Nick, if you wish. As far as he's capable of telling the truth, he'll corroborate my story. For that matter, you may ask Alicia as well. She's in Bradford."

"In Bradford?" I echoed. "I thought she was in France."

"She came with me to England. For obvious reasons, she didn't come all the way to Morton, and she's registered at the Bradford Inn under the name Mrs. Graves. Our family may be interesting, but there are certain situations that would be too awkward even for us."

I pondered this. The late-afternoon sunlight was fading, making the library look dim and grey. The air was stuffy too, and I felt as if Sir Peter and I had been closeted together for many hours.

"What do you want from me now?" I asked, glancing at the envelope on the table in front of me.

"Take it," he ordered, his tone changing as quickly as a flash of lightning.

I reached out slowly, but he didn't seem inclined to tease me with it this time. I took it and held it firmly in both hands.

"I want you to finish your work," he said. "When the new owner of Morton signs the necessary papers, you will carry out your duties as any conveyancer would so there are no difficulties with the title deed or other documents."

"Very well." I rose and took a step towards the door, but then stopped and turned back. "You said 'the new owner of Morton.' Did you mean 'when there is a new owner,' or has someone already made an offer?"

He smiled. "You'll find out soon enough."

His air of secrecy was maddening.

"If someone has made an offer," I said, trying to speak calmly, "Nick ought to be informed at once. He will need time to make arrangements to move elsewhere."

"*Nick?*" He smiled triumphantly as if he'd caught me in the act of committing a crime instead of merely using his brother's Christian name. "Tell me, Miss Springthorpe, what do you want from my brother? He'll never divorce Alicia, so marriage is out of the question. And he doesn't have enough of his own money to attract someone like you. Would it be enough for you just to share his bed?"

If I'd been a lady, no doubt I would have cried, "How dare you!" or made some other socially-acceptable expression of outrage. Instead, unsteady with shock and anger, I veered away from him and stumbled towards the library door.

He made no move to stop me but added calmly, "There's no need to take offence. I know you're not his mistress. I just thought you ought to know you have no hope of becoming that, either. Nick is very proud of his high moral standards, all the more to distinguish himself from me. You'll have better luck with almost any other man, despite your affliction."

If I could have slammed the heavy library door on my way out, I would have. I knew the faster I moved, the more awkward I looked, but all I could think about was getting away from him. I left the library and fled to my room, seeing nobody on the way there except a startled maidservant who had to leap out of my way.

I locked the door and sank into the armchair by the window, closing my eyes. My thoughts were whirling crazily in my head, and I pressed my fingers to my temples. Sir Peter's story about the sordid love triangle involving himself, Nick, and Alicia disturbed me, as did his accusations about Nick's somehow having had a hand in Frances's death. Part of me wanted to leave Morton and never look back. If only Joe would return and take me away with him.

But that wasn't true, either, not a reflection of my real feelings. With a guilty pang, I realized I'd hardly thought about Joe, aside from the mystery of his connection to Mrs. Wilson, since the night of our indoor picnic. That picnic seemed years instead of days ago. As unpleasant as Sir Peter's insinuations and insults had been, they forced me to be honest with myself. And being honest meant admitting that Nick was the only man I loved.

I couldn't admit it to anyone else, of course, and certainly not to Nick himself, but I was tired of denying my feelings, or, when that failed, trying to explain them away. My love for him had grown so quietly and gradually that I didn't know when it began. I worried about his health, cared too much about his opinions on every subject, and couldn't imagine my life without him. It was terrifying to realize how much power he had to affect my moods, my words, and my actions.

In short, I was miserable.

I couldn't understand why my heart was so perverse as to defy my mind, to overturn any shred of logic and reason. I did not want to love Nick. Not now. Not this way. If I could have trained my desires to seek Joe—or any other kind, available man—as their object, I would have. Or even better, train myself to have no desires at all.

And even though Sir Peter's words had helped me realize my true feelings, they also made it clear why I must not let Nick know what I felt for him. He was married, and just because he had kissed me in a moment of weakness didn't mean he had any serious intentions towards me. What had he meant when he said he could offer me nothing I would want? Was it a veiled invitation to become his mistress? Why couldn't he tell me plainly what he meant instead of speaking in riddles?

It was difficult to believe that Alicia was in Bradford. I had become accustomed to thinking of her as a ghost from Nick's past, not a real, living person. While I no longer thought she might be a corpse behind one of the locked doors in the house, my pet fancy about Nick as Bluebeard hadn't entirely dissipated. For one wild moment I convinced myself it was better for me that he was still married. Better to be Bluebeard's mistress than his wife.

"I've finally lost my mind," I said aloud. The bland green room seemed to silently accept the truth of this.

I took the envelope Sir Peter had given me and counted the bills as doggedly if my sanity depended on it. It was exactly half of what he owed me, just as he'd said.

I stayed in my room for the evening, pleading a headache when Betty knocked on the door to ask if I'd like dinner brought to me. I refused. I'd completely lost my appetite.

In the middle of the night I was awakened by the sound of a child crying. The sound made my stomach lurch, and everything in me wanted to ignore it. But then I realized that if it was coming from the wall behind Nick's room as it had done when I spent the night there, he would hear it too. If it was real and not a figment of my imagination, that is.

I got out of bed and put on my clothes. Taking a candle and a deep breath, I left my room and walked as quietly as possible down the corridor to Nick's room, but I was wearing my heavy shoes, so my progress wasn't very quiet at all.

I had been wrong about where the sound was coming from.

Now that I was in the corridor, the crying seemed to be coming from the stairs to the nursery, just as it had months ago when Nick was so ill and Mrs. Wilson had awakened me to ask for help.

Before I could decide whether or not to knock at Nick's door, it opened. He stood there, fully dressed and with his own candle, staring at me with a wild look, his hair dishevelled.

"Do you hear the crying?" he asked me.

"Yes. Are you going to the nursery?"

"Yes."

"May I come with you?"

"If you wish."

We walked together to the door leading to the second-floor stairs. The crying grew fainter, and I wondered again if we were looking in the right place. I looked back, towards Nick's room.

"Could there be a hidden room, a small one, attached to yours?" I asked. "When I was in your room the other night, I heard crying from the other side of the wall, behind your bed." I was still reluctant to admit that the child had talked to me, and especially reluctant to say her name.

"No," he said, "but there used to be a cupboard there when I was a child."

"Can we get to it?"

"Not from this floor, but there's a connection to it from the day nursery upstairs that might explain why it's so loud on this floor. I'll show you."

He opened the door to the staircase, then turned to me, his face flickering eerily in the light of our candles. "The stairs are steep, but perhaps if I hold your hand . . . ."

"If we hold hands, we can't carry both candles," I pointed out. "At least one of us must hold on to the balustrade, too."

"Let's take just the one candle, then. If you were to fall, I'd never forgive myself."

He went first, holding the candle in one hand and my hand in the other. With my free hand I held the balustrade, and we made slow progress up the uneven wooden stairs. Nick looked back to check on me every few steps.

An image rose unbidden to my mind, of Mrs. Wilson falling down the stairs in the east wing. Was it possible Nick could have arranged that accident? Were my feelings for him clouding my judgment so much that I too might be falling into a trap? I tightened my grip on the balustrade, which wasn't as sturdy as I'd hoped.

We managed to reach the top of the staircase, but by then the crying sound had ceased.

"Bloody hell," Nick muttered.

We stood on the landing for a moment. It was hard to catch my breath in the hot, stale air. I pushed a loose strand of hair out of my eyes and looked around.

On our left was the day nursery, a big, open room with cupboards, a large table in the middle, and a long window seat with cushions. Moonlight streamed through the windows, adding an eerie illumination to the smaller light of Nick's candle. On the right were two closed doors.

"Where do those lead?" I whispered, pointing to the closed doors.

"One used to be the night nursery when Peter and I were children. The other was a servant's room. There is nothing in them now, just old things nobody uses anymore." He went to the doors and opened them as if to prove to me that he wasn't lying. The doors swung open to reveal the evidence: old iron bedsteads, boxes, unidentifiable pieces of furniture.

There was no reason to whisper, but the oddly expectant quality of the silent room seemed to demand it. I would almost have preferred the crying sound.

"This is what I want you to see," Nick said, turning back to the big, open room. He pulled a small cupboard away from the wall and showed me what I never would have noticed on my own: a small door in the wall. It was about three feet square. I couldn't even see a way to open it until he reached underneath the bottom edge and pulled.

The door came open easily, and Nick said, "That's odd. As a child I used to have to work to open it: it was always sticking." Holding his candle inside the opening, he beckoned to me.

I knelt on the floor, trying to keep my fear at bay, and looked inside, trying to shake the horrifying possibility of finding a dead child there. But it was just an empty space that was very narrow. Despite my short stature, I knew I wouldn't fit. Only a small child could manage it.

"I still don't see how this could lead downstairs," I said.

"Look at the far end of the space, to the left."

I did so. There was a round opening there, smaller than the circumference of my head, but I would have needed to go inside the cramped space to see it properly.

"It's far too small," I said, leaning back and looking up at Nick.

"Not for a child. I spent a good deal of time in there when I was a lad. It was a wonderful hiding place. And that round opening leads down to the first floor: I have no idea what its original use would have been. What I remembered about it tonight is that I'd crawl into the larger space, pull the door to, and shout or even whisper into the opening, to frighten Peter. His room was next to mine when we were children, and when his bullying became more than I could take, I crept up here and made ghostly sounds to frighten him. That's all coming back to haunt me now, of course. Pun intended."

"Ah, you weren't always the innocent victim in those childhood stories, then," I said. "He must have been terrified indeed."

"I think he was." He smiled, but the next instant he was serious again. "Vaughan, I have a confession to make."

I stood up unsteadily.

"Let's open a window," he said. "The air is oppressive in here."

He walked to the window seat, picking his way around various toys—a rocking horse, a top, a loose deck of cards. Several marbles were scattered among the other toys. They looked exactly like the ones that had caused Mrs. Wilson's fall, and I shivered.

He set down his candle and struggled with the latch on the casement window. "Bloody thing hasn't been touched in years," he murmured. When he finally forced the window open, a breeze wafted in, cooling my parched skin.

We sat side by side on the window seat, close but not touching.

"What do you need to confess?" I asked.

"The other day, when you asked if I've heard the child crying lately, I said I hadn't. That was a lie. I've heard her speak, too. I just didn't want you to think me mad."

My relief made me light-headed. "I lied to you too. For the same reason."

"What did she say to you?"

"Her voice was muffled, so I couldn't hear everything she said, but she said, 'I can't get out.' I took that to mean she was trapped somewhere."

He was silent for a moment. "Did she say anything else?"

"She told me her name."

"What is it?"

I hesitated, then said, "Frances. That's another reason I didn't tell you."

He took my hand and squeezed it. "Don't worry. I've heard her, too, and she's told me the same things."

I clung to his hand as if it were a lifeline. "I've always refused to consider the existence of ghosts, and now it's the only explanation for this. Isn't it?"

"No. I don't believe that."

I turned to look at him. "Do you think there's a real child in this house, then?"

"No. I know every nook and cranny of this house, and since my health has improved, I've looked everywhere, even my childhood hiding places, but I've found nothing. And whoever is making these sounds can't be my daughter." With a tremor in his voice, he added, "I was with her when she died. Besides, if she had lived, she'd be sixteen now, not a child any longer."

I was surprised at this lapse in my own reasoning abilities: Frances's real age if she were alive had never occurred to me. "But," I stammered, "how do you explain the fact that you and I have both heard and spoken to this child, and she's told us the same things, including her name?"

"The only explanation is *folie á deux*."

"I don't understand."

"You and I are under a shared delusion. We both believe the same lie, and we both hear the same things that aren't real. It's been the same since you first came to Morton: even when we disliked each other, we both heard the same sounds. We're connected at a very deep level, you and I."

Our hands were still entwined. I wasn't convinced by his explanation of the child, but I couldn't deny the deep connection he spoke of.

Before I could reply, a loud sob burst out from a dark corner of the nursery, about twenty feet away. Nick and I sprang to our feet, and he stepped protectively in front of me to face the direction of the sound, holding his candle higher. There was a tall, ornate coat stand in the corner, and what looked like a pile of clothing at the foot of it.

"Who's there?" he demanded.

The only response was more sobbing, this time muffled but still coming from the same corner. Nick motioned for me to stay where I was and began to advance in the direction of the sound. I ignored his signal and followed him.

When we were about ten feet away, it was clear that what I'd mistaken for a pile of clothing was a huddled figure in a fluffy pink wrapper, her face hidden in her hands. A long blonde plait was coming loose over her shoulder.

"Show yourself." Nick spoke less sharply than before, but whatever shock or anxiety he felt lent a harshness to his voice. "Who are you?"

She shrank back.

"Nick, you're frightening her," I said. Stepping forward, I said softly, "We won't hurt you. Please stand up."

She slowly uncurled herself and rose to her feet.

It was Mrs. Dixon.

She looked small and vulnerable, almost like the child I was half-expecting to see. And for one wild moment I wondered if she had been the one making the childlike sounds ever since I'd arrived at Morton, that she'd somehow moved between Netherton and Morton unseen. But then I noted her height, which was average for a woman but taller than mine—she couldn't have fit in the hidden space Nick had just shown me—and the fact that her sobbing sounded nothing like the child's crying I'd been hearing at Morton.

"I'm sorry," she said, struggling to compose herself. "I didn't mean to startle you."

"What are you doing here?" Nick asked her. He had softened his tone, but he still sounded suspicious.

"I . . . I couldn't sleep," she began. "I had a vivid dream about the years I worked at Morton, and I remembered coming up here, to the nursery." Wiping her eyes with the back of her hand, she looked up at Nick nervously. "You were still a child, but too old for the nursery back then, so nobody used it, and I oughtn't to have been up here, then or now, but . . . it was a wonderful place to be alone and think.

"After my dream, I wanted to see it again, to . . . relive the happy memories. But when I came up here, I wasn't expecting the toys . . . especially the dolls. The things a little girl would have played with. Your daughter."

I heard Nick catch his breath.

"I lost a daughter too," she said, her voice breaking. "A year ago. Her name was Dora."

I realized that seeing the nursery must have finally forced her to accept the reality of her daughter's death, and I stepped towards her to take her hand, but there was something in it. She was holding a small cloth doll that wore a ballerina dress, and she held it out to Nick.

"I was going to take this," she said. "I don't even know why. It belongs to your daughter."

"Keep it," he said gruffly, turning away.

"I'm sorry," she said again.

She gave the doll to me, and before I could say anything, she fled through the dark nursery, by some miracle managing not to trip over any of the toys, and down the stairs.

Nick's back was to me, but I saw him make a furtive swipe at his eyes. He returned to the window-seat, and I gave him a moment before I followed and sat down beside him.

"Are you all right?" I asked.

"Yes. It's just . . . that poor woman. She has suffered a great deal."

"So have you." I set down the doll on the seat beside me, then crossed my arms tightly to resist the temptation to embrace him.

"I try not to think about the day Frances died, but being in the nursery and listening to Mrs. Dixon brought everything back."

I waited.

"Alicia came to see me that day," he said. "It was the first time she'd returned to Morton since she had left me about a year earlier, and she gave me no warning. She didn't want the servants to see her, so she waited at the east end of the property near the pond and sent word for me to bring Frances to her. I shouldn't have brought the child with me, but I thought— stupidly, as it turned out—Alicia would be more likely to return to me if she saw Frances."

"You were still in love with her," I said quietly.

"Yes. Idiot that I was, I thought there was still hope. She was dressed in high style, perfectly polished, and on her best behaviour. I ought to have known immediately that she wanted something. Frances was overjoyed to see her, of course, but I sent her to play nearby where I could keep an eye on her and speak privately with Alicia at the same time.

"I won't repeat the tortured conversation that followed, nor—thank God—do I remember all the details. Suffice it to say that she wanted to take Frances away with her, and I refused. My pride was hurt more than anything, and I proceeded to make insulting comments about her and her latest lover. That's when I found out she had been protecting Peter all along, and he had always been her only lover, or so she said."

Nick ran a hand through his hair. "Can you believe Alicia and I had been married for more than ten years at that time, but I'd never suspected she and Peter had been lovers for nearly the same length of time? I didn't believe her at first. But we had forgotten about Frances in the heat of our argument. Alicia was the first to notice her absence, and she began calling out for her."

He dropped his head into his hands. "Oh, God. This part is difficult to tell you."

I shivered. The room was still warm, but I had become ice cold.

"I wish I could forget what I told Alicia," he went on, his voice so quiet I could barely hear him. "I said, 'She'd be better off dead than with a mother like you.'" He let out a breath, his head sinking deeper into his hands.

The wave of coldness passed, and I no longer felt confused or afraid or nervous. I reached out and put my hand on his back, letting it rest there lightly.

He flinched a little, as if he had expected me to strike him. In a hoarse voice he continued, "Alicia and I must have both thought of the pond at the same time. I couldn't move at first, shocked by my own words. I watched her walk down the path towards the pond, first slowly, then picking up her skirts and running. It was too quiet in that beautiful place. No bird calls, no humming of insects, not even leaves rustling in the breeze.

"Then Alicia screamed. It freed me from my frozen state. I ran to the pond, knowing that my words, my curse, had done their work. Frances was . . . lying face-down on the surface, floating in the muddy water, one little shoe on a lily pad. I haven't been able to look at a lily pad since then—not even an image of one—without feeling nauseated."

He swallowed hard. "I dived into the pond, but I knew it was too late. When I pulled Frances out, Alicia took her from me, sobbing. I sat on the bank and watched them. My clothes must have been soaked and muddy, but I didn't notice. I felt no emotion, just a blank where my feelings had been."

My sympathy for him nearly made me forget myself and the resolve I had made only hours earlier. I moved as if to embrace him, then jerked away and stood up, pretending to examine the wallpaper, an impossible task in the candlelight. I clenched my hands, my fingernails digging into my palms.

For a while Nick was silent and unmoving behind me. Then he said in a low voice, "I ought not to have burdened you with this story."

I wanted to say he hadn't burdened me, that it meant more than he could imagine that he trusted me enough to tell me about that horrible day, but it would only lead to more dangerous intimacy between us. It was better to let him think me unaffected.

"Let's go downstairs," he said. We rose and went to the landing in silence. I couldn't ignore his outstretched hand, so I took it and we made our way down the stairs slowly—much too slowly for me, considering the effort it took to suppress my feelings.

Once we reached the bottom, I withdrew my hand and started to turn away.

"Vaughan, will you wait just a moment?" he said quietly.

I turned back but kept my eyes averted.

"Peter said something about you earlier this evening," he began.

My heart nearly stopped. "What did he say?" I asked, surprised into meeting his eyes.

It was Nick's turn to look away. "We haven't fooled him into thinking we're just acquaintances. He said things I won't repeat—things no lady ought to hear."

Dear God. Must I endure this torture? If Peter had told Nick the same things he said to me—particularly his implication that I would be only too happy to be Nick's mistress—I didn't want to hear it, especially from Nick.

"I wanted to mention it," he said, taking a step back, "only because it made me realize I haven't treated you with the respect you deserve. I'll do better from now on. But Peter knows now that we are . . . friends, and we needn't try to hide that."

Nick was standing stiffly against the wall in an almost military posture. He couldn't mean to humiliate me, so he must be trying to tell me obliquely that friendship was all he could offer me.

"Please don't say more. I understand you," I said quickly. "Good night."

I turned away, and this time he didn't try to stop me.

23

Sir Peter drove off in his motorcar the next morning and didn't return until late afternoon. He had asked Nick to make the arrangements for Mrs. Wilson's funeral, which kept Nick busy most of the day. I wished he could have a more pleasant task after what must have been an emotionally exhausting experience the night before. I was also concerned about Mrs. Dixon, who looked shaky and pale as she went about her housekeeping duties.

"Is there anything I can help you with?" I asked, intercepting her in the kitchen, where she was at the table poring over menus. It was a rare quiet moment between meals, with no other servants present.

"No, thank you." She smiled wanly up at me and returned her gaze to the papers on the table. "I shouldn't have gone to Netherton yesterday. I ought to have been here when Sir Peter arrived to welcome him properly, the way the owner of a grand house ought to be welcomed."

"You needn't worry about that. He received the welcome due to him. It was more important for you to take care of your child."

She looked startled. "What do you mean?" she asked, giving me a strangely suspicious look.

"Your son. Billy. Didn't you go to Netherton because of some trouble he was in at school?"

Her face relaxed. "Oh, yes, of course. He's fine. It was nothing. Would you like to see the menu I've planned for dinner this evening?"

I didn't, really, but I humoured her.

She told me we would have three courses served *á la russe*. The first two courses alone included green pea soup, salmon with lobster sauce, roast lamb, boiled capon with white sauce, and braised ham.

"It sounds delicious," I said, "but it's quite a lot for only three people, isn't it?"

"Perhaps, but I want to make up for my absence yesterday."

"I'm sure Sir Peter will understand."

She gathered up the menus and rose from the table. "I must get back to work. There's so much to do today."

"Don't you think you ought to rest?" I asked her. "Last night must have been difficult for you."

"Last night?" She looked at me blankly.

"In the nursery." I didn't want to cause her more pain, but I was baffled by her strange responses to what I thought were perfectly reasonable questions.

"Oh. That. I oughtn't to have been up there. I'll apologise to Mr. Spencer."

"No, that's not what I meant. It must have been difficult for you when you realized Dora was dead."

I realised with dismay that I was no better at comforting grieving people than I had been before my father died. Perhaps I was worse.

"You forget I'm used to death, Vaughan," she said in a calm, flat voice. "As a midwife, I've seen more than my share of it. Mothers dying in childbirth. Some of their wee babes, too, either born dead or dying within hours of the birth."

The horror of what she must have witnessed was sobering. I'd always thought of the work of a midwife as pleasant and joyful at best and tiring at worst. It hadn't occurred to me how sad it would be to see a mother or baby, or both, die despite one's best efforts. All the same, surely the deaths of other people's children would be quite different from losing one's own child, and I was puzzled by her lack of emotion. Perhaps she was simply exhausted and didn't want to think about upsetting subjects.

I left after extracting a promise that she'd ask me for help if she needed it, then went to my room.

When Sir Peter returned later that afternoon, he sent word that I was to dress for dinner. I considered ignoring his message and wearing my everyday blouse and skirt, but some perverse impulse made me choose the cream and gold dress. Perhaps it was because the last time I'd worn it, the night of the indoor picnic, was the last time I felt relaxed and happy. I'd been wearing the amber pendant since that night, too, underneath my clothes. I considered removing it because it would be exposed in this dress, but at the last minute I decided to leave it on.

In the dining room, two of Sir Peter's footmen, impeccable in blue livery, waited to serve us. Sir Peter sat at the head of the table, and Nick and I sat at his left and right, across from each other. Nick's black coat had seen better days and looked a little shabby next to the sheen of his brother's burgundy satin waistcoat. Nevertheless, I thought Sir Peter and his servants overdressed—laughably so, considering it was only a family dinner. And Nick always looked elegant, if a bit gaunt, no matter what he wore.

Just before the first course was served, the door opened and

Mrs. Dixon came in. She was wearing a dark blue silk dress, and her hair was plaited and wound round her head like a coronet. I was reminded of my first meeting with her when I'd thought she looked like a lost princess in a fairy tale.

Sir Peter exclaimed, "Rosie! What are you doing here?"

"I didn't have the chance to welcome you when you arrived," she said, apparently unsurprised by this extraordinary greeting. "I hope you'll forgive my absence yesterday and enjoy the special dinner I've planned."

He stared at her with a look I couldn't interpret, though confusion was certainly part of it. "How long have you been here?"

"I asked Mrs. Dixon to come here after Mrs. Wilson's accident," I interposed. "She kindly offered to take on the housekeeping duties and has been doing a splendid job."

"You ought to go home," Sir Peter said to her, abruptly but not unkindly.

"You ought to keep your promises," she said, quietly but firmly.

"Rosie, this is neither the time nor the place for such a discussion," he shot back with a flash of anger. "Go home."

Her face blanched and I could see her fighting back tears. Then with a stifled sob she ran from the room.

I rose to follow her, but Sir Peter said in an uncompromising tone, "Sit down, Miss Springthorpe."

I sat.

Looking at the footmen, he said, "You may serve the first course now."

"Wait," Nick said in an equally uncompromising tone. "I don't know what this is about, Peter, but if you don't go after that poor woman and apologise to her, I will. She has made herself indispensable here and you have no right to speak to her like that, much less order her to leave."

Nick rose from the table, placing his napkin beside his still-empty plate.

"Bloody hell," Sir Peter snapped. "I'll do it." He rose and left the room.

Nick sat down again and we exchanged equally baffled looks.

"They seem to know each other well," I observed.

"Indeed." Nick expression shifted from puzzled to suspicious.

Before we could discuss the situation further, Peter returned and sat down heavily in his chair, motioning to the servants to serve the first course.

"You were hardly gone long enough to speak to Mrs. Dixon," Nick said.

"I apologised to her," Sir Peter said, "and there's the end of the matter. It has nothing to do with you."

The two brothers stared each other down like two wild cats considering whether it was worthwhile to attack. Fortunately, they both seemed to decide in the negative, for Sir Peter applied himself vociferously to his meal, while Nick tapped a short, sharp rhythm on the table with the handle of his knife.

Nobody spoke for a while. I was glad I hadn't removed the amber pendant, because the only time during dinner that Nick didn't look grave and anxious was when I caught him looking at it. He met my eyes with the briefest of smiles, but it was enough to relax the tight knot of worry in my stomach.

"What will you do once you're finished your work at Morton, Miss Springthorpe?" Sir Peter asked between spoonfuls of pea soup.

"I haven't decided yet." I had been so caught up in the

Spencers' problems and the impending sale of the estate that I hadn't given much thought to my future. "I'll probably return to London and try to find conveyancing work there."

"You're really quite remarkable. An attractive woman with a head for business is a rarity."

I looked at him narrowly, not believing a word he said. He must have thought I'd appreciate the compliment, but to me it was empty flattery.

He seemed to be waiting for some response from me, and when I didn't reply, he shrugged and turned back to his soup.

The rest of the first course and most of the second passed in an uncomfortable silence. At least it was uncomfortable for me and for Nick, if the tension emanating from him was any indication. Sir Peter seemed merely intent on his meal.

As Sir Peter took a generous helping of roast lamb, he asked Nick, "Have you given any thought to what you'll do when Morton is sold?"

"No."

"If you want to return to politics—"

"I don't."

"Nevertheless, it might be useful for you to know I have a friend in London who's on good terms with Salisbury. He could help you. You'd give a whole new meaning to the term 'splendid isolation,' wouldn't you, Nick?" He laughed.

I had heard the words "splendid isolation" before in reference to England's foreign policy, but it meant nothing more to me. It was odd that Sir Peter knew his own brother so little as to suggest that he return to political life, but perhaps he had made the suggestion merely to antagonize Nick.

"What about a writing career?" Sir Peter persisted. "You used to write those satirical little essays for that student newspaper at Cambridge, didn't you? What was it called?"

Nick slammed his knife down on the table, making the dishes clatter. "I don't need your help, Peter."

"For the love of God, Nick, calm down. You're alarming the servants." Sir Peter waved them away. "We won't need anything else. You may go."

I was surprised. The third course hadn't been served yet. As Sir Peter wiped his mouth and set down his napkin, I felt uneasy enough to half-rise from my chair as if to leave, though I had no clear plan in my head.

"Sit down, Miss Springthorpe." Sir Peter's voice had lost its urbane smoothness. "I have an important announcement, and you must both hear it."

I was weary of being told to sit down, but I did so, anxious to hear the announcement.

Sir Peter rested his elbows on the table, bringing his fingers together in an arc. "I've found a buyer for Morton. His agent is coming with the papers tomorrow to complete the sale."

Tomorrow! I stared at Sir Peter in silent shock.

Nick shot to his feet, knocking over his water glass. "You bloody well ought to have prepared me for this."

"I didn't have time to write to you about it," Sir Peter said placidly, "so I'm telling you now. You've known for months I was planning to sell the property, so I don't know what you're so upset about."

I watched the water from Nick's overturned glass seep into the tablecloth, making a dark stain on the red fabric.

"You ought to have told me as soon as the buyer made an offer," Nick snapped.

Sir Peter shrugged. "I don't see what difference that would make. You can't stop the sale. Miss Springthorpe tried her best to convince me to compromise with you, but to no avail. I hope you appreciate her efforts. In truth, she's made an admirable effort to try to please both of us."

Nick looked at me as if he'd forgotten I was there. "There's no need for you to stay, Vaughan. This is between me and Peter."

"I'm not finished with Miss Springthorpe yet," Sir Peter interjected.

Nick slowly sat down again, looking dazed.

"Do you want your full salary?" Sir Peter asked me.

"I beg your pardon?" I said.

"Can I trust you to finalize the paperwork when the buyer's agent comes tomorrow? If you make a single mistake or refuse to complete the process, you won't receive the rest of the money."

I looked at Nick, who was staring at the tablecloth.

"Miss Springthorpe?" Sir Peter prompted.

I tore my eyes away from Nick's face and said in a choked voice, "I'll complete the work you asked me to do."

"I'm pleased to hear it," said Sir Peter. "Now, where were we with dinner? I'll ring the bell for our third course."

I couldn't even think of eating another bite. The food I'd already eaten, little as it was, was churning unpleasantly in my stomach. But I didn't want to leave Nick alone with his brother, not when he was so upset.

As if he'd read my mind, Nick said gently, "Leave us, Vaughan."

I didn't wait for Sir Peter's permission. I excused myself and left the room.

For a few minutes I hovered outside the dining room doors, unsure what to do and worried about the argument that would likely ensue between Sir Peter and Nick. Sir Peter was a large man, and Nick had so recently been ill, he could easily be overpowered by his brother. Should I stay close by in case Nick needed me? I listened for raised voices, but all was quiet within, and it occurred to me that I'd overlooked another way I might be able to help Nick.

I went to the library, lit the lamps, and surveyed the bookshelves. Nick had said he and Bedford had searched every book several times over for the amended will, but perhaps I would notice something they had missed. I went to the corner where the largest books and some maps were kept and began to sort through them. I was careful to turn every page and slide my fingers along the inside covers in case the will had become stuck inside.

As I searched, I thought about the story Nick had told me about the amended will and the night his father died. If he and Bedford had searched the library so many times, it seemed unlikely that the will was still there. Someone in the house that night must have taken it. It could have been Mrs. Wilson, who could no longer be questioned about it, but it also could have been Alicia Spencer. Nick had said she'd been feeling poorly and stayed in her room, but it was possible that she had left her room long enough to witness Bedford hiding the will. She and Peter would already have been lovers, so she would have had a motive to take it.

The more I thought about it, the more it seemed likely that Alicia either had the amended will or knew where it was. And it was my duty as a lawyer to ask her about it. All it would take was a trip to Bradford and a hopefully short conversation, but the very thought of meeting Nick's wife face to face made my stomach churn all over again. I had allowed my feelings for

Nick to interfere with my work, but it wasn't only my duty as a lawyer to speak to Alicia Spencer: it was my duty to him as well. If his father's intention was for Nick to inherit Morton, he ought to have it.

But the thought of even writing to Alicia Spencer was so unpleasant that I brushed it away. It was still possible that the will was in the library. After I had checked the largest books, I moved on to the middle shelves and began working more quickly, flipping the pages as Nick had done but trying to place the books neatly on the floor instead of letting them fall.

I lost track of time. I might have been in the library for an hour, perhaps two, but I was so intent on my task I didn't notice. My back began to ache after a while, so I sat on the floor, careless of my best dress.

"Vaughan?" It was Nick's voice. He was standing several few feet away, looking worried. "What are you doing? How long have you been here?"

I looked around me. I was surrounded by a sea of books and a wall of half–empty bookshelves. I had forgotten to put away the books I was finished with and merely kept removing them. A few heavy books lay on my skirt, pinning it down.

"I was looking for the amended will," I said, dazed. "I thought perhaps I might find something you and Bedford missed. Fresh eyes, you know."

Nick picked up the books at his feet, making his way towards me book by book. When he reached me, he removed the books from my skirt and helped me up. I was still holding the last tome I'd taken from the shelf.

"You've done enough," he said quietly, taking the book from me and setting it on top of the nearest pile. "It's time I accepted that the will won't be found and Morton will never be mine."

"How will you bear it?" I said. "Morton is everything to you."

"No, Vaughan." He reached out to place his palm against my cheek and gave me a look that made me tremble from head to foot. "*You* are everything to me. I love you."

He took my face in his hands and kissed my forehead, my eyelids, my cheeks, and finally, my mouth.

I was too stunned to register what was happening at first, but soon his kisses ignited the same passion in me as the first time, and I slipped my arms around his waist and leaned into him, giving myself up to his caresses.

When we finally stopped for breath, he gazed down at me with fierce intensity, and brushed a loose strand of hair out of my eyes.

"I've been a fool," he said. "I ought to have told you how I felt months ago."

"Months ago?" I echoed, amazed.

"Yes. I fell in love with you the first evening we read poetry together in the library. You were trying so hard not to be moved by that Wordsworth poem. You were utterly adorable."

"I didn't know."

"I didn't want you to know. I didn't want to fall in love or even care about anyone. For years I successfully avoided people and stayed hidden behind locked doors. If anyone came near Morton, I found ways to frighten them away, as you know."

"You couldn't frighten me away."

"No, thank God." He tightened his arms around me. "I've been fighting my feelings for a long time. I wasn't sure what you felt for me, either."

"Didn't you notice my response the first time you kissed me?"

"Ah, that." He smiled down at me. "Yes, but I took you by surprise, didn't I? You're a passionate woman, and you might have been confused."

"I *was* confused," I admitted. "I didn't realize until yesterday how much I love you."

His eyes filled with tears. "You don't know what it means to me to hear you say that," he said. "For a long time I assumed you loved Joe. How could I think anything else? The two of you seemed so comfortable together, and I didn't think I would fare well in any comparisons you might make between us. Only after that kiss did I allow myself to hope—"

I interrupted him by kissing him again, and he pulled me closer in a hungry, all-consuming embrace. He moved from my lips to my neck, trailing hot kisses down to the deep neckline of my dress, brushing aside the amber pendant to kiss the hollow between my breasts. I seemed to have forgotten how to breathe.

The only thing that brought me to my senses was remembering Sir Peter's insults and the fact that Nick was a married man. With some difficulty I extricated myself from his embrace and took a step back.

"Where are you going?" He caught my hand. "You can't leave me now."

"I'm not going anywhere. But I can't think when I'm so close to you."

He laughed. I hadn't heard such a sound from him before— a laugh of pure delight, a youthful laugh. It was incredible to me that I'd ever thought him old or sick or unattractive. He seemed as strong and virile as a man half his age.

"I'm glad of that," he said. "Stay and talk to me for a while longer. We have much to talk about."

I agreed, remembering that we were still standing in a sea of books with the library lamps blazing. We put out all the lamps except one, then went to our usual armchairs by the fireplace. Nick pushed the chairs together, and we sat with clasped hands, looking into each other's eyes.

"I have so little to offer you," he said. "I'm not young or wealthy or handsome, and my health is indifferent—good God, it's hardly to be imagined that you would accept me. I do expect to have enough means for us to live modestly in London, but I'll need time to establish myself in some profession."

I was confused. "We will live together? You and I?"

"I believe that's the generally accepted practice. Don't you want to? I know I can be difficult, but I hope I'm not impossible to live with."

I just looked at him, my brow furrowed. Was he asking me to be his mistress?

"Forgive me," he said. "I haven't made myself clear. I can't in good conscience ask you to marry me when I'm not free, but I will as soon as I divorce Alicia."

"But . . . are you certain you don't still love her, even a little?"

"Love her?" he exclaimed. "Why in the world would you think such a thing?"

"Because you wouldn't grant her a divorce when she wanted one. And because of her room." Seeing his blank look, I added, "The way her room is kept for her just the way it was when she left."

"You can't possibly have seen her room the way it was back then," he said. "It's the mineral room now: I had everything of hers removed years ago."

"Oh. I thought the room next to yours was her room. The one with the pink and white wallpaper."

Comprehension dawned on his face. "That was Frances's room. Some of Alicia's things are in there, now that I think of it. They seemed to comfort Frances after Alicia left. I feel like a coward to admit it, but I haven't been able to go into that room since Frances died."

"Then Mrs. Wilson lied to me." I tried to remember what she had said about the room, but I realized that I'd simply assumed it was Alicia's and she hadn't contradicted me.

"My poor girl, is that what's been troubling you?"

"Yes, a little. But it wasn't just the room. After all these years, you didn't divorce her, so I thought you must still have feelings for her."

"My refusal to divorce her was pure spite on my part, at least for the first few years. But I was also worried about the scandal it would cause, as well as losing the money she brought to our marriage. I'm not proud of the way I acted, but I've told you the truth. Do you understand?"

"Yes."

"Now that we've disposed of her, what else is troubling you?"

I doubted it would be so easy to dispose of Alicia, but there were other matters even less easily settled.

"What of Morton?" I asked. "Can you be happy in London, away from it?"

"I have no choice, do I? There. So much for Morton. What else?"

But a shadow passed over his face, just a flicker, that betrayed him. It wouldn't be easy for him to let Morton go, not even now.

"I must speak with Joe," I said.

Nick looked at me intently. "What are you going to tell him?"

"I can't break off an engagement that doesn't exist, but I'll tell him I can't marry him, of course. He is a good man, and I don't want to hurt him more than is necessary."

"Of course you don't."

We talked more about the events of the past week and the ways we had misunderstood each other. He told me that his uncertainty about my feelings and his long-held belief that he must remain married to Alicia to keep up appearances had held him back from declaring his love to me. He assured me that his conversations with Sir Peter about me, far from making me cheap in his eyes, gave him hope that I loved him, and he saw my ensuing evasions and attempts to suppress my feelings for what they were. Finally, seeing me in the library searching for the amended will for his sake had removed the last of his inhibitions.

When the grandfather clock in the corridor chimed midnight, I rose to my feet, exclaiming, "Is it so late? I must read over the papers for tomorrow, then go to bed. It will be a long, difficult day, and we both need our sleep."

"Yes, it will be difficult, but I can bear anything if you're with me." He rose too and slipped his arm around my waist. "Kiss me again before we part."

We shared a gentle, lingering kiss, more subdued than the last, as if we were both afraid of allowing ourselves to go too far.

Despite the late hour, when I went to bed I couldn't sleep. I lay awake thinking how amazing it was that the man I loved was just as much in love with me. This knowledge was strong enough to lull me into a sense of hopefulness and confidence that Nick and I could surmount whatever difficulties lay ahead.

24

When I awoke the next morning, my fears and general sense of uneasiness had returned. Never having been in love before, I didn't know if it was normal to feel so vulnerable, as if the slightest change in my circumstances or in Nick's opinion of me would be devastating. And as much as I loved him, I didn't know if I could put my life and my future in another person's hands. It felt rather like being on a train that had jolted off the tracks and was hurtling down a ravine.

Adding to my unease was my inability to ignore the likelihood that Alicia Spencer knew something about the amended will. I couldn't allow myself to become so caught up in my feelings that I shirked my duty as a lawyer. Thus, I forced myself to write her a note asking for a meeting at her hotel in Bradford the next morning. I told her the meeting was about the sale of Morton and asked her to keep both my note and the meeting confidential. I addressed her as Mrs. Spencer in the note, but I remembered just in time that Sir Peter had mentioned she was registered at the hotel as Mrs. Graves, so I used that name on the envelope.

I had slept late, and I was glad that nobody else was in the breakfast room when I went in. I didn't think I could behave casually in Nick's presence, and I had no desire to make conversation with Sir Peter. As soon as I'd eaten, I went outside, feeling the need for fresh air and solitude. I was unlikely to be intruded upon in the rose garden, so I went there and sat on the wrought-iron bench. But I hardly noticed the beauty of the roses or the fresh morning air because I was trying so hard to avoid imagining Alicia Spencer. Even though I knew Nick loved me, I feared that meeting her would lead to no good.

The intertwined initials of Nick and Alicia set in iron on the bench were digging into my back. I compressed my lips and rose to my feet, deciding that I'd be better off in the library preparing for what was bound to be a difficult meeting with Sir Peter, Nick, and the buyer's agent.

Before I had a chance to leave the garden, I heard the sound of a dog's bark nearby. A moment later—for I had left the gate open—Welkin bounded into the rose garden. Joe must have returned. I felt a mixture of emotions at the thought of seeing him again—curiosity, pleasure, trepidation. He had been away for only a week, but so much had happened since I saw him last that it felt like months.

I reached out to pat the dog, who was nearly jumping out of his skin with delight. "Welkin, you great big silly thing! I'm ever so glad to see you." I scratched his ears, looking at the open gate. "Where's your master? He must be here somewhere."

Strangely, I didn't see Joe, even when I left the rose garden and retraced my steps back to the house, Welkin at my side. The dog stopped obediently some ten yards from the house, and I went in alone. Bedford was still absent from his post at the front door.

As I made my way through the great hall, I saw a familiar tall frame just outside the drawing room.

"Joe, is that you?" I asked. "What are you doing in the shadows?"

He took a step towards me. "Vaughan, I'm glad to see you." His words were at odds with the pinched, tense tone of his voice. It was so unlike him to be anything but relaxed and comfortable that I was instantly alarmed.

"What's the matter?"

He took my hand and squeezed it, then said in a low voice, "I need to talk to you."

But he could say no more, for the drawing-room door opened and Sir Peter emerged. "There you are," he said to Joe. "Come in. You too, Miss Springthorpe. We're just waiting for my brother."

My mind seemed to stop, then start again slowly, like a defective machine. Why did Sir Peter want the gardener present? And where was the buyer's agent? I stared at Joe.

"Do sit down," Sir Peter said, settling himself in a large armchair, pulling out his pocket watch, and tapping it repeatedly with one finger.

Joe and I sat side by side on the sofa. I gave him a worried sidelong glance. He was staring at the floor and his shoulders were slumped forward.

A moment later, Nick strode into the room. He headed towards an armchair opposite to his brother's, but when he saw Joe he stopped short and asked, "What are you doing here?"

Joe slowly raised his head but looked at the curtains instead of Nick. He didn't speak.

I knew what Sir Peter would say before he said it. "I told you the buyer's agent would be here today."

Nick remained standing in the middle of the room. He looked at me. "Did you know?"

I shook my head mutely.

"Have you brought the papers?" Sir Peter asked Joe.

"Yes." Finding his voice at last, but still not looking at me or Nick, Joe reached inside his jacket, took out a sheaf of papers, rose, and handed them to Sir Peter.

The frozen silence was broken only by the sound of papers being shuffled.

"Well, everything seems to be here," Sir Peter said, "but of course Miss Springthorpe must confirm that." He held out the papers to me. "Tell me if Lord Brakehurst has signed all the necessary papers and if everything is in order."

I didn't move. Instead I said, "First I'd like an explanation of how your gardener came to be the buyer's agent. No doubt Mr. Spencer would appreciate an explanation as well."

"Certainly." Sir Peter gave me a condescending smile, put the papers on his lap, and looked at Joe. "Would you like to tell them or shall I?"

"May I speak to them alone first?" Joe asked. His manner was so unlike him, so cowed and small and weak, that I was shocked.

"Come, come," said Sir Peter in a tone of forced joviality. "This family has so many secrets already. Isn't it time to be frank with one another?"

"Oddly enough, I agree with my brother," said Nick with brittle emphasis. "Let us have no more secrets." He sat down in the armchair across from Sir Peter's, arms crossed.

After a pause, during which it became apparent Joe would not be forthcoming, Sir Peter said, "It's really very simple. I'm not so stupid as to hire a legal assistant sight unseen without arranging for someone I trust to be my eyes and ears. Especially when I knew very well that Nick, no matter how ill he pretended to be, would try to prevent the sale of the estate. Joe has worked for me in the past, and I knew he'd be more than capable of carrying out a variety of tasks for me."

"I knew it," Nick snapped. "I told Vaughan he wasn't what he seemed." To Joe he said, "I suppose you were laughing behind my back. I ought to have known you were nothing but a damnable spy."

"No." Joe looked at Nick and said evenly, "I'm a gardener. That's all I've ever wanted to be. I didn't lie to you."

"A sin of omission is still a sin," said Nick.

"Let him explain," I said quietly.

Nick gave me a piercing look. It was natural for him to be on edge, given the situation, but was this how we were going to support each other? Had our words of love the previous evening meant nothing?

"This is all very fascinating," Sir Peter interjected smoothly, sitting back and lacing his fingers over his brocade waistcoat. "It reminds me that Joe omitted quite a lot, though, in his letters to me. I suppose that's a compliment to the two of you. He didn't mention how . . . er, close you've all become, or your miraculous recovery, Nick."

Joe took a deep breath and turned to me. "I told him nothing personal, nothing that didn't relate to the sale of Morton."

"But the sale of Morton *is* personal," said Nick. "What benefit did you gain from it, Joe? That's what I want to know. Was it the money? Has Peter paid you well?"

Joe stared at his feet. I wished he would do something, be the man of action I had always thought him, instead of this guilty, quiet, creeping stranger.

"Lord Brakehurst has offered Joe a position he would be a fool to refuse," Sir Peter said. "He'll be the head gardener here, supervising a staff of fifteen under-gardeners. He'll be able to realize his plans for Morton's grounds, something he couldn't do with the small salary I've been paying him."

"I've heard enough," Nick said. He rose to his feet, adding to Sir Peter, "I assume you wanted me here just to witness your dramatic announcement. You'll excuse me if I don't applaud." He left the room.

"I haven't accepted Lord Brakehurst's offer," Joe said. "In fact, I've already started working as head gardener at another great house near Manchester."

"What are you talking about?" Sir Peter demanded. "They can't possibly have offered you as much as Lord Brakehurst has."

Joe didn't reply.

"Isn't it time you looked at these papers, Miss Springthorpe?" Sir Peter said, holding them out to me again.

I took them but set them down on the sofa beside me. "I need more time," I said, trying not to sound as desperate as I felt.

"What on earth for?"

I hesitated. I couldn't allow the sale of the estate to go forward without seeing Alicia first, but I couldn't tell Sir Peter that.

"I believe there may be a problem with the title," I said.

Sir Peter's eyebrows shot up. "When did this occur to you?"

"Earlier this morning."

"You've had several months to prepare the papers for this sale, Miss Springthorpe," he said sharply. "Either you are incompetent, or you are lying."

Being thought incompetent made my hackles rise enough that I almost admitted to lying. Catching myself before I could do so, I said as calmly as I was able, "The relevant file was in the wrong folder, so I didn't see it until today. I assure you I'll do everything I can to clear up the matter quickly."

Sir Peter looked at me appraisingly. Joe shifted in his seat and looked at me too, his eyes troubled.

"How quickly?" Sir Peter asked.

"By tomorrow afternoon. I promise you'll know everything then."

There was a brief silence. Then Sir Peter leaned towards me and said, "Very well, Miss Springthorpe. But you'll have twenty-four hours and not one minute more. And if I find out you've been lying to me, you'll be sorry. Very sorry." The menace in his tone and bearing made me believe him.

"Don't speak to Vaughan that way," Joe said firmly.

Before Sir Peter could reply, Joe took my hand and said, "You ought to know I've asked her to marry me."

A look of amazement appeared on Sir Peter's face. Then he laughed, loud and long.

Joe's expression became stony, and his grip on my hand tightened.

As soon as Sir Peter managed to control himself enough to speak, he wiped his eyes with his handkerchief and said, "Then you took my instructions too far, my boy. And you," he added, turning to me, "have played the seductress to good effect. A crippled solicitor's daughter managing to secure the . . . er, affections of not one but two men above her station . . . yes, that's impressive. I say, Joe, she's good enough for a dalliance, but more than that, I think not."

Two men above my station? Joe wasn't above my station. Perhaps the romantic atmosphere of Morton had addled my brain, but I expected Joe to knock Sir Peter down for insulting me. Instead, Joe released my hand, looking at me in confusion and said, "Two men? Who—"

This was neither the time nor the place to discuss my feelings for Nick. If Joe wouldn't stand up for me, I would. "Joe is a gardener," I said to Sir Peter. "He's hardly above me."

Sir Peter laughed again. "It seems even a clever woman can be slow to understand some things. Joe may wish to be only a gardener, but his pedigree is better than that."

I looked from Sir Peter to Joe and back again as an awful realization began to seep into my mind. Was it possible? Sir Peter's strangely familiar mannerisms—the way he held his head and moved his hands when he talked—were indeed similar to Joe's. But surely Joe was too old and Sir Peter too young . . .

"Is it so difficult to believe that Joe is my son?" Sir Peter said.

I kept looking from one to the other, though Joe had averted his face. They were both tall men with large frames, and I could imagine Joe looking very like Sir Peter in middle age if he lived a dissipated life and had no physical work to keep him fit. Most importantly, if Sir Peter was Joe's father, it explained the emotional interaction between Sir Peter and Mrs. Dixon in the dining room the previous day.

"You're a practical, grown-up woman, Miss Springthorpe," Sir Peter said, "not a sheltered girl just out of the schoolroom, so I assume the facts of the situation won't bring on an attack of the vapours."

"Go on," I said.

"I was only seventeen when I met Rosie," he continued. "I was besotted with her, but she was just a lower servant. Foolish boy that I was, I even entertained the idea of marrying her, but my father was understandably against the idea. Except for my father, nobody in my family knew about Rosie and me, and when she became pregnant, my father sent me to the Continent for what he called an early Grand Tour and arranged for her to marry John Dixon. He turned out to be a bad husband—"

"He was worse than a bad husband," Joe interjected with a frown.

"That wasn't my fault," Sir Peter said. "I pity Rosie, of course. She's had a difficult life, but my father was right to prevent us from marrying. I never forgot about the child, though. I saw him for the first time when he was about eight or nine—do you remember, Joe?"

"Yes." Joe's expression remained grim.

"He looked very like me at that age. I decided that, with Spencer blood in his veins, Joe could do great things in the world. I ensured that he would be well educated so he could work in any field—politics, the law, the church."

"You were the bachelor uncle," I said, half to myself.

"Well, he couldn't call me his father, could he?" Sir Peter shrugged. "Despite his education, Joe wanted to be just a gardener. So I've done my best to arrange opportunities for him. Naturally, I wish to see him do well in life."

"Nick ought to know about this," I said.

"If he hadn't stormed out of the room, he would have heard everything." Sir Peter stood up abruptly. "As much as I've enjoyed our little chat, it's time to let you clear up the problem with the title, Miss Springthorpe. Or have you already forgotten about it?"

"Of course not," I said, "but I'd like to speak to Joe alone for a few minutes."

"Very well," Sir Peter replied. He gave Joe a stern look. "You'd do well to ensure that Miss Springthorpe keeps her word to me. I hope I don't have to remind you what's at stake if you defy me."

"You don't," Joe said, his face blank.

"Good." Sir Peter left the room.

Anxious to waste no time finding out Joe's side of the story, I turned to him, but I was disconcerted by the sight of Sir Peter's features in his face and was momentarily struck dumb.

"Please don't look at me like that," he said, looking pained.

"What do you expect? It's quite a shock."

"I know. But I'm still the same man you know. I'm still Joe Dixon. And I'm not Sir Peter's puppet."

I wasn't convinced. "How could you betray Nick like this? You pretended to be his friend, and you know how much he loves Morton. To have a hand in taking the place away from him—I hadn't thought you capable of it."

"You don't know the whole story," he countered. "My family owes Sir Peter everything. He paid for my education. He paid for our house. He's been supporting our family ever since that monster John Dixon died. If I were the only person involved, I'd be willing to walk away from Sir Peter, but my family is dependent on his goodwill and his money. My mother has had two serious nervous illnesses, and in both cases he paid for her treatment in Switzerland.

"Besides," Joe added, looking earnestly into my face, "I haven't done everything he wanted me to do. I told him nothing about you or Nick that was personal, as I said. And Nick knew the estate would be sold. I've done nothing to hurry the process, and there's nothing I can do to stop Sir Peter from doing as he likes with his own property."

He took my hand. "I'm doing this to make a good life for us, too. The position I've been offered in Manchester comes with a lower salary than what Lord Brakehurst has offered me, but it's something I achieved on my own, and I can be proud of it. Vaughan, you will marry me, won't you?"

25

W hat's the matter?" Joe asked when I didn't respond.
"Surely this business about the sale of the estate
doesn't affect your feelings for me."

But I was thinking of what Sir Peter had said to Joe about
taking his instructions too far and the way Joe had flirted with
me from the beginning of my time at Morton. I pulled my hand
out of his grasp.

"Did Sir Peter tell you to flirt with me when I first arrived at
Morton?" I asked him.

"You don't understand," he said.

"That's not an answer."

"Very well. Yes, he did, but I didn't feel right about it. And
I developed real feelings for you quite early. When I kissed you
that first time, I already thought we'd be a good match."

I didn't know whether to believe him or not. "I can't think
of marriage right now," I said stiffly, "not when Morton is about
to be sold and there is so much to do in such a short time."

"But you do love me." He tried to make it a statement
instead of a question, but his tone fell somewhere between the
two.

"Joe . . ." I struggled to find the right words. "I care for you,
but . . . my feelings are those of a sister, not a wife."

He looked astonished. "Is it my position? Is the idea of being a gardener's wife degrading to you? Or is it finding out I'm Sir Peter's bastard son? I'm not proud of that." There was more than a hint of bitterness in his voice.

"No. Naturally, I'm surprised and disappointed by what I've learned about you today, but it hasn't changed my feelings." I laid my hand on his arm briefly. "And there would be nothing degrading in marrying you."

After a brief silence, Joe lifted his head and looked at me. "Sir Peter said something about your securing the affections of two men. Who is this other man?"

I was surprised that Joe didn't seem to have any idea who the other man might be. He knew how isolated Morton was—surely Nick was the only possibility. I tried to think of some way to evade his question. I had no desire to hurt him, and perhaps knowing the truth would upset him so much that he would make things worse for Nick.

"Tell me the truth," Joe said. "Are you in love with someone else?"

I bit my lip, then said, "Yes."

"Who?"

"Nick."

"Nick!" He stared at me. "But he's married. And old." In Joe's eyes was all the incredulity of a robust, attractive young man who had never imagined he could have a rival fourteen years his senior.

"He's only forty," I said. "And he's going to divorce his wife."

"Is that what he told you?"

"Joe—"

"I don't blame you," he said. "You've had little experience with men. But you can't tell me you have no doubts about his promises, not when his love for his wife is practically a legend around here. You're the only woman he's seen in years—no doubt he feels some attraction to you, but he's probably confused. You both are."

I tried to tell myself that Joe's shock and jealousy were making him say these things and there was no truth in them. But of course I had doubts. How could I not? My feelings for Nick were so new, our mutual understanding so recent, it seemed as though nearly anything could damage it.

"When you're away from Morton, you'll be able to think clearly," Joe continued, speaking slowly as if to an imbecile. "You'll see that Nick and this place have cast a spell on you. It's not real, Vaughan. Whatever you think you feel for Nick, it's not solid, not like what you and I have. Don't make the mistake of choosing an illusion over reality."

I saw no point in arguing with him when he was so convinced of my blindness. "I can't talk about this right now. I need to focus on the sale of the estate."

"Very well." He hesitated. "If there really is a problem with the title, I hope you can resolve it soon. Sir Peter can be unpleasant when he's crossed, and I don't want you to get hurt just because of this ridiculous estate business."

"This ridiculous estate business is my work." I tried not to sound as if I were chiding him, but I resented his overprotectiveness. Had he always been this way, or was he trying to prove how much he cared about me now that he knew he had a rival?

"I know," he said, "but I think I can safely say I know the Spencer family better than you do, and it'll be better for you not to become caught in their complicated relationships with one another and with this estate."

"So I should follow your example, then?" I couldn't help twisting the dagger just a little.

To his credit, he gave me a wry smile instead of becoming defensive. "No. Learn from my mistakes. Speaking of which . . . I need to see my mother. Do you know where she is?"

I realized that I hadn't seen Mrs. Dixon since her emotional exit from the dining room the day before.

"No," I said. "She's probably in her room, or in the kitchen. I'll help you find her."

As Joe and I made our way through the great hall to the back of the house, he muttered, "She shouldn't be here."

This was exactly what Sir Peter had said, and I was puzzled. "Why? She seems to love Morton."

"This place isn't good for her. I think she's spent too much time imagining what her life would have been like if she'd married Sir Peter and was the mistress of Morton."

"If her life with John Dixon was as terrible as you implied, can you blame her?"

"It was. And I don't. But it's still better for her to be in her own home."

"Some good things have come of her presence here," I ventured. "The other day she was in the nursery, and seeing Frances Spencer's toys helped her accept Dora's death. She knows your sister isn't coming back now. And Mrs. Wilson apologised before she died, so they had the chance to reconcile."

Joe stopped dead at the kitchen doorway. "What did you say?"

I didn't know which of my words he wanted me to repeat, so I just looked up at him in surprise.

"What did Mrs. Wilson apologise for?" he asked.

"I don't know, exactly. She wanted to speak to you, but your mother said she apologised to her instead, for some wrong she'd done to your family."

"I hear my son's voice!" Mrs Dixon called from within, and a second later she emerged from the kitchen, all smiles, to embrace Joe.

He returned the embrace, then pulled away so he could examine her face. "Mam, are you all right?" he asked.

"I'm fine, dear, but I missed you. You were in Manchester far too long."

I was relieved to see Mrs. Dixon looking composed, but it was strange to think of her and Sir Peter having been lovers. I wondered if she knew about Alicia.

"I know," Joe said. "I'm sorry. Are you ready to go home now? I can wait for you to pack your things."

She shook her head. "I can't go home now. I'm needed here."

"One of Sir Peter's servants can take over Mrs. Wilson's duties," he insisted. "And you're needed at home: Johnny can't care for Billy and David on his own much longer."

"All right," she said slowly, "but not today. I'm far too busy with dinner preparations, and I'll need to leave instructions for the staff. I'll go home tomorrow."

"I'll take care of the boys today, then, but I'll be back at three o'clock tomorrow to fetch you," Joe said firmly.

She agreed to this, and I left them, all too aware of the fact that the precious twenty-four hours Sir Peter had given me to complete my work were already slipping away.

A note came for me by the afternoon post from Alicia Spencer, in which she agreed to a meeting at her hotel the next morning. The note was brief, but I re-read it several times, as if it contained everything I needed to know about her. Her handwriting was elegant and feminine, with sweeping lines and loops. Was she the flighty, spoiled woman Mrs. Wilson had made her out to be? Was she so loyal to Sir Peter that she wouldn't tell me the truth about the amended will even if she knew where it was? If my trip to Bradford turned out to be fruitless, I was making myself anxious for nothing and making Sir Peter needlessly suspicious of me and my motives.

Hours went by as I sat at the desk in the library pretending to work, but I had nothing to show for them except tense shoulders and an aching back. Only gradually did I become aware of how quiet the house was. I didn't hear the usual footsteps of servants, the clatter of trays, or even muffled voices. Was I completely alone in the house?

I wondered where Nick was. Was he still so angry with Peter and Joe that he was refusing to speak to anyone? Although I could sympathize with him, I hadn't the patience to coax him out of his room. He could seek me out if he wished to see me. Whatever anger he felt with the others, surely he had nothing against me, especially after what had passed between us the previous evening.

Twice I left the library and peered down the corridor in the west wing. The first time I saw nobody. The second time I thought I saw a shadowy figure near the stairs to the nursery, but it moved out of sight so quickly that I couldn't be certain it was a person or just a trick of my imagination. I hoped it wasn't Sir Peter: I didn't like the idea of him standing in the corridor of the otherwise empty house, knowing I was in the library. Waiting for me to make a mistake.

My sense that I was alone in the house persisted, though I found Betty and Sir Peter's cook in the kitchen and decided to eat my dinner there. I asked where Mrs. Dixon was, and they said she was packing her things in preparation to return to Netherton the next day, but when I went to her door and knocked, there was no answer. I went in search of Nick then, but he was nowhere to be found. Bedford was just as impossible to locate, which was the strangest thing of all. Whatever mysterious appearances and disappearances might happen in the house, Bedford was always there.

I felt unnerved as well as trapped in the house. It had been a hot day, and the air indoors was oppressive and stale. Unable to bear the thought of returning to the library or to my room, I left the house. The cool evening air was a welcome relief, and now that I was outside I couldn't imagine ever going back in. I wandered among the hedges at the back of the house. After a while I sat on the bench by the broken fountain, facing the headless statue instead of sitting with my back to it as I used to do. I hoped the new owner of Morton would restore the fountain and the statue to their former glory.

A twig cracked behind me.

I turned around sharply.

It was Nick. "I'm sorry I startled you," he said. "May I join you?"

"Yes, of course."

He sat beside me on the bench, close but not touching me.

"Are you all right?" I asked.

"Yes. And you?"

I nodded.

"Will you tell me what happened in the drawing room after I left this morning?" he asked.

I gave him the essence of the conversation with Sir Peter and Joe, omitting my private conversation with Joe afterwards.

When I was finished, he shook his head in disbelief.

"Did you ever suspect that Joe was Sir Peter's son?" I asked.

"Never. My God. It seems my belief that nobody can be trusted is being confirmed."

"Don't you trust me?"

"Yes, of course I do." He took my hand and pressed it to his lips. "One thing I love about you is how utterly, painfully honest you are with me. It's the other people in this house who can't be trusted." He paused. "You said you told Peter there's a problem with Morton's title. Is that true?"

"There may be." I couldn't bring myself to tell him about my intended meeting with Alicia. Even though I knew he wouldn't tell his brother about it, I saw no reason to raise his hopes about the amended will. And part of me was afraid his eyes would light up at the sound of his wife's name.

He was looking at me expectantly, so I said, "You'll know everything tomorrow. I don't think it will make a difference in the long run. Morton will still be sold."

He shook his head. "That's not the point. Peter has been drinking more heavily than he used to—I noticed it from the day he arrived—and if you become the target of his anger . . ." He paused, then said, "You're in danger from several quarters, though I've taken care of one threat."

"What do you mean?"

"I spent the day with Bedford, arranging a new place for him to live. We had to go all the way to York."

Astonished, I exclaimed, "Why would you do such a thing? Morton is his life."

"Yes. Bedford is too much like me in that regard," he said ruefully. "The truth is, he was the one who put the marbles on the stairs in the east wing. They were meant for you. He admitted as much to me this morning."

I was silent.

"I didn't realize he was so upset by the increasing intimacy between you and me," Nick continued. "He was worried you'd take my attention away from Morton and be a bad influence on me. He was right on the first count, but he didn't realize that taking my focus off Morton was the best thing that could happen to me. In any case, I couldn't risk the possibility he would do something to hurt you again, so I had to remove him."

I felt like a fool. How could I have imagined that Nick had spent the day sulking somewhere? He had so much to worry about on his own account, but he had been thinking only of me. He was still holding my hand, and I tightened my fingers around his.

"Bedford told me something else too, something extraordinary," Nick said. "He said there was a real child in the house."

"A real child!" I exclaimed. "For how long?"

"On and off for the past year. Can you believe it? He said he didn't know whose child she was, but she was a little girl that Mrs. Wilson claimed she was keeping here at Morton for the child's own protection. He said he was opposed to the idea from the beginning, but Mrs. Wilson promised him the child wouldn't be here long."

"How could he agree to such a thing? For all he knew, Mrs. Wilson kidnapped this girl!" My questions tumbled over themselves in my haste to understand. "And I thought he was completely loyal to you: why would he agree to keep secret something that would be guaranteed to upset you, after what happened to your own daughter? Where is the child now? What's her name?"

"He didn't know her name. Mrs. Wilson had coached her to call herself Frances. He was remorseful about that, and about the fact that I heard the child making sounds in the house. He kept threatening Mrs. Wilson that he would tell me, and she kept pleading for more time, and finally, just before she died, she told him she'd sent the child to a family in Bradford, and that made an end of the matter."

I was speechless. Something didn't make sense about what Bedford had told Nick, but my mind was whirling with all the new revelations I'd heard that day, and I couldn't think clearly.

"I think you ought to leave Morton at once," he said.

"Now?" I exclaimed. "Why?"

"I told you, Peter could be dangerous. I don't want to risk his hurting you. If this problem with Morton's title prevents or even just delays the sale of the estate further, he'll blame you."

"But I'm not prepared . . . I haven't packed my things. Where would I go?"

"I can wait for you to pack. Then I'll take you to a hotel in Bradford where you can stay until your legal work is done."

As mad as everything at Morton was, as mad as Morton was making me, I wasn't ready to leave. I didn't want to stay in the same city as Alicia Spencer, and I didn't want to leave Nick, even for one night.

I said slowly, "I'll go if you think it's necessary."

"I don't know if it's necessary, my love," he said. "Perhaps if you leave tomorrow it will be soon enough. I'll stay awake tonight and keep watch."

"I'll stay awake with you." I knew what I was implying, but I had no more understanding of what motivated me to say it at that moment than the headless statue.

Nick looked at me intently, and I held my breath for a long, suspended moment. Then he took my hand and led me back into the house. Neither of us spoke as we entered the west wing and made our way down the corridor to my bedroom.

He dropped my hand to open the door, then turned to me with a question in his eyes. He was giving me a chance to behave properly, to bid him goodnight and close the door between us.

Instead, I took his hand again and led him inside. He closed and locked the door.

I flung myself at him as soon as he turned around, and his arms went around me as he kissed me passionately. I helped him pull the pins from my hair, and as he buried his hands in it, I slipped my hands underneath his shirt to caress the bare skin of his back.

He groaned and held me away from him, his hands on my shoulders.

"What's the matter?" I whispered.

He smiled, his eyes glittering down at me. "You must be aware how dangerous this is."

"I like this kind of danger."

"What happened to my sensible, practical Vaughan?" he teased me.

"She went away. Let her go." I tried to kiss him again, but he kept me at arm's length.

"One of us must be sensible," he insisted. "I want you. You know I do. But the temptation of going to bed with you is too great, and I don't want to begin our relationship that way."

I cast about for a solution to our problem. "What if we promise to keep our clothes on?"

He made a sound that was half laugh, half sigh, and pulled me into his arms again. "That might work," he said, his lips brushing the hair at my temple. "I'm willing to risk it."

We climbed into bed fully dressed and lay down together,

my head on his chest. It was both thrilling and comforting to be so close to him, listening to the strong, steady beating of his heart. We were silent for a long time.

After a while, he said, "You never did tell me if you have a Christian name. Is it really Vaughan?"

"No. It's Mary. Vaughan is my second name."

"Really?"

I raised my head to look into his eyes. "Yes."

"Mary." He traced my cheekbone with one finger. "No, it doesn't suit you."

"Couldn't you love Mary Vaughan Springthorpe?" I said with a smile.

"I love you no matter what your name is, but I'm going to continue calling you Vaughan."

I didn't care in the least what he called me, as long as he continued to hold me in his arms.

26

I'm here to see Mrs. Graves." I hoped the clerk didn't hear the tremor in my voice. In spite of my efforts to distance myself from the goings on at Morton and stay calm, I was so nervous that I'd tripped on the front steps of the hotel and would have fallen if a porter hadn't stepped forward to steady me. I clung to the possibility that the clerk would turn me away with a puzzled stare, claiming there was no Mrs. Graves registered at that hotel.

Instead, he said, "Yes, she's expecting you. The first door on the left at the top of the stairs."

My mind was spinning as I slowly mounted the stairs. I had awakened alone in my bed that morning, but there was a note from Nick: *I didn't want to awaken you, my love. I'll see you at breakfast.* But I didn't go down to breakfast. As soon as I had washed and dressed, I hired a fly to the station in time for the early train to Bradford, thinking it best to be alone and away from Morton to clear my head and prepare for this meeting. Nick's note was in my skirt pocket, and on the train I kept checking to ensure it was still there.

Now, as I reached the first-floor landing of the hotel, I told myself this was only a business meeting. I was there in a legal capacity to ensure that I'd gathered all the necessary information before completing the sale of the estate. Even so, my palms were damp and my heart was beating erratically.

I went to the first door on the left and took a deep breath before knocking. If I had hoped for another minute to compose myself, that hope was dashed, for a low, musical feminine voice called immediately, "Come in."

The room looked the way I assumed any private sitting room in any hotel would—devoid of personality. The floral curtains and upholstery gave it a vaguely feminine look, but otherwise it was a blank.

Alicia Spencer was sitting by the window at the far end of the room. In my anxiety I didn't look directly at her, but instead at the small, round table beside her upon which was a teapot, two cups, and a delicate gold cigarette case.

"Please sit down," she said. "Would you like a cup of tea?"

I sat in the chair opposite hers. "No, thank you."

She poured a cup of tea for herself. It shouldn't have surprised me that she wore a wedding ring, but it did: it was a simple gold band that looked old and too big for her delicate hands.

"We haven't got much time," I said, "so I'd like to get right to business, if you don't mind."

"I don't mind."

I looked directly at her face then and found I couldn't get right to business, after all. Since the previous day, I'd been preparing myself to see this woman who had always been just a story. A myth. I had also managed to convince myself that her beauty was part of that myth and that the Alicia I would meet today would be an ordinary middle-aged woman, not the spoiled young beauty of Mrs. Wilson's stories.

Alicia might be middle-aged, but she was anything but ordinary. Aside from the wedding ring, she wore no jewellery, just a simple, modest black dress with no adornments or trimmings. Her dark hair, sprinkled with grey, was swept back to reveal high cheekbones and almond-shaped black eyes. The fine lines around her eyes and mouth were like hairline cracks in a rare porcelain vase. She wasn't beautiful in the way I'd expected, not a fair pink-and-white English beauty like Rose Dixon, but she had an air of mystery, an allure that was evident without her needing to speak. No wonder Nick and Peter had both loved her. She had only to raise her hand, and a man would leave everything—wife, children, money, status—to go with her.

"You're not what I imagined," I blurted out, regretting the words as soon as they were spoken. The last thing I wanted to do was open the way for a personal conversation.

"Is that so?" she asked coolly but without rancour. "What did you imagine? A scarlet woman wearing nothing but feathers and beads?"

"No, I . . ." I was too surprised by her frankness to continue.

"You're not what I imagined, either," she said. She was clearly too well bred to tell me what she'd imagined, but I suspected it was similar to Sir Peter's caricature of me as a crone in tweeds.

I wondered which of us really was the scarlet woman. I certainly looked more like one than she did. I wasn't wearing beads and feathers, but I wished I had chosen more businesslike attire. The dress I was wearing showed more of my bosom than was appropriate for the time of day: my mother would have been horrified. I had also chosen to wear the shoe Joe had made for me instead of the more stable, heavier one and was now paying dearly for it with the pain that was throbbing in my hip. What had I been thinking? Had I been unconsciously trying to compete with the image of Alicia in my head? I thought with dismay how cheap I must look next to this elegant woman.

Pushing the thought aside, I said briskly, "I don't know how much you know about the sale of Morton Abbey, Mrs. Spencer, but I have some questions that I hope you can answer." Then, belatedly remembering the name by which Alicia was known at the hotel, I added, "Or would you prefer to be called Mrs. Graves?"

She waved her hand in a graceful, dismissive gesture. "Mrs. Graves was a private joke between me and Nick—Mr. Spencer—many years ago. He was always trying to make me smile, and he'd call me that when he thought I was too solemn. You may call me whatever you like."

The thought of a younger, light-hearted Nick teasing his solemn young wife made me feel queasy. I swallowed hard.

"You say 'the sale of Morton Abbey' as if the deal is done," Alicia said, looking worried. "Is it?"

Relieved to be speaking of business at last, I said, "I have all the papers and will finalize the sale today, unless your answers to my questions change that."

"I didn't realize Peter had found a buyer. Does he know you're here?"

"No, and I'd appreciate it if you don't tell him." I knew it was a risk to ask her to hide anything from Sir Peter, but she merely nodded as if keeping secrets from him was a matter of course.

"I'd like to ask you about the night old Sir Peter died," I began.

"Is this about the amended will?" she asked.

"Yes," I said, startled. "You knew it existed?"

Instead of answering, she reached for the cigarette case.

Taking a cigarette, she lit it and brought it to her lips. I had never seen a woman smoke, and I was hard pressed not to stare.

"Where do your loyalties lie, Miss Springthorpe?" she asked, giving me a sidelong look.

I blinked. "I don't know what you mean."

"Peter is your client, yet you've asked me not to tell him you're here. It makes me wonder, that's all."

"Sir Peter hired me to prepare the papers for the sale of the estate," I said, "but I need to ensure that the estate is in fact his to sell. I won't act against the law or my conscience. Beyond that, I wish to do what's best for the Spencer family."

"You speak convincingly. Though no doubt you're aware that Sir Peter and my husband would consider 'what's best for the Spencer family' quite different things."

"Yes." I didn't like her referring to Nick as her husband, despite its being the truth. "Will you tell me what you know about the amended will?"

"I knew something was going to happen that night. It wasn't just that my father-in-law was dying. Even the servants were behaving mysteriously, as if Nick had asked them to keep me in the dark, so naturally I was curious. I waited in the shadows outside my father-in-law's bedroom, and when I saw Bedford emerge with a paper in his hand, I followed him to the library. From the doorway I saw him hide the paper in a book. It was simple enough to go in after he had left and take the will. I intended to give it to Peter."

"Did you?"

She toyed with her cigarette. "When one is in love, one will do anything—or almost anything—for that person. I believed Peter was the rightful heir to Morton and that Nick had manipulated his father into changing the will. I didn't think a deathbed change of heart reflected what his father really would have wanted."

I was becoming impatient with her avoidance of my questions. All I wanted to know was what she'd done with the will, but I sensed that the more I pushed her for answers, the slower she would be to give them.

"What do you think now?" I asked.

Alicia shrugged, a slight, graceful movement of her slender shoulders. "I don't know. At that time all I wanted was to please Peter."

"When I first met Peter," she went on, "I thought him the most charming man I'd ever met. He seemed fearless. Exciting. Life with Nick was dull, just different variations of grey. With Peter the world was filled with brilliant colours."

What she said only confirmed that she had never understood Nick, not the way I did. I repeated, "Did you give the amended will to Sir Peter? Or destroy it?"

"He asked for it, but I still had a little of my own mind left. I told him I destroyed it, but I kept it with a vague notion it might be useful someday. Or perhaps my conscience wouldn't let me destroy it. I don't remember. Contrary to what some people think, Miss Springthorpe, one's conscience doesn't die easily. Even mine."

She put the cigarette to her lips again and inhaled slowly. Then, setting the cigarette carefully on the edge of her tea saucer, she reached into her reticule, which was on the floor beside her chair, and handed me an envelope.

I opened it, my fingers feeling clumsy in my haste, and pulled out a creased sheet of paper. It had been handled a great deal; it was crumpled and even torn at the bottom. I set it on the table and smoothed it with my fingers, my breath catching in my throat.

It was old Sir Peter Spencer's last will and testament, signed on the day he died and witnessed by Bedford and the maid, Susan Smith. Morton legally belonged to Nick.

"Peter has been talking about selling Morton for months," Alicia said, "but I didn't think he'd really do it. I'd been keeping the will in a safe at our house in France, but I thought I'd better bring it with me in case Peter was serious about selling the estate. I couldn't make up my mind whether or not to tell you about it. I didn't realize you knew about it already."

"Mr. Spencer told me." How strange that it was easy to call Nick "Mr. Spencer" in front of Alicia. Was I being a coward or only protecting our relationship? I couldn't tell.

"You may do as you like with the will," she said. "If you decide it's better for everyone if it's destroyed, I won't breathe a word to anyone."

I stared at the floral wallpaper behind Alicia's head. Of course I couldn't pretend the will never existed. Or could I? For a wild, reckless moment I imagined the advantages of doing exactly that. Sir Peter would pay my full salary if I completed the sale to Lord Brakehurst, and Nick would have to walk away from Morton, as he intended to do anyway. But could I look him in the eye again, knowing I had been the means of keeping the place he loved out of his hands?

"I can't do that," I said. "Now that I know about the will, I must stop the sale of the estate. It's possible the will isn't legal if old Sir Peter wasn't of sound mind when he signed it, so there may be an investigation, but I must act as if this is his final, official will."

Alicia nodded and lifted the cup of what now must be cold tea to her lips.

"I don't understand why you've shown me this," I persisted.

"Surely it will jeopardize your relationship with Sir Peter."

"My relationship with Peter is over," was the startling response. "Yes, I know it must not look that way. We were in France together and came here together, but I've had enough." Leaning forward, she added in a flippant tone that still managed to sound refined, "In these irreligious modern times, the lawyer is the new priest, isn't that so? You may hear my confession, but sadly, you haven't got the power to absolve me."

I didn't want to hear any personal confession from Alicia, but my blood was turning to ice, preventing me from moving or speaking.

"I no longer love Peter," Alicia continued, not seeming to notice my frozen state. "I haven't told him yet, though he must sense my feelings have changed. I've finally grown up, but he's remained a child in many ways. We had great fun together for years, and it didn't used to trouble me that I was living only for myself and for whatever pleasures were available to me. I thought it was my right. I was born into a privileged family, and when I was a girl my parents never denied me anything I wanted. Neither did Peter. Oh, I did feel some prickings of conscience when he and I first became lovers, but I felt so strongly we were meant to be together that nothing else mattered. I see no judgment in your eyes, Miss Springthorpe. Perhaps I shouldn't be surprised—you are, after all, a lawyer, not a priest."

I didn't feel like a priest or a lawyer at that moment. My feelings were a tangled jumble, and I just wanted her to stop talking.

"I've spent so many years avoiding my obligations as a wife and mother," Alicia went on. "My duty. What a quaint, old-fashioned word that is. But for the first time in my life I want to try to atone for my many sins. I've even wondered if perhaps Frances's death . . ." her voice caught on the name of her daughter, and she had to pause for a moment before continuing, ". . . if her death wasn't divine punishment for my relationship with Peter, but of course that too is a rather quaint, old-fashioned notion. It's to Nick's credit he never laid that burden upon me."

Alicia straightened up and took a deep breath. "To come to the point, Miss Springthorpe, I intend to break off with Peter and return to Nick, if he'll have me."

These were the words I knew somewhere deep inside me were coming. The words I had been dreading. My mouth went dry and the room seemed to quake around me.

Alicia rose abruptly and began to pace about the room, which was fortunate for me. If she had remained facing me, my eyes would doubtless have given me away. The only way I could remain calm was by repeating silently to myself, *He won't take her back. He loves me.*

"Nick may refuse, of course," Alicia said. "He may not forgive me for keeping the amended will all these years without telling him. But he is still my husband by law, and if he has any feelings left for me, he may take me back. Despite all his faults, he's a good man. He'll try to do what's right."

It was true. Nick was a good man, a moral man. I tried not to think of my attempt to seduce him the night before. He had stopped us from going too far, and I was glad of it now, in the light of day. Why had I been so willing to give myself to him? Perhaps this meeting with Alicia was the reason, though I hadn't thought of that at the time—I wasn't thinking at all at the time. My fears of what she might tell me, of what she would look like, *be* like—in fact, all the fears that were now realized— must have driven me to do what I did.

Alicia stopped in the middle of the room and turned to face me, her expression anxious and a little hopeful. "You can tell me if Nick is likely to accept my offer. Peter said he thinks Nick confides in you. Perhaps you are his substitute priest as well as mine."

I hadn't thought anything she could add would make me feel worse, but apparently it could. I found my voice at last, or at least a hollow, shaky version of it. "I don't know. You'll need to ask him yourself."

"I see you're as good at keeping the secrets of the confessional as any priest," she said, still apparently unaware of my distress. Were her own emotions blinding her to everything else, or was I managing to hide my own? "Well, I'll ask him. I've got nothing to lose. But I'd better wait until this legal business is sorted out and Peter leaves Morton, or even better, leaves the country. As for your part in all of this, I think it would be better for you not to return to Morton."

Stunned, I repeated, "Not to return to Morton? Ever?"

"Yes." Alicia returned to her chair. "You can have your things packed by one of the servants and sent to you here, or better yet, to a different hotel farther away from Peter. Then, when you've completed whatever work is necessary to validate the new will, you can go back to London without ever having to see Peter."

"Why is it so important that I don't see him?"

"For your safety, of course." She looked surprised that I would need to ask the question. "I'd forgotten how little you know Peter. He will naturally be very upset when he learns about the new will. When he's thwarted, he can be very unpleasant. Even violent." She glanced away. "Not to me, you understand. He's never laid a hand on me in anger, but I've seen him angry with others, and I wish to spare you that."

"I must go back to Morton," I insisted. "It would be irresponsible of me not to . . . complete my duties there." The truth was I couldn't imagine simply disappearing from Nick's life, although given what Alicia had told me, perhaps it would be better for everyone if I did. But I couldn't bear that thought. Everything was happening too quickly.

Alicia bit her lip. "If you insist on returning, I won't stop you. But you'd better not take the will with you. If Peter knows you have it—"

"I must tell him the sale is off, and he'll naturally want to know why. He'll need to know the truth eventually."

"Who will need to know the truth?" uttered a calm male voice from the doorway.

It was Sir Peter.

Both Alicia and I started violently.

She rose to her feet and took a step towards him, momentarily obscuring me from his view. I took the opportunity to slip the will into my skirt pocket.

"Peter, darling, what a fright you gave me!" exclaimed Alicia.

"I'm stealthy as a cat when I want to be," he said with a smile, coming forward to take her hand and kiss her offered cheek. He must have seen me, but he was taking his time acknowledging me. I wondered how much of our conversation he had heard.

I rose and assumed what I hoped was a pleasant expression.

"Miss Springthorpe, what a surprise to find you here," Sir Peter said smoothly. "I didn't know you ladies were acquainted. Sharing a bit of gossip over tea, are you? Why don't we go to the dining room for a celebratory late luncheon? I'm feeling generous now that Morton's all but sold, even though the purchase money isn't yet in my possession." He gave me a meaningful look.

Alicia and I exchanged quick, uneasy glances.

"Come now, why the long faces?" he demanded in the falsely jovial tone I was beginning to recognize. "I want to celebrate, and neither of you are fit companions, looking as you do." He slipped his arm around Alicia's waist. "Alicia, my dear, has Miss Springthorpe said anything to upset you? I'll get rid of her at once if she has."

"No, she's merely doing her job." Alicia made a slight movement, a half-step sideways as if to disengage herself from Peter's arm, but he didn't withdraw it.

"Sir Peter," I interposed, "There's a problem with the sale of Morton. Why don't we sit down and discuss it?"

"A problem? Didn't you say any potential problems would be cleared up today?" An edge was in his voice now.

"Peter, let's allow Miss Springthorpe to take her leave, and you and I will discuss the matter privately," Alicia said. "It doesn't really concern her."

I was amazed by the cool confidence in her voice.

"No, I don't like that idea, either," he said. "If she felt it necessary to come here to see you, she'll stay with us until I know what the problem is. I do like to have my legal counsel close at hand."

"Very well," Alicia said. "I've told Miss Springthorpe about your father's amended will."

"Is that all? What difference does it make?"

"I didn't destroy it."

"What?" He stared at her, his pleasant mask slipping. "I don't believe you."

"It's true." Taking advantage of his surprise, Alicia extricated herself from his encircling arm. "I couldn't bring myself to destroy it, but I didn't want Nick to find it either, so I thought the best thing was to hide it at Morton in a safe place where nobody would find it. It's still there."

"You lied to me." Sir Peter looked genuinely shocked. "I thought you were the only person in the world who would never lie to me."

I was also surprised Alicia had lied, not about the existence of the will but about its location. She knew I had the will. Was she trying to protect me or merely to avoid an ugly scene in the hotel?

Alicia put her hand on Peter's arm. "Peter, darling, I've never lied to you about anything else. I knew you'd be upset if I didn't destroy the will, but I simply couldn't do it."

Now he was the one to step away. His eyes were narrow and hard. "That's all very well, but why did you tell Miss Springthorpe about it?"

"I wanted to do the right thing. My conscience has been troubling me for years about that will, and if your father really wanted Nick to have Morton in the end, then he ought to have it. At the very least, it isn't right that you should receive all the purchase money for it."

"How inconvenient that you should have an attack of conscience now," he said. "And since when do you care about fairness to Nick? Might I remind you his welfare has never made a difference in any of your decisions before?"

"It isn't his welfare I'm concerned about. I just think if the estate is legally his—"

"The estate isn't his in any sense, and I'll see that it stays that way. Where is the will, exactly?"

Alicia was silent.

Turning to me, he said, "I assume she's told you. You'll be very sorry, Miss Springthorpe, if you don't tell me the truth."

Although his voice was still calm and even, there was something in his eyes that frightened me. Now I fully believed what Joe, Nick, and even Alicia had told me about Sir Peter's violent streak. My hand moved towards my pocket.

"It's in the library," Alicia said. "I haven't told Miss Springthorpe exactly where."

"Will you tell me exactly where?" he demanded.

She hesitated.

"Very well," he said. "I see that an immediate trip to Morton is in order. Shall I get your wrap, my dear?"

Alicia shook her head.

"Come along, then," he said doggedly, taking Alicia's arm and half-dragging her to the door. "You, too, Miss Springthorpe."

"She needn't come with us," Alicia said.

"She is most certainly coming with us."

Minutes later, I was in the back seat of Sir Peter's motorcar, clinging to the door and holding my hat as the vehicle careened wildly through the streets of Bradford. In some ways it was apt that this should be my first ride in a motorcar: the noise of the engine, the dust, and the wild, erratic movements fit my state of mind perfectly. My fear of a literal collision also momentarily took my mind off the emotional collision that couldn't fail to happen when the three of us arrived at Morton and saw Nick.

Sir Peter spoke only once during the journey, just as we entered the carriage drive after passing through Morton's main gates.

"How pleasant it will be," he said, "to have the whole family together again."

27

There was no opportunity to speak to Alicia alone. The moment we alighted from the motorcar, Sir Peter offered one arm to Alicia and the other to me, and the three of us marched solemnly into the house like a king with his harem, past several startled servants, straight to the library.

The library door was uncharacteristically wide open, and we passed through without hesitating. At the far end of the library by the long windows sat Nick and Joe, who appeared to be engaged in an intense conversation. It was difficult to tell who was more surprised by our grand entrance, but they both rose to their feet at once, and Nick's usually-guarded expression in the presence of his brother slipped away completely as he stared at us in shock.

I was afraid to look at him, afraid that any lingering feelings for the wife he hadn't seen in so many years would show on his face. But my eyes were irresistibly drawn to him. I saw nothing but astonishment in his expression, though his gaze seemed to rest longer on Alicia than on anyone else. When his eyes met mine, he took a step forward, then stopped, looking uncertain.

Joe did the opposite, taking a step back and looking around the room as if searching for a way of escape.

"How convenient that we should find you both here," Sir Peter purred, seeming perfectly at ease. "Do sit down, ladies. Scotch, anyone?"

Nobody answered him. I sank into the chair at the desk, but Alicia remained standing. She had lost her air of calm confidence and looked smaller and more fragile now. I realized that she probably hadn't been at Morton since her daughter died.

"Well, I certainly need a drink." Sir Peter went to the liquor cabinet in the near corner of the library and poured his Scotch, humming to himself.

Everyone remained in a frozen state except Alicia, who approached Nick and said something to him in a voice too low for anyone else to hear. He lowered his head to listen, then nodded.

I felt a pang of jealousy. Nick and Alicia looked comfortable together, as if they'd been separated for only days instead of years. And as if she had never betrayed him with his own brother.

Sir Peter took a liberal swallow of his Scotch. "We'll have no secrets any longer, Alicia," he said in a new, icy tone. It must have been a measure of the unreality of the situation that I didn't consider it strange to share Sir Peter's opinion, and perhaps his feelings too, at that moment.

Before Alicia could respond, Joe came forward and said, "I must leave."

Sir Peter stood in his way. Father and son stood eye-to-eye.

"You can't go just yet, Joe," Sir Peter said. "Where were you this morning? Surely it wouldn't have been difficult to keep watch over your beloved." He spoke the last word with a sneer and a glance in my direction.

"I was taking care of my brothers in Netherton." Joe was holding himself rigidly upright. I wondered if it was the only way he could keep his temper.

"You know how busy I am at the moment," Sir Peter continued. "Your laziness made it necessary for me to go to Bradford myself. I'm disappointed in you. After all I've done for you, you throw it all away just because of a scheming little common woman who doesn't even want you."

For a moment I thought Joe would strike his father, but then he turned and strode towards the door.

"Coward!" Sir Peter called after him. "You and the Dixons will get no further help of any kind from me." Lifting his glass, he drained it in one gulp.

"We don't need it," Joe shot back. The library door closed behind him with a resounding thud.

Although I understood why Joe wanted to leave, I couldn't help feeling abandoned. I wished he had stayed, if only to stand with the rest of us against Sir Peter.

Sir Peter returned to the liquor cabinet and poured himself another scotch.

"What do you want to discuss, Peter?" Nick asked. "Let's get on with it."

"Our conversation can be over in a matter of minutes, but that depends on Alicia, doesn't it, my dear?" Peter looked at Alicia over the rim of his glass. "Where is the document?"

My fingers brushed my skirt pocket where the will lay. The note Nick had left in bed for me that morning was in the same pocket, I realized. For some reason this struck me as amusing. I managed not to laugh, but I must have had a peculiar look on my face.

Alicia went to the corner of the library where the books on history and geography were shelved. She ran her fingers over the spines of a set of green leather-bound books, then chose one and opened it. I thought it was remarkably convincing the way she flipped the pages with apparently increasing consternation, then looked up, across the room at Sir Peter.

"It isn't here," she said.

Sir Peter cursed and strode to her side. Then in one sweeping movement, he pushed all the books from the shelf to the floor. They tumbled down heavily, one grazing Alicia's skirt. She stepped back hastily.

"Is someone going to tell me what in God's name is going on?" Nick demanded.

"Mrs. Spencer told Sir Peter about your father's amended will," I said, "and she said it's here in the library."

"You knew!" Nick exclaimed, staring at Alicia.

I opened my mouth to stop him from saying too much, but I was too late.

"The will isn't here," he said. "I've searched every book in this room."

"Why am I not surprised?" snapped Sir Peter. He drained his glass again, then looked down at Alicia, who was kneeling on the floor, looking through the books that had fallen. "Alicia, are you lying to me again?"

She didn't reply.

Sir Peter stalked back to the liquor cabinet and reached for the bottle of Scotch, but Nick intercepted him, taking the bottle before his brother reached it.

"You've had enough, Peter," Nick said.

"Who do you think you are? My nursemaid?" Sir Peter roared. "It's not for you to tell me when I've had enough." He lunged for the bottle but succeeded only in knocking it out of Nick's hand.

The bottle fell on the crimson Turkey carpet. It was heavy crystal and didn't break, but the liquor poured out of it, staining the carpet a darker red. The strong smell of whiskey permeated the room.

The two brothers faced each other, and I was afraid for Nick: they were not fairly matched, despite the whisky Sir Peter had consumed. But at that moment, a piercing cry came from Alicia, and everyone turned to look at her. She had one hand over her mouth and the other stretched out, pointing towards the long windows. Everyone's eyes followed the direction of her gaze, and we all froze.

Mrs. Dixon was running across the lawn, pulling a child by the hand. The little girl was wearing the pale blue silk frock with the matching pelisse I'd seen in the room I'd thought was Alicia's, and she could barely keep up with Mrs. Dixon's pace.

"Frances!" Alicia choked out. She and Nick both moved towards the windows as if in a trance. I thought they would walk right into the glass, they were so transfixed, but he was slightly ahead of her, and he braced one hand against the window and reached out the other to stop her. She caught his arm and leaned on him as they stood staring out the window, clearly unable to comprehend what they were seeing.

I felt another pang of jealousy, but suddenly my own arm was caught in an iron grip, and Sir Peter began to drag me away from the others, towards the door.

Before I could say a word or even try to pull away, he hissed in my ear, "You will come with me now without a struggle, or I swear to God I will break your arm."

I believed him.

Once Sir Peter and I were in the corridor outside the library, I said, "You're hurting me. Please let me go." My voice sounded strangely calm under the circumstances.

"I mean to hurt you." He spoke equally calmly, but his tone was chilling. "I'm going to take you somewhere that neither

Nick nor Alicia will think of. And even if they do think of it, they won't dare to follow us."

He dragged me through the great hall towards the back of the house. I cried out then, hoping someone would come to my aid, but my voice was breathless and thin. Only someone very close by would have heard me, and I saw nobody.

"Damn you, woman, keep your mouth shut!" he said roughly, giving me a shake that rattled every bone in my body. He opened a door near the kitchen that I'd thought led to servants' quarters, but it opened onto a dark passageway. I stumbled and fell, grazing my hands on the rough stone floor.

With another oath, Sir Peter pulled me up and dragged me along behind him this time. The passageway smelled mouldy and damp, and the floor was uneven, but I managed to stay upright. My lame leg was in excruciating pain from my fall and from being forced to walk so quickly.

At long last, Sir Peter pushed open a door and we were outside in the late-afternoon sunshine. I closed my eyes against the painful brightness. When I opened them again, I realized we were behind the house, not far from the broken fountain and headless statue.

Taking advantage of the fact that Sir Peter had slackened his hold on my arm, I pulled free and careened away from him, moving as fast as I dared. I screamed again, hoping one of the servants might see or hear me.

Sir Peter overtook me easily and grabbed my arm again, forcing me to face him. The last thing I saw was the look of rage on his face and his hand raised. Then I felt a blow to the side of my head that made my ears ring. I fell to the ground and was enveloped in blackness.

❧

When I opened my eyes again, I saw wispy clouds in a late-afternoon sky and the top of a willow tree. My left ear was throbbing painfully, as was my bad leg. Something sharp was digging into my back.

Slowly, I raised myself to a sitting position.

"I apologize for striking you," Sir Peter said, slurring his words a little. "It was the only way to ensure you wouldn't try to escape again."

He was sitting only a few feet from me, his back against a tree. He was very red in the face and breathing heavily.

"Where are we?" I asked in a voice that sounded too heavy and slow to be my own. But even as I asked the question, I knew. We were at the pond, not far from the water's edge. I could see the brown film on top of the water and some lily pads, which reminded me of what Nick had told me about Frances's death. Sir Peter had indeed taken me to the one place on the estate where Nick and Alicia wouldn't go. This was the place of their nightmares—and mine. I still didn't understand how I could have dreamed this place before I saw it.

"I think Alicia is protecting you, Miss Springthorpe. You have the will, or you know exactly where it is. Am I right?"

When I didn't reply, he grabbed my chin, forcing me to look at him. "It will be easy enough to find out if the will is on your person," he continued. "I'm prepared to search you thoroughly by removing each layer of your clothing, with or without your help. Is that what you want?"

"No." My throat closed so that I could hardly get the word out. With a shaking hand, I pulled the paper out of my pocket and handed it to him.

He skimmed the document, then smiled. "This is indeed what I've been looking for. Just think of the trouble you would have saved us all by giving it to me at the hotel."

I struggled to my feet, then turned and began to limp away, my whole body aching with every step.

"Where do you think you're going?" he demanded.

"You have what you want. You don't need me anymore."

"On the contrary. Did you really think I'd let you walk away after all the trouble you've caused? Will you sit down or must I make you sit?"

I sat. With a sinking heart, I watched Sir Peter tear the will into tiny pieces, slowly and deliberately, then stand up and toss them into the pond. Then he came over to me and looked down at me thoughtfully.

"It's unfortunate that you've seen the will, Miss Springthorpe," he said. "I can't risk your telling anyone it existed."

"What does it matter? Nobody would believe my word against yours."

"I'd like to believe that, but I can't take the risk." He bent down and pulled up the hem of my skirt.

I kicked at him with my good foot, but he pinned my legs down with his arm.

"Stop struggling," he snapped. "I'm not interested in your body, so you can set your mind at ease on that score. I just want to look at your shoe."

I was still wearing the shoe Joe had made for me, and Sir Peter tapped it with his finger. "Hmm. Not as heavy as I'd hoped. I thought your shoe would take you down like an anchor. Well, no matter."

He pulled me upright and dragged me to the water's edge.

"Nick and Mrs. Spencer know about the will," I said shakily. "Will you murder them too?" My recurring nightmare was coming back to me in all its terrifying detail: the darkness, the choking, the helplessness.

He didn't reply. Instead, I heard a muffled thud, and he suddenly let go of me. I fell just inches from the water, and I dug my fingers into the ground and clung there for a terrified moment before I could move again.

As I slowly pulled myself up to a seated position, I saw Mrs. Dixon holding a large rock and standing over Sir Peter, who was lying face down on the ground a few feet away, unmoving.

In the same instant, I became aware of a child crying somewhere nearby. After all these months, I recognized that sound and knew it was the same child.

It had always been the same child.

"Stay where you are, Dora, love," Mrs. Dixon called to her daughter, who was standing on the other side of the pond, under the willow tree, with tears streaming down her cheeks. She did look like the Pears soap girl, with a cherubic face, rosy cheeks, and golden-brown curls. Frances must have been thinner and taller, for Dora looked pinched and uncomfortable in the other girl's clothes.

I realized then what hadn't made sense when Nick told me Bedford's story about the child Mrs. Wilson had been hiding at Morton. Bedford had said the child had been sent to a family in Bradford just before Mrs. Wilson died, but Nick and I heard the child crying *after* Mrs. Wilson died, the night we went upstairs to the nursery. Dora had been crying in Frances's room, but we had become disoriented in the corridor because we'd both heard louder crying from the nursery and mistook it for the same sound. But the louder crying hadn't been a child. It had been Rose Dixon, trying to draw our attention away from Dora.

"Are you all right, Vaughan?" Mrs. Dixon asked me.

"Yes, I think so," I said shakily. My bruised body was

slowing down my mind. "Is he . . . dead?"

"I don't know." She stared down at him. "I always said he was the best of men. He *was* the best of the men I knew, but it turns out he wasn't a good man at all."

I couldn't fathom what she was trying to say. All I could think was that she was in danger if he regained consciousness. She was standing too close to him.

I struggled to my feet. "Let's go back to the house with Dora. Mr. Spencer will know what to do."

"No." She looked down at her old lover. The back of his head where she'd hit him was oozing blood. "I can't do this anymore. I can't fight all of them. I can't save any more little girls."

I didn't know what she meant, and I was too worried about her proximity to Sir Peter to try to figure it out.

"Come here, please," I said, "in case he wakes up and hurts you."

"Peter wouldn't hurt me," she said, lowering the rock to her side and looking down at him with something resembling affection.

I took two steps back, shaking violently. "Mrs. Dixon, think of Dora," I pleaded. "She needs you. Sir Peter tried to kill me. He's dangerous."

Very softly she said, "Peter isn't dangerous, just misguided. My husband, now, he was dangerous. He tried to kill me, in fact. I've cleaned up my own blood from the kitchen floor more times than I can count."

"Mam!" cried Dora from the other side of the pond. Her mother didn't seem to hear her.

"Don't think of that now. You're safe," I said, shaken by the vacant look on her face.

"I have something to discuss with Peter, but you'll take Dora, won't you?"

"No. Let's go to Netherton if you don't want to return to the house. Just you, me, and Dora. Please."

She sighed. "I'm tired, Vaughan. My work has not been easy. I told you about the bad men in Netherton. They would make their wives pregnant, and their wives would give birth to girls, and I was the only one who could save them. Do you know how exhausting such work can be? Nobody helped me: in fact, Jane even tried to stop me. She didn't understand."

I didn't understand, either.

Sir Peter groaned faintly and braced his hands against the ground, starting to sit up.

I cried out to warn Mrs. Dixon, and she took hold of her rock with both hands and shouted, "Don't move!"

He ignored her and sat up slowly, looking dazed. "What the devil are you doing, Rosie? Are you mad?"

"Why did you take Dora away from me?" she cried.

"What are you talking about? I didn't take your daughter."

"Don't lie to me!" her voice went higher. "I thought you were different from other men, but you're as bad as any of them. You took my innocence. And then your brother's wife. And now my only daughter."

"I told you, I didn't take your daughter—"

Mrs. Dixon tried to hit him with the rock again, but he deflected the blow and grabbed her ankle, pulling her down on top of him. They began to struggle, and I took a step towards them, trying to think of a way to save Mrs. Dixon without putting myself in jeopardy.

Dora had begun to scream hysterically, and now she was running towards her mother from the other side of the pond.

She was too close to the water, and I decided my chances of saving her were better than those of saving her mother. I ran towards her as fast as my bruised body would allow.

I tried to speak soothingly to Dora even as I ran towards her, but when I had nearly reached her, I heard a splash behind me. Glancing over my shoulder, I saw Mrs. Dixon and Sir Peter thrashing about in the pond. Dora tried to leap towards her mother, and I was close enough to catch her, but I was off balance, and we fell into the pond together. Something slimy wound itself around my ankles, and some of the rank, stale water went into my mouth and nose.

Dora was fighting me, and I knew I couldn't keep either of our heads above water. My skirt was clinging to my legs, but I kicked as hard as I could and pushed the child up as I went down, hoping by some miracle she would be saved and that the end would come quickly for me.

Did one continue to have nightmares after death? My head was above the water now, and a man was behind me, holding my arms, trying to push me under again. Was it Sir Peter? Oddly, Sir Peter was in the water with me but he was too far away to touch me. In fact, he was floating face-down on the surface of the pond. I slowly realized that the man holding me wasn't trying to push me underwater—instead, he was trying to hold me still. But why? It would be easier to drown me if he just let me go.

"Vaughan, you're safe now," he said in Joe's voice. "I'm here. Stop struggling." But how could it be Joe? He had walked out of the library without looking back, which seemed a long time ago.

Nevertheless, I did stop struggling, and it was indeed Joe who lifted me out of the pond and set me gently on the bank. I couldn't stop coughing, as if I had forgotten how to breathe air, as if I had become a water creature and could no longer live on land.

When my coughing fit ended, I became aware of Joe's coat around me and was grateful for its warmth. I was shivering uncontrollably. Looking up, I saw that Joe had moved to the edge of the pond a few feet away and was looking at two bodies floating on the surface.

I looked wildly around for the little girl. Further along the bank, Nick and Alicia were kneeling on the ground. He was holding Dora as his wife leaned on his arm, peering down into the child's face with a look of utter absorption.

"I need help," Joe called to them. "We can't leave them in the pond."

Nick shifted Dora to Alicia's lap and rose to his feet. "I'll help," he said. To Alicia he said, "Don't let the child see this."

Joe and Nick dived into the pond and struggled to retrieve the bodies of Sir Peter and Mrs. Dixon. Pulling out Sir Peter was obviously the most difficult work, and I watched in silent horror until the old lovers were reunited in what looked to my exhausted mind like a parody of Romeo and Juliet, lying together in death.

My hand went to my neck where the amber pendant ought to have been, but it was gone. It must have come off while I was struggling with Dora in the pond.

I remember very little of what happened after that, except that Nick did come to me at last to see if I was all right, and he kissed my hands and promised to take me back to the house. But then he and Alicia took Dora away, and Joe came and picked me up in his arms, and I let my head fall against his shoulder and relaxed into oblivion.

28

I awoke to bright sunlight in my own room, though at first I didn't recognize it, expecting the smaller room in the east wing where I'd spent my first months at Morton. There was a vase of wildflowers on the dressing table and a light morning breeze wafting through the room from the open window.

My head was throbbing where Sir Peter had struck me, and my body was a mass of dull pain. I must be bruised all over, judging from the way I felt just from shifting slightly in the bed. My memory of the previous day's events began to return, though what happened when we all returned to the house wasn't clear. I did remember Joe carrying me inside and the doctor examining me, but nothing after that. My clearest memory was of Mrs. Dixon at the pond, especially the look of desperation on her face.

I slowly raised myself to a sitting position, which added dizziness to the other unpleasant sensations. I took a few deep breaths, trying not to think of anything in particular, but my mind kept returning to what Mrs. Dixon had said about saving little girls. I hadn't understood at the time, but now I was beginning to. She hadn't been saving them. She'd been killing them.

I rang for Betty, who came in with a look of concern.

"How are you feeling?" she asked, helping to arrange the pillows behind me so I could sit up.

"I hardly know. Not well."

"You must be hungry. Would you like some beef tea?"

"Yes, please." I didn't remember the last time I'd eaten, and I was ravenous. "Betty, how long was I asleep?"

"Since yesterday evening. About twelve hours." She rose and said, "Joe Dixon is downstairs. He's been waiting to see you. Shall I send him in?"

"Yes." Joe was exactly the person I needed to see.

She took a step towards the door, then looked back at me. "Shall I brush your hair first?"

"Oh." I put my hand to my hair, which was a tangled mess. "Yes, thank you."

Betty gently brushed my hair and tied it back with a ribbon, then left with a promise to return quickly with the beef tea.

When Joe came in, I held out my hand to him. He looked as though he hadn't slept the night before: his hair was unruly and his clothing rumpled.

He drew up a chair beside my bed and took my hand. His eyes were bloodshot.

"How are you?" we asked each other at the same time.

I answered first. "Mostly just aches and pains. I'm a little dizzy, though."

"It must be the effects of the sleeping draught the doctor gave you last night."

"I don't remember taking a sleeping draught."

"You were exhausted. I'm not surprised you don't remember."

I squeezed his hand. "Are you all right, Joe?"

"Yes, just tired. The police detective is downstairs, and I've been answering his questions. He'll want to talk to you, too. Do you think you're up to it?"

"I think so. How is Dora? Is she . . ." I was hoping he hadn't lost three members of his family in one afternoon.

"She's shaky and frightened, but fine physically. Nick and his wife have been watching her all night." Seeing me stiffen, he added, "I needed their help."

"Of course," I said, but all I could think of was the hungry way Nick and Alicia had looked at Dora when they were holding her by the pond.

"And your . . . parents?" I ventured.

He looked puzzled, as though he didn't know who I meant. "I never thought of Sir Peter as a father. He was always pushing me. Manipulating me. I'm glad he's gone. But my mother . . ." his voice broke, and he looked away. "She didn't deserve to die that way."

"I'm so sorry, Joe. I didn't realize how fragile she was. I wish I had done more to help her."

"That's kind of you," he said. "Not everyone would feel that way about someone who . . . did what she did."

Betty returned with the beef tea, which I accepted gratefully, and with a quick glance from my face to Joe's, she slipped out of the room.

"What she did was wrong, of course," I replied, "but she really believed she was saving those babies. How did she . . . kill them?"

"I don't know." He pulled his hand out of my grasp and dropped his head into his hands. "It's hard to talk about this. Mrs. Wilson believed the method she used most often was an overdose of laudanum. I don't know if I believe that."

I said nothing, but I thought it was likely. It would be the easiest way for a midwife to kill babies without being caught. Laudanum was so commonly prescribed for mothers and babies that an overdose would be difficult to detect even if it was suspected.

"Did Sir Peter know what your mother was doing?" I asked. "Or that Dora was being hidden at Morton?"

"No." Joe raised his head. "He knew my mother's nerves were delicate, but he wasn't interested in the Dixon family apart from their relationship to me. He was adept at manipulating my feelings for my mother and siblings to serve his ends. And he knew nothing about Dora's presence here."

"So you and Mrs. Wilson agreed together to hide Dora at Morton."

"Yes. A year ago, Dora witnessed my mother . . . smothering a newborn baby and told Mrs. Wilson about it. She wanted to go the police, but I couldn't bear the thought of my mother in gaol or in an asylum. She wouldn't have survived either of those places. I thought if I could just keep a close eye on her and stop her from working as a midwife, she wouldn't be a danger to more children." He took a deep, ragged breath and dropped his head into his hands again. "It's my fault. I don't know how many babies she killed. Not as many as Mrs. Wilson believed. But I ought to have done more to stop her."

I set my untouched beef tea on the side table by the bed and reached out to put my hand on his head, like a benediction. "You made a mistake, yes," I said, "but the scarcity of little girls in Netherton couldn't have been all your mother's doing. Someone would have become suspicious and said something."

He raised his head again and made a swipe at his eyes. "I'm not the only person in Netherton who was protective of my mother. Everyone hated John Dixon, and they felt sorry for her.

And I still believe what I told you before: the stories circulating about Frances Spencer's death and the first couple of babies who died in Netherton spooked families with little girls, and they moved away."

He took a deep breath and looked directly at me. "I'm sorry I lied to you about Dora's death, Vaughan. I lied to everyone about it because I thought it would protect her and my mother, but it only caused more trouble."

"Did you know that Nick and I could hear the sounds Dora was making? Especially her crying in the night. For Nick especially, given his history, it was traumatic."

"I didn't know, not at first. Mrs. Wilson thought Frances's room was the safest place to keep Dora at night because Nick never went there, and she also thought it best to dress her in Frances's clothes to frighten away anyone who might see her. When you came, and Mrs. Wilson realized you had gone into Frances's room, she kept Dora upstairs in the nursery. I took her out sometimes just so she could get some air, but I had to ensure that nobody saw us. Of course I knew our solution wasn't perfect, and I was trying to find a family who could keep Dora, but it was difficult to find a good family who wouldn't ask uncomfortable questions about her origins. We did find a family at last, and I thought Mrs. Wilson had already sent Dora there when I left for Manchester."

A wave of anger washed over me as I thought about the extent of the deception Joe and Mrs. Wilson had practiced. And for what? His mother was dead and his sister had been taken from her home and further traumatized.

"I'm sorry, Vaughan," he said again. "I never meant to frighten or hurt anyone."

"You ought to apologise to Nick, too."

"I will."

"What will you do now?" I asked him.

"I'm going to take my brothers to Manchester with me and settle there. I don't want to return to Netherton, and I can't wait to get away from Morton Abbey."

"What about Dora?"

He ignored my question and took my hand. "Will you come with me?"

"To Manchester?" I stared at him.

"Not as my wife. I know you don't want that, but perhaps you could make a new start there too."

"No, I can't."

A look of disbelief appeared on his face. "Surely you don't intend to stay here at Morton with Nick and his wife. Does he have so much power over you still?"

I didn't flinch at this blow, but I withdrew my hand from his. "You're mistaken, Joe. I intend to return to London and try to find work there, just as I always planned. I think you're mistaken about Nick and Mrs. Spencer, too. He won't want her to stay here." But my voice didn't sound as confident as I wanted it to.

"I don't think he has much choice. Morton is hers now: apparently Sir Peter left Morton to her in his will. Now that he's gone, Nick probably thinks he can win her back."

I swallowed hard to keep back the humiliating tears that rose in my throat.

"You didn't answer my question about Dora," I said, but I suspected the answer a second before he gave it.

"Mrs. Spencer offered to take care of her here at Morton until I'm settled in Manchester with the boys."

"That's a terrible idea," I said. "This place has been a prison to that poor child. You ought to take her with you to Manchester."

"I may do that. I'm going to need help, though, so I need to consider other possibilities."

"Please go now," I said stiffly, averting my face. I could no longer keep the tears back, but he didn't need to see the extent of my pain.

"Forgive me," he said, sounding genuinely contrite. "I shouldn't have told you so much. You probably think I'm just jealous. I *am* jealous, but I don't want to see you hurt, either."

I didn't reply.

When he had gone, I closed my eyes and lay back against the pillows, concentrating on my physical scrapes and bruises to distract myself from the emotional ones. But it took too much effort, and what Joe had said about Nick, Alicia, and Dora kept invading my mind. And what made everything worse was that Joe didn't even know about Alicia's intention to return to Nick.

Joe's words might have been coloured by his jealousy, but what he said didn't change the fact that Sir Peter was dead, leaving the way clear for Alicia and Nick to stay together. Nick loved her once, and if I was out of the way, perhaps he could love her again. Especially if being with her meant keeping Morton. I couldn't let myself dwell on the possibility that they might want to raise Dora together, but it seemed like the perfect solution to Joe's problems and theirs: after all, they'd already mistaken her for their dead daughter. I had half a mind to kidnap her myself and escape from the prison of Morton with her.

I tried to force myself to think clearly, but my mind kept going in circles. Betty came in again with a tray of food and told me the detective would like to see me as soon as I was ready. This time I was able to eat. The cold roast beef, cheese, and fresh bread were delicious, and I felt steadier afterwards. Betty helped me dress and pinned my hair in a loose knot at the nape of my neck. When I looked at myself in the mirror, I was shocked by how normal I looked. Tired, certainly, but otherwise calm and in my right mind. None of the bruises— mental or physical—showed.

I asked Betty to send the detective up to my room, not ready to risk a chance meeting with Nick or Alicia. Mr. Williams was a wiry man whose bushy moustache dominated his face and whose questions were curt, direct, and predictable. I told him everything I remembered about the events of the previous day and asked if I could leave Morton. He had no objection as long as I gave him an address where I could be reached. I wrote down my sister's address, and he left.

The interview with the detective helped clear my mind: even though I'd had to relive the events of the previous day, his emotionless, objective presence steadied me as much as the food had, and I realized there was only one thing left for me to do.

I called Betty into the room again and asked, "Will you help me pack my things? I'm leaving Morton today."

"Today, miss? Don't you think you ought to go tomorrow, after you've had more rest?"

"No. I need to leave today." I could neither rest nor think clearly until I was away from Morton.

When my things were packed and I'd asked Betty to hire a carriage for me, I put on my hat and my light cloak and went downstairs, slowly and shakily. I half-expected to see Nick with Alicia somewhere in the house, holding Dora in their arms as they had at the pond. Instead, he was standing in the great hall speaking to the detective, who appeared to be taking his leave.

Nick didn't seem to notice my presence until the detective shook his hand and walked out of the house.

Then he gave me a sweeping, comprehensive look that took in my cloak, hat and reticule, and he looked more surprised than I thought he ought to, considering the circumstances.

"Where are you going?" he asked.

"I'm returning home. To London."

"You ought to be resting, not travelling," he said. When I didn't reply, he added, "We haven't had a chance to talk. Come and sit in the library with me for a few minutes so we can make plans for the future."

"I can't." The thought of sitting in the library with him, in the armchairs where we'd spent whole evenings reading and talking, was insupportable. Taking a deep breath, I added, "Your future is here, but mine is not. Besides, it's rather crowded here at present."

After glancing at a servant's retreating back, he took a step towards me. "Vaughan, I know it must be difficult for you with Alicia here, and I can imagine what you're thinking. Give me a chance to explain."

"You don't need to," I replied, taking a step back. "You have a great deal of unfinished business to attend to, and I don't want to get in the way of that. Besides," I added as he started to protest, "I have my own unfinished business in London, and I need to work it out on my own."

"What sort of business?"

"Do you remember chiding me about having no dreams?"

He nodded.

"I do have a dream now. It's not much more than a tiny wisp of one, but I want to help other women with my legal knowledge. I don't know how I'll do that, but I need to find out."

"I understand," he said slowly, "but is there no room in that dream for me?"

"I don't know," I replied, unable to meet his eyes, "but I do know there's no room for Morton in my dream. And I don't want to come between you and your first love."

"I don't love Alicia."

"I wasn't speaking of Alicia." I looked steadily at him then. The answer was so obvious to me that I saw no reason to spell it out, and eventually I saw that he understood.

"Would it be so terrible to live here with me?" he said in a low voice.

I hated to hurt him, but I owed him the truth. "Yes," I said as gently as I could. "This place would suffocate me."

"I see," he said. "Then it seems there's nothing more to say. But you'll write to me, won't you? And send me your address once you're settled in London."

"I don't know. I need time to think about that, too."

"Is it that bad? You want nothing more to do with me?" A muscle in his jaw twitched. "But I'm not being fair, am I? Of course you must do what seems best to you."

"Thank you. I . . . I do wish you happiness, Nick," I said, turning away as my vision blurred with tears.

That day I left Morton Abbey behind forever.

29

LONDON: FEBRUARY 1898 (EIGHT MONTHS LATER)

I took the fountain pen I kept in the chatelaine at my belt, smoothed out the page, and finished the last sentence of the contract. With a sigh of satisfaction, I sat back in my chair, only to see my partner, Eliza Orme, watching me suspiciously over the rim of her round glasses from the other side of the office.

"Vaughan, is that copy work?" she asked. "Why don't you give it to Martin?" Martin was our clerk.

"I gave him the day off."

She frowned.

"He was sneezing all over the papers yesterday," I said. "We don't want to catch whatever he has. Besides, I don't mind a bit of copying now and then."

"As long as you don't stay late today. You haven't forgotten the party, have you?"

I stared at her blankly.

"You *have* forgotten. Mr. Phipps is counting on us to be there. We can't disappoint him."

Mr. Phipps was a wealthy client of ours, the head of a publishing house, and as much as I would have liked to start sneezing in imitation of poor Martin as an excuse to avoid the party, I felt I had no choice. Mr. Phipps had been one of our first clients and had done more to advertise our services among his acquaintances than anyone else. We owed our success, however modest, largely to him.

"I have nothing to wear," I protested weakly.

Eliza gave me an exasperated look. She had curly fair hair that by the end of the day sprang into wild wisps all over her head, no matter what she did to smooth it down. "The burgundy dress you wore at the last party will do nicely."

The last party was months ago, and the dress she was referring to hadn't been in fashion even then. But I hadn't the time or the money to obtain a new one by this evening, so it would have to do.

"By the way," Eliza added, "do you know where the Blackwell contract is? I was looking for it yesterday."

I thought for a few seconds. "It's in one of the 'to be shelved' piles. Fifth pile from the front window."

I watched Eliza leave her desk, where her electric reading lamp was perched precariously on a pile of papers, and pick her way carefully through the maze of papers stacked on the floor until she found the one I mentioned. Like a pearl diver she swooped down, then came back up again looking triumphant and waving the contract over her head.

"How do you do that?" she exclaimed. "I wish I had your memory."

"I wish I had your tolerance for clutter," I replied, smiling to soften my words.

"I can't help it. The more tidying I try to do, the more papers seem to appear out of nowhere." Catching sight of the wall clock, Eliza exclaimed, "Five o'clock already! I've got to go, or I'll never be ready for the party." She took her coat from the peg and pulled it on as she made her way to the front door. "Are you coming?"

"No, I want to finish a few things first. I won't stay long." Seeing her sceptical look, I added, "I promise."

I kept my word. Twenty minutes after Eliza had left, I put on my coat, gloves, and hat and went out into the cold wind. That morning when I had walked to the office, limp snowflakes were drifting lazily to the ground, but now the snow eddied wildly around my feet. I had to watch my step because of some slippery patches, and I only just avoided a collision with a well-dressed gentleman who was walking in the opposite direction.

"I beg your pardon, madam," he said in a low, cultured voice, touching the brim of his hat before moving on.

I turned to stare after him. Something about his voice and bearing reminded me of Nick. But as I watched him walk away, it was clear he was taller than Nick, and his walk was different.

I continued to my lodgings, which were only a twenty-minute walk from our office in Chancery Lane. I wondered when I would stop seeing Nick's features in passers-by. It had been worse when I first left Morton and came to London, partly because I had no occupation for the first month and lived with Mother and my sister. So much worse, in fact, that I didn't leave the house for a week just so I wouldn't feel the searing disappointment of mistaking strangers for Nick.

After that horrible first month, I began looking for work again. A former colleague of Father's introduced me to Eliza, one of the few women solicitors in London who had struck out on her own. She'd attended university but had little practical experience, and she was looking for a partner. My years of experience with Father made up for my shortcomings of education, and she and I began to work together. I began as a sort of glorified clerk, but I soon gained clients as well as confidence. Although I needed to budget carefully, I was finally independent from my family and could support myself. And best of all, most of our clients were women. I had found my purpose at last: helping women understand the legal language relating to contracts and their rights over their own property.

Eliza had also become a friend, and I was even more grateful for her friendship than for her willingness to take me on as a business partner. I had come to the conclusion that my sanity could be maintained only if I kept my visits to my family brief and sporadic, so without Eliza my life would have been unbearably solitary.

A letter was waiting for me at my lodgings. I recognized Joe's handwriting at once and hurried to my room to read it. Joe was still in Manchester, and we had exchanged a few letters since leaving Morton. I was always glad to hear from him.

Dear Vaughan,

I hope you're well and prospering in your new business. I hope also that the bustling life of the city is a welcome relief after the quiet of Morton. You'll forgive me for mentioning that place, but I do have news concerning it, which I'll relate presently.

As you probably guessed from my last letter, I've enjoyed good fortune in Manchester so far, but it's even better now—I've met a wonderful girl who's agreed to marry me. Louisa is the daughter of the village doctor and has an enviable combination of beauty and intelligence that so few women possess (save one—I'll let you guess who I mean!). She doesn't even mind having a ready-made family to care for.

But before I wax eloquent on my Louisa's attributes and bore you to death in the process, I'll proceed to my news. I went to Morton Abbey last week. I wanted to see how Nick was getting on and what he'd done with the place, but it turns out Morton has a new owner, someone unknown to me. One of the servants told me his master bought the place in September, so Nick wasn't there more than a few months after you and I left. Nobody seems to know where Nick went, though the servant I spoke to was under the impression he'd moved to London. Have you heard from him?

I stopped reading and stared at the letter as if the words had suddenly transformed from English into Russian. Why would Nick have sold Morton? Was it Alicia's influence? I knew they were no longer caring for Dora because Joe had written shortly after I left Morton that he'd brought her to live with him. I wouldn't have admitted it to anyone, but I still scoured the daily papers, hoping for news of Nick and Alicia's divorce. So far I had been disappointed.

I had written to Nick once, just before Christmas, and I'd convinced myself there could be no harm in sending a card with vague good wishes of the season. He would learn nothing from my message, but he would at least have my address if he wished to write to me. He didn't reply, and I berated myself for my weakness for weeks afterwards, my mind filled with tortuous images of Nick and Alicia laughing at my transparent attempt to communicate with him. Joe's new information made me feel both better and worse: better because if Nick had no longer been living at Morton when I sent the card, he likely hadn't received it, and worse because now I had no way of finding him.

Sometimes I felt as if nothing had changed, that despite the relentlessly modern life I was living, I was still doing the same work I had done when Father was alive and that my time at Morton had been only a brief, wild dream in the midst of a mundane life. Yes, I was supporting myself through my legal work, but this achievement, and the satisfaction of helping other women, didn't lessen my loneliness. Eliza, who had a wide circle of friends, was always telling me I needed to meet more people, but I found her friends overwhelming. They moved quickly, talked loudly, and didn't seem interested in discussing ideas.

I no longer dreamed of Nick or Morton. For all the trouble those dreams caused me in the past, I was sorry I couldn't experience them again. I didn't miss the nightmares, of course, but I did miss the vivid sensations: the scent of summer roses, the fresh breeze from the moor, the smell of sandalwood soap on Nick's skin. Of course it was better for me that I didn't dream of him. I knew it was. Perhaps in time I would really believe that.

Oddly, I did dream of Rose Dixon and sometimes of Netherton. I dreamed scenes of her life that I'd never witnessed but that she had alluded to at the pond: Rose as a hopeful young woman with dreams of being loved; Rose as the beaten wife of a drunkard; Rose as a midwife who saw the dangers men posed; Rose becoming the heroine who "saved" their tiny daughters. These dreams were often disturbing, but they also kept the purpose of my own work clearly before me.

That evening I put on my burgundy dress, which I decided was acceptable after all. I would never dress in the height of fashion, and I didn't want to stand out. I still dreaded the party, though, and during the cab ride to Mr. Phipps' house, I was already counting the minutes until I could go home.

Eliza was already there when I arrived, but she was in the middle of a lively group of people, so I merely waved at her from across the room. It was a larger gathering than I was expecting, which didn't help my nerves. After greeting our host, I looked with dismay at the crowd in the large drawing room. There must be thirty people, talking in groups of three or four and looking as though they'd known one another for years.

I spied a quiet corner with a few empty chairs, and I went around the perimeter of the room to get there, sinking into one of the chairs with relief. I could sit unnoticed in the shadows and watch everyone, which was exactly what I wanted.

As I observed the animated conversations and speculated about who the guests might be—for I knew nobody but Eliza and Mr. Phipps—I saw a man disengage himself from a group and head in my direction. Once again it seemed that my eyes were playing tricks on me, for he looked so much like Nick that I caught my breath. I reminded myself of the many times this sort of thing had happened before. Soon his face or mannerisms or walk would be wrong, and the resemblance would disappear.

But this time the resemblance didn't disappear. He continued to look like Nick, from the dark hair greying at his temples to his upright bearing and thin frame.

I remained still as he approached me, thinking perhaps he hadn't even seen me and was merely coming to look at a painting on the wall behind me. But he faced me and stopped only a few feet away. It was indeed Nick. I couldn't breathe, and my heart thudded so loudly in my chest that I was sure he must be able to hear it.

"You've found the best spot in the room," he said. "I wouldn't blame you if you don't want to share it, but may I join you?"

"Yes, of course." My voice sounded wooden, but at least it was audible. I began to breathe again, albeit unevenly.

He pulled up a chair beside mine, not too close, but close enough for a quiet conversation.

Neither of us spoke for a moment. His eyes flickered away from me, and he took a sip from the drink he was holding. Then he said, "Forgive me. I ought to have asked if you would like anything to drink."

"No, thank you."

We didn't quite meet each other's eyes. I tried desperately to think of something to say, worried he would tire of the awkward silence and leave.

"How are you?" he asked.

"I'm well. And you?"

"Also well." He gave a low laugh. "It's silly, but I've thought a great deal about what I'd say to you if I ever saw you again, and now that I have the chance, all I can think of are vapid pleasantries."

"I know." I smiled. "I was thinking the same thing. About myself, that is."

He looked directly at me. I had forgotten how all-consuming, how intense, his gaze was. And how beautiful his eyes were, light grey framed by impossibly long black eyelashes. I thought he might be diminished somehow when he was away from Morton, as if the place was what infused him with personality and energy, but he was the same man I remembered, though a little thinner and paler.

"I must confess," he said, "I knew—or rather, I was hoping—you'd be here. Mr. Phipps is a business acquaintance of mine and when he mentioned his solicitor was a woman, I asked questions. I knew he invited you here tonight."

"Then you have the advantage," I replied. "I had no idea you knew him, or that you'd be here."

"I hope you don't mind."

"Why should I mind?" Taking care to keep my voice steady, I asked, "Is your wife here? I didn't see her."

He hesitated. "Alicia and I divorced a few months ago."

I stared at him, then quickly lowered my eyes. Why hadn't he told me?

"We wanted to have it done quietly to keep it out of the papers," he said. "It took longer than we expected. There were legal complications with Peter's will, and we had to work out what to do with Morton first."

"I heard you sold Morton," I said.

"Yes. How did you know?"

"Joe told me in a letter."

"Oh." He took another sip of his drink. "How is Joe?"

"He seems happy. He's engaged to a doctor's daughter from Manchester."

"I see."

I couldn't tell from his tone what he was feeling. He still sounded formal and polite, and his face gave nothing away. "Why did you sell the place?" I asked.

"Many reasons. It was filled with so many sad memories, so many tragedies. You were right to leave when you did. You were right about many things."

I didn't dare ask what else I was right about. "Where are you living now?"

"Here in London. I have a house in Bloomsbury. It isn't large, but I don't need a large place." He smiled. "Lest you think I've degenerated into a gentleman of leisure, I can assure you I've been keeping busy. I've finished my *Life of Wordsworth*, and Phipps is going to publish it. That's how I met him."

"That's wonderful."

"We've talked enough about me," he said. "Tell me how you are. Do you enjoy your work?"

"Yes. I'm very fortunate to work with Miss Orme, and I like the work itself. Most of our clients are women, and it's very satisfying when I can help them understand what their legal rights are."

"That sounds perfect for you," he exclaimed, smiling. "It's important work, too."

He asked me more questions about my work, and I answered them, sounding to myself as if I were reciting answers by rote, like a catechism. I wished he would cast off his reserve and speak frankly to me. I wished I knew how he felt about his life. About the past. About me.

"I want to thank you for the Christmas card," he said abruptly.

My eyes flew to his face. "You received it?"

"Yes." He looked a little abashed. "I arranged for any letters mistakenly sent to Morton to be delivered to my London address."

He was divorced, living in London, and had been in possession of my address for at least two months but hadn't written or tried to see me. I waited for an explanation, but none came.

Instead, he reached into the pocket of his coat, took out a small box, and offered it to me. "I found something that belongs to you."

I took it from him and opened it. Inside lay the amber pendant, attached to a fine gold chain. My breath caught in my throat.

"I found it in the grass by the side of the pond a few days after you left Morton," he said. "The chain was broken and couldn't be mended, so I bought a new one. The pendant itself was unharmed."

"Thank you." I looked at him searchingly. Was he merely, as he said, returning something that belonged to me, or did his gesture mean more than that?

As if to prevent any further confusion on my part, he rose to his feet and said briskly, "Well, I've done what I came to do, and I've monopolized you long enough. There must be others here you wish to speak to."

I was so startled by his abruptness that I made no reply.

"It was good to see you," he said gravely. Then he was gone, his polite words lingering in my ears. The words any acquaintance might have said, sincerely or not.

He'd said nothing about wanting to see me again. Was this all he wanted, to return the pendant and have a few minutes' conversation in a public place to learn the superficial facts of my life? Had he come to believe that his feelings for me weren't real, just the product of our being together in an isolated place? Would he have felt the same about any woman in the same situation?

I forced myself to leave the safety of my nook and engage in polite conversation with a few other people, but after a quarter of an hour I could no longer sustain the charade. I needed to go home to think and be alone.

Spying Eliza near the main entrance, I took her aside and said, "I'm feeling a little unwell. I'm going home."

"How unfortunate! You do look a bit peaky. I'll make your apologies to Mr. Phipps, if you wish."

"Apologies? What apologies?" Mr. Phipps himself, a jovial little man, appeared at Eliza's elbow, peering at me with bright black eyes. "Is something the matter?"

I repeated what I'd told Eliza.

"I'm sorry to hear it," he said. "As it turns out, Mr. Spencer is also leaving. He tells me the two of you are friends, so I'll ask if he would mind taking you home in his carriage. No point taking a cab if you don't need to."

"Oh, no," I protested, mortified. "Please don't—"

But he had already gone in search of Nick. I considered fleeing, but I wouldn't have gotten far and would only make myself ridiculous.

"That poor man," Eliza said, interrupting my panicky thoughts.

"Who? Mr. Phipps?"

"No, Mr. Spencer. I didn't know you were his friend, so you must know about his illness, but Mr. Phipps just told me."

A shiver snaked up my spine. "I didn't know," I said.

"He has a serious condition that disables him for weeks at a time. Apparently he rarely leaves his house. I'm glad he was well enough to come to the party."

Before this information could penetrate my mind, Mr. Phipps returned with Nick, who had already put on his greatcoat and muffler.

"Please allow me to see you home," Nick said. "It's a cold night, and my carriage will be warmer than a cab."

"Thank you," I managed.

In a daze I said farewell to Eliza and my host and accompanied Nick downstairs to collect my coat, hat, and gloves.

Nick's carriage was a brougham with a plush interior. We sat beside each other, and I was glad he couldn't see my face clearly in the dim light filtering through the windows from the lampposts.

"I'm glad we have another chance to talk," Nick said when the carriage began to move.

"Yes."

Despite our agreement on this point, we were silent for some time. The rhythmic clop of the horse's hooves and the clatter of the carriage wheels on the cobblestone street seemed to come from far off.

When I found my voice again, I asked, "What is your illness?"

"Oh. That." He picked at a loose thread on one of his gloves.

"Is it the same as what you had before, when I was at Morton?"

"Yes, mostly." He took a deep breath. "The attacks are more frequent now, and they last longer. I've seen another specialist, not an oculist this time but a neurologist. He diagnosed me with hemiplegic migraine. It was a relief to find out the eye disturbances and paralysis were connected to my headaches, but there is no effective treatment, and no cure. It's not fatal," he added hastily, "lest you think I'm telling you the same story as when you first came to Morton."

"Is your illness the reason you sold Morton and moved to London?"

"No. I sold Morton mainly because of the furniture."

"I beg your pardon?" I risked a glance at his face.

With a wry smile, he said, "Do you remember the chair you used to sit on when we used to read together in the library?"

"Of course."

"I had it removed and stored away on the second floor. I did the same with the furniture in your old room in the east wing, then with the furniture in your west wing room. You've become the ghost that haunts me: I kept seeing things you used, seeing you, everywhere. The servants must have been worried I'd have the walls knocked down where your skirt had brushed them."

In a trembling voice I ventured, "Why didn't you write to me?"

"I wanted to. But as I said, the divorce was dragging out longer than I expected, and I wanted to wait until it was finalized to seek you out honourably, as a free man. But then my condition became more debilitating." He turned to me. "I won't hide the truth from you any longer. I can live a relatively normal life between attacks, but during an attack I can't get out of bed, often for several days. The specialist says the symptoms will likely worsen as I age."

I took his hand in both of mine and gripped it tightly. "I'm so sorry. Why didn't you tell me sooner?"

"This is why," he said quietly, pulling his hand from my grasp just long enough to remove his gloves, then reaching up to brush away the tears running down my cheeks. "Because I knew you'd pity me, and I didn't want that. The last thing you need is to be dragged away from the work you love to play nursemaid to a sick man. It would be the early days at Morton all over again. Your life would be diminished because of me."

"The early days at Morton?" I repeated, laughing through my tears. "Are you saying I'd have to submit to your insults while trying to label minerals in the dark? Are you saying you still think of me as an ugly—"

"If you dare to repeat the horrible things I said to you back then," he exclaimed, "I'll—"

"You'll what?"

"I don't know. But it will be something you don't like."

"That's a poor answer," I replied. "I can issue threats too, Mr. Spencer."

"Is that so? Let's hear one, then."

I considered his challenge for a few seconds, then said, "If you don't kiss me immediately, I won't marry you."

To my surprise, his only response was to turn away from me and rap the ceiling of the carriage twice with his walking stick. The carriage pulled over and stopped so quickly that I nearly fell from my seat.

Had I offended him? Was he going to order me out of the carriage? I waited with a quaking heart.

Not waiting for the coachman to open the door, Nick got out, then held out his hand to me. "Come," he said.

I put my hand in his, trying to read his face, but it was impassive.

When we were standing on the street face to face, he said, "Let's do this properly, Vaughan, without threats, however charmingly issued."

Still holding my hand, he knelt before me, paying no heed to the wet pavement or the curious stares of passers-by, and asked, "Will you marry me?"

He gave me only a few seconds to answer before taking me in his arms and kissing me in front of the astonished coachman.

Author's Note

All characters in *The Curse of Morton Abbey* are fictional except Eliza Orme, who was the first woman in Britain to obtain a law degree in 1888. However, women were not admitted to the bar or allowed to qualify as solicitors until the Sex Disqualification (Removal) Act was passed in 1919, so Orme had to practice law unofficially. She opened a law office in Chancery Lane with a female partner, working as junior legal counsel ("devilling") for qualified male lawyers and specializing in conveyancing, patents, and estates work. In addition to her successful law practice, Orme became a prominent public figure, earning the admiration of well-known writers and political activists such as George Gissing, Beatrice and Sidney Webb, and George Bernard Shaw. Despite her extraordinary career, Orme had fallen into such obscurity by her death in 1937 that nobody wrote her obituary.

Acknowledgments

The inspiration for this novel came to me many years ago in a most unlikely place: a stuffy campus classroom where my students were feverishly writing the final exam for my children's literature course. I watched them fidget and stare into space or at the ceiling as if hoping the answers would magically appear there, likely dreaming of the summer and freedom awaiting them on the other side of the door. Some students finished early, unable to resist the siren song of freedom even though their answers would likely be incomplete and rushed. I started marking those. One essay answer was about Frances Hodgson Burnett's *The Secret Garden*. In the middle of the essay I looked up and stared into space myself, arrested by an idea: What if the child protagonists of Burnett's novel were adults? What would they be like? And my brain exploded with ideas. If I could remember which student wrote that exam, I'd thank her by name for sparking what became *The Curse of Morton Abbey*!

Many people have helped me with countless drafts of this book over the years. For advice on early drafts, I am grateful to members of the London Writers Society critique groups, especially Jo Ogaick, Leanne Olson, and Buddy Young, with whom I debated levels of creepiness and the extent to which I could demonize the hero or humanize the villain.

For later drafts, I am indebted to the eagle eyes and brilliant advice of Kris Waldherr, Dianne Freeman, Carrie Callaghan, and Christine Thorpe. Special thanks to Ellen Keigh (Kay

Henden) for answering my legal history questions and to Mimi Matthews for going above and beyond with her excellent suggestions about the story as well as the business side of publishing. I also appreciate the entertaining and suspiciously informative conversations about methods of murder with Jannay Thiessen and Theresa Therrien. All mistakes are my own.

I would not be a productive or happy author without the support of my husband Michael, who read this book more than once and patiently listened to my plotting problems despite his dislike of gothic novels.

Finally, I couldn't ask for a better agent than the amazing Laura Crockett of TriadaUS Literary Agency. This book is for you.

Milton Keynes UK
Ingram Content Group UK Ltd.
UKHW040659191023
430917UK00004B/248